FAR THOUGHTS AND
PALE GODS

FAR THOUGHTS AND PALE GODS

THE COMPLETE SHORT FICTION OF
GREG BEAR
VOLUME TWO

OPEN ROAD

INTEGRATED MEDIA

NEW YORK

Cover art by Greg Bear

"Heads" © 1990 by Greg Bear
"The Wind From A Burning Woman" originally appeared in *Analog*, 1978
"A Plague of Conscience" originally appeared in *Murasaki*, edited by Robert Silverberg, 1992
"Scattershot" originally appeared in *Universe 8*, 1978
"Petra" originally appeared in *Omni*, 1992
"Mandala" originally appeared in *New Dimensions 8*, 1978

Cover design by Mauricio Díaz

978-1-5040-2147-0

Published in 2016 by Open Road Integrated Media, Inc.
345 Hudson Street
New York, NY 10014
www.openroadmedia.com

Pit; the force disorder pumps with their constant sucking silence; the dissolving ghost of my sister, Rho; and William Pierce's expression when he faced his lifetime goal, in the Quiet . . .

I believe that Rho and William are dead, but I will never be sure. I am even less sure about the four hundred and ten heads.

Fifty meters beneath the cinereous regolith of Ocean Procellarum, in the geographic center of the extensive and largely empty Sandoval territories, the Ice Pit was a volcanic burp in the Moon's ancient past, a natural bubble almost ninety meters wide that had once been filled with the aqueous seep of a nearby ice fall.

The Ice Pit had been a lucrative water mine, one of the biggest pure water deposits on the Moon, but it had long since tapped out. Loath to put family members out of work, my family, the binding multiple of Sandoval, had kept it as a money-losing farm station. It supported three dozen occupants in a space that had once housed three hundred. It was sorely neglected, poorly managed, and worst of all for a lunar establishment, its alleys and warrens were *dirty*. The void itself was empty and unused, its water-conserving atmosphere of nitrogen long since leaked away and its bottom littered with rubble from quakes.

In this unlikely place, my brother-in-law, William Pierce, had proposed seeking absolute zero, the universal ultimate in order, peace, and quiet. In asking for the use of the Ice Pit, William had claimed he would be turning a sow's ear into a scientific silk purse. In return, Sandoval BM would boast a major scientific project, elevating its status within the Triple, and therefore its financial standing. The Ice Pit Station would have a real purpose beyond providing living space for several dozen idled ice miners masquerading as farmers. And William would have something uniquely his own, something truly challenging.

Rho, my sister, supported her husband by using all her considerable energy and charm—and her standing with my grandfather, in whose eyes she could do no wrong.

Despite grandfather's approval, the idea was subjected to rigorous examination by the Sandoval syndics—the financiers and entrepreneurs, as well as the scientists and engineers, many of whom had worked with William and knew his extraordinary gifts. Rho skillfully navigated his proposal through the maze of scrutiny and criticism.

By a five-four decision of the syndics, with much protest from the financiers and grudging acceptance from the scientists, William's project was approved.

Thomas Sandoval-Rice, the BM's director and chief syndic, gave his own approval reluctantly, but give it he did. He must have seen some use for a high-risk, high-profile research project; times were hard, and prestige could be crucial even for a top-five family.

Thomas decided to use the project as a training ground for promising young family members. Rho spoke up on my behalf, without my knowledge, and I found myself assigned to a position far above what my age and experience deserved: the new station's chief financial manager and requisitions officer.

I was compelled by family loyalties—and the pleas of my sister—to cut loose from formal schooling at the Tranquil and move to the Ice Pit Station. At first I was less than enthusiastic. I felt my calling to be liberal arts rather than finance and management; I had, in family eyes, frittered away my education studying history, philosophy, and the Terrestrial classics. But I had a fair aptitude for the technical sciences—less aptitude for the theoretical—and had taken a minor in family finances. I felt I could handle the task, if only to show my elders what a liberal mentality could accomplish.

Ostensibly I was in charge of William and his project, answerable to the syndics and financial directors alone; but of course, William quickly established his own pecking order. I was twenty years old at the time; William, thirty-two.

Inside the void, foamed rock was sprayed to insulate and seal in a breathable atmosphere. I oversaw the general cleanup, refitting of existing warrens and alleys, and investment in a relatively Spartan laboratory.

Large refrigerators stored at the station since the end of ice mining had been moved into the void, providing far more cooling capacity than William actually needed for his work.

Vibration is heat. The generators that powered the Ice Pit laboratory lay on the surface, their noise and vibration isolated from the refrigerators and William's equipment and laboratory. What vibration remained was damped by suspension in an intricate network of steel springs and field levitation absorbers.

The Ice Pit's heat radiators also lay near the surface, sunk six meters deep in the shadow of open trenches, never seeing the sun, faces turned toward the all-absorbing blackness of space.

Three years had passed since the conversion. Again and again, William had failed to meet his goal. His demands for equipment had become more extravagant, more expensive, and more often than not, rejected. He had become reclusive, subject to even wider mood swings.

I met William at the beginning of the alley that led to the Ice Pit, in the main lift hollow. We usually saw each other only in passing as he whistled through the cold rock alleys between home and the laboratory. He carried a box of thinker files and two coils of copper tubing and looked comparatively happy.

William was a swarthy stick of a man, two meters tall, black eyes deep-set, long narrow chin, lips thin, brows and hair dark as space, with a deep shadow on his jaw. He was seldom calm or quiet, except when working; he could be rude and abrasive. Set loose in a meeting, or conversing on the lunar com net, he sometimes seemed contentious to the point of self-destruction, yet still the people closest to him loved and respected him. Some of the Sandoval engineers considered William a genius with tools and machines, and on those rare occasions when I was privileged to see his musician's hands prodding and persuading, seducing all instrumentality, designing as if by willing consensus of all the material parts, I could only agree; but I loved him much less than I respected him.

In her own idiosyncratic way, Rho was crazy about him; but then, she was just as driven as William. It was a miracle their vectors added.

William and I matched step. "Rho's back from Earth. She's flying in from Port Yin," I said.

"Got her message," he said, bouncing to touch the rock roof three meters overhead. His glove brought down a few lazy drifts of foamed rock. "Got to get the arbeiters to spray that." His distracted tone betrayed no real intent to follow through. "I've finally straightened out the QL, Micko. The interpreter's making sense. My problems are solved."

"You always say that before some new effect cuts you down." We had come to the large, circular, white ceramic door that marked the entrance to the Ice Pit and stopped at the white line that William had crudely painted there, three years ago. The line could be crossed only on his invitation.

The hatch opened. Warm air poured into the corridor; the Ice Pit was always warmer than ambient, being filled with so much equipment. Still, the warm air *smelled* cold; a contradiction I had never been able to resolve.

"I've licked the final source of external radiation," William said. "Some terrestrial metal doped with twentieth century fallout." He zipped his hand away. "Replaced it with lunar steel. And the QL is really tied in. I'm getting straight answers out of it—as straight as quantum logic can give. Leave me my illusions."

"Sorry," I said. He shrugged magnanimously. "I'd like to see it in action."

He screwed up his face in irritation, then slumped. "I'm sorry, Mickey. I've been a real wart. You fought for it, you got it for me, you deserve to see it. Come on."

I followed William over the line and across the forty-meter-long, two-meter-wide wire and girder bridge into the Ice Pit. He walked ahead of me, between the force disorder pumps. I stopped to look at the bronze torii mounted on each side of the bridge. They reminded me of massive abstract sculptures, but they were among the most sensitive and difficult of William's tools, always active, even when not connected to William's samples. Passing between them, I felt a twitch in my interior, as if my body were a large ear listening to something it could barely hear: an elusive, sucking silence.

William looked back at me and grinned sympathetically. "Spooky feeling, hm?"

"I hate it," I said.

"So do I, but it's sweet music, Micko. Sweet music indeed."

Beyond the pumps, connected to the bridge by a short, narrow walkway and enclosed in a steel Faraday cage, hung the Cavity. Inside the Cavity, embedded in a meter-wide sphere of perfect, orbit-fused quartz, hidden by a flawless mirror coating of niobium, rested eight thumb-sized ceramic cells, each containing approximately a thousand atoms of copper. Each cell was surrounded by its own superconducting electromagnet. These were the mesoscopic samples, large enough to experience the macroscopic qualities of temperature, small enough to lie within the microscopic realm of quantum forces. They were never allowed to reach a temperature greater than one millionth of a degree Kelvin.

The T-shaped laboratory lay at the end of the bridge: a hundred square meters of enclosed work space made of thin shaped steel framing covered by black plastic wall. Suspended by vibration-damping cords and springs and field levitation from the high dome of the Ice Pit, three of the four cylindrical refrigerators surrounded the laboratory like the pillars of a tropical temple, overgrown by a jungle of pipes and cables. Waste heat was conveyed through the rubble net at the top of the void and through the foamed rock roof beyond by flexible tubes; the buried radiators on the surface then shed that heat into space.

The fourth and final and largest refrigerator lay directly above the Cavity, sealed to the upper surface of the quartz sphere. From a distance, the refrigerator and the Cavity might have resembled a squat, old-fashioned mercury thermometer, with the Cavity serving as bulb.

Almost from the beginning of the project, William had maintained to the syndics—through Rho and myself; we never let him appear in person—that his equipment could not be perfectly tuned by even the most skilled human operators, or by the most complicated of computer controllers. All of his failures, he said in his blackest moods, were due to this problem: the inability of macroscopic controllers to ever be in sync with the quantum qualities of the samples.

What he—what the *project*—needed was a Quantum Logic thinker. Yet these were manufactured only on Earth and were not being exported. Because so few existed, the black market of the Triple had none to offer, and even could we find one for sale, the costs of purchase, avoiding Earth authorities, and shipping to the Moon would be enormous. Rho and I could not convince the syndics to even contemplate making the effort.

William had seemed to blame me personally.

Our break came with news of an older-model QL thinker being offered for sale by an Asian industrial consortium. William determined that this thinker would suit our needs—but it was suspiciously cheap, and almost certainly obsolete. That didn't bother William.

The syndics approved this request, to everybody's surprise, I think. It might have been Thomas's final gift and test for William—any more expensive requisitions without at least the prospect of a success and the Ice Pit would be closed.

Rho traveled to Earth to strike a deal with the Asian consortium. The thinker was packaged, shipped, and arrived six weeks later. I had not heard from her between the time of the purchase and her message from Port Yin that she had returned to the Moon.

She had spent four weeks extra on Earth, and I was more than a little curious to find out what she had been doing there.

The laboratory had four rooms, two in the neck of the T, one extending on each side to make the wings. William led me through the laboratory door—actually a flexible curtain—into the first room, which was filled with a small metal table and chair, a disassembled nano-works arbeiter, and cabinets of cubes and disks. In the second room, the QL thinker occupied a central platform about half a meter on a side. On the wall to the left of the table were a manual control board—seldom used now—and two windows overlooking the Cavity.

The QL room was quiet and cool, like what I imagine a monk's cell off a cloister would be like. (We have monks, but we don't have cloisters on the Moon.) The QL itself covered perhaps a third of the platform's surface. Beneath the platform lay the QL's separate power supplies; by Triple common law, all thinkers were equipped with supplies capable of lasting a full year without outside replenishment.

William leaned over and patted the QL proudly. "It's running almost everything now," he said. "If we succeed, the QL will take a large share of the credit."

I hunkered to the QL's level to peer at its white cylindrical container. "Who'll get the Nobel, you or it?" I asked.

William shook his head. "Probably doesn't matter. Nobody off Earth has ever gotten a Nobel, anyway," he said. I felt the most affection for my brother-in-law when he reacted positively to my acidulous humor. "But surely I get some credit for pointing the QL in the right direction!"

"What about this?" I asked, touching the interpreter with a finger. Connected to the QL by fist-thick optical cables, covering another half of the platform, the interpreter was a thinker in itself. It addressed the QL's abstruse contemplations and rendered them, as closely as possible, in language humans could understand.

"A marvel all by itself."

"Tell me about it," I said.

"You didn't study the files," William chided.

"I was too busy fighting with the syndics," I said. "Besides, you know theory's never been my strong suit."

William knelt behind the opposite side of the table, his expression contemplative, almost reverent. "Did you read about Huang-Yi Hsu?"

"Educate me," I said.

He sighed. "You paid for all this out of ignorance, Mickey. I could have misled you grievously."

"I trust you, William."

He accepted that with generous dubiety. "Huang-Yi Hsu invented post-Boolean three-state logic before 2010. Nobody paid much attention to it until 2030. He was dead by then; had committed suicide rather than submit to Beijing's Rule of Seven. Brilliant man, but I think a true anomaly in human thought. Then a few physicists in the University of Washington's Cramer Lab Group discovered they could put Hsu's work to use solving problems in quantum logic. Post-Boolean and quantum logic were made for each other. By 2060, the first QL thinker had been built, but nobody thought it was successful.

"Fortunately, it was against the law by then to turn off activated thinkers without a court order, but nobody could even *talk* to it. Its grasp of human languages was inadequate; it couldn't follow their logic. It was a mind in limbo, Mickey; brilliant but totally alien. So it sat in a room at Stanford University's Thinker Development Center for five years before Roger Atkins—you know about Roger Atkins?"

"William," I warned.

"Before Atkins found the common ground for any functional real logic, the Holy Grail of language and thought . . . His CAL interpreter. Comprehensible All Logics. Which lets us talk to the QL. He died a year later." William sighed. "Swan song. So this,"

Rho was something of a lunar princess. Biologically of the Sandoval line, great-grand-child of Robert and Emilia Sandoval, her future was the concern of far too many, and in response, she developed a closeted attitude of defiance. That she should reach out for the hand of a Pierce was both expected, considering her character and upbringing, and shocking.

But old prejudices had softened considerably. Despite the doubts of Rho's very protective "aunts" and "uncles", and the strains of initiation and marriage, and despite his occasional reversion to prickly form, William was quickly recognized as a valuable adjunct to our family. He was a brilliant designer and theoretician. For four years he contributed substantially to many of our scientific endeavors, yet adjunct he was, playing a subservient role that must have deeply galled him.

I was fifteen when Rho and William married, and nineteen when he finally broke through this more or less obsequious mask to ask for the Ice Pit. I had never quite understood their attraction for each other; lunar princess drawn to son of outcast family. But one thing was certain: whatever William did to strain Rho's affections, she could return with interest.

I walked to the Ice Pit with Rho after an hour of helping her prepare her case.

She was absolutely correct; as Sandovals, we had a duty to preserve the reputation and heirs of the Sandoval BM, and even by an advocate's logic that would include the founders of our core family.

That we were also taking in four hundred and eight outsiders was quite another matter . . . But as Rho pointed out, the Society could hardly sell individuals. Surely nobody would think it a *bad* idea, bringing such a wealth of potential information to the Moon. Tired old Earth didn't want it; just more corpsicles on a world plagued by them. Anonymous heads, harvested in the mid-twenty-first century, declared dead, stateless, very nearly outside the law, without rights except under the protection of their money and their declining foundation.

The StarTime Preservation Society was actually not *selling* anything or anyone. They were transferring members, chattels and responsibilities to Sandoval BM pending dissolution of the original Society; in short, they were finally, after one hundred and ten years, going cold blue belly up. Bankruptcy was the old term; pernicious exhaustion of means and resources was the new. Well and good; they had guaranteed to their charter members only sixty-one years (inclusive) of tender loving care. After that, they might just as well be out in the warm.

"The societies set up in 2020 and 2030 are declaring exhaustion at the rate of two and three a year now," Rhosalind said. "Only one has actually buried dead meat. Most have been bought out by information entrepreneurs and universities."

"Somebody hopes to make a profit?" I asked.

"Don't be noisy, James," she said, by which she meant incapable of converting information to useful knowledge. "These aren't just dead people; they're huge libraries. Their memories are theoretically intact; at least as intact as death and disease allow them to be. There's maybe a five percent degradation; we can use natural languages algorithms to check and reduce that to maybe three percent."

"Very noisy," I said.

"Nonsense. That's usable recall. Your memories of your seventh birthday have degraded by fifty percent."

I tried to remember my seventh birthday; nothing came to mind. "Why? What happened on my seventh birthday?

"Not important, Mickey," Rho said.

"So who wants that sort of information? It's out of date, it's noisy, it's going to be hard to prove provenance . . . Much less check it out for accuracy."

She stopped, brow cloudy, clearly upset. "You're resisting me on this, aren't you?"

"Rho, I'm in charge of project finances. I *have* to ask dumb questions. What value are these heads to us, even if we can extract information? And—" I held up my hand, about to make a major point, "What if extraction of information is intrusive? We can't dissect these heads—you've assumed the contracts."

"I called Cailetet from Tampa, Florida, last week. They say the chance of recovery of neural patterns and states from frozen heads is about eighty percent, using non-intrusive methods. No nano injections. Lamb shift tweaking. They can pinpoint every molecule in every head from *outside* the containers."

However outlandish Rho's schemes, she always did a certain amount of longer-range planning. I leaned my head to one side and raised both hands, giving up. "All right," I said. "It's fascinating. The possibilities are—"

"Luminous," Rho finished for me.

"But who will buy historical information?"

"These are some of the finest minds of the twentieth century," Rho said. "We could sell shares in future accomplishments."

"*If* they're revivable." We were coming up to the white line and the big porcelain hatch to the Ice Pit. "They're currently not very active and not very creative."

"Do you doubt we'll be able to revive them . . . someday? Maybe in ten or twenty years?"

I shook my head. "They talked revival a century ago. High-quality surgical nano wasn't enough to do the trick. You can make a complex machine shine like a gem, fix it up so that everything fits, but if you don't know where to kick it to start it chugging . . . And we don't. Long time passes, no eyelids crack to the new day."

Rho palmed the hatch guard. William took his own sweet time answering. "I'm an optimist," she said. "I always have been."

"Rho, you've come when I'm busy," William said over the com.

"Oh, for Christ's sake, William. I'm your wife and I've been gone for three months." She wasn't irritated; her tone was playfully piqued. The hatch opened, and again I caught the smell of cold in the outrush of warm.

"The heads are ancient," I said, stepping over the threshold behind her. "They'll need re-training, re-everything. They're probably elderly, inflexible . . . But those are hardly major handicaps when you consider that right now, they're *dead*."

She shrugged this off and walked briskly across the steel bridge. She'd once told me that William, in his more tense and frustrated moments, enjoyed making love on the bridge. I wondered about harmonics. "Where's the staff?" she asked.

"William told me to let them go. He said we didn't need them with the QL in control." We had been working for the past three years with a team of young technicians chosen from several other families around Procellarum. William had informed me two days after the QL's installation that these ten colleagues were no longer needed. He was coldly blunt about it, and he made no dust about the fact that I was the one who would have to arrange for their severance.

His logic was strong; the QL would not need additional human support, and we could use the BM exchange for other purchases. Despite my instincts that this was bad manners between families, I could not stand alone against William; I had served the notices and tried to take or divert the brunt of the anger.

Rho cringed as she sidled between the disorder pumps, whether in reaction to her husband's blunt efficiency or the pumps' effect on her body. She glanced over her shoulder sympathetically. "Poor Micko."

William opened the door, threw out his arms in a peremptory fashion, and enfolded Rho.

I love my sister. I do not know whether it was some perverse jealousy or a sincere desire for her well-being that motivated my feeling of unease whenever I saw William embrace her.

"I've got something for us," Rho said, looking up at him with high-energy, complete-equality adoration.

"Oh," William said, eyes already wary. "What?"

I lay in bed, unable to purge the noiseless suck of the pumps from my thoughts, from my body. After a restless time I began to slide into my usual lunar doze, made a half-awake comparison between seeing William embrace Rho and feeling the pumps embrace me; thought of William's reaction to Rho's news; smiled a little; slept.

William had not been pleased. An unnecessary intrusion; yes there was excess cooling capacity; yes his arbeiters had the time to construct a secure facility for the heads in the Ice Pit; but he did not need the extra stress now nor any distractions because he was *this close* to his goal.

Rho worked on him with that mix of guileless persuasion and unwavering determination that characterized my sister. I have always equated Rho with the nature-force shakers of history; folks who in their irrational stubbornness shift the course of human rivers, whether for good or ill perhaps not even future generations can decide.

William had given in, of course. It was after all a small distraction, so he finally admitted; the raw materials would come out of the Sandoval BM contingency fund; he might even be able to squeeze in some mutually advantageous equipment denied him for purely fiscal reasons.

"I'll do it mostly for the sake of your honored ancestors, of course," William had said.

The heads came by shuttle from Port Yin five days later. Rho and I supervised the deposit at Pad Four, closest to the Ice Pit lift entrance. Packed in steel boxes with their own refrigerators, the heads were slightly bulkier than Rho had estimated. Six cartloads and seven hours after landing, we had them in the equipment lift.

"I've had Nernst BM design an enclosure for William's arbeiters to build," Rho said. "These will keep for another week as they are." She patted the closest box, peering through her helmet with a wide grin.

"You could have chosen someone cheaper," I groused. Nernst had gained unwarranted status in the past few years; I would have chosen the more reasonable, equally capable Twinning BM.

"Nothing but the best for our progenitors," Rho said. "Christ, Mickey. Think about it." She turned to the boxes, mounted in a ring of two crowded stacks in the round lift, small refrigerators sticking from the inward-pointing sides of the boxes.

We descended in the shaft. I could not see her face, but I heard the emotion in her voice. "Think of what it would mean to actually access them, *talk* to them . . ."

I did not like that thought at all. I walked around and between the boxes. High quality, old-fashioned bright steel, beautifully shaped and welded. "A lot of garrulous old-timers," I said, trying to sound calm.

"Mickey." Her chide was mild. She knew I was thinking.

"Are they labelled?" I asked.

"That's one problem," Rho said. "We have a list of names, and all the containers are numbered; but StarTime says it can't guarantee a one-to-one match. Records were apparently jumbled after the closing date."

"How could that happen?" I was shocked by the lack of professionalism more than by the obvious ramifications.

"I don't know."

"What if StarTime goofed in other ways, and they really *are* just cold meat?" I asked.

Rho shrugged with a casualness that made me cringe, as if, after all her efforts and the expenditure of hard-earned Sandoval capital, such a thing might not be disastrous. "Then we're out of some money," she said. "But I don't think they made that big a goof."

We slowly pressurized at the bottom of the shaft. Rho watched the containers for buckling. There was none; they had been expertly packed. "Nernst BM says it will take two days for William's machines to make their enclosure. Can you supervise? William refuses . . ."

I pulled off my helmet, kicked some surface dust from my boots into a vacuum nozzle, and grinned miserably. "Sure. I have nothing better to do."

Rho put her gloved hands on my shoulders. "Mickey. Brother."

I looked at the boxes, my spooky intrigue growing alarmingly. What if they were alive inside there, and could—in their own deceased way—tell us of their lives? That would be extraordinary; historic. Sandoval BM could gain an enormous amount of publicity, and that would reflect on our net worth in the Triple. "I'll supervise," I said. "But you get Nernst BM to send a human over here and not just an engineering arbeiter. It should be in the contract; on completion, I want someone to personally inspect."

"No fear," Rho said. Gloves removed but skinsuit still on, she gave me a quick hug. "Let's roll!" She guided the first cartload of stacked boxes through the gate into the Ice Pit storage warren, where they'd be kept for the time being.

The first sign of trouble came quickly. Barely six hours after the unloading of the heads, Janis Granger, assistant to Fiona Task-Felder, requested a formal visit to the Ice Pit. Janis, like her boss and "sister" Fiona, was a member of Task-Felder BM. Fiona's election to president of the Multiple Council was a political move I would have thought impossible just a year before.

Task-Felder had been founded five decades ago, on Earth, as a lunar BM, an unorthodox procedure that had raised eyebrows on both worlds. Membership was allegedly limited to Logologists—nobody knew of any exceptions, at any rate—which made it the only lunar BM founded on religious principles. For these reasons, Task-Felder had for years been comparatively powerless in lunar politics, if such could be called politics: a weave of mutual advantage, politeness, and small-community cooperation in the face of clear financial pressures.

The Task-Felder Logologists had tended their businesses carefully, played their parts with scrupulous attention to detail and quality, and had carefully distributed favors and loans to other BMs and the council, working their way slowly and deliberately up the ladder of lunar acceptance, all at the same time they believed six impossible things before breakfast.

And then—Fiona had won their first big prize.

I didn't have the slightest idea what Granger wanted to talk about, but I could hardly refuse to speak with a council representative. Her private bus arrived at Pad Three seven hours after we spoke. I received her in my spare but spacious formal office in the farm management warrens.

Granger was twenty-seven, black-haired, with Eurasian features and Amerindian skin—all genetically designed and tailored. She wore trim flag-blue denims and a white ruffled-neck blouse, the ruffles projecting a changing and delicate geometric pattern of white-on-white.

I did not receive her behind a desk; that was reserved for contract talks or financial dealings.

Granger sat gracefully, knees together, legs cocked at a prim angle, in the chair across from mine. "I've brought the status report on Ice Pit projects from the BM council," she said. "I wanted to discuss it with you, since you're project manager. We've got a consensus of the founding BMs to agree to consult on projects which could affect lunar standing in the Triple."

I had heard something about this council report, in its early drafts. It had seemed innocuous enough—just another BM mutual consent agreement. Why come all this way? Why hadn't she gone to the family syndics in Port Yin?

"Very good," I said. "I assume Sandoval's representative has looked over the report and the agreement."

"She has. She told me there might be a conflict with one current project—not your *primary* project. She advised me to send a representative of the president to talk with you; I decided this was important enough I would come myself."

Granger had an intensity that reminded me of Rho. She did not take her eyes off mine. She did not smile. She leaned forward, elbows still on the chair rests, and said, "Rhosalind Sandoval has signed a contract to receive terrestrial corpsicles."

"It's no secret. She's my direct sister, by the way."

Granger blinked. With any family-oriented BM member, such a comment would have elicited a polite "Oh, and how is your branch?" She neglected the pleasantry.

"Are you planning resuscitation?" she asked.

"No," I said. *Not yet.* "We're speculating on future value."

"If they're not resuscitated, they have no future value."

I disagreed with a mild shake of my head. "That's our worry, nobody else's."

"The Council has expressed concern that your precedent could lead to a flood of corpsicle dumping. The Moon can't possibly receive a hundred thousand dead. It would be a major financial drain."

"I don't see how precedent is established," I said, wondering where she was going to take this.

"Sandoval BM is a major family group. You influence new and offshoot families. We've already had word that two other families are considering similar deals, in case you're on to something. And all of them have contacted Cailetet BM. I believe Rhosalind Sandoval-Pierce has tried to get a formal exclusion contract with Cailetet. Have you approved all this?"

I hadn't; Rho hadn't told me she'd be moving so quickly, but it didn't surprise me. It was a logical step in her scheme. "I haven't discussed it with her. She has Sandoval priority approval."

This seemed to take Granger by surprise. "BM charter priority?"

"Yes."

"Why?"

I saw no reason to divulge family secrets. If she didn't already know, my instincts told me, she didn't need to know. "Family privilege, ma'am."

Granger looked to one side and thought this over for an uncomfortably long time, then returned her gaze to me. "Cailetet is asking for Council advice. On behalf of the president, I've issued a chair statement of disapproval. We think it might adversely affect our currency ratings in the Triple. There are strong moral and religious feelings on Earth now about corpsicles; revival has been outlawed in seven nations. We feel you've been taken advantage of."

"Really?" I said. "We don't think so."

"Nevertheless, the Council is considering issuing a restraining order against any storage or possible use of the corpsicles."

"Excuse me," I said. I reached across to the desk and took hold of my manager's slate. "Auto counselor, please," I requested aloud, then keyed in instructions I didn't want Granger to hear, asking for a legal opinion on this possible action.

The auto counselor quickly reported: "Not legal at this time," and gave a long list of citations.

"You can't restrain an autonomous chartered BM," I said. I read one of the citations, the one most on point. "Mutual benefit agreement 35 stroke 2111, reference to charter family agreements, 2102."

"If sufficient BMs can be convinced of the unwisdom of your actions, and if the financial result could be ruinous to any original charter BM, our council thinker has issued an opinion that you can be restrained."

It was my turn to pause and consider.

"Then it seems we might be heading for council debate," I said.

"I'd regret causing so much fuss," Granger said. "Perhaps we can reach an agreement outside of council."

"Our syndics can discuss it," I allowed. My backbone was

becoming stubbornly stiff. "But I think it should be openly debated in council."

She smiled. If, as was alleged by the Logologists, their philosophy removed all human limitations, judging by Janis Granger, I opposed such benefits. There was a control about her that suggested she had nothing to control, neither stray whim nor dangerous passion; automatonous. She chilled me.

"As you wish," she said. "This is really not a large matter. It's not worth a lot of trouble."

Then why bother?

"I agree," I said. "I believe the BMs can resolve it among themselves."

"The council represents the BMs," Granger said.

I nodded polite agreement. I wanted nothing more than to have her out of my office, and out of the Ice Pit Station.

"Thank you for your time," she said, rising. I escorted her to the lift. She did not say good-bye; merely smiled her unrevealing mannequin smile.

Back in my office, I put through a request for an appointment with Thomas Sandoval-Rice at Port Yin. Then I called Rho and William. Rho answered. "Mickey! Cailetet has just accepted our contract."

That took me back for a second. "I'm sorry," I said, confused. "What?"

"What are you sorry about? It's good news. They think they can manage it. They say it's a challenge. They're willing to sign an exclusive."

"I just had a conversation with Janis Granger."

"Who's she?"

"Task-Felder. Aide to the president of the council," I said. "I think they're going to try to shut us down."

"Shut down Sandoval BM?" Rho laughed. She thought I was joking.

"No. Shut down your heads project."

"They can't do that," she said, still amused.

"Probably not. At any rate, I have a call in to the director." I was thinking over what Rho had told me. If Cailetet had accepted our contract, then they were either not worried about the council debate, or . . .

Granger had lied to me.

"Mickey, what's this all about?"

"I don't know," I said. "I'll find out. The new Council president is a Task-Felder. You should keep up on these things, Rho."

"Who gives a rille? We haven't had any complaints from other BMs. We keep to our boundaries. Task-Felder, huh? Dust them, they're not even a lunar-chartered BM. Aren't they Logologists?"

"They have the talk seat in Council," I said.

"Oh, for the love of," Rho said. "They're crazier than mud. When did they get the seat?"

"Two months ago."

"How did they get it?"

"Careful attention to the social niceties," I said, tapping my palm with a finger.

Rho considered. "Did you record your meeting?"

"Of course." I filed an automatic BM-priority request for Rho and transferred the record to her slate.

"I'll get back to you, Mickey. Or better yet, come on down to the Ice Pit. William needs someone besides me to talk to, I think. He's having trouble with the QL again, and he's still a little irritated about our heads."

My brother-in-law was in a contemplative mood. "On Earth," he said, "in India and Egypt, centuries before they had refrigerators, they had ice, cold drinks. Air conditioning. All because they had dry air and clear night skies."

I sat across the metal table from him in the laboratory's first room. William sat in a tattered metal sling chair, leaving me the guest's cushioned armchair. Outside, William's arbeiters were busily, noisily constructing an enclosure for Rho's heads, using the Nernst BM design.

"You mean, they used storage batteries or solar power or something," I said, biting on his nascent anecdote.

He smiled pleasantly, relaxing into the story. "Nothing so obvious," he said. "Pharaoh's servants could have used flat, broad, porous earthenware trays. Filled them with a few centimeters of water, hoping for a particularly dry evening with clear air."

"Cold air?" I suggested.

"Not particularly important. Egypt was seldom cold. Just dry air and a clear night. Voila. Ice."

I looked incredulous.

"No kidding," he said, leaning forward. "All done by evaporation and radiation into empty space. Under totally cloudless, black, starry skies, and given almost no humidity, evaporation cools the tray and the water, temperature of the liquid drops, and the water in the tray freezes solid. Harvest the ice in the morning, fill the tray again for the next night. You could have had air conditioning, if you laid out enough surface area, filled enough trays, and used caves to store the ice."

"It would have worked?"

"Hell, Micko, it *did* work. Before there was electricity, that's how they made ice. Anyplace dry, with clear night skies . . ."

"Lose a lot of water through evaporation, wouldn't you?"

William shook his head. "You haven't a gram of romance in you, Micko. Not at all tempted by the thought of a frosty mug of beer for the Pharaoh."

"Beer," I said. "Think of all the beer you could store in Rho's annex." Beer was a precious commodity in a small lunar station.

He made a face. "I saw the CV of that Granger woman. Is she going to give Rho trouble?"

I shook my head.

"Serves Rho right," William said. "Sometimes . . ." He stood and wiped his face with his hands, then squeezed thumb and pointing finger together, squinting at them. "You were right. A new problem, Micko, a new *effect*. The QL says the disorder pumps have to be retuned. It'll take a week. Then we'll hit the zeroth state of matter. Nothing like it since before we were all a twinkle in God's eye."

We had been through this before. My teasing seemed a necessary anodyne to him when he bumped up against another delay. "Violation of Third Law," I said casually.

He waved that away. "William, you're an infidel. The Third Law's a mere bagatelle, like the sound barrier—"

"What if it's more like the speed of light?"

William shut one eye half-way and regarded me balefully. "You've laid out the money. If I'm a fool, you're a worse fool."

"From your point of view, I wouldn't find that reassuring," I said, smiling. "But what do I know. I'm a dry accountant. Set me out under a clear terrestrial night sky and my brain would freeze."

William laughed. "You're smarter than you need to be," he said. "Violating the Third Law of thermodynamics—no grief there. It's a sitting duck, Micko. Waiting to be shot."

"It's been sitting for a long time. Lots of hunters have missed. *You've* missed for three years now."

"We didn't have quantum logic thinkers and disorder pumps," William said, staring out into the darkness beyond the small window, face lit orange by flashes of light from the arbeiters at work in the pit below.

"Those pumps make me twitch," I confessed, not for the first time.

William ignored that and turned to me, suddenly solemn. "If the council tries to stop Rho, you'd better fight them with all you've got. I'm not a Sandoval by birth, Mickey, but by God, this BM better stand by her."

"It won't get that far, William," I said. "It's all dust. A burble of politics."

"Tell them to cut the damned politics," William said softly.

This was the rallying cry of all the Moon's families, all our tightly-bound, yet ruggedly individual citizens; how often had I heard that phrase? "This is Rho's project. If I—if *we* let her have the Ice Pit for her heads, nobody should interfere. Damn it, that's what the Moon is all about. Do you believe all you hear about the Logologists?"

"I don't know," I said. "They certainly don't think like you and I."

I joined William at the window. "Thank you," I said.

"For what?"

"For letting Rho do what she wants."

"She's crazier than I am," William said with a sigh. "She says you weren't too pleased at first, either."

"It's pretty gruesome," I admitted.

"But you're getting interested?"

"I suppose."

"That Task-Felder woman made you even more interested."

I nodded.

William tapped the window's thick glass. "Mickey, Rho has always been protected by Sandoval, by living here on the Moon. The Moon has always encouraged her; free spirit, small population, place for young minds to shine. She's a little naive."

"We're no different," I said.

"Maybe you aren't, but I've seen the rough side of life."

I tilted my head, giving him that much. "If by *naive*, you mean she doesn't know what it's like to be in a scrap, you're wrong."

"She knows intellectually," William said. "And she's sharp enough that may be all she needs. But she doesn't know how dirty a fight can get."

"You think this is going to get dirty?"

"It doesn't make sense," William said. "Four hundred heads is gruesome, but it isn't dangerous, and it's been tolerated on Earth for a century . . ."

"Because nothing ever came of it," I said. "And apparently the toleration is wearing thin."

William rubbed thumb and forefinger along his cheeks, narrowing his already narrow mouth. "Why would anyone object?"

"For philosophical reasons, maybe," I said.

William nodded. "Or religious. Have you read Logologist literature?"

I admitted that I hadn't.

"Neither have I, and I'm sure Rho hasn't. Time we did some research, don't you think?"

I shrugged dubiously, then shivered. "I don't think I'm going to like what I find."

William clucked. "Prejudice, Micko. Pure prejudice. Remember *my* origins. Maybe the Task-Felders aren't all that forbidding."

Being accused of prejudgment irritated me. I decided to change the subject and scratch an itch of curiosity. He had shown the QL to me earlier, but had seemed to deliberately avoid demonstrating the thinker.

"Can I talk to it?"

"What?" William asked, then, following my eyes, looked behind him at the table. "Why not? It's listening to us now. QL, I'd like to introduce my friend and colleague, Mickey Sandoval."

"Pleased to meet you," the QL said, its voice gender neutral, as most thinker voices were. I raised an eyebrow at William. Normal enough, house-trained, almost domestic. He understood my expression of mild disappointment.

"Can you describe Mickey to me?" he asked, challenged now.

"In shape and form it is not unlike yourself," the thinker said.

"What about his extensions?"

"They differ from yours. Its state is free and dynamic. Its link with you is not primary. Does he want controlling?"

William smiled triumphantly. "No, QL, he is not an instrumentality. He is like myself."

"You are instrumentality."

"True, but for convenience's sake only," William said.

"It thinks you're part of the lab?" I asked.

"Much easier to work with it that way," William assured me.

"May I ask another question?"

"Be my guest," William said.

"QL, who's the boss here?"

"If by boss you mean a node of leadership, there is no leader here. The leader will arise at some later date, when the instrumentalities are integrated."

"When we succeed," William explained, "then there will be a boss, a node of leadership; and that will be the successful result itself."

"You mean, QL thinks that if you achieve absolute zero, that will be the boss?"

William smiled. "Something like that. Thank you, QL."

"You're welcome," the QL replied.

"Not so fast," I said. "I have another question."

William extended his hand, be my quest.

"What do you think will happen if the cells in the Cavity reach absolute zero?"

The interpreter was silent for a moment, and then spoke in a subtly different voice. "This interpreter is experiencing difficulties translating the QL thinker's response," it said. "Do you wish a statement in post-Boolean mathematical symbols by way of direct retinal projection, or the same transferred to a slate address, or an English interpretation?"

"I've already asked this question, of course," William told me. "I have the mathematics already, several different versions, several different possibilities."

"I'd like an English interpretation," I said.

"Then please be warned that response changes from hour to hour in significant ways," the interpreter said. "This might indicate a chaotic wave-mode fluctuation of theory within the QL. In other words, it has not yet formulated an adequate prediction, and cannot. This thinker will present several English language responses, but warns that they are inadequate for full understanding, which may not be possible for organic human minds at any rate. Do you wish possibly misleading answers?"

"Give us a try," I said, feeling a sting of resentment. William sat at the manual control console, willing to let this be my own contest.

"QL postulates that achievement of absolute zero within a significant sample of matter will result in a new state of matter. Since there is a coupling between motion of matter in spacetime and other forces within matter, particularly within atomic nuclei—the principle upon which the force disorder pumps operate—then this new state of matter may be stable, and may require substantial energy input to return to a thermodynamic state. There is a small possibility that this new state may be communicable by quantum forces, and may induce a similar state in closely associated atoms."

I glanced at William.

"A very small possibility," William said. "And I've protected against it. The copper atoms are isolated in a Penning trap and can't come in contact with anything else."

"Please go on," I told the interpreter.

"Another possibility is a hitherto undiscovered coupling between states of spacetime itself and the thermodynamic motion of matter. If thermodynamism ceases within a sample, the nature of spacetime around the sample might change. Quantum ground states could be affected. Restraints on probabilities of atomic positions could induce an alignment of virtual particle activities, with amplification of other quantum effects, including remote release of quantum information normally communicated between particles and inaccessible to non-communicants."

"All right," I said, defeated. "William, I need an interpreter for your interpreter."

"What the math says—" William said, eyes shining with what must have been joy or pride, it could not have been sadness, "—is that spacetime just *might* crystallize."

"So?"

"Spacetime is naturally amorphous, if we can poetically use terms reserved for matter. Crystallized space would have some interesting properties. Information of quantum states and positions normally communicated only between particles—through the so-called exclusive channels—could be leaked. There could even be propagation of quantum information backwards in time."

"That doesn't sound good," I said.

"It would be purely local," William said. "Fascinating to study. You could think of it as making space a superconductor of information, rather than the highly limited medium it is now."

"But is that likely?"

"No," William said. "From what I can understand, no QL prediction is likely or unlikely at this point."

The Ice Pit farms and support warrens occupied some thirty-five hectares and employed ninety family members. That was moderately large for an isolated research facility, but old habits die hard—on the Moon, each station, large and small, is designed to be autonomous, in case of emergency, natural or political. Stations are more often than not spread so far apart that the habit makes hard sense. Besides, each station must act as an independent social unit, like a village on Earth. The closest major station to us, Port Yin, was six hours away by shuttle.

I had been assigned twelve possible in-family girlfriends at the age of 13. Two resided at the Ice Pit. I had met one only casually, but the other, Lucinda Bergman-Sandoval, had been a love friend since we were sixteen. Lucinda worked on the farm that grew the station's food. We saw each other perhaps once a month now, my focus having shifted to extra-family women, as was expected when one approached marriage age. Still, those visits were good times, and we had scheduled a chat dinner date at the farm cafe this evening.

I've never cared much what women look like. I mean, extraordinary beauty has never impressed me, perhaps because I'm no platinum sheen myself. The Sandoval family had long since accepted pre- and post-birth transforms as a norm, like most lunar families, and so no son or daughter of Sandoval BM was actively unpleasant to look at. Lucinda's family had given her normal birth, and she had chosen a light transform at age seventeen: she was black-haired, coffee-skinned, purple-eyed, slender and tall, with a long neck and pleasant, wide face. Like most lunar kids, she was bichemical—she could go to Earth or other higher gravity environments and adjust quickly.

We met in the cafe, which overlooked the six hectare farm spread on the surface. Thick field-reinforced windows separated our table from high vacuum; a brass bar circled the enclosure to reassure our instincts that we would not fall off to the regolith or the clear polystone dome below.

Lucinda was a quiet girl, quick and sympathetic. We talked relationships for a while—she was considering an extra-family marriage proposal from a Nernst engineer named Hakim. I had some prospects but was still barn dancing a lot.

"Hakim's willing to be name-second," she said. "He's very generous."

"Wants kids?"

"Of course. He told me they could be ex-utero if I was squeamish." Lucinda smiled.

"Sounds rad," I said.

"Oh, he's not. Just . . . generous. I think he's really sweet on me."

"Advantage?"

She smirked lightly. "Lots. His branch controls Nernst Triple Contracts."

"Nernst's done some work for us," I said.

"Do tell," she instructed me in a friendly but pointed tone.

"I probably shouldn't. I haven't even thought it through . . ."

"Sounds serious."

"It could be, I suppose. The council president may try to stop something my blood-sister is doing."

The enormous hologram had been the last of the True Humans, and the crystal she had given him had helped him unlock the power of his mind. He published and promoted the book personally. It sold ten thousand copies the first year, and five hundred thousand copies the next. Later editions revised the name and some of the doctrines of the cosmic science: it became Logology, his final break with even the name *psychology.*

The Old and the New Human Race was soon available not just in paper, but in cube text, LitVid, Vid, and five interactive media.

Through a series of seminars, he converted a few disciples at first, then multitudes, to the belief that humanity had once been godlike in its powers, and was now shackled by ancient chains that made us small, stupid, and dependent on our bodies. Thierry said that all humans were capable of transforming themselves into free-roving, powerful spirits. The crystal told him how to break these chains through a series of mental exercises, and how to realize that humanity's ancient enemies—all but one, whom he called Shaytana—were already dead, and powerless to stop our self-liberation. All one's personal liberation required was concentration, education, and discipline—and a lifetime membership in the Church of Logology.

Shaytana was Loki and a watered-down Satan combined, too weak to destroy us or even stop strong individuals from breaking free of the chains, wily enough and persistent enough to convince the great majority of humans that death was our destiny and weakness our lot. Those who opposed Thierry were dupes of Shaytana, or willing cohorts (as Freud, Jung, Adler, and all other psychiatrists and psychologists had been). There were many other dupes of Shaytana, including presidents, priests, and even his fellow prophets.

In 1997, Thierry tried to purchase a small South Pacific island to create a community of Unchained. He was rebuffed by the island's inhabitants and forced to move his seedling colony to Idaho, where he started his own small town, Ouranos, named after the progenitor of human consciousness. Ouranos became a major political center in Idaho; Thierry was in part responsible for the separation of the state into two sections in 2012, the northern calling itself Green Idaho.

He wrote massively, still made movies occasionally. His later books covered all aspects of a Logologist's life, from prenatal care to funeral rites and design of grave site. He packaged LitVids on such topics as world economics and politics. Slowly, he became a recluse; by 2031, two years before his death, he saw no one but his mistress and three personal secretaries.

Thierry claimed that a time of crisis would come after his own "liberation," and that within a century he would return, "freed of the chains of flesh," to put the Church of Logology into a position of "temporal power over the nations of the Earth." "Our enemies will be cinderized," he promised, "and the faithful will see an eon of spiritual ecstasy."

At his death, he weighed one hundred and seventy-five kilograms and had to move with the aid of a massive armature part wheel-chair, part robot. Press releases, and reports to his hundreds of thousands of disciples in Ouranos and around the world, described his death as voluntary release. He was accompanying the spirit who had first appeared to him on the beach in California on a tour of the galaxy.

His personal physician—a devoted disciple—claimed that despite his bulk, he was in perfect health, and that his body had changed its internal constitution in such a way as to build up massive amounts of energy necessary to power him in the first few years of his spiritual voyage.

Thierry himself they called the Ascended Master. Allegedly he had made weekly reports to his mistress on his adventures. She lived to a ripe old age, eschewed rejuvenation legal or otherwise, grew massive in bulk and so the story went, joined her former lover on his pilgrimage.

A year after his death, one of his secretaries was arrested in

Green Idaho on charges of child pornography. There was no evidence that Thierry had ever participated in such activities; but the ensuing scandal nearly wrecked the Church of Logology.

The Church recovered with remarkable speed when it sponsored a program of supporting young LitVid artists. Using the program as a steppingstone to acceptance among politicians and the general public, Logology's past was soon forgotten, and its current directors—anonymous, efficient, and relatively colorless—finished the job that Thierry had begun. They made Logology a legitimate alternative religion, for those who continued to seek such solace.

The church prospered and made its beginning moves on Puerto Rico. Logologists established a free hospital and "psychiatric" training center on the island in 2046, four years before Puerto Rico became the 51st state. The island was soon controlled by a solid 60% majority population of Logologists, the greatest concentration of the religion on Earth. Every Puerto Rican representative in the United States Congress since statehood had been a Logologist.

The rest was more or less familiar, including an in-depth history of the Io purchase and expedition.

When I finished poring over the massive amounts of material, I was drained and incredulous. I felt that I understood human nature from a somewhat superior perspective—as someone who was not a Logologist, who had not been taken in by Thierry's falsehoods and fantasies.

Arrogance can swing both ways.

Already, something was haunting me.

I dreamed that night of walking along an irrigation canal in Egypt. Dawn came intensely blue in the east, stars overhead still shining like little needles. The canal had frozen during the night, which pleased me; it lay in jumbled cubes of ice, clear as glass, and the cubes were rearranging themselves like living things into perfect flat sheets.

Order, I thought. *The Pharaoh will be pleased.*

But as I looked into the depths of the canal, I saw fish pinned under the cubes, unable to move, gills flexing frantically, and I realized that I had sinned. I looked up to the stars, blaming them, but they refused to accept responsibility; then I looked to the sides of the canal, among the reeds, and saw a copper torus on each side, sucking soundlessly.

All my dream-muscles twitched and I came awake.

It was eight hundred hours and my personal line was blinking politely. I answered; there were two messages, one from Rho, left three hours earlier, and one from Thomas Sandoval-Rice, an hour after hers.

Rho's message was voice only, and brief. "Mickey, the director wants to meet with both of us today in Port Yin. He's sending an executive shuttle for us at ten hundred."

The director's message was extensive text and a vocal request from his secretary. "Mickey, Thomas Sandoval-Rice would like you meet with him in Port Yin as soon as possible. We'd like Rhosalind to be there as well."

Accompanying the message was text and LitVid on Logology—much of the same material I'd already studied.

I cleared my schedule for the day and canceled a meeting with family engineers on generator maintenance.

Rho was uncharacteristically somber as we waited in the Pad Four lounge. Outside, it was lunar night, but the brilliant glow of landing field lights blanked out the stars. Earth was at full above us, a double-thumbnail-sized spot of bluish light through the overhead ports. All we could see through the lounge windows was a few hectares of ashen churned lunar soil, a pile of rubble dug out from the Ice Pit warrens decades before, and the featureless gray concrete of the field itself.

"I feel like they're shoving my nose in it," Rho said. The lights of the executive bus became visible above the horizon. "Pretty fancy treatment. The director never paid us so much attention before."

I tried to reassure her. "You've never reeled in Great-Grandma and Grandpa before," I said.

She shook her head. "That isn't it. He sent a stack of research on Logologists."

I nodded. "Me, too. You've read it?"

"Of course."

"What did you think?"

"They're odd, but I can't find anything that would make them object to this project. They say death isn't liberation unless you're enlightened—so frozen heads could just be more potential converts . . ."

"Maybe Thomas knows something more," I said.

The bus landed, sleek and bright red, an expensive, full-pressure, full-cabin late model Lunar Rover. I had never ridden on the Sandoval limo before. The interior was impressive: automatically adjusting seats, a hot and cold restaurant unit—I'd already eaten breakfast, but nibbled on Rho's eggs and mock ham—and a complete communications center. We could have called Earth or Mars or any of the asteroids using Lunar Cooperative or even the Triple satellites if we'd wished.

"Makes you realize how far out of the Sandoval mainstream we are at the Ice Pit," I said as Rho slipped her plate into the return.

"I haven't missed it," she said. "We get what we need."

"William might not agree."

Rho smiled. "It's not luxury he's after."

Port Yin was Procellarum's main interplanetary commerce field and largest city, hub for all the stations in the ocean. Procellarum was the main territory of Sandoval BM, though we had some twenty stations and two smaller ports in the Earthside highlands. Besides being a transportation hub, Port Yin was surrounded by farms. We fed much of the Earthside Moon south and west of the ocean. For lunar citizens, a farm station of sufficient size also acts as a resort—a chance to admire forests and fields.

We passed over the now-opaqued rows of farm domes, thousands of hectares spaced along the southeast edge of the port, and came in at the private Sandoval field half an hour before our appointment. That gave us little time to cross by rail and walkway through Yin City's crowds to Center Port.

The director's secretary led us down the short hall to his small personal office, centrally located among the Sandoval syndic warrens.

Thomas Sandoval-Rice was trim, resolutely gray-haired, with a thin nose and ample lips, a middling seventy-five years old, and he wore a formal black suit with red sash and mooncalf slippers. He stood to greet us. There was barely room for three chairs and a desk; this was his inner sanctum, not the show office for Sandoval clients or other BM reps.

Rho looked at me forlornly as we entered; this did indeed seem like the occasion for a dressing-down.

"I'm pleased to see both of you again," Thomas said as he offered us chairs. "You're looking well. Mickey, it's been three years, hasn't it, since we approved your position at the Ice Pit?"

"Yes, sir," I said. "Thank you."

"No need. You've done well." Thomas noticed Rho's wary expression and smiled reassurance. "This is not a visit to the dentist," he said. "Rho, I smell a storm coming, and I'd like to have you tell me what kind of storm it might be, and why we're sailing into it."

"I don't know, sir," Rho said steadily.

"Mickey?"

"I've read your text, sir. I'm puzzled, as well."

"The Task-Felder BM is behind all this, everybody's assured me of that. I have friends in the United States of the Western Hemisphere Senate. Friends who are in touch with California Logology, the parent church, as it were. Task-Felder BM is less independent than they want to appear; if California Logology nods its hoary head, Task-Felder jumps. Now, you know that no lunar BM is supposed to operate as either a terrestrial representative or to promote purely religious principles . . . That's in the Lunar Binding Multiples Agreements. The Constitution of the Moon."

"Yes, sir," I said.

"But Task-Felder BM has managed to avoid or ignore a great many of those provisions, and nobody's called them on it, because no BM likes the image of making a council challenge of another fully chartered BM, even one with terrestrial connections. Bad for business, in brief. We all like to think of ourselves as rugged individualists, family first, Moon second, Triple third . . . and to hell with the Triple if push comes to shove. Understood?"

"Yes, sir," I said.

"I've served as chief syndic and director of Sandoval BM for twenty-nine years, and in that time, I've seen Task-Felder grow powerful *despite* the distaste of the older, family-based binding multiples. They're sharp, they're quick learners, they have impressive financial backing, and they have a sincerity and a drive that can be disconcerting."

"I've noticed that, sir," I said.

Thomas pursed his lips. "Your conversation with Janis Granger was not pleasant?"

"No, sir."

"We've done something to offend them, and my sources on Earth tell me they're willing to take off their gloves, get down in the dust and spit up a volcano if they have to. Mud, mud, crazier than mud."

"I don't understand why, sir," Rho said.

"I was hoping one or both of you could enlighten me. You've gone through the brief on their history and beliefs. You don't find anything suggestive?"

"I certainly don't," Rho said.

"Our frozen great-grandma and great-grandpa never did anything to upset them?"

"Not that we know of."

"Rho, we've had some two-facing from our fellow BMs, haven't we? Nernst and Cailetet are willing to design something for us and take our cash, but they may not stand up for us in the Council." He rubbed his chin for a moment with his finger, making a wry face. "Is there anyone else interesting in the list of heads, besides Great-Grandma and Great-Grandpa?"

"I've brought along my files, including the list of individuals preserved by StarTime. There's a gap I was not aware of, sir—three intact individuals, not named—and I've asked StarTime's advocate in New York for an accounting, but I have yet to get an answer."

"You've correlated the list?"

"Pardon?" Rho asked.

"You've run cross-checks between Logology connections and the list? In history?"

"No," Rho said.

"Did you, Mickey?"

"No, sir."

Thomas glanced at me reproachfully. "Let's do it now, then," he said. He took Rho's slate and plugged it into his desktop thinker. With a start, I realized this small green cube was Ellen C, *the* Sandoval thinker, advisor to all the syndics. Ellen C was one of the oldest thinkers on the Moon, somewhat obsolete now, but definitely part of the family. "Ellen, what do we have here?"

"No interesting strikes or correlations in the first or second degree," the thinker reported. "Completed."

Thomas raised his eyebrows. "Perhaps a dead end."

"I'll look into the unnamed three," Rho said.

"Do that. Now, I'd like to rehearse a few things with you folks. Are you familiar with our weaknesses—or your own? What about the many weaknesses and failures of the lunar BM political system?"

I could not, in my naïveté, come up with any immediate answers. Rho was equally blank.

"Allow an older fool to lecture you a bit. First, let's get personal. Grandpa Ian Reiker-Sandoval favored Rho, doted on her. Gave her anything she wanted. So Rho got the man she wanted, someone from outside who didn't meet the usual Sandoval criteria for eligible matches. And she got him his project."

Rho looked stubbornly unperturbed.

Thomas smiled. "Still, William has done his work admirably, and the project is interesting. We all look forward to a breakthrough. However—"

"You're saying I'm spoiled," Rho anticipated.

"Let's say . . . that you've had a rich girl's leeway, without the corruption of free access to fabulous wealth," Thomas said. "Nevertheless, you have substantial BM resources at your disposal, and you have a way of getting us into trouble without really seeing it coming."

"I'm not sure that's fair," I said.

"As judgments go, it's extremely fair," Thomas said, staring at me with no further humor. "This is not the first time . . . or are memories short in the younger Sandovals?"

Rho looked up at the ceiling, then at me, then at Thomas. "The tulips," she said.

"Sandoval BM lost half a million Triple dollars. Fortunately, we were able to convert the farms to tailored pharmaceuticals. That was before your marriage to William . . . Although typical of your early adventures. You've matured considerably, as I'm sure you'll both agree. Still, Rho has never been caught up in a freefall scuffle. She has always had Sandoval BM firmly behind her. To her credit, she's never brought in the kind of trouble that could reflect badly on the BM. Until now, and I can't pin the blame on her for this, except to say she's not terribly prescient."

"You blame her for *any* aspect of this?" I asked, still defensive before Thomas's gaze.

"No," he said after a long pause. "I blame *you*. You, my dear lad, are a focused dilettante, very good in your area, which is the Ice Pit, but not widely experienced. You don't have Rho's ambition, and neither have you shown signs of her innovative spark . . . You've never even taken advantage of your Earth sabbatical. Micko, if I may be familiar, you've managed the Ice Pit well enough, certainly nothing for us to complain about, but you've had little experience in the bigger arena of the Triple, and you've grown soft sitting out there. You didn't check out Rho's scheme."

I straightened in my chair. "It had BM charter—"

"You should *still* have checked it out. You should have smelled something coming. There may be no such thing as prescience, but honed instincts are crucial in our game, Micko. You've cultivated fine literature—terrestrial literature—fine music, and a little history in the copious time you've had between your bursts of economic activity. You've become something of a lady's man in the barn dances. Fine; you're of an age where such things are natural. But now it's time that you put on some muscle. I'd like you to handle this matter as my accessory. You'll go to the council meetings—one is scheduled in a couple of days—and you'll study up on the chinks in our system's armor."

I settled back, suddenly more than just uneasy, and not about my impending debut in larger BM politics. "You think we're approaching a singularity?"

Thomas nodded. "Whatever your failings, Micko, you are sharp. That's exactly right. A time when all the rules could fail, and all our past oversights come back to haunt us. It's a good possibility. Care to lecture *me* for a minute?"

I shrugged. "Sir, I—"

"Stretch your wings, lad. You're not ignorant, else you wouldn't have made that last remark. What singularity faces the BMs now?"

"I can't really say, sir. I don't know which weakness you're referring to, specifically, but—"

"Go on." Thomas smiled like a genial tiger.

"We've outgrown the lunar constitution. Two million people in fifty-four BMs, that's ten times as many as lived on the Moon when the constitution was written. And actually, it was never written by an individual. It was cobbled together by a committee intent on not stretching or voiding individual BM charters. I think that *you* think Task-Felder isn't above forcing a constitutional crisis."

"Yes?"

"If they are planning something like that, now's the time to do it. I've been studying the Triple's performance for the past few years. Lunar BMs have gotten increasingly conservative, sir. Compared with Mars, we've been . . ." I was on a nervous high; I waved my hands, and smiled placation, hoping not to overwhelm or offend.

"Yes?"

"Well, a little like you accuse me of being, sir. Self-contented, taking advantage of the lull. But the Triple is going through a major shake-up now, Earth's economy is suffering its expected forty-year cyclic decline, and the lunar BMs are vulnerable. If we stop cooperating, the Moon could be put into a financial crisis worse than the Split. So everybody's being very cautious, very . . . conservative. The old rough-and-tumble has given way to don't-prick-the-seal."

"Good," Thomas said.

"I haven't been a worm, sir," I said with a pained expression.

"Glad to hear it. And if Task-Felder convinces a significant number of BMs that we're rocking the boat in a way that could lower the lunar rating in the Triple?"

"It could be bad. But why would they do that?" I asked, still puzzled.

Rho picked up my question. "Tom, how could a few hundred heads bring this on? What's Task-Felder got against us?"

"Nothing at all, dear daughter," Thomas said. BM elders often referred to family youngsters as if they were their own children. "That's what worries me most of all."

Rho returned to the Ice Pit to supervise completion of the chamber for the heads; I stayed behind to prepare for the council meeting. Thomas put me up in Sandoval guest quarters reserved for family, spare but comfortable. I felt depressed, angry with myself for being so vulnerable.

I *hated* disappointing Thomas Sandoval-Rice.

And I took no satisfaction in the thought that perhaps he had stung me to get my blood moving, to spur me to action.

I wanted to avoid any circumstance where he would need to sting me again.

Thomas woke me from an erratic snooze of one hour, post twelve hours of study. My head felt like a dented air canister. "Tune to general net lunar news," he said. "Scroll back the past five minutes."

I did as he told me and watched the LitVid image.

News of the quarter-hour. Synopsis: Earth questions jurisdiction of Moon in Sandoval BM buy-out of StarTime Preservation Society Contract and transfer of corpsicles.

Expansion 1: The United States Congressional Office of Triple Relations has issued an advisory alliance alert to the Lunar Council of Binding Multiples that the Sandoval BM purchase of preservation contracts of four hundred and ten frozen heads of deceased twenty-first century individuals may be invalid, under a late twentieth century law regarding retention of archaeological artifacts within cultural and national boundaries. StarTime Preservation Society, a deceased-estate financed partnership group now dissolved on Earth, has already transferred "members, chattels, and responsibilities" to Sandoval BM. Sandoval Chief Syndic Thomas Sandoval-Rice states that the heads are legally under control of his binding multiple, subject to . . .

The report continued in that vein for eight thousand words of text and four minutes of recorded interviews. It concluded with a kicker, an interview with Puerto Rican Senator Pauline Grandville: *"If the Moon can simply ignore the feelings and desires of its terrestrial forebears, then that could call into question the entire matrix of Earth-Moon relations."*

I transferred to Thomas's line. "That's amazing," I said.

"Not at all," Thomas said. "I've run a search of the Earth-Moon LitVids and terrestrial press. It's in your hopper now."

"I've been reading all night, sir—"

Thomas glared at me. "I wouldn't have expected any less. We don't have much time."

"Sir, I'd be able to pinpoint my research if you'd let me know your strategy."

"I don't have one yet, Micko. And neither should you. These are just the opening rounds. Never fire your guns before you've chosen a target."

"Did you know about this earlier? That California would tell Puerto Rico to do something like this?"

"I had a hint, nothing more. But my sources are quiet now. No more tattling from Earth, I'm afraid. We're on our own."

I wanted to ask him why the sources were quiet, but I sensed I'd used up my ration of questions.

Never in my life had I faced a problem with interplanetary implications. I finished a full eighteen hours of research, hardly more enlightened than when I had started, though I was full of facts: facts about Task-Felder, facts about the council president and her aide, yet more facts about Logology.

I was depressed and angry. I sat head in hands for fully an hour, wondering why the world was picking on me. At least I had a partial answer to Thomas's criticisms—short of actual precognition, I didn't think anybody could have intuited such an outcome to Rho's venture.

I lifted my head to answer a private line call, routed to the guest quarters.

"I have a live call direct from Port Yin for Mister Mickey Sandoval."

"That's me," I said.

The secretary connected and the face of Fiona Task-Felder, president of the council, clicked into vid. "Mr. Sandoval, may I speak to you for a few minutes?"

I was stunned. "I'm sorry, I wasn't expecting . . . a call. Not here."

"I like to work direct, especially when my underlings screw up, as I trust Janis did."

"Uh . . ."

"Do you have a few minutes?"

"Please, Madame President . . . I'd much rather hold this conversation with our chief syndic tied in . . ."

"I'd rather not, Mr. Sandoval. Just a few questions, and maybe we can patch all this up."

Fiona Task-Felder could hardly have looked more different from her aide. She was gray-haired, in her late sixties, with a muscular build that showed hours of careful exercise. She wore stretch casuals beneath her short council collar and seal. She looked vigorous and friendly and motherly, and was a handsome woman, but in a natural way, quite the reverse of Granger's studied, artificial hardness.

I should have known better, but I said, "All right. I'll try to answer as best I can . . ."

"Why does your sister want these heads?" the president asked.

"We've already explained that."

"Not to anyone's satisfaction but your own, perhaps. I've learned that your grandparents—pardon me, your great-grandparents—are among them. Is that your sole reason?"

"I don't think now's the time to discuss this, not without my sister, and certainly not without our director."

"I'm trying hard to understand, Mr. Sandoval. I think we should meet casually, without noise from aides and syndics, and straighten this out quickly, before somebody else screws it up out of all proportion. Is that possible?"

"I think Rho could explain—"

"Fine, then, bring her."

"I'm sorry, but—"

She gave me a motherly expression of irritation, as if with a

wayward son—or an irritating lover. "I'm giving you a rare opportunity. In the old lunar spirit of one-on-one, and cut the politics. I
think we can work it out. If we work fast."

I felt way out of my depth. I was being asked to step outside
of formal procedures . . . To make a decision immediately. I knew
the only way to play *that* game was to ignore her unexpressed
rules.

"All right," I said.

"I have an appointment available on the third at ten hundred.
Is that acceptable?"

That was three days away. I calculated quickly; I'd be back in
the Ice Pit station by then, and that meant I'd have to hire a special
shuttle flight. "I'll be there," I said.

"I'm looking forward to it," Fiona Task-Felder said, and left me
alone in the guest room to think out my options.

I did not break the rules of her game. I did not talk to Thomas
Sandoval-Rice. Nor did I tell Rho what I was doing. Before leaving
Port Yin for a return trip to the Ice Pit, I secretly booked a non-
scheduled round-trip shuttle, spending a great deal of Sandoval
money on one passenger; thankfully, because of my position at the
station, I did not have to give details.

I doubted that Thomas or Rho would look for me during the
time I was gone; six hours going, a few hours there, and six back.
I could leave custom messages for whoever might call, including
Rho or Thomas or—much less likely—William.

To this day I experience a sick twist in my stomach when I ask
myself why I did not follow through with my original thought,
and tell Thomas about the president's call. I think perhaps it was
youthful ego, wounded by Thomas's dressing-down; ego plus a
strange gratification that the council *president* was going to see me
personally, to put aside a block of her time to speak to someone
not even an assistant syndic. Me. To speak to *me.*

I knew I was not doing what I should be doing, but like a mouse entranced by a snake, I ignored them all—a tendency of behavior I have since learned I was not unique in possessing. A tendency common in some lunar citizens.

We habitually cry out, "Cut the politics." But the challenge and intrigue of politics seduces us every time.

I honestly thought I could beat out Fiona Task-Felder.

As our arbeiters executed the Nernst design, the repository for the heads resembled a flattened doughnut lying on its side: a wide, circular passageway with heads stored in seven tiers of cubicles around the outer perimeter. It would lie neatly in the bottom cup of the void, seven meters below the laboratory, out of range of whatever peculiar fluctuations might occur in the force disorder pumps during William's tests, and easily connected to the refrigerators. Lunar rock would insulate the outer torus; pipes and other fittings could be neatly dropped from the refrigerators above. A small elevator from the side of the bridge opposite the Cavity would give access.

It was a neat design, as we expected from Nernst BM. Our arbeiters performed flawlessly, although they were ten years out of date. Not once did anyone mention problems with the Council. I started to feel cocky; my plan of conferring with Thomas about the visit with the president faded in and out with my mood. I could handle her; the threat was minimal. If I was sufficiently cagey, I could drop right in, leap right out, no harm, although perhaps no benefit, either.

The day after I finished oversight and inspection on the chamber, and received a Nernst designer's inspection report, and after the last of Rho's heads had been installed in their cubicles, I stamped my approval for final payment to Nernst, called in the Cailetet consultants to look over the facilities, packed my travel bag, and was off.

There is a gray sameness to a lunar ocean's surface that induces a state of hypnosis, a mix of fascination at the lifeless expanse, never quite encompassed by memory, and incredible boredom. Crater walls, rilled terrain, the painted flats of ancient vents. Parts of the moon are beautiful in a rugged way, even to a citizen.

Life on the Moon is a process of turning inward, toward interior living spaces, an interior *you*. Lunar citizens are exceptional at introspection and decoration and indoor arts and crafts. Some of the finest craftsmen and artists in the solar system reside on the Moon; their work commands high prices throughout the Triple.

Two hours into the journey, I fell asleep and dreamed again of Egypt, endless dry deserts beyond the thin greenbelts of the Nile, deserts populated by mummies leading trains of camels. Camels carrying trays of ice, making sounds like force disorder pumps . . .

I awoke quickly and cursed William for that story, for its peculiar fascination. What was so strange about space sucking heat from trays of water? That was the principle behind our own heat exchangers on the surface above the Ice Pit. Still, I could not conceive of a sky on Earth as black as the Moon's, as all forgiving, all absorbing.

The shuttle made a smooth landing minutes later at Port Yin, and I disembarked, part of me still believing I would go to Thomas's office first, an hour before my appointment.

I did not. I spent that hour shopping for a birthday present for a girl in Copernicus Station. A girl I was not particularly courting at the time; something to pass an hour. My mind was blank.

The offices of the council president were located in the council annex to Port Yin's western domicile district; in the suburbs, as it were, and away from the center of BM activity, as befitted a political institution. The offices were numerous but not sumptuous; the syndics of many small BMs could have displayed more opulence.

I walked and took the skids, using the time to prepare myself. I was not stupid enough to believe there was no danger; I even felt with one part of my mind that what I was doing was more likely to turn out badly than otherwise. But I skidded along toward the council president's offices regardless, and in my defense I must say that my self-assurance still overcame my doubts. On the average, I felt more confident than ill-at-ease.

It was after all just *politics*. My entire upbringing had ingrained in me the essential triviality of lunar politics. Council officers were merely secretaries to a bunch of congenial family businesses, dotting the i's and crossing the t's of rules of cooperation that probably would have been followed anyway, out of simple courtesy and for the sake of mutual benefit.

Most of our ancestors had been engineers and miners exported from the Earth; conservative and independent, suspicious of any authority, strongly convinced that large groups of people could live in comparative peace and prosperity without layers of government and bureaucracy.

My ancestors worked to squash the natural growth of such layers: "Cut the politics" was their constant cry, followed by shaking heads and raised eyes. Political organization was evil, representative government an imposition. Why have a representative when you could interact personally? Keep it small, direct, and uncomplicated, they believed, and freedom would necessarily follow.

They couldn't keep it small. The moon had already grown to such a point that layers of government and representation were necessary. But as with sexual attitudes in some Earth cultures, necessity was no guarantee of responsibility and planning.

From the beginning, our prime families and founders—including, I must say, Emilia and Robert—had screwed up the lunar constitution, if the patched-up collations of hearsay and station charters could even be called such.

When complex organization did come, it was haphazard, unenthusiastically organic, undisciplined. When the Split broke our economic supply lines with Earth, and when the first binding multiples came, the Moon was a reservoir of naively amenable suckers, but blessedly lucky—at first. The binding multiples weren't political organizations—they were business families, extensions of individuals, the Lunars said. Lunar citizens saw nothing wrong with family structures or even syndicates; they saw nothing wrong with the complex structures of the binding multiples, because somehow they did not qualify as government.

When the binding multiples had to set up offices to work with each other, and share legal codes written and unwritten to prevent friction, that was not government; it was pragmatism. And when the binding multiples formed a council, why, that was nothing more sinister than business folks getting together to talk and achieve individual consensus. (That oxymoron—individual consensus—was actually common then.) The Council of Binding Multiples was nothing more than a committee organized to reduce frictions between the business syndicates—at first. It was decorative and weak.

We were still innocent and did not know that the price of freedom—of individuality—is attention to politics, careful planning, careful organization; philosophy is no more a barrier against political disaster than it is against plague.

Think me naive; I was. We all were.

I entered the reception area, a cubicle barely four meters square, with a man behind a desk to supplement an automated appointments system.

"Good day," the man said. He was perhaps fifty, gray-haired, blunt-nosed, with a pleasant but discriminating expression.

"Mickey Sandoval," I said. "I have an invitation from the president."

"Indeed you do, Mr. Sandoval. You're about three minutes early, but I believe the president is free now." The automated appointments clerk produced a screenful of information. "Yes, Mr. Sandoval. Please go in." He gestured toward a double door on his left, which opened to a long hallway. "At the end. Ignore the mess, please; the administration is still moving in."

Boxes of information cubes and other files lined the hallway in neat stacks. Several young women in Port Yin drabs—a style I did not find attractive—were moving files into an office along the hallway by electric cart. They smiled at me as I passed. I returned their smiles.

I was full of confidence, walking into the attractive, the seductive and yet trivial inner sanctum. These were all doubtless Logologists. The council presidents could choose all staff members from their own BM if they so desired. Binding multiples worked together; there would never be any accusations of nepotism or favoritism in a political climate where such was the expected, the norm.

Fiona Task-Felder's office was at the end of the hall. Wide lunar oak doors opened automatically as I approached, and the president herself stepped forward to shake my hand.

"Thanks for shuttling in," she said. "Mr. Sandoval—"

"Mickey, please," I said.

"Fiona to you, as well. We're just getting settled here. Come sit; let's talk and see if some sort of accommodation can be reached between the council and Sandoval."

Subtly, she had just informed me that Sandoval was on the outs, that we somehow stood apart from our fellow BMs. I did not bristle at the suggestion. I noted it, but assumed it was unintentional. Lunar politics was almost unfailingly polite, and this seemed too abrupt.

"Fruit juice? That's all we're serving here," Fiona said with a smile. She was even more fit-looking in person, solid and square-shouldered, hair strong and stiff and cut short, eyes clear blue and surrounded by fine wrinkles, what my mother had once called "time's dividends." I took a glass of apple juice and sat at one end of the broad curved desk, where two screens and two keyboards waited.

"I understand the installation is already made, and that Cailetet is beginning its work now," the president said.

I nodded.

"How far along?" she asked.

"Not very," I said.

"Have you revived any heads?"

That set me aback; she knew as well as I, she *had* to know, that it was not our plan to revive any heads, that nobody had the means to do so. "Of course not," I said.

"If you had, you'd have violated council wishes," she said.

From the very beginning, she had me off balance. I tried to recover. "We've broken no rules."

"Council has been informed by a number of syndics that they're concerned about your activities."

"You mean, they're worried we might try to bring more corpsicles from Earth."

"Yes," she said, nodding once, firmly. "That will not be allowed if I have anything to do with it. Now, please explain what you plan to do with these heads."

I was aghast. "Excuse me? That's—"

"It's not confidential at all, Mickey. You've agreed to come here to speak with me. A great many BMs are awaiting my report on what you say."

"That isn't what I understood, Fiona." I tried to keep my voice calm. "I'm not here testifying under oath, and I don't have to reveal family business plans to any council member, even the president." I settled more firmly into my seat, trying to exude the confidence I had already scattered to the winds.

Her face hardened. "It would be simple courtesy to your fellow BMs to explain what you intend to do, Mickey."

I hoped to give her a tidbit sufficient to put her off. "The heads are being preserved in the Ice Pit, in the void where my brother does his work."

"Your brother in-law, you mean."

"Yes. He's family now. We dispense with modifiers." *When talking with outsiders*, I might have added.

She smiled, but her expression was still hard. "William Pierce. He's doing BM funded research on extremely low temperatures in copper, no?"

I nodded.

"Has he been successful?"

"Not yet," I said.

"It's simple coincidence that his facilities are capable of preserving the heads."

"I suppose so, yes. My sister probably would not have brought them to the Moon otherwise. I think of it more as opportunity than coincidence."

Fiona instructed the screens to bring up displays of lunar binding multiples who were pushing for an investigation of the Sandoval corpsicle imports. They were platinum names indeed: the top four BMs, except for Sandoval, and fifteen others, spaced around the Moon, including Nernst and Cailetet. "Incidentally," she said, "You know about the furor on Earth."

"I've heard," I said.

"Did you know there's a ruckus starting on Mars now?"

I did not.

"They want Earth's dead kept on Earth," the president said. "They think it's bad precedent to export corpsicles and make the outer planets responsible for the inner's problems. They think the Moon must be siding with Earth in some fashion to get rid of this problem."

"It's not a problem," I said, exasperated. "Nobody on Earth has made a fuss about this in decades."

"So what's causing the fuss now?" she asked.

I tried to think my way through to a civil answer. "We think Task-Felder is behind it," I said.

"You accuse me of carrying my BM's interests into the council with me, despite my oath of office?"

"I'm not accusing anybody of anything," I said. "We have evidence that the representative, the . . . the . . . United States national assembly representative from Puerto Rico—"

"Congressional representative," she corrected.

"Yes . . . You know about that?"

"He's a Logologist. So is most of Puerto Rico. Are you accusing members of my religion of instigating this?"

She spoke with such complete shock and indignation that I thought for a moment, could we be wrong? Were our facts misleading, poorly analyzed? Then I remembered Janis Granger and her tactics in our first interview. Fiona Task-Felder was no more gentle, no more polite. I was here at her invitation to be raked over the coals.

"Excuse me, Madame President," I said. "I'd like for you to get to your point."

"The point is, Mickey, that you've agreed by coming here to testify before the full council and explain your actions, your intentions, everything about this mess, at the next meeting, which will be in three days."

I smiled and shook my head, then brought up my slate. "Auto counselor," I said.

Her smile grew harder, her blue eyes more intense.

"Is this some new law you've cooked up for the occasion?" I asked, trying for a tough and sophisticated manner.

"Not at all," she said with an air of closing claws on the kill. "You may think what you wish about Task-Felder BM, or about Logologists—about my people—but we do not play outside the rules. Ask your auto counselor about courtesy briefings and formal council meetings. This is a courtesy briefing, Mickey, and I've logged it as such."

My auto counselor found the relevant council rules on courtesy briefings, and the particular rule passed thirty years before, by the council, that mandated the council's right to hear just what the president heard, as testimony, under oath. A strange and parochial law, so seldom invoked that I had never heard of it. Until now.

"I'm ending this discussion," I said, standing.

"Tell Thomas Sandoval-Rice that you and he should be at the

next full council meeting. Under council agreements, you don't have any choice, Mickey."

She did not smile. I left the office, walked quickly down the hall, and avoided looking at anyone, especially the young women still moving files.

"She's snared her rabbit," Thomas said as he poured me a beer. He had been unusually quiet all evening, since I had announced myself at his door and made my anguished confession of gross ineptitude. Far worse than being blasted by his rage was facing his quiet disappointment. He seemed somehow deflated, withdrawn, like an aquarium anemone touched by an uncaring finger. "Don't blame yourself entirely, Micko. I should have guessed they'd try something like this."

"I feel like an idiot."

"That's the third time you've said that in the past ten minutes," Thomas said. "You have been an idiot, of course, but don't let that get you down."

I shook my head; I was already down about as far as it was possible to fall.

Thomas lifted his beer, inspected the large bubbles, and said, "If we don't testify, we're in much worse trouble. It will look as if we're ignoring the wishes of our fellow BMs, as if we've gone renegade. If we do testify, we'll have been maneuvered into breaking the BM's sacred right to keep business and research matters private . . . and that will make us look like weaklings and fools. No doubt about it, she's pushed us into a deep rille, Mickey. If you had refused to go in, and had claimed family privilege, she'd have tried something else . . .

"At least now we can be sure what we're in for. Isolation, recrimination, probable withdrawal of contracts, maybe even boycott of services. That's never happened before, Micko. We're going to make history this week, no doubt about it."

"Is there anything I can do?"

Thomas finished his glass and wiped his lips. "Another?" he asked, gesturing at the keg. I shook my head. "Me neither," he said around a restrained belch. "We need clear heads, Micko, and we need a full family meeting. We're going to have to build internal solidarity; this has gone way beyond what the director and all the syndics can handle by themselves."

I flew back from Port Yin, head cloudy with anguish. It seemed somehow I had been responsible for all of this. Thomas did not say as much, not this time; but he had hinted it before. I halfway hoped the shuttle would smear itself across the regolith; that the pilot would survive and I would not. Then, anguish began to be replaced by a grim and determined anger. I had been twisted around by experts; used by those who had no qualms about use and abuse. I had seen the enemy and underestimated the strength of their resolve, whatever their motivations, whatever their goals. These people were not following the lunar way; they were playing us all, all of the BMs—me, Rho, the Triple, the Western Hemispheric United States, the corpsicles—like fish on a line, single-mindedly dedicated to one end. The heads were just an excuse. They had no real importance; that much was obvious.

This was a power play.

The Logologists were intent on dominating the Moon, perhaps the Earth. I hated them for their ambition, their evil presumption, for the way they had lowered me in the eyes of Thomas.

Having erred on the side of underestimation, I was now swinging the opposite direction, equally in error; but I would not realize that for a few more days yet.

I came home, and knew for the first time how much the station meant to me.

I met a Cailetet man in the alley leading to the Ice Pit. "You're Mickey, right?" he asked casually. He held a small silver case in front of him, dangling from one hand. He seemed happy.

I looked at him as if he might utter words of absolute betrayal.

"We've just investigated one of your heads," he said, only slightly put off by my expression. "You've been shuttling, eh?"

I nodded. "How's Rho?" I asked, somewhat irrelevantly; I hadn't spoken to anybody since my arrival.

"She's ecstatic, I think. We've done our work well."

"You're sticking with us?" I asked suspiciously.

"Beg your pardon?"

"You haven't been recalled by your family syndics?"

"No-o-oo," he said, drawling the word dubiously. "Not that I've heard."

The families were being incredibly two-faced. "Just curious," I said. "What's it going to cost us?"

"In the long term? That's *right*," he said, as if the reason for my surliness had finally been solved. "You're financial manager for the Ice Pit. I'm sorry; I'm a bit slow. Believe me, we're interested in this as a research project. If we perfect our techniques here, we can market the medical applications all over the Triple and beyond. We're charging you expenses and nothing else, Mickey. This is platinum opportunity."

"Does it work?" I asked, still sullen.

He thumped the case. "Data right here. We're checking it with history on Earth. I'd say it works, yes. Talking with the dead—I don't think anybody's done that before!"

"Who was it?" I asked.

"One of the three unknowns. Rho decided we'd work with them first, to help solve the mystery. Please go right in, Mickey. Nernst has designed a very nice facility. Ask questions, see what they're doing. They're working on unknown number two right now."

"Thanks," I said, wondering what distortion of protocol could lead this man to invite me into my own BM's facility. "I'm glad it's working."

"All right," the man said, with a short intake of breath. "Must be off. Check this individual out, correlate . . . on our own nickel, Mickey. Good to have met you."

I stopped at the white line and called for access.

"Goddamn it, yes!" William's voice roared from the speaker. "It's open. Just cross and stop bothering me."

"It's me, Mickey," I said.

"Well then, come and join the party! Everybody else is here."

William had locked himself in the laboratory. Three Onnes and Cailetet techs were on the bridge standing well away from the force disorder pumps, chatting and eating lunch. I passed them with casual nods.

William sounded in no mood for visitors—this time of day was usually his phase of most intense activity. I swung onto the lift and descended to Rho's facility, twenty feet below the laboratory. The Ice Pit echoed with voices from above and below; the sounds seemed to come from all directions as I descended in the open lift, first to the right, then the left, canceled, returned, grew soft, then immediate.

Rho came through the hatch at the top of the chamber and rushed forward excitedly. "William's pissed, but we're leaving him alone, mostly, so it'll pass." She fairly brewed over with enthusiasm. "Oh, *Mickey!*" She threw her arms around me.

"What?"

"Did you hear upstairs? We tuned in to a head! It works! Come on in. We're working on the second head now."

"An unknown," I said with polite interest, her enthusiasm not infecting me. (How much could I blame *her* for these problems?)

"Yes. Another unknown. I still can't get a response from the StarTime trustees. Do you think they've lost all their backup records? That would be something, wouldn't it?" She ushered me down the hatch into the chamber. Within the chamber, all was quiet but for a faint song of electronics and the low hiss of refrigerants.

I recognized Armand Cailetet-Davis, the balding, slight-figured powerhouse of Cailetet research. Beside him stood Irma Stolbart of Onnes, a lunar-born reputed superwhiz whom I had heard of but never met: thirty or thirty-five, tall and thin with reddish brown hair and chocolate skin. They stood beside a tripod-mounted piece of equipment, three horizontal cylinders strapped together, pointed at the face of one of the forty stainless steel boxes mounted in the racks.

Rho introduced me to them. Penetrating my dark mood, I felt a small thrill at the confirmation, the solid realization, of what was actually going on here.

"We're selecting one of the seventy-three known natural mind languages," Armand explained, pointing at a thinker prism in Irma Stolbart's hands. She smiled, quick glance at me, at Armand, distracted, then continued to work on her thinker, which was about a tenth the size of William's QL and easily portable. "We'll test some uploaded data for patterns—"

"Patterns from the head," I said, stating the obvious.

"Yes. A male individual, age sixty-five at death—apparently in good condition considering medical standards of the time. Very little deterioration."

"Have you looked inside?" I asked.

Rho lifted her brows. "Brother, *nobody* looks inside. Not by actually opening the box. We don't care what they look like." She laughed nervously. "It's not the head that interests us, it's the mind, the memory—it's what's locked up in the *brain*."

A soul?

Now I was shivering from fatigue, as well as something like superstitious awe. "Sorry," I said to nobody in particular. They ignored me, concentrating on their work.

"We find northern Europeans tend to cluster in these three program areas," Stolbart explained. She showed me a slate screen on which a diagram had been sketched. The diagram showed twelve different rectangles, each labeled with a cultural-ethnic group. Her finger underlined three boxes: *Finn/ Scand/ Teut/.* "Mind-memory storage languages are among the genetic traits most rigidly adhered to. We think they change very little across thousands of years. That makes sense, considering the necessity of immediate infant adaptation to its milieu."

"Indeed," Rho said, smiling and gently squeezing my arm again. "So he's of northern European stock?"

"He's definitely not Levantine, African, or Asian," Irma Stolbart said. I watched her curiously, focusing on her face, lean and intent, with lovely, skeptical brown eyes.

"Have you spoken with your syndics?" I asked out of the blue, startling even myself.

Armand had clearly earned his position in Cailetet through quick thinking and adaptability. With no hesitation whatsoever, he said, "We work here until somebody tells us to leave. Nobody has yet. Maybe you administrators can work it all out in the council."

You administrators. That put us in our place. Paper pushers, bureaucrats, politicians. Cut the politics. We were the ones who stood in the way of the scientist's goal of unrestrained research and intellection.

"I see a fourteen Penrose cipher trace algorithm in the cerebral cortex," Irma said. "Definitely Northern European."

Rho looked troubled, examined my face for signs. With a tug of my ear and a gesture up into the air I indicated that we should talk. She drew me aside. "Are you tired?" she asked.

"Dead on my feet," I said. "I'm an idiot, Rho, and maybe I've augured this whole thing right into a rille."

"I have faith in the family. We'll make it. I have faith in you, Micko," she said, grasping my arm. I felt vaguely sick, seeing her expression of support, her trust. "I'd like you to stay and watch. This is really something . . . if you're up to it?"

"Wouldn't miss it," I said.

"It's almost religious, isn't it?" she whispered in my ear.

"All right," Armand said. "We have locale. Let's take a picture, upload into the translator, and see if we can draw a name from the file."

Armand adjusted the position on the triple cylinders and tuned his slate to their output, getting a picture of a vague gray mass suspended by a thin sling in a sharp black square—the head resting in its cubicle and cradle within the larger box. "We're centered," he said. "Irma, if you could . . ."

"Field guide on," she said, flipping a switch on a tiny disk taped to the box.

"Recording," Armand said nonchalantly. There was no noise, no visible or audible sign that anything was happening. Squares appeared on Armand's slate in the upper right hand portion of the mass. I was able to make out that the head had slumped to one side, whether facing us or not, I could not tell. I kept staring at the image, the squares flashing one by one in sequence around the cranium, and I realized with a gruesome tingle that the head had become misshapen, that during its decades in storage it had deformed in the presence of Earth gravity, nestling deeper into its sling like a frozen melon.

"Got it," Armand said. "One more—the third unknown—and we'll call it a session."

For Rho's sake, I stayed to watch the third head be scanned and its neural states and patterns recorded. I kissed Rho's cheek, congratulated her, and took the lift to the bridge. Again, the voices flowed around me, soft technical chatter from the chamber below, the technicians on the bridge above.

I went to my water tank room and collapsed.

Strangely enough, I slept well.

Rho came into my room and woke me up at twelve hundred, eight hours after I'd dropped onto my bed. Obviously, she had not slept at all. Her hair was matted with finger-tugs and rearrangement, her face shiny with the long hours.

"We got a name on the number one unknown," she said. "It's a female, we think. But we haven't done a chromosome check. Irma located a few minutes of pre-death short-term memory and translated it into sound. We heard . . ." She suddenly wrinkled her face, as if about to cry, and then lifted her head and laughed. "Micko, we *heard* a voice, it must have been a doctor, a voice speaking out loud, 'Inchmore, can you hear me? Evelyn? We need your permission. . .'"

I sat up on the bed and rubbed my eyes. "That's . . ." I couldn't find a good word.

"Yeah, amen," Rho said, sitting on the edge of the bed. "Evelyn Inchmore. I've sent a query to StarTime's trustees on Earth. Evelyn Inchmore, Evelyn Inchmore . . ." She spoke the name out loud several more times, her voice dropping in exhaustion and wonder. "Do you know what this means, Micko?"

"Congratulations," I said.

"It's the first time anybody has ever communicated with a corpsicle," Rho said distantly.

"She hasn't answered back," I said. "You've just accessed her memories." I shrugged my shoulders. "She's still dead."

"Yeah," Rho said. "'*Just* accessed her memories.' Wait a minute." She looked up at me, startled by some inner realization. "Maybe it's a male after all. We thought the name was female . . . But didn't Evelyn used to be a male's name? Wasn't there a male author centuries ago named Evelyn?"

"Evelyn Waugh," I said.

"We could have it all wrong again," she said, too tired to build up much concern. "I hope we can straighten it out before this goes to the press."

My level of alertness went up several notches. "Have you told Thomas what's happened?"

"Not yet," she said.

"Rho, if word gets out that we've already accessed the heads . . . But who's going to stop Cailetet or Onnes from trumpeting this?"

"You think it would cause problems?" Rho asked.

I felt vaguely proud that finally I was starting to anticipate trouble, as Thomas would want me to. "It would probably cook off the bomb," I said.

"All right, then. I don't want to cause more trouble." She looked at me with loving sympathy. "You've been in a rough, Micko."

"You heard what happened in Port Yin?"

"Thomas talked to me while you were shuttling home." She pushed out her lips dubiously and shook her head. "Fapping pol. Someone should impeach her and take away the Task-Felder charter."

"I appreciate the sentiments, but neither is likely. Could you keep this quiet for a few more days?"

"I'll do my damnedest," Rho said. "Cailetet and Onnes are under contract. We control the release of the results, even if they eventually get full scientific credit. I'll tell them we want to confirm with the Earth trustees, back up our findings, analyze the third unknown head . . . Work on a few known heads and see if the process is reliable."

"What about Great-grandmother and Great-grandfather?" I asked.

Rho's smile was conspiratorial. "We'll save them until later," she said.

"We don't want to experiment on family, right?"

She nodded. "When we're sure the whole thing works, we'll do something with Robert and Emilia. As for me, Micko, in a few minutes I'm going to get some forced sleep. Right after I reiterate our rules to the Cailetet and Onnes folks. Now. William wants to talk with you."

"About the interruptions?"

"I don't think so. He says work is going well."

She hugged me tightly and then stood. "To sleep," she said. "No dreams, I think . . ."

"No ancient voices," I said.

"Right."

William seemed tired but at peace, pleased with himself. He sat in the laboratory control center, patting the QL thinker as if it were an old friend.

"It did me proud, Micko," he said. "It's tuned everything to a fare-thee-well. It keeps the universe's quantum bugs from nibbling at my settings, controls the rebuilt disorder pumps, anticipates virtual fluctuations and corrects for them. I'm all set now; all I have to do is bring the pumps to full capacity."

I tried to show enthusiasm, but couldn't. I felt sick at heart. The disaster in Port Yin, the upcoming council meeting, Rho's success with the first few heads . . .

With a little time to think about what had happened, I realized now that it all felt *bad*. Thomas was scrambling furiously to convince the council to reverse its action. And here I was, cut out of the drift of things, watching William gloat about an upcoming moment of triumph. William caught my mood and reached out to tap my hand.

"Hey," he said. "You're young. Fapping up is part of the game."

I screwed my face up at first in anger, then in simple grief, and turned away, tears running down my cheeks. To have William name the card so openly—*fapping up*—was not what I needed right now. It was neither circumspect nor sensitive. "Thank you so very much," I said.

William kept tapping my hand until I jerked it away. "I'm sorry, Micko," he said, his tone unchanged—telling it like it is. "I've never been afraid to admit when I've made a mistake. It nearly drives me nuts sometimes, making mistakes. I keep telling myself I should be perfect, but that isn't what we're here for. Perfection isn't an option for us; perfection is death, Micko. We're here to learn and change and that means making mistakes."

"Thanks for the lecture," I said, glancing at him resentfully.

"I'm twelve years older than you. I've made maybe twelve times more major mistakes. What can I tell you? That it gets any easier to fap up? Well, yes, it gets easier and easier with more and more responsibilities—but hell, Micko, it doesn't feel any better."

"I can't just think of it as a mistake," I said softly. "I was betrayed. The president was dishonest and underhanded."

William leaned back in his chair and shook his head, incredulous. "Hay-soos, Micko. Who expects anything different? That's what politics is all about—coercion and lies."

Suddenly my anger reached white heat. "Goddamn it, *no*, that isn't what politics is all about, William, and people thinking that it is has gotten us into this mess!"

"I don't understand."

"Politics is management and guidance and feedback, William. We seem to have forgotten *that* on the Moon. Politics is the art of managing large groups of people in good times and bad. When the people know what they want and when they don't know what they want. 'Cut the politics. . .' Hay-soos yourself, William!" I waved my arm and shook my fist in the air. "You can't get rid of politics, any more than you can . . ." I struggled to find a metaphor. "Any more than you can cut out *manners* and *talking* and all the other ways we interact."

"Thanks for the lecture, Micko," William said, not unpleasantly.

I dropped my fist on the table.

"What you're saying is, the whole Moon is screwing this up," William said. "I agree. And the Task-Felder BM is leading us all into temptation. But my point is, I'm never going to be a politician or an administrator. Present company excepted, I hate the breed, Micko. They're put on this Moon to stand in my way. This council stuff only reinforces my prejudices. So what can you do about it?" He looked at me with frank inquiry.

"I can wise up," I said. "I can be a better . . . administrator, politician."

William smiled ironically. "More devious? Play their own game?"

I shook my head. Deviousness and playing the Task-Felder game were not what I meant. I was thinking of some more idealistic superiority, playing within the ethical boundaries as well as the law.

William continued. "We can plan ahead for the worse yet to

come. They might cut off our resources, beyond just stopping other BMs from helping us. We can survive an interdict for some time, maybe even forge a separate business alliance within the Triple."

"That would be . . . very dangerous," I said.

"If we're forced into it, what can we do? We have business interests all over the Triple. We have to survive."

The QL toned softly on the platform. "Temperature stability has been broken," it said.

William jerked up in his chair. "Report," he said.

"Unknown effect has caused temperature to rotate in unknown phase. The cells have no known temperature at this time."

"What's that mean?" I asked.

William grabbed his thinker remote and pushed through the curtain to the bridge. He walked out to the Cavity and I followed, glad to have an interruption. The Cailetet and Onnes techs had retired to get some rest; the Ice Pit was quiet.

"What's wrong?" I asked.

"I don't know," William said in a low voice, concentrating on the Cavity's status display. "There are drains on four of the eight cells. The QL refuses to interpret temperature readings. QL, please explain."

The remote said, "Phase rotation in lambda. Fluctuation between banks of four cells."

"Shit," William said. "Now the other four cells are absorbing, and the first four are stable. QL, do you have any idea what's happening here?" He looked up at me with a worried expression.

"Second bank is now in down cycle of rotation. Up cycle in three seconds."

"It's reversed," William said after the short interval had passed. "Back and forth. QL, what's causing a power drain?"

"Temperature maintenance," the QL said.

"Explain, please," William pursued with waning patience.

"Energy is being accepted by the phase down cells in an attempt to maintain temperature."

"Not by the refrigerators or the pumps?"

"It is necessary to put energy directly into the cells in the form of microwave radiation to try to maintain temperature."

"I don't understand, QL."

"I apologize," the QL said. "The cells accept radiation to remain stable, but they have no temperature this thinker can interpret."

"We have to *raise* the temperature?" William guessed, face slack with incredulity.

"Phase down reversal," the QL said.

"QL, the temperatures have jumped to *below* absolute zero?"

"That is an interpretation, although not a very good one."

William swore and stood back from the Cavity.

The QL reported, "All eight cells have stabilized in lambda phase down. Fluctuation has stopped."

William went pale. "Micko, tell me I'm not dreaming."

"I don't know what the hell you're doing," I said, frightened.

"The cells are draining microwave energy and yet maintaining a stable temperature. Christ, they must be accessing new spin dimensions, radiating into a direction outside status geometry . . . does that mean they're operating in negative time? Micko, if any of Rho's outsiders have messed with the lab, or if their goddamn equipment is causing this . . ." He balled his fists and shook them at the darkness above. "God help them! I was this close, Micko . . . All I had to do was connect the pumps, align the cells, turn the magnetic fields off . . . I was going to do that tomorrow."

"I don't think anybody's messed with your equipment," I told him, trying to calm him. "These are pros, William, and besides, Rho would kill them . . ."

William lowered his head and swung it back and forth helplessly. "Micko, something has to be wrong. Negative temperature is meaningless."

"It didn't *say* temperatures were negative," I reminded him.

"This thinker does not interpret the data," the QL chimed in.

"That's because you're a coward," William accused it.

"This thinker does not relay false interpretation," it responded.

Suddenly, William laughed, a rocking angry laugh that seemed to hurt. He opened his eyes wide and patted the QL remote with gritted-teeth paternalism. "Micko, as God is my witness, nothing on this Moon is ever easy, no?"

"Maybe you've found something even more important than absolute zero," I suggested. "A new state of matter."

The idea sobered him. "That . . ." He ran his hand through his hair, making it even more unruly. "A big idea, that one."

"Need help?" I asked.

"I need time to think," he said softly. "Thanks, Micko. Time without interruptions . . . a few hours at least."

"I can't guarantee anything," I said.

He squinted at me. "I'll let you know if I've discovered something big, okay? Now get out of here." He pushed me gently along the bridge.

The Council Room was circular, paneled with lunar farm oak, centrally lighted, with a big antique display screen at one end, lovingly preserved from the year of the Council's creation. Politicians like to keep an eye on each other; no corners, no chairs facing away from the center.

I shuffled in behind Thomas and two freelance advocates from Port Yin, hired by Thomas to offer him extra-familial advice. Within the Triple it has often been said that lunar advocates are the very worst money can rent; there is some truth to that, but Thomas still felt the need of an objective and critical point of view.

The room was mostly empty. Three representatives had already taken their seats—interestingly enough, they were from Cailetet, Onnes, and Nernst BMs. Other representatives talked in the hall outside the room. The president and her staff would not enter until just before the meeting began.

The council thinker, a large, antique terrestrial model encased in gray ceramic, rested below the president's dais at the north end of the room. Thomas nudged me as we sat, pointed at the thinker, and said, "Don't underestimate an old machine. That son of a glitch has more experience in this room than anybody. But it's the president's tool, not ours; it will not contradict the president, and it will not speak out against her."

We sat quietly while the room slowly filled. At the appointed time of commencement, Fiona Task-Felder entered through a door behind the president's dais, Janis Granger and three council advocates in train.

I knew many of the BM representatives. I had spoken to ten or fifteen of them over the years while doing research for my minor; others I knew by sight from lunar news reports and council broadcasts. They were honorable women and men all; I thought we might not do so badly here after all.

Thomas's frown revealed a less favorable opinion.

The Ice Pit controversy was not first on the council agenda. There were matters of who would get contracts to parent lucrative volatiles supply deliveries from the Outer; who had rights in a BM border dispute to sell aluminum and tungsten mining claims to Richter BM, the huge and generally silent tri-family merger that had taken over most lunar mining operations. These problems were discussed by the representatives in a way that struck me as exemplary. Resolutions were reached, contracts vetted and cleared, shares assigned. The president remained silent most of the time. When she did speak, her words were well-chosen and to the point. She impressed me.

Thomas seemed to sink into his chair, chin in hand, gray hair in disarray. He glanced at me once, gave me something like a leer, and retreated into glum contemplation.

Our two outside advocates sat plumb-line in their chairs, hardly blinking.

Janis Granger read out the next item on the agenda: "Inter-family disputes regarding purchase by Sandoval BM of human remains from terrestrial preservation societies."

Societies. That was a subtlety that could speak volumes of mis-interpretation. Thomas closed his eyes, opened them again after a long moment.

"The representative from Gorrie BM would like to address this issue," the president said. "Chair allots five minutes to Achmed Bani Sadr of Gorrie BM."

Thomas straightened, leaned forward. Bani Sadr stood with slate held at waist-level for prompting.

"The syndics of Gorrie BM have expressed some concern over the strain on Triple relations this purchase might provoke. As the major transportation utility between Earth and Moon, and on many translunar links, our business would be very adversely affected by any shift in terrestrial attitudes . . ."

And so it began. Even I in my naïveté could see that this had been brilliantly orchestrated. One by one, politely, the BMs stood in council and voiced their collective concern. Earth had rattled its pocketbooks at us; Mars had chided us for rocking the Triple boat in a time of economic instability. The United States of the Western Hemisphere had voted to restrict lunar trade if this matter was not resolved to its satisfaction.

Thomas's expression was intense, sorrowful but alert. He had not been inactive. Cailetet expressed an interest in pursuing poten-tially very lucrative, even revolutionary, research on the deceased; Onnes BM testified that there was no conceivable way these heads could be resurrected and made active members of society within the next twenty years; the technology simply did not yet exist, despite decades of promising research.

Surprisingly, the representative from Gorrie BM reversed

himself and expressed an interest in the medical aspects of this research; he asked how long such work might take to mature, in a business sense, but the president—not unreasonably—ruled that this was beyond the scope of the present discussion.

The representative from Richter BM expressed sympathy for Sandoval's attempts to open a new field of lunar business, but said that disturbances in lunar raw materials supply lines to Earth could be disastrous in the short term. "If Earth boycotts lunar minerals, the Outer can supply them almost immediately, and we lose one third of our gross lunar export business."

Thomas requested time to speak in reply. The president granted him ten minutes to state Sandoval's case. He conferred briefly with the advocates. They nodded agreement to several whispered comments, and he stood, slate at waist-level—the formal posture in this room—to begin his response.

"Madame President, honored Representatives, I'll be brief and I'll be blunt. I am ashamed of these proceedings, and I am ashamed that this council has been so blind as to make them necessary. I have never, in my thirty-nine years of service to the Sandoval BM, and in my seventy-five years of lunar citizenship, felt the anguish I feel now, knowing what is about to happen. Knowing what is about to be done to lunar ideals in the name of expediency.

"Sandoval BM has made an entirely reasonable business transaction with a fully authorized terrestrial legal entity. For reasons none of us can fathom, Task-Felder BM, and Madame President, have raised a flare of protest and carefully planned and executed a series of maneuvers to force an autonomous lunar family to divest itself of legally acquired resources. To my knowledge, this has never before been attempted in the history of the Moon."

"You speak of actions not yet taken, perhaps not even contemplated," the president said.

Thomas looked around the room and smiled. "Madame President, I address those who have already received their instructions."

"Are you accusing the president of participating in this so-called conspiracy?" Fiona Task-Felder continued.

Calls of, "Let him speak," "Let him have his say." She nodded and motioned for Thomas to resume.

"I have not much more to say, but to recount a tale of masterful politics, conducted by an extra-lunar organization across the Solar System, in support of a policy that has nothing to do with lunar prosperity. Even my assistant, Mickey Sandoval, has been trapped into giving testimony on private family affairs, through a ruse involving an old council law not invoked since its creation. My fellow citizens, he will testify under protest if this council so wishes—but think of the precedent! Think of the power you give to this council, and to those who have the skills to manipulate it—skills which we have not ourselves acquired, and are not likely to acquire, because such activity goes against our basic nature. We are naive weaklings in such a fight, and because of our weakness, our lack of foresight and planning, we will give in, and my family's activities will be interfered with, perhaps even forbidden—all because a religious organization, based on our home planet, does not wish us to do things we have every legal right to do. I voice my protest now, that it may be put in the record before the council votes. Our shame will be complete by day's end, Madame President, and I will not wish to show my face here thereafter."

The president's face was cold and pale. "Do you accuse me, or my chartered BM, of being controlled by extra-lunar interests?"

Thomas, who had sat quickly after his short talk, stood again, looked around the council, and nodded curtly. "I do."

"It is not traditional to libel one's fellow BMs in this council," the president said.

Thomas did not speak.

"I believe I must reply to the charge of manipulation," the president said. "At my invitation, Mickey Sandoval came to Port Yin to render voluntary testimony to the president. Under old council rules, designed to prevent the president from keeping information that rightfully should be given to the council, the president has the duty to request testimony be given to the council as a whole. If that is manipulation, then I am guilty."

Our first extra-familial advocate stood up beside Thomas. "Madame President, a tape of Mickey Sandoval's visit to your office is sufficient to fulfill the requirements of that rule."

"Not according to the council thinker's interpretation," the president said. "Please render your judgment."

The thinker spoke. "The spirit of the rule is to encourage more open testimony to the council than to the president in private meetings. A voluntary report to the president implies willingness to testify in full to the council. Such testimony must always be voluntary, and not under threat of subpoena." Its deep, resonating voice left the council room in silence.

"So much for our auto counselors," the first advocate muttered to Thomas. Again he addressed the council. "Mickey Sandoval's testimony was solicited under guise of casual conversation. He was not aware he would later be forced to divulge family business matters to the entire council."

"The president's conversations on council matters can hardly be called casual. I am not concerned with your assistant's lack of education," the president said. "This council deserves to hear Sandoval BM's plans for these deceased individuals."

"In God's name, why?" Thomas stood, jaw outthrust. "Who asks these questions? Why is private Sandoval business of concern to anyone but us?"

The president did not react as strongly to this outburst as I expected. I cringed, but Fiona Task-Felder said, "The freedom of any family to swing its fist ends at our nose. How the inquiry has arisen is irrelevant; what *is* relevant is the damage that might occur to lunar interests. Is that enough, Mr. Sandoval-Rice?"

Thomas sat again. I looked at him curiously; how much of this was show, how much loss of control? Seeing his expression, I realized that show and inner turmoil were one. Only then did center of my life, but he was, and I needed above all else to find out how his project was proceeding. There seemed something almost holy and pure in his quest, above human quibbling; I sensed I could take comfort in his presence, in his words.

But William himself was not comfortable. He looked a wreck. He, too, had not slept. I entered the laboratory, ignoring the soft voices from the chamber below, and found him standing by the QL thinker, eyes closed, lips moving as if in prayer. He opened his eyes and faced me with a jerk of his shoulders and head. "Christ," he said softly. "Are they done down there?"

I shook my head. "I'm afraid I've set them on to something new."

"I heard you've been checkmated," he said.

I shrugged. "And you?"

"My opponent is far more subtle than any human conspiracy," he said. "I've gone so far as to be able to switch between plus and minus." He chuckled. "I can access this new state at will, but there's real resistance to reaching the no man's land between. I have the QL cogitating now. It's been working five hours on the problem."

"What's the problem?" I asked.

"Micko, I haven't even engaged the force disorder pumps to achieve this new state. No magnetic field cut-off, no special efforts—just a sudden jerk-down to this negative state, absorbing energy to maintain an undefined temperature."

"But why?"

"The best the QL can come up with is we're approaching some key event that sends signals back in time, affecting our experiment now."

"So neither of you know what's actually happened?"

He shook his head. "It's not only undefined, it's incomprehensible. Even the QL is befuddled and can't give me straight answers."

I sat on the edge of the QL's platform and caressed the machine with an open palm as if in sympathy. "Everything's screwed, top to bottom," I said. "The center cannot hold."

"Ah, Micko—there's the question. What *is* the center? What is this event we're approaching that can reach back subtle fingers and diddle us now?"

I smiled. "We're a real pair of loons," I said.

"Speak for yourself," William said defensively. "I'll break this dustover, by God, Micko." He pointed down. "Solve your little problem, and I'll solve mine."

As if on cue, Rho stood in the open laboratory door, face ashen. "Mickey," she said. "How did you know?"

The shock of confirmation—and confirmation was not in doubt—made me tremble. I glanced at William. "A little ghost told me. A fat nightmare on ice."

"We don't have too much translated," she said. "But we know his name."

"What are you talking about?" William asked.

"Our third unknown," I explained. "We have three unknown heads below, three among four hundred and ten. Alleged bad record keeping."

"Do you know something, Mickey?" Rho asked.

"There were four Logologists employed by StarTime Preservation between 2079 and 2094," I said. "Two worked in records, two were in administration. None were ever given access to the heads themselves; those were kept in cold vaults in Denver."

"You think they screwed up the records?"

"It was the most they could manage."

"It's so *cynical*," Rho said. "I can't believe such a thing. It would be like our . . . like trying to kill Robert and Emilia. It's sickening."

William uttered a wordless curse of frustration. "Damn it, Rho, what are you talking about?"

"We know why we're having such problems with Task-Felder," she said. "I've really hit the jackpot this time, William. I've invited a snapping, snarling wolf into our corral. I apologize."

"What wolf?"

"K. D. Thierry," I said, the breath going out of me. I didn't know whether I might laugh or cry. "Founder of Logology."

"I will not listen to you unless you are willing to testify, in open session."

"Please."

"That's my requirement, Mickey. It would be best if you consulted with your syndics before you went any further." She stood to dismiss me.

"All right," I said. "I'll let you judge whether you want me to testify."

"I'll record this as a voluntary meeting, just like the last time you were here."

"Fine," I said, caving in disconsolately.

"I'm listening."

"We've started accessing the patterns, the memories inside the heads," I said.

She seemed to swallow something bitter. "I hope all of you know what you're doing," she said slowly.

"We've discovered something startling, something we didn't expect at all . . ."

"Go on," she said.

I told her about StarTime's apparent bookkeeping errors, I told her about learning the names of the first two unknowns from short-term memory and other areas in the dead but intact brains.

She showed a glimmer of half-fascinated, half disgusted interest.

"Only a couple of days ago, we learned who the third unknown was." I swallowed. Drew back before leaping into the abyss. "He's Kimon Thierry. K.D. Thierry. He joined StarTime."

Fiona Task-Felder rocked back and forth slowly in her chair. "You're lying," she said softly. "That is the foulest, most ridiculous story I've . . . It's more than I imagined you were capable of, Mr. Sandoval. I am . . ." She shook her head, genuinely furious, and stood up at her desk. "Get out of here."

I laid a slate on her desk. "I d-don't think you should d-dismiss me," I said, shaking, stuttering, teeth knocking together. My own contradictory emotions again supported my play-acting. "I've put together a lot of evidence, and I have recordings of Mr. Thierry's . . . last moments."

She stared at me, at the slate. She sat again but still said nothing.

"I can show you the evidence very quickly," I said, and I laid out my trail of facts. The employment of the Logologists, Frederick Jones's suit against the church, the three unknown members of the group of dead transported from Earth, our triumph in playing back and translating the last memories of each. I thought there might be other facts and remembrances clicking, meshing, in her head, but her face betrayed nothing but cold, tightly controlled rage.

"I see nothing conclusive here, Mr. Sandoval," she said when I had finished.

I played her a tape made by Thierry when he'd been alive, in his later years. Than I played the record of his last moments, not just the short-term memories of sounds, but the visual memories, which Rho had clumsily processed and translated at Thomas's request. Faces, oddly inhuman at first, and then fitting a pattern, being recognized; the memories not refined by the personal mind's own interpreters; raw and immediate and therefore surprisingly crude. The office where he died, his bulky hands on the table, the twitching and shifting of his eyes from point to point in the room, difficult to follow. The fading. The end of the record.

The president looked down at the slate, eyebrows raised, hands tightly clenched on the desktop.

I leaned forward to retrieve the slate. She grabbed it herself, held it shakily in both hands, and suddenly threw it across the office. It banged against a foamed rock wall and caromed to the metabolic carpet.

"It's not a hoax," I said. "We were shocked, as well."

"Get out," she said. "Get the hell out, now."

I turned to leave, but before I could reach the door, she began to cry. Her shoulders slumped and she buried her face in her hands.

I moved toward her to do something, to say I was sorry again, but she screamed at me to leave, and I did.

"How did she react?" Thomas asked. I sat in his private quarters, my mind a million miles away, contemplating sins I had never imagined I would feel guilty for. He handed me a glass of terrestrial Madeira and I swallowed it neat, then looked over the cube files on his living room wall.

"She didn't believe me," I said.

"Then?"

"I convinced her. I played the tape."

Thomas filled my glass again.

"And?"

I still would not face him.

"Well?"

"She began to cry," I said.

Thomas smiled. "Good. Then?"

I gave him a look of puzzlement and disapproval. "She wasn't faking it, Thomas. She was devastated."

"Right. What did she do next?"

"She ordered me out of her office."

"No setup for a later meeting?"

I shook my head.

"Sounds like you really knocked a hole in her armor, Mickey."

"I must have," I said solemnly.

"Good," Thomas said. "I think we've got our extra time. Go home now and get some rest. You've redeemed yourself a hundred times over."

"I feel like a shit, Thomas."

"You're an honorable shit, doing only when others do unto you," Thomas said. He offered his hand to me but I did not accept it. "This is for your *family*," he reminded me, eyes flinty.

I could not forget the tears coming, the fierce, shattering anger, the dismay and betrayal.

"Thank you again, Micko," Thomas said.

"Call me Mickey, please," I said as I left.

Alienation without must be accompanied by alienation within; that is the law for every social level, even individuals. To harm one's fellows, even one's enemies, harms you, takes away some essential element from your self respect and self image. This must be the way it is when fighting a full-fledged war, I told myself, only worse. Gradually, by killing your enemies, you kill your old self. If there is room for a new self, for an extraordinary redevelopment, then you grow and become more mature, though sadder.

If there is no room, you die inside or go crazy.

Alone in my dry, warm water tank, creature comforts aplenty and mind in a state of complete misery, I played my own Shakespearean scene of endless, unvoiced soliloquy. I held a party of all my selves and we gathered to argue and fight.

I felt badly for my anger toward Thomas. Still, he had turned me into a weapon and I had been effective, and that hurt. I learned the hard way that Fiona Task-Felder was not a heartless monster; she was a human, playing her cards as she thought they must be played, not for reasons of self-aggrandizement, but following orders.

What effect would our news have on her superiors, the directors of the political and secular arms of the Logologist Church?

If Thomas actually leaked the news to the public of the Triple, what would the effect be on millions of faithful Logologists?

Logology was a personal madness expanded by chance and the laws of society into an institution, self-perpetuating, even growing with time. We could eventually tap the experiences, the memories, of the man at the fount of the madness. We could in time disillusion the members, perhaps even destroy the Church. None of this gave me the least satisfaction. I longed for the innocence I had known but not been aware of, three months past.

We had bought our extra time, and here it was; the Task-Felder arm of Logology was quiet. On the Triple nets, there was nary a murmur from the Earthside forces.

Ten hours after returning from Port Yin, I left my water tank to cross the white line. William was jubilant. "You just missed Rho," he told me as I entered the lab. "She'll be back in an hour. I have it now, Micko. Tomorrow I'll do the trial run. Everything's stable—"

"Did you find out what caused your last problem?"

William pursed his lips as if I'd mentioned something dirty. "No," he said. "I'd just as soon forget it. I can't reproduce the effect now, and the QL is no help."

"Beware those ghosts," I said mordantly. "They come back."

"You're *both* so cheerful," he said. "You'd think we were all awaiting doomsday. What did Thomas have you do, assassinate somebody?"

"No," I said. "Not literally."

"Well, try to cheer up a little—I'd like to have both of you help me tomorrow."

"Doing what?" I asked.

"I'll need more than one pair of hands, and I'll also need official witnesses. The record-keepers aren't emotionally satisfying; real human testimony can shake loose more grant money, I suspect, especially if you and Rho are giving the testimony to possible financiers."

We'll be too controversial to squeeze dust from any financiers, I thought. "Are we going to market absolute zero?"

"We'll market something new and rare. Never in the history of the universe—until tomorrow—has matter been cooled and tricked to reach a temperature of zero Kelvin. It will make the nets all over the Triple, Mickey. It might even take some of the heat off Sandoval BM, if I may pun. But you know that; why are you being *so* pessimistic?"

"My apologies, William."

"Judging from your face, you'd think we've already lost," he said.

"No. We may have won," I said.

"Then cheer up a little, if only to give me some breathing room in all this gloom."

He returned to work; I walked out on the bridge and deliberately stood between the force disorder pumps to punish my body with that fingernail-on-slate sensation.

Rho and I joined William in the Ice Pit laboratory at eight hundred. He assigned Rho to monitoring the pumps, which he ramped to full activity. I sat watch on the refrigerators. There didn't seem to be any real need for either Rho or I to be there. It soon became obvious we had been invited more to provide company than to help or witness.

William was outwardly calm, inwardly very nervous, which he betrayed by short bursts of mild pique, quickly apologized for and retracted. I didn't mind him; somehow it all made me feel better, took my mind off events outside the Ice Pit.

We were a strange crew; Rho even more subdued than William, unaffected by the grating of the disorder pumps; I getting progressively drunker and drunker with an uncalled-for sense of separation and relief from our troubles; William making a circuit of all the equipment, ending at the highly polished Cavity containing the cells, mounted on levitation absorbers just beyond the left branch of the bridge.

Far above us, barely visible in the spilled light from the laboratory and the bridge, hung the dark gray vault of the volcanic void, obscured by a debris net.

At nine hundred, William's calm cracked wide open when the QL announced another reverse in the lambda phase, and conditions within the cells that it could not interpret. "Are they the same conditions as last time?" William asked, fingers of both hands drumming the top surface of the QL.

"The readings and energy requirements are the same," the QL

said. Rho pointed out that the force disorder pumps were showing chaotic fluctuations in their "draw" from the cells. "Has that happened before?"

"I've never had the pumps ramped so high before. No, it hasn't happened," William explained. "QL, what would happen to our cells if we just turned off the stabilizing energy?"

"I cannot guess," the QL replied. It flatly refused to answer any similar questions, which irritated William.

"You said something earlier about this possibly reflecting future events in the cells," I reminded him. "What did you mean by that?"

"I couldn't think of any other explanation," William said. "I still can't. QL won't confirm or deny the possibility."

"Yes, but what did you *mean?* How could that happen?"

"If we achieved some hitherto unknown state in the cells, there could be a chronological backwash, something echoing into the past, our now."

"Sounds pretty speculative to me," Rho commented.

"It's more than speculative, it's desperate dust," William said. "Without it, however, I'm lost."

"Have you correlated times between the changes?" Rho asked.

"Yes," William said, sighing.

"Ok. Then try changing your scheduled time for achieving zero."

William looked across the lab at his wife, both eyebrows raised, mouth open, giving his long face a simian appearance. "What?"

"Re-set your machines. Make the zero-moment earlier or later. And don't change it back again."

William produced his most sardonic, pitying smile. "Rho, my sweet, but you're crazier than I am."

"Try it," she said.

He swore but did as she suggested, setting his equipment for five minutes later.

The lambda phase reversal ended. Five minutes later, it began again.

"Christ," he whispered. "I don't dare touch it now."

"Better not," Rho said, smiling. "What about the previous incident?"

"It was continuous, no lapses," he said.

"There. You're going to succeed, and this is a prior result, if such a thing is possible in quantum logic."

"QL?" William queried the thinker.

"Time reverse circumstances are only possible if no message is communicated," it said. "You are claiming to receive confirmation of experimental success."

"But success at what?" William said. "The message is completely ambiguous . . . We don't know what our experiment will do to cause this condition in the past."

"I'm dizzy, having to think with those damned pumps going," I said.

"Wait until they're completely tuned to the cells," William warned, enjoying my discomfort. His grin bared all his teeth. He made final preparations, calling out numbers and settings to us, all superfluously. We repeated just to keep up his morale. From here on, the experiment was automatic, controlled by the QL.

"I think the reversal will end in a few minutes," William said, standing beside the polished Cavity. "Call it a quantum hunch."

A few minutes later, the QL reported yet again the end of reversal. William nodded with mystified satisfaction. "We're not scientists, Micko," he said cheerily. "We're magicians. God help us all."

The clocks silently counted their numbers. William walked down the bridge and made a final adjustment in the right hand pump with a small hex wrench. "Cross your fingers," he said.

"Is this it?" Rho asked.

"In twenty seconds I'll tune the pumps to the cells, then turn off the magnetic fields . . ."

"Good luck," Rho said. He turned away from her, turned back

and extended his arms, folding her into them, hugging her tightly. His face shined with enthusiasm; he seemed gleeful, childlike.

I clenched my teeth when he tuned the pumps. The sensation was trebled; my long bones seemed to become flutes piping a shrill, unmelodic quantum tune. Rho closed her eyes and groaned. "That's *atrocious*," she said.

"It's sweet music," William said, shaking his head as if to rid himself of a fly. "Here goes." He beat the seconds with his upheld finger. "Field . . . off." A tiny green light flashed in the air over the main lab console, the QL's signal.

"Unknown phase reversal. Lambda reversal," the QL announced.

"God damn it all to hell!" William shrieked, stamping his foot.

Simultaneously with his shout, there came the sound of four additional footstamps above the cavern overhead, precisely as if gigantic upstairs neighbors had jumped on a resonant floor. William held his left foot in the air, astonished by what seemed to be echoes of his anger. His expression had cycled beyond frustration, into something like expectant glee: *Yes by God, what next?*

Rho's personal slate called for her attention in a thin voice. My own slate chimed; William was not wearing his.

"There is an emergency situation," our slates announced simultaneously. "Emergency power reserves are in effect." The lights dimmed and alarms went off throughout the lab. "There have been explosions in the generators supplying power to this station."

Rho looked at me with eyes wide, lips drawn into a line.

The mechanical slate voices announced calmly, in unison, "There has been damage to components above the Ice Pit void, including heat radiators." This information came from sentries around the station. Every slate in the station—and emergency speaker systems throughout the warrens and alleys—would be repeating the same information.

A human voice interrupted them, someone I did not recognize, perhaps the station watch attendant. Somebody was always assigned to observe the sentries, a human behind the machines. "William, are you all right? Anybody else in there with you?"

"Mickey and I are in here with William. We're fine," Rho said.

"A shuttle dropped bombs into the trenches. They've taken out your radiators, William, and all of our generators are damaged. Your pit is drawing a lot more power than normal—I was worried—"

"It shouldn't be," William said.

"William says it shouldn't be drawing more power," Rho informed the anonymous watch attendant.

"But it is," William continued, turning to look at his instruments.

"Phase down lambda reversal in all cells," the QL announced.

"—you folks might be injured," the voice concluded, overlapping.

"We're fine," I said.

"You'd better get out of there. No way of knowing how much damage the void has sustained, whether—"

"Let's go," I said, looking up.

Chunks of rock and dust drifted into the overhead net, making it undulate like the upside-down bell of a jellyfish.

"Lambda reversal ending in all cells," the QL said.

"Wait—" William said.

I stood on the bridge between the Cavity and the disorder pumps. The refrigerators hung motionless in their intricate suspensions. Rho stood in the door to the lab. William stood beside the Cavity.

"Zero attained," the QL announced.

Rho glanced my way, and I started to speak, but my throat caught. The lights dimmed all around.

Distantly, our two slates said, "*Time to evacuate . . .*"

I turned to leave, stepping between the pumps, and that saved my life . . . or at any rate made it possible for me to be here, now, in my present condition.

The pump jackets fluoresced green and vanished, revealing spaghetti traceries of wire and cable and egg-shaped parcels. My eyes hurt with the green glare, which seemed to echo in glutinous waves from the walls of the void. I considered the possibility that something had fallen and hit me on the head, making me see things, but I felt no pain, only a sense of being stretched from head to feet. I could not see Rho or William, as I was now facing down the bridge toward the entrance to the Ice Pit. I could not hear them, either. When I tried to turn around again, parts of my being seemed to separate and rejoin. Instinctively, I stopped moving, waiting for everything to come together again.

It was all I could do to concentrate on one of my hands grasping the bridge railing. The hand shed dark ribbons that curled toward the deck of the bridge. I blinked and felt my eyelids separate and rejoin with each rise and fall. Fear deeper than thought forced me to stop all motion until only my blood and the beat of my heart threatened to sunder me from the inside.

Finally I could stand it no more. I slowly turned in the deepening quiet, hearing only the slide of my shoes on the bridge and the serpent's hiss of my body separating and rejoining as I rotated.

Please do not take my testimony from this point on as having any kind of objective truth. Whatever happened, it affected my senses, if not my mind, in such a way that all objectivity fled.

The Cavity sphere had cracked like an egg. I saw Rho standing between the Cavity and the laboratory, perfectly still, facing slightly to my left as if caught in mid-turn, and she did not look entirely real. The light that reflected from her was not familiar, not completely useful to my eyes, whether because the light had changed or my eyes had changed, I do not know. In addition there came from her—radiated is not the right word, it is deceptive, but perhaps there is no better—a kind of communication of her presence that I had never experienced before, a shedding of skins that *lessened* her as I watched. I think perhaps it was the information that comprised her body, leaching away through a new kind of space that had never existed before: space made crystalline, a superconductor of information. With the shedding of this essence Rho became less substantial, less real. She was dissolving like a piece of sugar in warm water.

I tried to call out her name, but could make no sound. I might have been caught in a vicious gelatin, one that stung me whenever I tried to move. But I could not see myself dissolving, as I saw Rho. I seemed immune at least to that danger.

William stood behind her, becoming more visible as Rho dissipated. He was farther from the Cavity; the effect, whatever it might be, had not worked quite as strongly on him. But he too began to shed this essence, the hidden music that communicates each particle's place and quantum state to other particles, that holds us in one shape and one condition from this moment to the next. I think he was trying to move, to get back inside the laboratory, but he succeeded only in evaporating this essence more rapidly, and he stopped, then tried to reach out for Rho, his face utterly intent, like a child facing down a tiger.

His hand passed through her.

I saw something else flee from my sister at that moment. I apologize in advance for describing this; I do not wish to spread any more or less hope, to offer encouragement to mystical interpretations of our existence, for as I said, what I saw might be a function of hallucination, not objective reality.

But I saw two, then three, versions of my sister standing on the bridge, the third like a cloud maintaining its rough shape, and this cloud-shape managed to move toward me, and touch me with an outstretched limb.

Are you all right, Micko? I heard in my head if not in my ears. *Don't move. Please don't move. You seem to be . . .*

Suddenly I saw myself from her perspective, her experience leaching from her, passing into me, like a taste of her dissipating self in the superconducting medium.

The cloud passed through me, carried by some unknown momentum of propagation, then through the bridge rail and out over the void where it fell like rain.

Was I to fade as well? The other images of Rho and William had become mere blurs against the laboratory which was itself blurring, casting away fluid tendrils.

Oddly, the Cavity containing the copper samples—I assumed they were the cause of this, their new condition, announced by the QL, *zero* Kelvin—seemed more solid and stable than anything else, despite the fine cracks across its surface.

Because of my position between the disorder pumps—and I repeat, this is only my speculation—I seemed to have suffered as much dissolution as I was due, whereas everything else became even less real, less material.

The bridge slumped, stretching as if I stood on a sheet of rubber. I performed some gymnastic and caught the rails with both hands, but could not stop my fall toward the lower framework built to support the heads. I tried to climb but could not gain purchase with my feet.

My descent continued until the bridge and my legs actually passed through the ceiling of the lower chamber. A sharp pain shoved like a spear through both limbs, gouging through my bones into my hips. Looking up for some new handhold, some way of stalling my fall, I saw the laboratory rotating loosely at the center of the void, shedding vapors. Rho and William I could not see at all.

A sensation of deep cold surrounded me, then faded. The refrigerators tumbled silently all around, passing through the chamber and casting slow ripples of some cold blue liquid that had filled the bottom of the pit. The liquid washed over me.

I describe the rest knowing perfectly well it cannot be anything more than delirium. How is it that instinct can be aware of dangers from a situation no human being could ever have faced before? I felt a terrified loathing of that wash of unknown liquid, abhorrence so strong I crushed the bridge railing between my hands like thin aluminum. Yet I knew that it was not liquefied gas from the refrigerators; *I was not afraid of being frozen.*

My feet pulled up from the mire and I hooked one onto a stanchion, lifting myself perhaps a meter. Still, I was not out of that turbulent pool, and it seeped into me. I filled with sensations, remembrances not my own. Memories from the dead. From the heads, four hundred and ten of them, leaking their patterns and memories across crystalline spacetime, the information condensing into a thick lake not of matter, not of anything anyone had ever experienced before, like an essence or cold brew.

I carry some of these memories with me still. In most cases I do not know who or what they come from, but I see things, hear voices, remember scenes on Earth I could not possibly know. I have never sought verification, for the same reasons I have never told this story until now—because if I am a chalice of such memories, they have changed *me*, replacing parts of my own memories I shed in the first few instants of the Quiet—and I do not wish that confirmed.

There is one memory in particular, the most disturbing I think, that I must record, even though it is not verifiable. It must have come from Kimon Thierry himself. It has a particular flavor that matches the translated voices and visual memories I played for Fiona Task-Felder.

I believe that in this terrible cold blue pond, the last thoughts of his dying moment permeated me. I loathe this memory: I loathe *him.* To suspect, even deeply believe in, the duplicity and the malice and the greed—in the *evil*—of others is one thing. To know it for a fact is something no human being should ever have to face.

Kimon Thierry's last thoughts were not of the glorious journey awaiting him, the translation to a higher being. He was terrified of retribution. In his last moment before oblivion, he knew he had constructed a lie, knew that he had convinced hundreds of thousands of others of this lie, had limited their individual growth and freedom, and he feared going to the hell he had been taught about in Sunday school . . .

He feared another level of lie, created by past liars to punish their enemies and justify their own petty existences.

The memory ends abruptly with, I suppose, his death, the end of all recorded memories, all physical transformations. Of that I am left with no impressions whatsoever.

I rose above this hideous pool by climbing up the stanchions, finding the bars stronger the farther from the Cavity they had initially been, stronger but losing their strength and shape rapidly. I scrambled like an insect, mindless with terror, and somehow I climbed the twenty yards to the lip of the doorway in complete silence. Perhaps three minutes had elapsed since the bombing, if time had any function in the Ice Pit void. A group of rescuers found me crawling over William's white line. When they tried to go through the door and rescue the others, I told them not to, and because of my condition, they did not need much persuasion.

I had lost the first half centimeter of skin around my body from the neck down, and all my hair, precisely as if I had been sprayed with supercold gas.

For two months I lay in dreamless suspended sleep in the Yin City Hospital, wrapped in healing liquid, skin-cells and muscle cells and bone cells migrating under the guidance of surgical nano machines, re-knitting my surface. I came awake at the end of this time, and fancied myself—with not a hint of fear, as if I had lost all my emotions—still in the Ice Pit, floating in the pool, spreading through the spherical void like water through an eager sponge, dissolving slowly and peacefully in the Quiet.

Thomas came to my room when I had a firmer grasp of who I was, and where. He sat by my cradle and smiled like a dead man, eyes glassy, skin pale.

"I didn't do so well, Mickey," he told me.

"We didn't do so well," I said in a hoarse whisper, the strongest I could manage. My body felt surrounded by ice cubes. The black ceiling above me seemed to suck all my substance up and out, into space.

"You were the only one who escaped," Thomas said. "William and Rho didn't make it."

I had guessed that much. Still, the confirmation hurt.

Thomas looked down at the cradle and ran his gnarled, pale hand along the suspension frame. "You're going to recover completely, Mickey. You'll do better than I. I've resigned as director."

His eyes met mine and his mouth betrayed the presence of an ironic smile, fleeting, small, self-critical. "The art of politics is the art of avoiding disasters, of managing difficult situations for the benefit of all, even for your enemies, whether they know what's good for them or not. Isn't it, Mickey?"

"Yes," I croaked.

"What I had you do . . ."

"I did it," I said.

He acknowledged that much, gave me the gift of that much complicity but no more. "The word has spread, Mickey. We really hurt them, worse than they know. They hurt themselves."

"Who dropped the bombs?"

He shook his head. "It doesn't matter. No evidence, no arrests, no convictions."

"Didn't somebody see?"

"The first bomb took out the closest surface sentries. Nobody saw. We think it was a low-level shuttle. By the time we were able to get a search team off, it must have been hundreds of klicks away."

"No arrests . . . what about the president? Who's going to make her pay?"

"We don't know she ordered it, Mickey. Besides, you and I, we really zapped her. She's no longer president."

"She resigned?"

Thomas shook his head. "Fiona walked out of an airlock four days after the bombing. She didn't wear a suit." He rubbed the back of one hand with the fingers of his other hand. "I think I can take the blame for that."

"Not just you," I said.

"All right," he said, and that was all. He left me to my thoughts, and again and again, I told myself:

William and Rho did not escape.

Only I remember the pool.

Whether they are dead, or simply dissolved in the Ice Pit, floating in that incomprehensible pond or echoing in the space above, I do not know. I do not know whether the heads are somehow less dead than before.

There is the problem of accountability.

In time, I was interrogated to the limits of my endurance, and still there were no prosecutions. The obvious suspicions—that the bombers had acted on orders from Earth, if not from Fiona Task-Felder herself—were never formalized as charges. The binding multiples wished to return to normal, to forget this hideous anomaly.

But Thomas was right. The story made its rounds, and it became legend: of Thierry's having himself harvested and frozen, an obvious apostasy from the faith he had established, and of the violent reluctance of his followers to have him return in any form. In the decades since, that has hurt the faith he founded in ways that even a court case and conviction could not have. Truth is a far less vigorous prosecutor than legend. Neither masterful politics nor any number of great lies can stand against legend.

Task-Felder ceased being a Logologist multiple twenty years ago. The majority of members voted to open it to new settlers, of all faiths and creeds. Their connections with Earth were broken.

I have healed, grown older, worked to set lunar politics

aright, married and contributed my own children to the Sandoval family. I suppose I have done my duty to family and Moon, and have nothing more to be ashamed of. I have watched lunar politics and the lunar constitution change and reach a form we can live with, ideal for no one, acceptable to most, strong in times of crisis.

Yet until this record I have never told everything I knew or experienced in that awful time. Perhaps my experience in the Quiet was an internal lie, my own fantasy of justification, my own kind of revenge dreamed in a moment of pain and danger.

I still miss Rho and William. Writing this, I miss them so deeply I put my slate aside and come back to it only after grieving all over again. The sorrow never dies; it is merely pearled by time.

No one has ever duplicated William's achievement, leading me to believe that had it not been for the bombs, perhaps he would have failed, as well. Some concatenation of his brilliance, the guidance of a perverse QL thinker, and an unexpected failure of equipment—a serendipity that has not been repeated—led to his success, if it can be called that.

On occasion I return to the blocked-off entrance of the Ice Pit. Before I began writing I went there, passing the stationed sentries, the single human guard—a young girl, born after the events I describe. As director of Sandoval BM, participant in the mystery, I am allowed this freedom. The area beyond the white line is littered with the deranged and abandoned equipment of dozens of fruitless investigations.

I have gone there to pray, to indulge in my own apostasy against rationalism, to hope that my words can reach into the transformed matter and information beyond. Trying to reconcile my own feeling that I sinned against Fiona Task-Felder, as Thierry had sinned against so many . . .

I cannot make it sensible.

No one will understand, not even myself, but when I die, I

want to be placed in the Ice Pit with my sister and William. God forgive me, even with Thierry, Robert and Emilia, and the rest of the heads . . .

In the Quiet.

AFTERWORD:

Writing "Heads"

One of the strengths of nineteenth and twentieth century lit has been the emphasis on the little guy, the underdog. Dickens, Joyce, Faulkner, Steinbeck, James Jones, Vonnegut, Pynchon, King, William Gibson—all focus their attentions and sympathies on characters at the bottom of political and economic (or metaphysical) forces. The problems of leaders, politicians, robber barons—people wielding real power—are not dealt with nearly as often, perhaps because writers naturally feel themselves to be "put upon," at the receiving end of the forces of history and nature. Some—Vidal and Drury come to mind—have written about the corridors of power. In science fiction, however, the literature of masters and power-wielders is even sparser. Popular fiction almost demands an underdog as a main character.

Never willing to give in to the obvious, or to popular wisdom—and following the lead of Poul Anderson and Shakespeare, among others—I often choose people in positions of responsibility and power as sympathetic central characters. They're human, too, and their internal conflicts are just as complex. Leadership is a dirty job, but somebody has to do it—even though he or she may, with the best of intentions, leave crushed bodies and broken souls strewn across the landscape.

In *Heads*, the opening sentences define the conflict and theme: "Order and cold, heat and politics. The imposition of wrong order: anger, death, suicide and destruction." Politics is a kind of ordering, with the laws of human behavior and interaction giving shape to the social body much as chemical bonds, hormones, and enzymes give shape to the individual. Wrong order—the rule of the incompetent or the corrupt—is a constant danger, akin to cancer or disease. But unlike the individual body, society is made what it is by decisions both instinctive and conscious. Will and resolve and training are important aspects; the people in power must be vigilant, educated, and resourceful. The people who are governed must also be informed and responsible, especially in a democracy. The failure to take these responsibilities seriously inevitably leads to calamity.

Mickey Sandoval, the narrator of *Heads*, is a leader-in-training. His instincts are good; he passionately believes that politics is a necessity, when his lunar society—made up of rugged individualists, descendants of settlers and miners—tends to discredit all politics. Such disdain is a reflection of opinions generally held in the United States, where a substantial portion of the population never votes, and believes in letting somebody else take the blame for everything.

But what immediately brought these facts home to me—and probably led to this story being written—was seven years of service to the Science Fiction Writers of America. I served on the grievance committee, edited a publication, acted as vice president and finally as president; and there are few individualists more rugged and contentious, or more suspicious of politics and politicians, than writers.

The level of political naiveté in the SFWA—my own as well as others'—was astonishing. Constantly heart-rending were the letters which arrived from member writers, claiming, in paraphrase, "I can't serve as an officer, or in any other capacity, because I am unqualified by reason of my philosophical opposition to governments and politics—but here's what I think *you* should do . . ." When important votes came up (or, at least, votes which *I* thought were important), much less than half of the active membership voted.

Tossed through the muse's meat-grinder, the emotions and frustrations aroused by this service emerged as *Heads.*

The other aspects of *Heads*—the echoing themes of science, nature, and human nature so important in science fiction—came from reading science magazines. An article on the search for absolute zero in *The Sciences*—unfortunately, the issue is not immediately at hand, nor the author's name—kicked off idea and plot. Reading the entry for *Principles of Thermodynamics* in the *Encyclopedia Britannica* (1986) provided the wonderfully evocative picture of ancient Egypt and ice trays. Ice, freezing, the ideas of order and disorder, information and nonsense . . . *What if?*

I've also expelled a hairball associated with young religious groups, one of which—undecided as to whether it is a science or a religion—has tried to have an impact on science fiction, in the name of its founder. This group represents just the sort of "wrong order" which must *not* gain power. Complacency and over-tolerant pluralism—which not just tolerates, but tacitly condones—could lead to political disaster. We've seen it happen before, and the beginnings are often deceptively benign.

As Deep Throat is alleged to have said, *Follow the money . . .*

None of this was on my mind when Deborah Beale of Legend proposed I should write a novella for their line. But what irks me for a long enough time will inevitably emerge.

Often, the origins seem remote from the final product, as wine is remote from microbes and grape juice. Less remote, I think, in *Heads.*

Simply put twelve hundred science fiction and fantasy writers on the Moon, expand them two or three thousandfold, and stir . . .

THE WIND FROM A BURNING WOMAN

This story is the first in my longest and most successful sequence of stories and novels—the Thistledown series. The asteroid starships described here will later form the setting for Eon, Eternity, *and portions of* Legacy, *as well as the novella "The Way of All Ghosts."*

"Wind" was written in Long Beach and first published in Analog. It was bought by Ben Bova, who gave it a fine cover and interior illustrations by Mike Hinge. It would become the title story for my first collection from Arkham House, and thereby hangs another tale.

Jim Turner, at that time the editor of Arkham House, the most venerable small press publisher in SF and fantasy, was one of the most important people in my career. In 1980, he wrote a letter asking if I had a short story collection in the works. Jim had this silly notion that he wanted to publish SF writers, and not just modern horror. (Some horror writers regarded this as a gross betrayal of Arkham House's roots as the publisher of H. P. Lovecraft, Robert E. Howard, and Clark Ashton Smith. But in fact August Derleth, co-founder of the small press, had published science fiction long before—notably, A.E. Van Vogt's SLAN.)

I was not just an avid fan of Lovecraft et. al, I was a collector of Arkham House books, and I was thrilled when Jim approached me about a collection of short fiction—thrilled and amazed, as I was still pretty much an unknown. We assembled a tentative collection, but he wanted to top it off with something phenomenal—a story better than anything I had ever done before. I obliged with "Hardfought," which left him nonplussed for a couple of months—until he decided it met his requirements. The collection was finally published in 1983, and sold out its first printing faster than any previous book in Arkham House's history.

The irony of course was that Jim had approached a virtual unknown rather than the obvious up-and-comers and the established giants of the field. A then-famous agent asked him, point-blank, "Why Greg Bear? Who's he? Why not so-and-so or so-and-so?"

Jim just grinned—and passed the comment on to me, just to keep me in my place.

He continued to do that, surprising people and grinning at their reactions, publishing collections from promising new SF writers as well as neglected established writers, along with the core program at Arkham House of keeping Lovecraft and Clark Ashton Smith in print.

Jim was a visionary in a very restricted pond, and what he did must have rankled many, but he was right. He pulled Arkham House up in the seventies and eighties from a publisher of old classics and collectibles to one of the major forces in small-press publishing, doing, in his own way, just what Derleth had done in the thirties and forties.

I had read a poem by Michael Bishop that contains the line, "The wind from a burning woman is always a Chinook." I knew instantly I had the title for the following story, so I asked permission from Michael to use part of the line, which he very kindly gave me. Later, in his scrupulous attention to details and permissions, Jim Turner wrote to Michael. They struck up a friendship, and Jim bought two collections and a novel from Michael.

Jim Turner was a remarkable man, a conscientious editor, a fine raconteur, prickly and contentious on the surface and loving under-neath. I will miss him.

Five years later the glass bubbles were intact, the wires and pipes were taut, and the city—strung across Psyche's surface like a dewy spider's web wrapped around a thrown rock—was still breathtaking. It was also empty. Hexamon investigators had swept out the final dried husks and bones. The asteroid was clean again. The plague was over.

Giani Turco turned her eyes away from the port and looked at the displays. Satisfied by the approach, she ordered a meal and put her work schedule through the processor for tightening and trimming. She had six tanks of air, enough to last her three days. There was no time to spare. The robot guards in orbit around Psyche hadn't been operating for at least a year and wouldn't offer any resistance, but four small pursuit bugs had been planted in the bubbles. They turned themselves off whenever possible, but her presence would activate them. Time spent in avoiding and finally destroying them: one hour forty minutes, the processor said. The final schedule was projected in front of her by a pen hooked around her ear. She happened to be staring at Psyche when the readout began; the effect—red numerals and letters over gray rock and black space—was pleasingly graphic, like a film in training.

Turco had dropped out of training six weeks early. She had no need for a final certificate, approval from the Hexamon, or any other nicety. Her craft was stolen from Earth orbit, her papers and cards forged, and her intentions entirely opposed to those of the sixteen corporeal desks. On Earth, some hours hence, she would be hated and reviled.

The impulse to sneer was strong—pure theatrics, since she was alone—but she didn't allow it to break her concentration. (Worse than sheep, the cowardly citizens who tacitly supported the forces that had driven her father to suicide and murdered her grandfather; the seekers-after-security who lived by technology but believed in the just influences: Star, Logos, Fate, and Pneuma. . .)

To calm her nerves, she sang a short song while she selected her landing site.

The ship, a small orbital tug, touched the asteroid like a mote settling on a boulder and made itself fast. She stuck her arms and legs into the suit receptacles, and the limb covers automatically hooked themselves to the thorax. The cabin was too cramped to get into a suit any other way. She reached up and brought down the helmet, pushed until all the semifluid seals seized and beeped, and began the evacuation of the cabin's atmosphere. Then the cabin parted down the middle, and she floated slowly, fell more slowly still, to Psyche's surface.

She turned once to watch the cabin clamp together and to see if the propulsion rods behind the tanks had been damaged by the unusually long journey. They'd held up well.

She took hold of a guide wire after a flight of twenty or twenty five meters and pulled for the nearest glass bubble. Five years before, the milky spheres had been filled with the families of workers setting the charges that would form Psyche's seven internal chambers. Holes had been bored from the Vlasseg and Janacki poles, on the narrow ends of the huge rock, through the center. After the formation of the chambers, materials necessary for atmosphere would have been pumped into Psyche through the bore holes while motors increased her natural spin to create artificial gravity inside.

In twenty years, Psyche's seven chambers would have been green and beautiful, filled with hope—and passengers. But now the control bubble hatches had been sealed by the last of the investigators. Since Psyche was not easily accessible, even in its lunar orbit, the seals hadn't been applied carefully. Nevertheless it took her an hour to break in. The glass ball towered above her, a hundred feet in diameter, translucent walls mottled by the shadows of rooms and equipment.

Psyche rotated once every three hours, and light from the sun was beginning to flush the tops of the bubbles in the local cluster. Moonlight illuminated the shadows. She pulled away the rubbery cement seals and watched them float lazily to the pocked ground. Then she examined the airlock to see if it was still functioning. She wanted to keep atmosphere inside the bubble, to check it for psychotropic chemicals; she would not leave her suit at any rate.

The locked door opened with a few jerks and closed behind her. She brushed crystals of frost off her faceplate and the port of the inner lock door. Then she pushed the button for the inner door. Nothing happened. The external doors were on a separate power supply, which was no longer working or, she hoped, had only been switched off. From her backpack she removed a half-meter pry bar. The break-in took fifteen minutes.

She was five minutes ahead of schedule.

Across the valley, the fusion power plants that supplied power to the Geshel populations of Tijuana and Chula Vista sat like squat mountains of concrete. By Naderite law, all nuclear facilities were enclosed by multiple domes and pyramids, whether they posed any danger or not. The symbolism was two-fold—it showed the distaste of the ruling Naderites for energy sources that were not nature-kinetic, and it carried on the separation of Naderites-Geshels.

Farmer Kollert, advisor to the North American Hexamon and ecumentalist to the California corporeal desk, watched the sun set behind the false peak and wondered vaguely if there was symbolism in the scene. Was not fusion the source of power for the sun? He smiled. Such things seldom occurred to him; perhaps it would amuse a Geshel technician.

His team of five Geshel scientists would tour the plants two days from now and make their report to him. He would then pass on *his* report to the desk, acting as interface for the invariably clumsy, elitist language the Geshel scientists used. In this way, through the medium of advisors across the globe, the Naderites oversaw the production of Geshel power. By their grants and control of capital, his people had once plucked the world from technological overkill, and the battle was ongoing still—a war against some of mankind's darker tendencies.

He finished his evening juice and took a package of writing utensils from the drawer in the veranda desk. The reports from last month's balancing of energy consumption needed to be revised, based on new estimates—and he enjoyed doing the work himself rather than giving it to the persona in the library computer. It relaxed him to do things by hand. He wrote on a positive feedback slate, his scrawly letters adjusting automatically into script, with his tongue between his lips and a pleased frown creasing his brow.

"Excuse me, Farmer." His ur-wife, Gestina, stood by the French doors leading to the veranda. She was as slender as when he had married her, despite fifteen years and two children.

"Yes, cara, what is it?" He withdrew his tongue and told the slate to store what he'd written.

"Josef Krupkin."

Kollert stood up quickly, knocking the metal chair over. He hurried past his wife into the dining room, dropped his bulk into a chair, and drew up the crystalline cube on the alabaster tabletop. The cube adjusted its picture to meet the angle of his eyes and Krupkin appeared.

"Josef! This is unexpected."

"Very," Krupkin said. He was a small man with narrow eyes and curly black hair. Compared to Kollert's bulk, he was dapper—but thirty years behind a desk had given him the usual physique of a Hexamon backroomer. "Have you ever heard of Giani Turco?"

Kollert thought for a moment. "No, I haven't. Wait—Turco. Related to Kimon Turco?"

"Daughter. California should keep better track of its radical Geshels, shouldn't it?"

"Kimon Turco lived on the Moon."

"His daughter lived in your district."

"Yes, fine. What about her?" Kollert was beginning to be perturbed. Krupkin enjoyed roundabouts even in important situations and to call him at this address, at such a time, something important had happened.

"She's calling for you. She'll only talk to you, none of the rest. She won't even accept President Praetori."

"Who is she? What has she done?"

"She's managed to start up Psyche. There was enough reaction mass left in the Beckmann motors to alter it into an Earth-intersect orbit." The left side of the cube was flashing bright red, indicating the call was being scrambled.

Kollert sat very still. There was no need acting incredulous. Krupkin was in no position to joke. But the enormity of what he said—and the impulse to disbelieve, despite the bearer of the news—froze Kollert for an unusually long time. He ran his hand through lank blond hair.

"Kollert," Krupkin said. "You look like you've been—"

"Is she telling the truth?"

Krupkin shook his head. "No, Kollert, you don't understand. She hasn't claimed these accomplishments. She hasn't said anything about them yet. She just wants to speak to you. But our tracking stations say there's no doubt. I've spoken with the officer who commanded the last inspection. He says there was enough mass left in the Beckmann drive positioning motors to push—"

"This is incredible! No precautions were taken? The mass wasn't drained, or something?"

"I'm no Geshel, Farmer. My technicians tell me the mass was left on Psyche because it would have cost several hundred million—"

"That's behind us now. Let the journalists worry about that, if they ever hear of it." He looked up and saw Gestina still standing near the French doors. He held up his hand to tell her to stay where she was. She was going to have to keep to the house, incommunicado, for as long as it took to straighten this out.

"You're coming?"

"Which center?"

"Does it matter? She's not being discreet. Her message is hitting an entire hemisphere, and there are hundreds of listening stations to pick it up. Several aren't under our control. Once anyone pinpoints the source, the story is going to be clear. For your convenience, go to Baja Station. Mexico is signatory to all the necessary pacts."

"I'm leaving now," Kollert said. Krupkin nodded, and the cube went blank.

"What was he talking about?" Gestina asked. "What's *Psyche?*"

"A chunk of rock, dear," he said. Her talents lay in other directions—she wasn't stupid. Even for a Naderite, however, she was unknowledgeable about things beyond the Earth.

He started to plan the rules for her movements, then thought better of it and said nothing. If Krupkin was correct—and he would be—there was no need. The political considerations, if everything turned out right, would be enormous. He could run as Governor of the Desk, even President of the Hexamon . . .

And if everything didn't turn out right, it wouldn't matter where anybody was.

Turco sat in the middle of her grandfather's control center and cried. She was tired and sick at heart. Things were moving rapidly now, and she wondered just how sane she was. In a few hours she would be the worst menace the Earth had ever known, and for what cause? Truth, justice? They had murdered her grandfather, discredited her father and driven him to suicide—but all seven billion of them, Geshels and Naderites alike?

She didn't know whether she was bluffing or not. Psyche's fall was still controllable, and she was bargaining it would never hit the Earth. Even if she lost and everything was hopeless, she might divert it, causing a few tidal disruptions, minor earthquakes perhaps, but still passing over four thousand kilometers from the Earth's surface. There was enough reaction mass in the positioning motors to allow a broad margin of safety.

Resting lightly on the table in front of her was a chart that showed the basic plan of the asteroid, an egg-shaped chunk of nickel-iron and rock. The positioning motors surrounded a crater at one end. Catapults loaded with huge barrels of reaction mass had just a few hours earlier launched a salvo to rendezvous above the crater's center. Beckmann drive beams had then surrounded the mass with a halo of energy, releasing its atoms from the bonds of nature's weak force. The blast had bounced off the crater floor, directed by the geometric patterns of heat-resistant slag. At the opposite end, a smaller guidance engine was in position, but it was no longer functional and didn't figure in her plans. The two tunnels that reached from the poles to the center of Psyche opened into seven blast chambers, each containing a fusion charge. She hadn't checked to see if the charges were still armed.

There were so many things to do.

She sat with her head bowed, still suited up. Though the bubbles contained enough atmosphere to support her, she had no intention of unsuiting. In one gloved hand she clutched a small ampoule with a nozzle for attachment to air and water systems piping. The Hexamon Nexus's trumped-up excuse of madness caused by near-weightless conditions was now a shattered, horrible lie. Turco didn't know why, but the Psyche project had been deliberately sabotaged, and the psychotropic drugs still lingered.

Her grandfather hadn't gone mad contemplating the stars. The asteroid crew hadn't mutinied out of misguided Geshel zeal and space sickness.

Her anger rose again, and the tears stopped. 'You deserve whoever governs you," she said quietly. "Everyone is responsible for the actions of their leaders."

The computer display cross-haired the point of impact. It was ironic—the buildings of the Hexamon Nexus were only sixty kilometers from the zero point. She had no control over such niceties, but nature and fate seemed to be as angry as she was.

"Moving an asteroid is like carving a diamond," the Geshel advisor said. Kollert nodded his head, not very interested. "The charges for initial orbit change—moving it out of the asteroid belt—have to be placed very carefully or the mass will break up and be useless. When the asteroid is close enough to the Earth-Moon system to meet the major crew vessels, the work has only begun. Positioning motors have to be built—"

"Madness," Kollert's secretary said, not pausing from his monitoring of communications between associate committees.

"And charge tunnels drilled. All of this was completed on the asteroid ten years ago."

"Are the charges still in place?" Kollert asked.

"So far as I know," the Geshel said.

"Can they be set off now?"

"I don't know. Whoever oversaw dismantling should have disarmed to protect his crew—but then, the reaction mass should have been jettisoned, too. So who can say? The report hasn't cleared top secrecy yet."

And not likely to, either, Kollert thought. "If they haven't been disarmed, can they be set off now? What would happen if they were?"

"Each charge has a complex communications system. They were designed to be set off by coded signals and could probably be set off now, yes, if we had the codes. Of course, those are top secret, too."

"What would happen?" Kollert was becoming impatient with the Geshel.

"I don't think the charges were ever given a final adjustment. It all depends on how well the initial alignment was performed. If they're out of true, or the final geological studies weren't taken into account, they could blow Psyche to pieces. If they are true, they'll do what they were intended to do—form chambers inside the rock. Each chamber would be about fifteen kilometers long, ten kilometers in diameter—"

"If the asteroid were blown apart, how would that affect our situation?"

"Instead of having one mass hit, we'd have a cloud, with debris twenty to thirty kilometers across and smaller."

"Would that be any better?" Kollert asked.

"Sir?"

"Would it be better to be hit by such a cloud than one chunk?"

"I don't think so. The difference is pretty moot—either way, the surface of the Earth would be radically altered, and few life forms would survive."

Kollert turned to his secretary. "Tell them to put a transmission through to Giani Turco."

The communications were arranged. In the meantime Kollert tried to make some sense out of the Geshel advisor's figures. To Kollert, the Geshel mathematics was irritatingly dense and obtuse. He was very good at mathematics, but in the past sixty years many physics and chemistry symbols had diverged from those used in biology and psychology.

He put the paper aside when Turco appeared on the cube in front of him. A few background beeps and noise were eliminated, and her image cleared. "Ser Turco," he said.

"Ser Farmer Kollert," she replied several seconds later. A beep signaled the end of one side's transmission. She sounded tired.

"You're doing a very foolish thing."

"I have a list of demands," she said.

Kollert laughed. "You sound like the Good Man himself, Ser Turco. The tactic of direct confrontation. Well, it didn't work all the time, even for him."

"I want the public—Geshels and Naderites both—to know why the Psyche project was sabotaged."

"It was not sabotaged," Kollert said calmly. "It was unfortunate proof that humans cannot live in conditions so far removed from the Earth."

"Ask those on the Moon!" Turco said bitterly.

"The Moon has a much stronger gravitational pull than Psyche. But I'm not briefed to discuss all the reasons why the Psyche project failed."

"I have found psychotropic drugs—traces of drugs and containers in the air and water the crew breathed and drank. That's why I'm maintaining my suit integrity."

"No such traces were found by our investigating teams. But, Ser Turco, neither of us is here to discuss something long past. Speak your demands—your price—and we'll begin negotiations." Kollert knew he was walking a loose rope. Several Hexamon terrorist team officers were listening to everything he said, waiting to splice in a timely splash of static. Conversely, there was no way to stop Turco's words from reaching open stations on the Earth. He was sweating heavily under his arms. Stations on the Moon—the bastards there would probably be sympathetic to her—could pick up his messages and relay them back to the Earth. A drop of perspiration trickled from armpit to sleeve, and he shivered involuntarily.

"That's my only demand," Turco said. "No money, not even amnesty. I want nothing for myself. I simply want the people to know the truth."

"Ser Turco, you have an ideal platform from which to tell them all you want them to hear."

"The Hexamons control most major reception centers. Everything else—except for a few ham and radio-astronomy amateurs—is cabled and controlled. To reach the most people, the Hexamon Nexus will have to reveal its part in the matter."

Before speaking to her again, Kollert asked the advisors if there was any way she could be fooled into believing her requests were being carried out. The answer was ambiguous—a few hundred people were thinking it over.

"I've conferred with my staff, Ser Turco, and I can assure you, so far as the most privy of us can know, nothing so villainous was ever done to the Psyche project." At a later time, his script suggested, he might indicate that some tests had been overlooked, and that a junior officer had suggested lunar sabotage on Psyche. That might shift the heat. But for the moment, any admission that drugs existed in the asteroid's human environments could backfire.

"I'm not arguing," she said. "There's no question that the Hexamon Nexus had somebody sabotage Psyche."

Kollert held his tongue between his lips and punched key words into his script processor. The desired statements formed over Turco's image. He looked at the camera earnestly. "If we had done anything so heinous, surely we would have protected ourselves against an eventuality like this—drained the reaction mass in the positioning motors—" One of the terrorist team officers scowled and waved frantically at him. The screen's words showed red where they were being covered by static. There would be no mention of how Turco had gained control of Psyche. The issue was too sensitive, and blame hadn't been placed yet. Besides, there was still the option of informing the public that Turco had never gained control of Psyche at all. If everything worked out, the issue would be solved without politically costly admissions.

"Excuse me," Turco said seconds later.

The time lag between communications was wearing on her nerves, if Kollert was any judge. "Something just got lost there."

"Ser Turco, your grandfather's death on Psyche was accidental, and your recent actions undermine the creed of the Geshels. Destroying the Hexamon Nexus"—much better than saying *Earth*—"would be a meaningless act of inhuman cruelty." He leaned back in the seat, chewing on his index finger. This gesture had been approved an hour before the talks began, but it was nearly genuine. His usual elegance seemed to be wearing thin in this encounter. He'd already made several embarrassing misjudgments.

"I'm not doing this for logical reasons," Turco finally said. "I'm doing it out of hatred for you and all the people who support you. What happened on Psyche was purely evil—useless, motivated by the worst intentions, resulting in the death of a beautiful dream, not to mention people I loved. No talk can change my mind about those things."

"Then why talk to me at all? I'm hardly the highest official in the Nexus."

"No, but you're in an ideal position to know those high officials. You're a respected politician. And I suspect you had a great deal to do with devising the plot. I just want the truth. I'm tired. I'm going to rest for a few hours now."

"Just a moment," Kollert said sharply. "We haven't discussed the most important issues."

"I'm signing off. Until later."

The team leader made a cutting motion across his throat that almost made Kollert choke. Kollert shook his head and held his fingertips to his temples. "We didn't even have time to start," he said.

The team leader stood and stretched his arms.

"You're doing reasonably well so far, Ser Kollert," he said. "It's best to ease into these things."

"I'm *Advisor* Kollert to you, and I don't see how we have the time to *ease into things.*"

"Yes, sir. Absolutely. Apologies."

Turco needed the rest, but there was far too much to do. She pushed off from the seat and floated gently for a few moments before drifting down. Psyche's pull was weak, but just enough to remind her there was no time for rest.

One of the things she had hoped she could do—checking the charges deep inside the asteroid to see if they were armed—was impossible. The main computer and the systems board indicated the transport system through the bore holes was no longer operative. It would take her days to crawl or float the distance down the shafts, and she wasn't about to take the small tug through a tunnel barely fifty meters wide. She wasn't that good a pilot.

So she had a weak spot. The bombs couldn't be disarmed from where she was. They could be set off by a ship positioned along the axis of the tunnels, but so far none had shown up. That would take another twelve hours or so, and by then time would be running out. She hoped that all negotiations would be completed.

Turco drifted for more long minutes, vacillating, and finally groaned and slapped her thigh with a gloved palm. "I'm *tired*," she said. "Not thinking straight." She felt like a ball of tacky glue wrapped in wool. She desperately wanted out of the suit. The catheters and cups were itching. Her eyes were stinging from strain and sweat buildup. One way or another, she had to clean up—and there was no way to do that unless she risked exposure to the residue of drugs.

She looked at the computer. There was a solution, but she couldn't see it clearly. "Come on, girl. So simple. But what?"

The drug would probably have a limited life, in case the Nexus wanted to do something with Psyche later. But how limited? Ten years? She chuckled grimly. She had the ampoule and its cryptic chemical label. Would a Physician's Desk Reference be programmed into the computers?

She hooked herself into the console. "Medical, pharmacy, PDR," she said. The screen blanked, then brightened and said, "Ready."

"Iropentaphonate," she said. "Two-seven diboltene."

The screen scrolled down the relevant data. She searched through the technical maze for a full minute before finding what she wanted. "Effective shelf life, four months two days from date of manufacture."

She tested the air again—it was stale but breathable—and unhooked her helmet. It was worth any risk. A bare knuckle against her eye felt so good.

The small lounge in the Baja Station was well-furnished and comfortable, but suited more for Geshels than Naderites—bright rather than natural colors, abstract paintings of a mechanistic tendency, modernist furniture. To Kollert it was faintly oppressive. The man sitting across from him had been silent for the past five minutes, reading through a sheaf of papers.

"Who authorized this?" the man asked.

"Hexamon Nexus, Mr. President."

"But who proposed it?"

Kollert hesitated. "The advisory committee."

"Who proposed it to the committee?"

"I did."

"Under what authority?"

"It was strictly legal," Kollert said defensively. "Such activities have been covered under the emergency code, classified section fourteen."

The president nodded. "She came to the right man when she asked for you. I wonder where she got her information. None of this can be broadcast. Why was it done?"

"There were a number of reasons, among them financial—"

"The project was mostly financed by lunar agencies. Earth had perhaps a five percent share, so no controlling interest—and there was no connection with radical Geshel groups, therefore no need to invoke section fourteen on revolutionary deterrence. I read the codes, too, Farmer."

"Yes, sir."

"What were you afraid of? Some irrational desire to pin the butterflies? Jesus God, Farmer, our Naderite beliefs don't allow anything like this. But you and your committee took it upon yourselves to covertly destroy the biggest project in the history of mankind. You think this follows in the tracks of the Good Man?"

"You're aware of lunar plans to build particle guidance guns. They're canceled now because Psyche is dead. They were to be used to push asteroids like Psyche into deep space, so advanced Beckmann drives could be used."

"I'm not technically minded, Farmer."

"Nor am I. But such particle guns could have been used as weapons—considering lunar sympathies, probably *would* have been used. They could cook whole cities on Earth. The development of potential weapons *is* a matter of concern for Naderites, sir. And there are many studies showing that human behavior changes in space. It becomes less Earth-centered, less communal. Man can't live in space and remain human. We were trying to preserve humanity's right to a secure future. Even now the Moon is a potent political force, and a future war has been studied by our best strategists. It's a dire possibility. All this because of the perverse separation of an intellectual class of humans from the parent body—from wise government and safe creed."

The president shook his head and looked away. "I am ashamed such a thing could happen in my government. Very well, Kollert, this remains your ball game until she asks to speak to someone else. But my advisors are going to go over everything you say. I doubt you'll have the chance to botch anything. We're already acting with the Moon to stop this before it gets any worse. And you can thank God—for your life, not your career, which is already dead—that our Geshels have come up with a way out."

Kollert was outwardly submissive, but inside he was fuming. Not even the President of the Hexamon had the right to treat him like a child or, worse, a criminal. He was an independent advisor, of a separate desk, elected by Naderites of high standing. The ecumentalist creed was apparently much tighter than the president's. "I acted in the best interests of my constituency," he said.

"You no longer have a constituency, you no longer have a career. Nor do any of the people who planned this operation with you, or those who carried it out. Up and down the line. A purge."

Turco woke up before the blinking light and moved her lips in a silent curse. How long had she been asleep? She panicked briefly— a dozen hours would be crucial—but then saw the digital clock. Two hours. The light was demanding her attention to an incoming radio signal.

There was no video image. Kollert's voice returned, less certain, almost cowed.

"I'm here," she said, switching off her camera as well. The delay was a fraction shorter than when they'd first started talking.

"Have you made a decision?" Kollert asked.

"I should be asking that question. My course is fixed. When are you and your people going to admit to sabotage?"

"We'd—I'd almost be willing to admit, just to—" He stopped. She was about to speak when he continued. "We could do that, you know. Broadcast a worldwide admission of guilt. A cheap price to pay for saving all life on Earth. Do you really understand what you're up to? What satisfaction, what revenge, could you possibly get out of this? My God, Turco, you—" There was a burst of static. It sounded suspiciously like the burst she had heard some time ago.

"You're editing him," she said. Her voice was level and calm. "I don't want anyone editing anything between us, whoever you are. Is that understood? One more burst of static like that, and I'll . . ." She had already threatened the ultimate. "I'll be less tractable. Repeat what you were saying, Ser Kollert."

The digital readout indicated one-way delay time of 1.496 seconds. She would soon be closer to the Earth than the Moon was.

"I was saying," Kollert repeated, something like triumph in his tone, "that you are a very young woman, with very young ideas—like a child leveling a loaded pistol at her parents. You may or may not be a fanatic. But you aren't seeing things clearly. We have no evidence here on Earth regarding your accusations, and we won't have evidence—nothing will be solved—if the asteroid collides with us. That's obvious. But if it veers aside, goes into a wide Earth orbit, then—"

"That's not one of my options," Turco said.

"—an investigating team could reexamine the crew quarters," Kollert continued, not to be interrupted for a few seconds. "They could perform a more detailed search. Your accusations might be verified."

"I can't go into Earth orbit without turning around, and this is a one-way rock, Ser Kollert. Remember that. My only other option is to swing around the Earth, be deflected a couple of degrees, and go into a solar orbit. By the time any investigating team reached me, I'd be on the other side of the sun, and dead. I'm the daughter of a Geshel, Ser Kollert. I have a good technical education, and my training under Hexamon auspices makes me a competent pilot and spacefarer. Too bad there's so little long-range work for my type, just Earth-Moon runs. But don't try to fool me or kid me. I'm far more expert than you are. Though I'm sure you have Geshel people on your staff." She paused. "Geshels! I can't call you traitors—you in the background—because you might be thinking I'm crazy, out to destroy all of you. But do you understand what these men have done to our hopes and dreams? I've never seen a finished asteroid starship, of course—Psyche was to have been the first. But I've seen good simulations. It would have been like seven Shangri-las inside, hollowed out of solid rock and metal—seven chambers separated by walls four kilometers high, each self-contained, connected with the others by tube trains. The chambers would be like deep valleys, their floors stretching up to the sky, everything wonderfully topsy-turvy. And quiet—so much insulation none of the engine sounds would be heard inside."

She was crying again.

"Psyche would consume herself on the way to the stars. By the time she arrived, there'd remain a cylinder thirty kilometers wide and two hundred ninety long. Like the core of an apple, and the passengers would be luxurious worms—star travelers. Now ask why, why did these men sabotage such a marvelous thing? Because they are blind, blind unto pure evil—ugly-minded, weak men who hate greatness and exploration, who hate all great ideas . . ." She paused. "I don't know what you think of me and what I've done, but remember, they stole something magnificent from us all. I know. I've seen the evidence here. Sabotage and murder." She pressed the button and waited wearily for a reply.

"Ser Turco," Kollert said, "you have ten hours to make an effective course correction. We estimate you have enough reaction mass left to extend your orbit and miss the Earth by about four thousand kilometers. There is nothing we can do here but try to convince you—"

She stopped listening, trying to figure out what was happening behind the scenes. Earth wouldn't take such a threat without exploring a large number of alternatives. Kollert's voice droned on as she tried to think of the most likely action, and the most effective.

She picked up her helmet and sent a short message, paying no attention to the transmission from Earth. "I'm going outside for a few minutes."

The large cargo transport was fully loaded with extra fuel—and a substantial bulk William Porter was reluctant to contemplate.

His acceleration had been steady for two hours, but now the weightlessness was just as oppressive. With the ship reversed for course correction, he could see a hair-thin silvery crescent—the Moon, its inner shadow relieved by light from Earth.

He had about half an hour to relax before the real work began, and he was using it to read an excerpt from a novel by Anthony Burgess. He'd been a heavy reader all his memorable life, and now he allowed himself a possible last taste of pleasure.

Like most inhabitants of the Moon, Porter was a Geshel, with a physicist father and a geneticist mother. He'd chosen a career as a pilot rather than a researcher out of romantic predilections established long before he was ten years old. There was something immediately effective and satisfying about piloting, and he'd turned out to be well suited to the work. He'd never expected to take on a mission like this. But then, he'd never paid much attention to politics, either. Even if he had, the last remaining disputes between Geshels and Naderites had been settled, most experts claimed, fifty years before, when Naderites emerged as Earth's ruling class. Few Geshels still bothered to complain. Responsibility had been lifted from their shoulders.

Most of the populations of both Earth and Moon were now involved in technical and scientific work, yet the mistakes they made would be blamed on Naderite policies—and the disasters would likewise be absorbed by the leadership. It wasn't a hard situation to get used to.

William Porter wasn't so sure, now, that it was the ideal. He had two options to save Earth, and one of them meant he would die.

He'd listened to the Psyche-Earth transmissions during acceleration, trying to make sense out of Turco's position, to form an opinion of her character and sanity, but he was more confused than ever. If she was right—and not a raving lunatic, which didn't seem to fit the facts—then the Hexamon Nexus had a lot of explaining to do and probably wouldn't do it under the gun. The size of Turco's gun was far too imposing to be rational—the destruction of the human race, the wiping of a planet's surface.

He played back the computer diagram of what would happen if Psyche hit the Earth. At the angle it would strike, it would speed the rotation of the Earth's crust and mantle by an appreciable fraction. The asteroid would cut a gouge from Maine to England, several thousand kilometers long and at least a hundred kilometers deep. The impact would vault hundreds of millions of tons of surface material into space, and that would partially counteract the speedup of rotation. The effect would be a monumental jerk, with the energy finally being released as heat. The continents would fracture in several directions, forming new faults, even new plate orientations, which would generate earthquakes on a scale never before seen. The impact basin would be a hell of molten crust and mantle, with water on the perimeter bursting violently into steam, altering weather patterns around the world. Decades would pass before the Earth would cool and again return to a restless sort of stability.

Turco may not have been raving, but she was coldly suggesting a cataclysm to swat what amounted to a historical fly. That made her a lunatic in anyone's book, Geshel or Naderite. And his life was well worth the effort to thwart her.

That didn't stop him from being angry, though.

Kollert impatiently let the physician check him over and administer a few injections. He talked to his wife briefly, which left him more nervous than before, then listened to the team leader's theories on how Turco's behavior would change in the next few hours. He nodded at only one statement: "She's going to see she'll be dead, too, and that's a major shock for even the most die-hard terrorist."

Then Turco was back on the air, and he was on stage again.

"I've seen your ship," she said. "I went outside and looked in the direction where I thought it would be. There it was—treachery all around. Goddamned hypocrites! Talk friendly to the little girl, but shiv her in the back! Public face cool, private face snarl! Well, just remember, before that ship can kill me, I can destroy the controls to the positioning engines. It would take a week to replace them. You don't have the time!"

The beep followed.

"Giani, we have only one option left, and that's to do as you say. We'll admit we played a part in the sabotage of Psyche. It's confession under pressure, but we'll do it." Kollert pressed his button and waited, holding his chin with one hand.

"No way it's so simple, Kollert. No public admission and then public denial after the danger is over—you'd all come across as heroes. No. There has to be some record-keeping, payrolls if nothing else. I want full disclosure of all records, and I want them transmitted around the world—facsimile, authenticated. I want uninvolved government officials to see them and sign off that they've seen them. And I want the actual documents put on display where anyone can look at them—memos, plans, letters, whatever. All of it that's still available."

"That would take weeks," Kollert said, "even if they existed."

"Not in this age of electronic wizardry. I want you to take a lie detector test, authenticated by half a dozen experts with their careers on the line—and while you're at it, have the other officials take tests, too."

"That's not only impractical, it won't hold up in a court of law."

"I'm not interested in formal courts. I'm not a vengeful person, no matter what I may seem now. I just want the truth. And if I still see that goddamn ship up there in an hour, I'm going to stop negotiations right now and blow myself to pieces."

Kollert looked at the team leader, but the man's face was blank.

"Let me talk to her, then," Porter suggested. "Direct person-to-person. Let me explain the plans. She really can't change them any, can she? She has no way of making them worse. If she fires her engines or does any positive action, she simply stops the threat. So I'm the one who holds the key to the situation."

"We're not sure that's advisable, Bill," Lunar Guidance said.

"I can transmit to her without permission, you know," he said testily.

"Against direct orders, that's not like you."

"Like me, hell," he said. "Listen, just get me permission. Nobody else seems to be doing anything effective." There was a few minutes' silence, then Lunar Guidance returned.

"Okay, Bill. You have permission. But be very careful what you say. Terrorist team officers on Earth think she's close to the pit."

With that obstacle cleared away, he wondered how wise the idea was in the first place. Still, they were both Geshels—they had something in common compared to the elite Naderites running things on Earth.

Far away, Earth concurred and transmissions were cleared. They couldn't censor his direct signal, so Baja Station was unwillingly cut from the circuit.

"Who's talking to me now?" Turco asked when the link was made.

"This is Lieutenant William Porter, from the Moon. I'm a

pilot—not a defense pilot usually, either. I understand you've had pilot's training."

"Just enough to get by." The lag was less than a hundredth of a second, not noticeable.

"You know I'm up here to stop you, one way or another. I've got two options. The one I think more highly of is to get in line-of-sight of your bore holes and relay the proper coded signals to the charges in your interior."

"Killing me won't do you any good."

"That's not the plan. The fore end of your rock is bored with a smaller hole by thirty meters. It'll release the blast wastes more slowly than the aft end. The total explosive force should give the rock enough added velocity to get it clear of the Earth by at least sixty kilometers. The damage would be negligible. Spectacular view from Greenland, too, I understand. But if we've miscalculated, or if one or more charges doesn't go, then I'll have to impact with your aft crater and release the charge in my cargo hold. I'm one floating megaboom now, enough to boost the rock up and out by a few additional kilometers. But that means I'll be dead, and not enough left of me to memorialize or pin a medal on. Not too good, hm?"

"None of my sweat."

"No, I suppose not. But listen, sister—"

"No sister to a lackey."

Porter started to snap a retort, but stopped himself. "Listen, they tell me to be soft on you, but I'm under pressure, too, so please reciprocate. I don't see the sense in all of it. If you get your way, you've set back your cause by God knows how many decades— because once you're out of range and blown your trump, they'll deny it all, say it was manufactured evidence and testimony under pressure—all that sort of thing. And if they decide to hard-line it, force me to do my dirty work, or God forbid let you do yours— we've lost our homeworld. You've lost Psyche, which can still be salvaged and finished. Everything will be lost, just because a few men may or may not have done a very wicked thing. Come on, honey. That isn't the Geshel creed, and you know it."

"What is our creed? To let men rule our lives who aren't competent to read a thermometer? Under the Naderites, most of the leaders on Earth haven't got the technical expertise to . . . to . . . I don't know what. To tie their goddamn shoes! They're blind, dedicated to some half-wit belief that progress is the most dangerous thing conceived by man. But they can't live without technology so we provide it for them. And when they won't touch our filthy nuclear energy, we get stuck with it—because otherwise we all have to go back four hundred years, and sacrifice half the population. Is that good planning, sound policy? And if they do what I say, Psyche won't be damaged. All they'll have to do is fetch it back from orbit around the sun."

"I'm not going to argue on their behalf, sister. I'm a Geshel, too, and a Moonman besides. I never have paid attention to Earth politics because it never made much sense to me. But now I'm talking to you one-to-one, and you're telling me that avenging someone's irrational system is worth wiping away a planet?"

"I'm willing to take that risk."

"I don't think you are. I hope you aren't. I hope it's all bluff, and I won't have to smear myself against your backside."

"I hope you won't, either. I hope they've got enough sense down there to do what I want."

"I don't think they have, sister. I don't put much faith in them, myself. They probably don't even know what would happen if you hit the Earth with your rock. Think about that. You're talking about scientific innocents—flat-Earthers almost, naive. Words fail me. But think on it. They may not even know what's going on."

"They know. And remind them that if they set off the charges, it'll probably break up Psyche and give them a thousand rocks to contend with instead of one. That plan may backfire on them."

"What if they—we—don't have any choice?"

"I don't give a damn what choice you have," Turco said. "I'm not talking for a while. I've got more work to do."

Porter listened to the final click with a sinking feeling. She was a tough one. How would he outwit her? He smiled grimly at his chutzpah for even thinking he could. She'd committed herself all the way—and now, perhaps, she was feeling the power of her position. One lonely woman, holding the key to a world's existence. He wondered how it felt.

Then he shivered, and the sweat in his suit felt very, very cold. If he would have a grave for someone to walk over . . .

For the first time, Turco realized they wouldn't accede to her demands. They were more traitorous than even she could have imagined. Or—the thought was too horrible to accept—she'd misinterpreted the evidence, and they weren't at fault. Perhaps a madman in the Psyche crew had sought revenge and caused the whole mess. But that didn't fit the facts. It would have taken at least a dozen people to set all the psychotropic vials and release them at once—a concerted preplanned effort. She shook her head. Besides, she had the confidential reports a friend had accidentally plugged into while troubleshooting a Hexamon computer plex. There was no doubt about who was responsible, just uncertainty about the exact procedure. Her evidence for Farmer Kollert's guilt was circumstantial but not baseless.

She sealed her suit and helmet and went outside the bubble again, just to watch the stars for a few minutes. The lead-gray rock under her feet was pocked by eons of micrometeoroids. Rills several kilometers across attested to the rolling impacts of other asteroids, any one of which would have caused a major disaster on Earth. Earth had been hit before, not often by pieces as big as Psyche, but several times at least, and had survived. Earth would survive Psyche's impact, and life would start anew. Those plants and animals—even humans—that survived would eventually build back to the present level, and perhaps it would be a better world, more daunted by the power of past evil. She might be a force for positive regeneration.

The string of bubbles across Psyche's surface was serenely lovely in the starlight. The illumination brightened slowly as Earth rose above the Vlasseg pole, larger now than the Moon. She had a few more hours to make the optimum correction. Just above the Earth was a tiny moving point of light—Porter in his cargo vessel. He was lining up with the smaller bore hole to send signals, if he had to.

Again she wanted to cry. She felt like a little child, full of hatred and frustration, but caught now in something so immense and inexorable that all passion was dwarfed. She couldn't believe she was the controlling factor, that she held so much power. Surely something was behind her, some impersonal, objective force. Alone, she was nothing, and her crime would be unbelievable— just as Porter had said. But with a cosmic justification, the agreeing nod of some vast, all-seeing God, she was just a tool, bereft of responsibility.

She grasped the guide wires strung between the bubbles and pulled herself back to the airlock hatch. With one gloved hand she pressed the button. Under her palm she felt the metal vibrate for a second, then stop. The hatch was still closed. She pressed again and nothing happened.

Porter listened carefully for a full minute, trying to pick up the weak signal. It had cut off abruptly a few minutes before, during his final lineup with the Vlasseg pole bore hole. He called his director and asked if any signals had been received from Turco. Since he was out of line-of-sight now, the Moon had to act as a relay.

"Nothing," Lunar Guidance said. "She's been silent for an hour."

"That doesn't make sense. We've only got an hour and a half left. She should be playing the situation for all it's worth. Listen, LG, I received a weak signal from Psyche several minutes ago. It could have been a freak, but I don't think so. I'm going to move back to where I picked it up."

"Negative, Porter. You'll need all your reaction mass in case Plan A doesn't go off properly."

"I've got plenty to spare, LG. I have a bad feeling about this. Something's gone wrong on Psyche." It was clear to him the instant he said it. "Jesus Christ, LG, the signal must have come from Turco's area! I lost it just when I passed out of line-of-sight from her bubble."

Lunar Guidance was silent for a long moment. "Okay, Porter, we've got clearance for you to regain that signal."

"Thank you, LG." He pushed the ship out of its rough alignment and coasted slowly away from Psyche until he could see the equatorial ring of domes and bubbles. Abruptly his receiver again picked up the weak signal. He locked his tracking antenna to it, boosted it, and cut in the communications processor to interpolate through the hash.

"This is Turco. William Porter, listen to me! This is Turco. I'm locked out. Something has malfunctioned in the control bubble. I'm locked out . . ."

"I'm receiving you, Turco," he said. "Look for me above the Vlasseg pole. I'm in line-of-sight again." If her suit was a standard model, her transmissions would strengthen in the direction she was facing.

"God bless you, Porter. I see you. Everything's gone wrong down here. I can't get back in."

"Try again, Turco. Do you have any tools with you?"

"That's what started all this, breaking in with a chisel and a pry bar. It must have weakened something, and now the whole mechanism is frozen. No, I left the bar inside. No tools. Jesus, this is awful."

"Calm down. Keep trying to get in. I'm relaying your signal to Lunar Guidance and Earth." That settled it. There was no time to waste now. If she didn't turn on the positioning motors soon, any miss would be too close for comfort. He had to set off the internal charges within an hour and a half for the best effect.

"She's outside?" Lunar Guidance asked when the transmissions were relayed. "Can't get back in?"

"That's it," Porter said.

"That cocks it, Porter. Ignore her and get back into position. Don't bother lining up with the Vlasseg pole, however. Circle around to the Janacki pole bore hole and line up for code broadcast there. You'll have a better chance of getting the code through, and you can prepare for any further action."

"I'll be cooked, LG."

"Negative—you're to relay code from an additional thousand kilometers and boost yourself out of the path just before detonation. That will occur—let's see—about four point three seconds after the charges receive the code. Program your computer for sequencing; you'll be too busy."

"I'm moving, LG." He returned to Turco's wavelength. "It's out of your hands now," he said. "We're blowing the charges. They may not be enough, so I'm preparing to detonate myself against the Janacki pole crater. Congratulations, Turco."

"I still can't get back in, Porter."

"I said, congratulations. You've killed both of us and ruined Psyche for any future projects. You know that she'll go to pieces when she drops below Roche's limit? Even if she misses, she'll be too close to survive. You know, they might have gotten it all straightened out in a few administrations. Politicos die, or get booted out of office—even Naderites. I say you've cocked it good. Be happy, Turco." He flipped the switch viciously and concentrated on his approach program display.

Farmer Kollert was slumped in his chair, eyes closed but still awake, half-listening to the murmurs in the control room. Someone tapped him on the shoulder, and he jerked up in his seat.

"I had to be with you, Farmer." Gestina stood over him, a nervous smile making her dimples obvious. "They brought me here to be with you."

"Why?" he asked.

Her voice shook. "Because our house was destroyed. I got out just in time. What's happening, Farmer? Why do they want to kill me? What did I do?"

The team officer standing beside her held out a piece of paper, and Kollert took it. Violence had broken out in half a dozen Hexamon centers, and numerous officials had had to be evacuated. Geshels weren't the only ones involved—Naderites of all classes seemed to share indignation and rage at what was happening. The outbreaks weren't organized—and that was even more disturbing. Wherever transmissions had reached the unofficial grapevines, people were reacting.

Gestina's large eyes regarded him without comprehension, much less sympathy. "I had to be with you, Farmer," she repeated. "They wouldn't let me stay."

"Quiet, please," another officer said. "More transmissions coming in."

"Yes," Kollert said softly. "Quiet. That's what we wanted. Quiet and peace and sanity. Safety for our children to come."

"I think something big is happening," Gestina said. "What is it?"

Porter checked the alignment again, put up his visual shields, and instructed the processor to broadcast the coded signal. With no distinguishable pause, the ship's engines started to move him out of the path of the particle blast.

Meanwhile Giani Turco worked at the hatch with a bit of metal bracing she had broken off her suitpack. The sharp edge just barely fit into the crevice, and by gouging and prying she had managed to force the door up half a centimeter. The evacuation mechanism hadn't been activated, so frosted air hissed from the crack, making the work doubly difficult. The Moon was rising above the Janacki pole.

Deep below her, seven prebalanced but unchecked charges, mounted on massive fittings in their chambers, began to whir. Four processors checked the timings, concurred, and released safety shields.

Six of the charges went off at once. The seventh was late by ten thousandths of a second, its blast muted as the casing melted prematurely. The particle shock waves streamed out through the bore holes, now pressure release valves, and formed a long neck and tail of flame and ionized particles that grew steadily for a thousand kilometers, then faded. The tail from the Vlasseg pole was thinner and shorter, but no less spectacular. The asteroid shuddered, vibrations rising from deep inside to pull the ground away from Turco's boots, then swing it back to kick her away from the bubble and hatch. She floated in space, disoriented, ripped free of the guide wires, her back to the asteroid, faceplate aimed at peaceful stars, turning slowly as she reached the top of her arc.

Her leisurely descent gave her plenty of time to see the secondary plume of purple and white and red forming around the Janacki pole. The stars were blanked out by its brilliance. She closed her eyes. When she opened them again, she was nearer the ground, and her faceplate had polarized against the sudden brightness. She saw the bubble still intact, and the hatch wide open now. It had been jarred free. Everything was vibrating . . . and with shock she realized the asteroid was slowly moving out from beneath her. Her fall became a drawn-out curve, taking her away from the bubble toward a ridge of lead-gray rock, without guide wires, where she would bounce and continue on unchecked. To her left, one dome ruptured and sent a feathery wipe of debris into space. Pieces of rock and dust floated past her, shaken from Psyche's weak surface grip. Then her hand was only a few meters from a guide wire torn free and swinging outward. It came closer like a dancing snake, hesitated, rippled again, and looped within reach. She grabbed it and pulled herself down.

*   *   *

"Porter, this is Lunar Guidance. Something went wrong. Earth says the charges weren't enough."

"She held together, LG," Porter said in disbelief. "Psyche didn't break up. I've got a fireworks show like you've never seen before."

"Porter, listen. She isn't moving fast enough. She'll still impact."

"I heard you, LG," Porter shouted. "I heard! Leave me alone to get things done." Nothing more was said between them.

Turco reached the hatch and crawled into the airlock, exhausted. She closed the outer door and waited for equalization before opening the inner. Her helmet was off and floating behind as she walked and bounced and guided herself into the control room. If the motors were still functional, she'd fire them. She had no second thoughts now. Something had gone wrong, and the situation was completely different.

In the middle of the kilometers-wide crater at the Janacki pole, the bore hole was still spewing debris and ionized particles. But around the perimeter, other forces were at work. Canisters of reaction mass were flying to a point three kilometers above the crater floor. The Beckmann drive engines rotated on their mountings, aiming their nodes at the canister's rendezvous point.

Porter's ship was following the tail of debris down to the crater floor. He could make out geometric patterns of insulating material. His computers told him something was approaching a few hundred meters below. There wasn't time for any second guessing. He primed his main cargo and sat back in the seat, lips moving, not in prayer, but repeating some stray, elegant line from the Burgess novel, a final piece of pleasure.

One of the canisters struck the side of the cargo ship just as the blast began. A brilliant flare spread out above the crater, merging with and twisting the tail of the internal charges. Four canisters were knocked from their course and sent plummeting into space. The remaining six met at the assigned point and were hit by beams from the Beckmann drive nodes. Their matter was stripped down to pure energy.

All of this, in its lopsided, incomplete way, bounced against the crater floor and drove the asteroid slightly faster.

When the shaking subsided, Turco let go of a grip bar and asked the computers questions. No answers came back. Everything except minimum life support was out of commission. She thought briefly of returning to her tug, if it was still in position, but there was nowhere to go. So she walked and crawled and floated to a broad view window in the bubble's dining room. Earth was rising over the Vlasseg pole again, filling half her view, knots of storm and streaks of brown continent twisting slowly before her. She wondered if it had been enough—it hadn't felt right. There was no way of knowing for sure, but the Earth looked much too close.

"It's too close to judge," the president said, deliberately standing with his back to Kollert. "She'll pass over Greenland, maybe just hit the upper atmosphere."

The terrorist team officers were packing their valises and talking to each other in subdued whispers. Three of the president's security men looked at the screen with dazed expressions. The screen was blank except for a display of seconds until accession of picture. Gestina was asleep in the chair next to Kollert, her face peaceful, hands wrapped together in her lap.

"We'll have relay pictures from Iceland in a few minutes," the president said. "Should be quite a sight." Kollert frowned. The man was almost cocky, knowing he would come through it untouched. Even with survival uncertain, his government would be preparing explanations. Kollert could predict the story: a band of lunar terrorists, loosely tied with Giani Turco's father and his rabid spacefarers, was responsible for the whole thing. It would mean a few months of ill-feeling on the Moon, but at least the Nexus would have found its scapegoats.

A communicator beeped in the room, and Kollert looked around for its source. One of the security men reached into a pocket and pulled out a small earplug, which he inserted. He listened, frowned, then nodded. The other two gathered close and whispered. Then, quietly, they left the room. The president didn't notice they were gone, but to Kollert their absence spoke volumes.

Six Nexus police entered a minute later. One stood by Kollert's chair, not looking at him. Four waited by the door. Another approached the president and tapped him on the shoulder. The president turned.

"Sir, fourteen desks have requested your impeachment. We're instructed to put you under custody, for your own safety."

Kollert started to rise, but the officer beside him put a hand on his shoulder.

"May we stay to watch?" the president asked. No one objected.

Before the screen was switched on, Kollert asked, "Is anyone going to get Turco, if it misses?"

The terrorist team leader shrugged when no one else answered. "She may not even be alive."

Then, like a crowd of children looking at a horror movie, the men and women in the communications center grouped around the large screen and watched the dark shadow of Psyche blocking out stars.

From the bubble window, Turco saw the sudden aurorae, the spray of ionized gases from the Earth's atmosphere, the awesomely rapid passage of the ocean below, and the blur of white as Greenland flashed past. The structure rocked and jerked as the Earth exerted enormous tidal strains on Psyche.

Sitting in the plastic chair, numb, tightly gripping the arms, Giani looked up—down—at the bright stars, feeling Psyche die beneath her.

Inside, the still-molten hollows formed by the charges began to collapse. Cracks shot outward to the surface, where they became gaping chasms. Sparks and rays of smoke jumped from the chasms. In minutes the passage was over. Looking closely, she saw roiling storms forming over Earth's seas and the spreading shock wave of the asteroid's sudden atmospheric compression. Big winds were blowing, but they'd survive.

It shouldn't have gone this far. They should have listened reasonably, admitted their guilt—

Absolved, girl, she wanted her father to say. She felt him very near. *You've destroyed everything we worked for—a fine architect of Pyrrhic victories.* And now he was at a great distance, receding.

The room was cold, and her skin tingled.

One huge chunk rose to block out the sun. The cabin screamed, and the bubble was filled with sudden flakes of air.

AFTERWORD

Researching this story in 1977 led me back to a science article by J.E. Enever, "Giant Meteor Impact," published in *Analog* in March of 1966. J. E. Enever—no biography or credentials are given in the magazine, and he published, as far as I can discover, only a couple of items later—started something really big with this piece. To my knowledge, nobody before the mysterious Mr. Enever had ever written realistically about the effects of a large rocky mass striking the Earth. It's hard to imagine now, but in those years, Catastrophism—the belief that the Earth had ever been subjected to short, sharp shocks—was not in favor in mainstream geology. Most geologists were only beginning to seriously consider the theory of continental drift, espoused by Alfred L. Wegener. It's possible Enever could not have published this article in any respectable science journal.

That left John W. Campbell, Jr., and *Analog.*

Within a few years, Walter Alvarez would begin thinking about giant asteroids and dinosaur extinction . . .

In his 1972 novel, *Rendezvous with Rama,* Arthur C. Clarke (now Sir Arthur) would propose Spaceguard, a security system designed to watch for meteorites and asteroids that could collide with Earth.

Jerry Pournelle and Larry Niven would write the bestselling *Lucifer's Hammer* . . .

Gregory Benford and William Rotsler would write *Shiva Descending.*

Scientists would begin looking for the Big Ones, the impact craters that would provide the evidence for Alvarez's hypothesis. They would find several such craters, and the public imagination would be altered forever. We would watch a calved comet fall into Jupiter's atmosphere, and imagine our own possible fate.

We would feel very mortal.

Decades later, *Deep Impact* and *Armageddon* would compete for big bucks in the movie marketplace. Nearly every documentary on dinosaurs would show them peering up, squinty-eyed, at that bright light descending from the sky . . .

Today (2004), Spaceguard exists, in a rudimentary form. It has been organized by J. R. Tate in the United Kingdom, where it is struggling to procure funding to *keep watching the skies.*

All, possibly, because of J. E. Enever.

PLAGUE OF CONSCIENCE

Poul Anderson was a master at building artificial worlds. With his wife, Karen, he devised a system of planets to serve as the setting for a collaborative novel/anthology entitled Murasaki. Fred Pohl, a master of sociology and cultural anticipations, and himself an expert planet-builder (see Jem) provided the cultural underpinnings for the inhabitants of these worlds. Robert Silverberg edited and organized. A number of prominent writers—Anderson, Pohl, Gregory Benford, David Brin, and Nancy Kress—were invited to contribute to the round robin, setting their individuals chapters on these planets.

"Plague of Conscience" was my portion.

It may be a little confusing without the other tales to provide background, but I think it works well by itself, though more as a segment of a novel than a complete story. At any rate, it's worthwhile finding Murasaki and reading the complete cycle.

The hardest theme in science fiction is that of the alien. The simplest solution of all is in fact quite profound—that the real difficulty lies not in understanding what is alien, but in understanding what is self. We are all aliens to each other, all different and divided. We are even aliens to ourselves at different stages of our lives. Do any of us remember precisely what it was like to be a baby?

To describe the alien, I tend to take an aspect from my own multiple selves, a manifold of personality traits, and expand upon it. It's not a bad technique, as long as I'm willing to look very closely at the truth of what I think I see . . .

*　　　*　　　*

Kammer looked worse than any corpse Philby had seen; much worse, for he was alive and shouldn't have been. This short wizened man with limbs like gnarled tree branches and skin like leather—what could be seen of his skin beneath the encrustations of brown and green snug—had survived ten Earthly years on Chujo without human contact. He could hardly speak English any more.

Kammer regarded Philby through eyes paled by some Chujoan biological adaptation—the impossible which had happened to him first, and then had spread so disastrously to the God the Physicist settlers and the Japanese stationed here. Three hundred dead, and it had certainly begun on Kammer's broken, dying body, pissed on by a Chujoan shaman, that benison, that curse.

The half-human coughed and his snug wrinkled and crawled in obscene patches, revealing yet more leather. "Not many people let to see me," Kammer said. "Why do you?"

"I come from Genji," Philby said, "with a message from the Irdizu to the Chujoan shamans."

"Ah, Christ," Kammer said roughly and spat a thin stream of green and red saliva on the rocky ground between them. "Pardon. No offense. I still hate the . . . taste. Keeps me alive, I think, my human thoughts think, but tastes like essence of crap profane."

"You know about the God the Physicist crew?" Philby asked.

"Bloody *criaock* and *oonshlr#hack*."

The translator could not work with his humanized pronunciation; little was known of Chujoan language anyway, the Masters being so spare with their communications. Philby jotted the words on his notepad in the Chujoan phonetic devised by the Japanese, who had dropped transmitters into the villages four years before Philby's ship arrived in the Murasaki system. The Chujoans had tolerated the transmitters, and what few phrases they uttered had been fed into their All Nihon shipboard supercomputers. The Japanese had been kind enough to share their knowledge with Philby.

They knew Philby would be useful. He was, after all, rational—unlike the God the Physicists.

"I've come to talk about Carnot," Philby said. Kammer said nothing, leaning on his thick, snug-encrusted stick. "He's using your name. Claims to have been blessed by you. He's spreading a religion, if you can call it that, around the Irdizu villages—"

"I know little about the Irdizu," Kammer said, voice cracking. "Do them seldom. Not been there." The leathery face seemed to half-smile.

"He claims to have met with you, talked about his version of Jesus with you. He says you have seen visions of Chujo and Genji united under the rule of Jesus, who will come to these planets when the time is right."

"We didn't talk much, doing the first," Kammer said.

Philby tried to understand what he meant, and decided to let context be his guide. The notepad was recording all sound—perhaps meaning could be extracted later.

"Doing the second, he was already ill. Could see that."

"You met with him twice?" Philby asked.

Kammer nodded. "Sick the second time. He was doing the wind."

"He was ill with the plague," Philby said, his skin crawling at the thought that Kammer had probably been the source of that plague.

"He was doing the wind," Kammer said. "Pardon me. He was almost dead. He was looking for signs. I did what I could."

"What was that?"

Kammer shook his head and lifted his stick. "Doing the foulness. I hit him." He brought the stick down on the ground with a sharp crack. Philby noticed there was snug on the stick as well. Some of the snug on the stick fell away in patches. "He got away before I could hit him again."

"Do you know where Carnot is hiding?" Philby asked, hoping that Kammer's reversion to Chujoan had reflected a personal distaste.

"Wonderful man," Kammer said, hawking again—his entire chest patch of snug heaving like a sewage-befouled sea—but not spitting. "I don't. Where he is. Who are you? Beg pardon. That means . . . What will you be doing here?"

General clean-up. Triage. Sanitizing.

"I'm here to interview the survivors of the wineskin plague," Philby said, adjusting his hydrator. "And to find Carnot."

Kammer laughed. "Thinks I'm something."

"I'm sorry, I don't understand."

"Risked doing martyr to the bullyboys. They dislike anything new. Do the thorn fence." Kammer made a disgusting excretory sound in his throat and rasped, "Knew. Knew."

Philby glanced at the line of Chujoans standing mute, motionless, six human paces east of them, and the bullyboys—what the early explorers had called trolls—standing with mindless patience at the edge of the village waiting for some biochemical sign of his alienness, his undesirability.

"He survived the plague," Philby said offhandedly, as if conveying sad news.

"Know that," Kammer said. "Vector of the cultural disease."

"Yes," Philby said, surprised that Kammer was so in tune with his own thoughts. "Then you agree with me, that he—that his people are a danger?"

"You try to block him?"

"Yes," Philby said.

"How?"

"By going from village to village among the Irdizu, and telling them the truth. Not mystical nonsense."

Kammer smiled, his teeth a ruin encrusted with gray. "Doing the good. I mean, that's good of you. What will you make of Carnot . . . doing with him when you find him?"

"Make him stop polluting these worlds," Philby said.

"Ah. Doing us all a service."

"You tried to stop him as well, didn't you? With your stick?"

"He's alive, isn't he? You'd better go now," Kammer said, turning his head and poking his raw-looking chin at their observers. "They'll make you do martyr soon. Best pass on your message from Heaven and do a . . . be a trotter. Trot off. You're beginning to *bore* them, you silly wretch."

"Do I bore you as well, Kammer?" Philby asked. He trusted the bullyboys would not detect or react to his human irritation.

Kammer said nothing, the whited eyes with their pastel green irises minus pupils moving back and forth independently, like a lizard's hunting for a flying insect.

"No, old fellow," Kammer said. "I'd really like to sit and do the speaking some more. But my skin tells me I'm not up to it. I always listen to my skin. Without it, I'm an indigestible memory."

Philby nodded, the gesture almost invisible behind his mask and hydrator. "Thank you, Mr. Kammer," he said.

Kammer had already turned and begun his limping retreat to the safety of the village. "Nothing, old folks," Kammer said. Lurching on his beggar's rearranged limbs, S-curved back hunched like a ridge of iron-rich mountains, without looking back Kammer added, "Hope you know what the Irdizy *fchix* are saying to these." He waved a thin crooked hand at the shaman and his attendants.

Philby didn't. He had to take that risk.

The shaman approached and without looking at him, as if direct eye contact was either unknown or an unspeakable breach, snatched the Irdizu package from Philby's grasp and walked away, quietly erecting his genitalia and pissing all over the sacred himatid pelt wrapper.

Philby, hair on his neck frizzing with fear of bullyboy teeth, walked away from the village to rejoin the transport crew on the cliff ledge a kilometer outside the village. The Japanese escort, an attractive middle-aged woman named Tatsumi, bowed deeply on his return. Sheldrake and Thompson, pilots from his own crew, stiffened perceptibly. They seemed surprised he had returned. He lifted his arms and they sprayed him down, just as a precaution. *Our own pissing ceremony.*

Kammer's spit had landed within a meter of his disposable boots.

"He's become the Old Man of the Mountain," Philby said, doffing the boots, tossing them into the scrub and climbing into the transport. Tatsumi, Sheldrake and Thompson followed. "He knows what I'm here for. I think he approves."

They all listened to the notepad playback.

Dream journey above the pastel land, dreary dry old Chujo, bleak waste of a world with a thin cloak of dry air and an illustrious past, if what the Japanese had witnessed years ago could be believed . . . No reason not to.

Edward Philby, First Planetfall Coordinator of the multinational starship *Lorentz*, who answered only to the Captain and First Manager, tried briefly to sleep but found himself staring over the mountains and once, briefly, a small pale green lake with ancient shores like lids around a diseased eye. *We have come so far and suffered so much to be here.*

He could not avoid the crooked shape of Kammer in his thoughts, broken and mummified, smelling like an unwashed tramp and yet also like something else: flowers. An odor of sanctity. Eyes like that lake.

The God the Physicists had come here to find something transcendental, their ragged ship surviving the voyage just barely, their faith strengthened in the great Betweens, knowing they could not return if they could not find It here, and they had been lucky. They had found It, and then It had killed them as mercilessly as the unthinking void . . .

The glory of Chujoan biology, the truly transcendental; that which takes a man and transforms him into a survivor and a symbol. Carnot had said: "He is resurrected. The old Kammer died, just as we thought. They resurrected him and imbued him with their spirit of Christ." A dirty, ragged, smelly sort of Christ.

Tatsumi saw that he was not asleep. "You are worried about the settlers on Genji," she said. "Your countrymen."

"They're not my countrymen," Philby said. "I'm English. They're bloody Southwesterners from the U.S.A."

"I beg your pardon."

"Easy mistake, we might as well be a state of the U.S.," he said. "Europe won't have us now. Or rather, *then* . . ." He waved a hand back behind him; time dilated by decades. He had not bothered to catch up on the thin messages from distant Sol, slender lifelines to farflung children.

She smiled and nodded: Earth history, all past for her as well.

"You believe they will do great damage," she offered cautiously, as if Philby might be offended to have a Japanese commenting upon people at least of his language and broad culture if not his nation.

"You know they will, Tatsumi-san," he said. "Kammer knows they will. He says he tried to kill Carnot and failed."

Tatsumi pursed her lips and frowned. She did not appear shocked. Philby tapped his finger on the edge of the couch, waiting for her reaction. "Carnot thinks Kammer is a . . . Jesus?"

"An avatar of the ancient spirituality of Chujo. Identical to Jesus. Jesus can be found in the universal ground state, where all our redemptions lie. God shows us the way through physics. Just what the Irdizu need—visitors from the sky able to carry messages to Heaven."

"So you take messages in his stead."

"They know I'm not a spirit. I'm a man of solid matter, not Physicist nonsense."

"And what will you do next?"

"Talk to Carnot, if I can find him."

Tatsumi frowned again, shaking her head. "He is not on Chujo?"

"I've been looking for him for the past three weeks."

"Then he must be on Genji. If he is there, I can find out where he is, and take you to him."

Philby hid his surprise. "I thought your people wanted to stay out of this."

"We thought all the cultists would die," Tatsumi said. "They did not."

"Pardon my inquisitiveness—"

"Your *inquisition*?" Tatsumi interrupted with a faint smile. He returned her smile, but with slitted eyes and an ironic nod.

"Believe me, I represent no religious authority on Earth."

"Of course not," Tatsumi said.

"I'm wondering just what your position is on these settlers."

"Earth will keep sending them," Tatsumi said sadly. "There is nothing we can do. Dialog takes decades. The nations of Earth have made the Murasaki system into a symbol of . . . manliness? National prestige? We cannot fight such a thing."

"There are two more ships on the way," Philby said.

Tatsumi nodded. "We hope they are as enlightened as your own expedition."

Irony? "Thank you," he said.

"But since dialog is so difficult, we wonder from whence you derive your authority. You represent no church, and any government is too far away to instruct you. Who gives you orders to quell the God the Physicists?"

Philby shook his head. "Nobody outside of the Murasaki system."

"Then you perform your duty autonomously?"

"Yes."

"Self-appointed."

He flinched and his face reddened. "Your people should remember the effect of a cultural plague. The nineteenth century . . . Admiral Perry?"

"Nobody forces the Irdizu to accept our commercial products. There are none yet to force upon them. And the West came to

Nihon before Perry. We had Christians in our midst for centuries before Perry. They were persecuted, tortured, murdered . . . yet fifty thousand still lived in Japan when Perry arrived."

"What Carnot wants to force upon the Irdizu could lead to war, death, destruction on a colossal scale."

"Carnot seems to want to re-establish the ancient links between Chujo and Genji," Tatsumi said.

Thompson, who had listened attentively and quietly in the seat behind Tatsumi, leaned forward. "We're here to preserve Irdizu self-rule. Carnot is a kind of missionary. We can't allow the kind of desecration of native cultures that happened on Earth."

"Oh, yes, that is true," Tatsumi said. She appeared mildly flustered. "I do not wish to be flippant, Mr. Philby, Mr. Thompson."

"They're out of their minds," Philby said, grimacing. Listening to Thompson, though, he realized how much they sounded as if *they* were mouthing a party line, rehearsed across centuries; how much it sounded as if they might be the persecutors, the inquisitors, as Tatsumi had so pointedly punned. "They really are."

"A cultural plague," Tatsumi said, attempting to mollify when in fact no umbrage had been taken.

"Precisely," Philby said. *What Kammer said. Have the Japanese spoken to Kammer?*

Sheldrake had kept his silence, as always, a young man with a young face, born on the journey and accelerated to manhood, but still looking boyish.

"What do you think, Mr. Sheldrake?" Tatsumi asked him.

Sheldrake gave a sudden, sunny smile. "I'm enjoying the landscape," he said in his pleasant tenor.

"Please be open with us," Tatsumi pursued, very uncharacteristically for a Japanese, Philby thought.

"It's not their war," Sheldrake said, glancing at Philby. "It's ours. No matter what we do, we're imposing. I think we just have to reduce that imposition to a minimum."

"I see," Tatsumi said. "Do you know the story of a man named Joseph Caiaphas?" she asked him.

"No," Philby said. She queried the others with a look as they seated themselves in the tiny cockpit. None of them did.

Across the channel between the two worlds, on clouded and storm-wracked Genji, Robert Carnot walked around the temple site, watching the Irdizu workers stalk on strong high chicken-legs around the site of the temple, carrying bricks and mortar and buckets of sloshing paste-thick paint. He rubbed his neck beneath the pressure seal, wondering how much longer this shift before he could take a rest, lie down. He disliked Genji's gravity and climate intensely. His back ached, his legs ached, his neck and *shoulders* ached from the simple weight of his arms. He looked longingly up at the point in the sky where Chujo would be, if they could see it through the rapidly scudding gloom.

The boss of the temple construction crew, a sturdy female named Tsmishfak, approached him with a pronounced swag-ger of pride. It was good that they should feel proud of what they had accomplished; their pride was good, not the civilized, stately antithesis of resentment that had so often brought Car-not's kind low.

"Tzhe in spatch endED," Tsmishfak told him, eyes glancing back and forth on her sloping fish head. The Irdizu had adapted quickly to this kind of pidgin, much more merciful to their man-ner of speech than to the humans'. The Japanese had never thought of creating a pidgin; the rationals would despise Carnot for doing so. But at least human and Irdizu could talk without translators intervening.

"Tzhe in spatch finitchED?" he asked, using an Irdizu inquisi-tive inflection.

"FinitchED," Tsmishfak confirmed.

"Then let me see, and if it matches the Chujoan dimensions—which I'm sure it does—we'll begin the consecration, and I can move on to the next village." Tsmishfak understood most of this unpidgined speech.

She guided him through the fresh pounding rain—each drop like a strike of hail—to the site he had laid out two weeks before. The temple's exterior was still under construction; when completed, the walls would be smooth and white and square, sloping to the broad foundations to withstand the tidal inundations Tsmishfak's village experienced every few Genjian years. Muddy rain fell along the unplastered bricks in gray runnels; clay scoured by clouds from the high mountains above the village's plateau. He would be a Golem-like mess before this day was over.

The in spatch—inner space, interior—was indeed finitchED. Within the temple, out of the sting of clayed rain, the walls were painted a dreadful seasick green, the paint pigments mixed from carpet whale slime and algoid dyes. Tsmishfak had assured him this was a most desirable color to the Irdizu, a sacred color, as yellow might be to a human. Carnot pretended to admire the effect, then noticed he was dripping mud on the clean green floor. Tsmishfak was as well.

"Lengd it," Carnot said, which meant simply, "I will length it," or "I will measure it." Tsmishfak backed away, awed by this moment.

Carnot wiped mud from his face plate and produced a simple string coiled on a spool in his pocket. The string unwound from the two halves of the spool into two lengths; he had made up this device several months before, aware that the temples were nearing completion and some sort of masonic service would be necessary.

By hand gestures up, Carnot indicated that the spool came from Chujo. That was a lie. No matter. What was important was the spiritual import.

He stretched one string along the north wall, found it matched precisely, then stretched the second string along the east wall. The second string was the same length as the first; the second wall was the same length as the first. He then produced a simple metal protractor, machined aboard their ship in orbit at his request, and measured the angles of each corner. Ninety degrees. A fine square box painted sick green. Perfect.

He raised his hands. "In the name of the great ground of all existence, that which is called Continuum, which breathes with the life of all potential, which creates all and sees all, in the name of the human Kammer who has survived the bonding of human and Chujoan, in the name of the Irdizu Christ called Dsimista, who tells us that all worlds shall be one, I consecrate this temple, which is well-built and square and essential. May no one who does not believe in the Ground, in Kammer, and in Dsimista enter into this place."

Tsmishfak found this eminently satisfactory, particularly as she only understood about a third of what Carnot had said. She echoed, in pidgin, his last commandment, stalked around the walls, then clacked her jaws to summon workers. The workers cleaned up the mud and the in spatch smelled of Irdizu, a not unpleasant smell to Carnot, though pungent.

"Ny mer dert," Tsmishfak promised him as they returned to the exterior. The clayed rain had let up; now there was only drizzle. *Like living at the bottom of a fishbowl.*

"No more dirt, that's fine," Carnot said. "You've din guud, *akkxsha hikfarinkx.*"

Tsmishfak accepted this with a slight swagger.

Good, good, all is well.

"Must move on now," he said in plain English, walking to the edge of the plateau and trying to find his wife and the ship's second officer in the crowded beach area below. "Ah. There are my people." He nodded cordially to the solicitous Tsmishfak. "Must go."

"Dthang u," Tsmishfak said. "Dum Argado."

She was using both English and the Japanese she had acquired.

"You're most welcome," Carnot said. He felt he would die if he could not soon rest his leaden arms and relieve the weight on his back.

Tsmishfak bounced off on spring-steel legs to her workers near the temple, swagger lessened but tentacle arms curling enthusiastically. *Big lumbering thing. Something out of Bosch; fish with legs, but eyes above and below the jawline . . . anatomically improbable. Not easy to love them, but I do, Jesus, I do.*

Carnot found his wife by the ichthyoid pens, standing with the second officer on a wicker frame, nodding to some point of technicality being explained by a small male Irdizu. Not much call for the kind of work she was skilled in, helping poor natives feed themselves. The Irdizu did well enough at that. But scratch beneath their quiet strength and you found a well of anguish; paradise lost and set high in the sky. Connections broken with their distant relations, the Chujoans, millennia past . . .

Desire to rise to heaven and be one with another race. Another species. What if his theories were correct? The rationalists would never accept that intelligent cultures—technological cultures—could rise and fall like fields of wheat coming in and out of season. Perhaps that was why they were looking for him, why he was finding it necessary—through the inner suspicion of aching instinct—to hide . . .

Madeline saw his wave and gently broke off her conversation with the pen manager. It seemed eternities as they made their way back to the ship along the beach. The transport's struts were awash with thick swells of water—no spray under these conditions, only a fine mist like smoke around the sharp rocks. They waded through the swell, more eternities, then the second officer lifted the transport from the beach, its name becoming visible as it rose to a level with him: *2T Benevolent.* Second transport of the starship *Benevolent.*

They touched down again near the lip of the plateau overlooking the beach, and he climbed through the door, wheezing into his respirator. "Enough," he said. "They'll do fine without us. Let's move on."

Madeline touched him solicitously. "You're hurting, poor dear."

"I'm fine," he said, but her touch and sympathy helped. Madeline, thin small strong Madeline, so perfectly adapted to life aboard the *Benevolent*, could crawl into cubbies where large, lumbering Carnot could not hope to find comfort. Cramped starship, crowded with pilgrims. Madeline who had married him en route and did not share in the sexual-spiritual profligacy, even when her new husband did. Madeline of the bright intense gaze and extraordinary sympathetic intelligence; his main crutch, his main critic. He smiled upon her and she smiled back like a tough-minded little girl.

"I'd enjoy studying their fish farming methods," she said. "We *might* be able to give them benefit of our own experiences on Earth."

The second officer, thin black African Asian, Lin-Fa Chee by name, did not share Madeline's interest. "They don't farm fish, madame," he observed. "And these people have farmed the ichthyoids for who knows how many thousands of years."

"Millions, perhaps," Carnot said. "Lin-Fa is right, Madeline."

"Still, they need us in many ways," Madeline said, staring through the window as the transport lifted and flew out across the oily rain-dappled sea. "They need *you*, Robert." She smiled at him and he could read the unfinished message: "*Why shouldn't they need me, as well?*"

"Look," Chee said, pointing from his pilot's seat. "Carpet whales."

Carnot looked down upon the huge multi-colored leviathans with little interest. *Great flat brutes. Not even Madeline would wish to help them.*

Suzy Tatsumi watched the distance lessen between the orbital shuttle and Genji. Chujo grew small as a basketball held at arm's length, visible through the shuttle's starboard windows. She pushed her covered plate of food—sticky rice and bonito flakes topped with thick algal paste—down the aisle between the twenty seats and sat beside Thompson, who had already eaten from a refillable paste tube.

"Fruit yogurt," he said, lifting the empty tube disconsolately. "Supplemented. All we brought with us."

"I would gladly share . . ." Tatsumi said, but that was forbidden. They were still not sure of all the vectors a new wineskin plague might follow, so intimate contact between those who had lived long on Chujo, partaking of its few edibles—or the transfer of food possibly grown on Chujo—was against the rules.

The known forms of the plague had been conquered, but once Chujo's micro-organisms had discovered how to take advantage of the ecological niche offered by humans, they had proven to be remarkably inventive. More mutations might yet occur. Casual contact had not yet shown itself to be dangerous among those protected against the plague, but even so . . .

"I know how your people conquered the plague," Philby said to her. "A remarkable piece of work. But how did Carnot and the last of his people survive?"

Tatsumi shook her head. "We doubt they had any native ability to resist. We still do not know . . . They were already cured by the time our doctors went among them. But they had suffered terrible losses, on the planet and on their ship . . . there are only twenty of the original two hundred left alive."

"Could they have found the same substances you did?" Thompson asked.

"They did not have our expertise. Nor did they equip themselves with the sophisticated biological equipment we carried . . . the food synthesizers, large molecule analyzers, and the computer programs to run such devices. They arrived here in a weakened state, their ship crippled. We do not know how they survived."

"They get along with the Irdizu," Philby mused. "Maybe the Irdizu helped them."

"The Irdizu have not the biological mastery of the Chujoans," Tatsumi said.

"Still, there might have been a folk remedy, something serendipitous."

Tatsumi was not familiar with that word. Her translator quickly explained it to her: fortunate, unexpected. "Perhaps," she said. "It was *serendipitous* that we found our own remedy in Chujo's deep lake muds. An antibiotic grown by anaerobic microbes, used to defend their territories against other microbes, and not poisonous to human tissues . . . Most fortunate. Most unexpected. We all thought we would die."

Philby smiled. "Luck favors those who are prepared . . . Which is why all of Carnot's people should have died. They're as innocent as children."

Tatsumi raised her eyebrows. "You admire strength and their luck?"

"What I admire has nothing to do with what damage they can do here."

"No, indeed," Tatsumi said, feeling dreadfully aware that she had irritated this strange man yet again. She had met Carnot only once, when the *Benevolent* first arrived in orbit around Genji, but she thought these two were well-matched as opponents. Determined, opinionated, they might be brothers in some strange Western tale of Cain and Abel, or *East of Eden*, which she had read as a girl back on Earth.

"Do you believe Genji and Chujo are so closely connected, biologically?" Thompson asked.

"They must be," quiet Sheldrake said from behind them all. He had finished his yogurt without complaint or comment.

"What mechanism would bring organisms from Chujo to Genji?" Philby challenged with professorial glee. Tatsumi had noted that these people enjoyed debating, and seemed not to understand boundaries of politeness in such discussions. She had heard them argue violently among themselves without anyone losing face or apologizing.

"Besides the rocket balloons from Chujo . . ." Thompson said.

"I don't yet accept those as fact," Philby said. He glanced at Tatsumi. "Your people didn't actually see rockets . . . just balloons."

"It seems pretty certain the elder Chujo civilizations were capable of rockets," Sheldrake said. Tatsumi was attracted by the young tenor's calm, confident reserve. A child quickly, artificially raised to manhood in space . . . What strange wisdoms might he have acquired in those years? "But I was thinking of cometary activity—"

"Rare in the Murasaki system," Thompson noted.

"Or even extreme volcanic events. Chujo's ejecta might have carried spores into the upper atmosphere . . . and beyond."

"Not likely," Philby snorted. "There's no easy mechanism, none that doesn't stretch credibility."

"Nevertheless," Tatsumi said, enjoying the spirit of this debate, "the genetic material is very closely related in many primitive organisms on Chujo and Genji."

"There's no denying that," Philby said. "I wish your people had solved this riddle before we arrived . . . there's too many other problems to take care of."

"You did not come here to find and solve such problems?"

"I did," Sheldrake said. "I'm not sure Edward did . . ."

"Essence of crap profane," Philby said, not unpleasantly.

"What's that?" Thompson asked. Philby was not usually so expressive.

"Something Kammer said. He said his mouth tasted like essence of crap profane. After he expectorated red and green saliva."

Tatsumi wrinkled her nose despite herself. "Our biologists would love to be allowed to study him," she said. "We might have saved lives, had we been allowed to . . ."

"Nobody's going to study him without killing a lot of Chujoans," Philby said. "And that we will not allow."

A planetary consciousness . . . Something that united both worlds, something only vaguely felt by either the Irdizu or the Chujoans. If he could prove its existence, as one might prove the psychic link between two twins, then all of his beliefs would fall into place . . .

Carnot tossed in his cylindrical bed, drifting slowly between the limits of the elastic net. He did not sleep well in microgravity, but it was important that he maintain contact with the ship's captain, who had suffered horribly from the plague, and might even now be insane.

When Carnot thought of what they had lost, of the price paid by two hundred and forty-five of the *Benevolent*'s crew, he felt a sick darkness curl inside him. Not all the faith, not all the conviction of forty years' service to Jesus the Ground of All Being could erase his sense of loss. From here on in, his life would be a scarred, dedicated emptiness; he knew he would be little more than an efficient shell; the old Carnot had been burned out, leaving fire-hardened wood.

He could not even find the fierce love he had once felt for his wife. He needed her; he paid her the minimum due of affection, all she seemed to require now. She, too, had been burned hollow. Sex between them was at an end. Sex had always been a kind of play, and this close to the truth, this close to the death and disfigurement of their people, no play could be allowed.

And now to be hunted . . .

He closed his eyes tighter, hoping to squeeze a tear or some other sign of his humanity between the lids, but he could not. He thought of the Earth and his young adulthood and the simple miseries that had filled him then. Had his people suffered any more than others had suffered for their faiths? Was he being pressed any harder than any other leader of peoples who believed in pattern and justice and order? These events had been enough to drain him of the pleasures of simply existing; was that the sure sign of his ultimate weakness, that he could no longer take satisfaction in serving Jesus? That he could no longer take satisfaction in having a wife, in breathing in and out, in not being hungry or in having survived that which had turned so many of his people into pain-wracked monsters?

Now he found his one tear, and he let it roll from his left eye, a true luxury. Deep inside, a younger voice said, *You're goddamned right you've had it hard. Space was supposed to be clean and clear-cut, with sharp dividing lines between life and death. It wasn't supposed to be this way, tending this ship like a leaky tub across five years, and then arriving on the inconceivably far shore and finding disease and hideous death. Not supposed to be that way at all. You've been pushed. Don't expect joy when you've been pushed this hard; do not be so demanding as to expect joy after what you've experienced.*

Carnot opened his eyes and saw Captain Plaissix floating in the shadow of the hatch to his cabin. Beyond Plaissix, through the transparent blister of the central alley's cap, Carnot saw Genji's blue-gray surface fall perpetually beneath them. "The Japanese have sent a message," Plaissix said. "They wish to speak directly with you."

Half of the Captain's face had crumpled inward. The wineskin plague had been made up of Chujoan bacterioids particularly well-adapted to living on minerals; they had devoured much of the calcium in his bones, and in his nerves, as well.

"All right," Carnot said, giving up yet another attempt at sleep. He slid from the net and floated past Plaissix, who tracked him with off-center haunted eyes.

The ship's communications center was in a constant state of repair. George Cluny, the last remaining engineer, moved to one side to give Carnot room. The image of a young Japanese woman floated a few hands away from its normal position; Cluny shrugged in apology, best he could do with what they had. Her voice was distant but clear.

"Carnot here."

"My name is Suzy Tatsumi," the woman said. "I've just traveled to Chujo and back with Edward Philby. We would like to arrange a meeting between your group and his . . . To settle your disputes."

Carnot smiled. "I don't believe we've met, Tatsumi-san. I've been working with Hiroki-san of Station Hokkaido on Genji."

"He has transferred his responsibilities to me."

Apparently the conflict between Carnot's expedition and the

rationalists was beginning to worry the Japanese. Until now, they had been content to let the two stand separate and not intervene in any disputes. Had this Tatsumi woman already been poisoned by Philby and his representatives?

"I have no time to meet with the rationalists," Carnot said. "They are physically stronger than we are. They would have attacked us by now, if it weren't for their lack of offensive weapons . . . They cannot harm our ship in orbit." Actually, he was not sure of that.

"I think it would be good for you to begin speaking to each other," Tatsumi said.

"You have remained neutral until now," Carnot said through tight lips. "I can only trust you will not join up with them, against us."

"There are many problems we can solve, Mr. Carnot. We are very far from home, and it is ridiculous to fight among ourselves, when we have faced so many common dangers."

"Tatsumi-san, you underestimate the depth of divisions between our kind. I have already had my dialogues with Edward Philby. We know where we stand. If you will not take sides—" *and damn you if you stay neutral!* "—then please leave us to our histories," he fumbled for what he wanted to say, "our destinies. For what lies ahead."

Tatsumi regarded his image with sad, serious eyes. "Mr. Carnot, Edward Philby has spoken with Kammer. He says that Kammer tried to kill you. If the man you consider so vital a link, if he himself believes you are wrong . . ."

"Please do not argue my faith with me, Tatsumi-san. He struck me with his stick. He did *not* kill me."

Tatsumi said nothing, puzzled into silence, trying to riddle this human mystery.

"His *stick*, Tatsumi-san," Carnot said sharply, surprised they had not guessed by now. "He blessed me with his greatest gift. Because of that blow, some of my people are alive now." He was too weary to waste his time with her any longer. "Good-bye, Tatsumi-san. If you wish to offer us help, we are not too proud to accept."

He ordered Cluny to cut the transmission. The engineer did so and stared at him as if awaiting more instructions. Captain Plaissix had come into the communications room and simply floated there, his deformity an accusation.

Carnot had applied the crushed and writhing balm of a patch of Kammer's symbiotic snug, embedded by the stick in his own skin, first upon his wife, and then upon the others. By circumstance Plaissix had been last. Surely by circumstance and not by Carnot's own subconscious planning. Plaissix had been the most doubtful of Carnot's revelation regarding Kammer. The one most likely to frustrate their designs, after they had come so far . . .

Casual contact with the avatar was death; the Japanese had learned that much. But to arouse the avatar's passion, and be struck by him, was *to live.*

"Who is the fanatic, then?" Eiji Yoshimura asked. "And who is the aggressor?" The director of Hokkaido station rose from his stone desk, cut from Genji's endless supply of slate, and stood by a rack of laboratory equipment. By trade Yoshimura was an agricultural biologist; he had never wished to be a politician, but deaths at the station during the plague had forced this circumstance upon him.

Tatsumi tried to say something, but Yoshimura was angry and raised his hand. "They are all fools. This Englishman Philby, by what right does he dictate his philosophies?"

"I regret Philby's determination—" Tatsumi began.

"They are all troublemakers!" Yoshimura shouted.

"Director, please hear me out," Tatsumi said, her own voice rising the necessary fraction of a decibel to break through her superior's indignation.

"My apologies," Yoshimura said, glancing at her from the corner of his eye. "I am not angry with you, nor critical of the work you have done."

"I understand, sir. Philby's fears are well-founded. Already Carnot has spread his religious beliefs to nine Genji villages. Already nine temples to their version of Jesus, and to Kammer, have been built. Carnot will soon have a broad enough base of support to endanger our own mission, should he so choose—using Irdizu as his soldiers."

Yoshimura considered this with deep solemnity. "Do you believe Carnot will go that far?"

"He has been pushed beyond reason," Tatsumi said. "By the plague, and now by the rationalists."

"I once would have counted myself among the rationalists," Yoshimura said. "But I have never tried to impose my will upon those who disagreed. Has Carnot made any converts in our camp?"

Tatsumi reacted with some surprise to this question, which had not occured to her. "Not to my knowledge," she replied.

"I will inquire discreetly. You look shocked, Suzy."

"I find it hard to believe any of our people would believe such drivel," she said, with more heat than she intended.

Yoshimura smiled sagely. "We are human, too. We are in a strange land, far from home, and we can lose our bearings as quickly as anyone else. We do have some Christians among us—Aoki, for example."

"Aoki is very circumspect," Tatsumi said. "Besides, traditional Christians would hardly recognize the beliefs of the God the Physicists."

"Such an awkward name," Yoshimura said. "Still, I would hate to face an army of Irdizu—led by the females, no doubt." His expression slumped once more into solemnity and he seemed very old and tired. "Try to reason with Carnot again. If he is still unwilling to meet with Philby, then ask him if he will meet with our people—with you."

"I do not believe he will. He is exhausted and depressed, sir."

"Do you know that for certain?"

"It's obvious."

"Then he's even more dangerous," Yoshimura said. "But we will try anyway."

Tatsumi sighed.

Philby stood up under Genji's excessive affection, muscles aching from the hour of acclimatizing exercise. With most of his time spent on kinder, simpler Chujo, the storms and thickness and heaviness of Genji was like being immersed in nightmare; but here was the core of their problem, among the apparently gullible Irdizu, who were building temples to Kammer—and to Carnot's Jesus.

Theresa O'Brien joined him in the makeshift gymnasium, dressed in exercise tights, short hair frizzed with moisture. "How's the tummy, Edward?" she asked.

"Ah, tight as a drum," Philby responded, thwupping his abdomen with a thumb-released finger. "I've never been in better shape."

O'Brien shook her head dubiously. "You've always inclined to more muscle than you needed, then neglected, then to gut."

"Brutal Theresa," Philby said drily, continuing his leg-lifts.

"When are you leaving for the temple site?"

"In four hours," Philby said.

"I've come from Diana's bungalow," O'Brien said, squatting slowly, carefully beside him. Exercise on Genji seemed ridiculously slow; anything faster and they might injure themselves. She sat and watched his red face. "Don't overdo it."

"What, the exercise, or . . . ?" Philby didn't finish.

"We don't like what Carnot's doing any more than you do," O'Brien said. "But the Japanese concern us, too. We're making an impression here, not just with the Irdizu and the Chujoans—with our fellow humans, as well."

"They seem to be on our side, certainly more than on Carnot's side," Philby said, stopping to devote his full attention to their conversation. "I hope Diana's not re-thinking our plans."

"It seems to some of us that you're the one doing the re-thinking."

"Diana put me in charge of relations with the *Benevolent*. We've all agreed they're dangerous; I'm following through."

O'Brien nodded. "Edward, it sometimes seems you're the aggressor, not them. What will the Irdizu think if . . ." She shook her head and didn't finish.

"If Carnot's made such an impression on them, and we constrain him?" Philby finished for her. She raised her chin in the slightest nod, as if wary of him.

"I apologize, Theresa," Philby said. "You know my temperament better than anybody. I'm thorough, but I'm not a loose beam. Reassure Diana for me."

"She's on the ship now, arranging for a reception. The Japanese are coming—and she tells me they're trying to get Carnot to come, as well."

"I'm always a man for dialogue," Philby said. He replaced the padded bench and weights and wiped his face with a towel. "But Carnot . . . I think he is not."

"Will you listen to Carnot if the Japanese convince him to come?"

"What will he . . ." Philby realized he was being excessively contrary, and that more argument might tip the balance in O'Brien's eyes. "Of course. I'll listen."

She turned to leave, and he could not restrain himself from saying, "But Theresa, there must be constraint on their part. That should be clear to all of us. We are *protecting* the Irdizu from the worst parts of ourselves."

"Are we?" O'Brien asked over her shoulder.

"Yes," Philby said after a pause. "Any doubts on that score and we might all be lost."

"I do not doubt Carnot is a danger," O'Brien said, and closed the door behind her.

That evening, the communications manager on their starship

told Philby something extraordinary, and the wheels began to turn in his mind. If he must meet with Carnot, then he would be prepared to shatter that little plaster prophet once and for all. Now, he might have the hammer to do so.

When traveling at close to lightspeed, our geometry is distorted, such that, to an outside observer, we reveal aspects of our shapes that are not usually seen . . . around curves, edges. We are warped in ways we cannot feel . . . Is this also not true of our souls?

Philby inspected the fourth finished temple, his legs and feet aching abominably. He used two canes now to support his weight; to the Irdizu, he called them "Kammerstaffs."

He had begun to spread the story of Kammer's striking him. He had found an interesting analogy to his contretemps with Kammer in Irdizu storytelling, a resonance he could take advantage of. Indeed, this was very the village, so said Irdizu legend, where the angelic Szikwshawmi had landed in ancient times and struck the female warriors with staffs of ice to give them superior strength. At the same time, the Szikwshawmi had frozen the tongue-penises of the males, making intercourse in both senses of the word impossible. The females had gone out in their frustration and gathered in new males from distant villages, leaving the females of those villages frustrated, and they had gone forth and done likewise . . . and so on, a great wave of Sabine rapes.

It was hardly a precise analogy. In some respects it was embarrassingly inappropriate; but the Irdizu found it a compelling comparison, and when searching for mythic roots, one had to bend, and to be bent.

The temple, constructed in a thick patch of manzanitas-like beach forest, deep in a shadowy hollow filled with drifting mist, sea-spray, and dark tidal pools, was certainly the gloomiest that had been built so far. The Irdizu in this village were larger, more sullen, more suspicious than any they had encountered before. The females certainly seemed more brusque and dominating.

The village had been visited by humans—Japanese—only once, years before. Yet still the stories of Jesus and Kammer and Carnot and the Chujo connection had spread even into these shadows, and taken root.

The temple matched the necessary specifications. Carnot blessed it, and moved on.

There was a disturbing trend. Five villages had so far refused Carnot, and rejected his doctrines. All of these villages had been visited by Philby and his agents, spreading rationalist doctrine. Carnot had only heard bits and pieces of this antithesis to his thesis: Philby was apparently feeding them visions of a potential future, when Genji and Chujo would be united, not in any mystical sense, but politically, in league with human advisors.

A dry, deadly sort of myth, Carnot thought. To tell the truth, he wasn't sure *what* role humans would play in his own scheme; perhaps none at all. There were so few of his people left. They could find comfort in a small corner of Chujo, perhaps acting as the spiritual advisors, setting up a center for pilgrims. They would certainly not stride hand-in-hand into a bright future with the rationally corrected and technologically equipped Irdizu and Chujoans . . .

And yet still the Japanese tried to arrange a meeting, and still Philby's people visited village after village, creating territories where he could not operate.

It was a war.

Carnot realized how reluctant he had been, until now, to accept that fact. He had always felt hunted, opposed; he had never devised a strategy whereby he might counterstrike. But it was clearly becoming necessary.

"You have done well," Carnot told the chief females, who bounced and swaggered solemnly on their large chicken legs, horizontal bodies quivering. He cringed inside, craving the company of humans, wishing to be relieved of this burden; and he retreated on his Kammerstaffs to the ship, where Madeline and Lin-Fa Chee waited.

"Another message from the Japanese," Madeline said quietly when they were settled, and the transport had lifted off. The ship's engines made a high-pitched whickering noise and one side settled as they rose; Lin-Fa Chee corrected, and the transport gained altitude, but more slowly.

"Of course," Carnot said.

"The Captain thinks we should talk to them."

Carnot lifted an eyebrow. "Yes?"

"We need to barter," Lin-Fa Chee said. "We need spare parts."

"The Captain has spoken with the Japanese, with Suzy Tatsumi. She says they will trade or manufacture spare parts for us . . ."

"Generous," Carnot said, closing his eyes.

"If we meet with them, and with the rationalists," Madeline concluded.

Carnot pretended to sleep.

"Robert, we have to make a decision soon," Madeline said. "There's a lot at stake here."

"We'll meet," he said softly. "How many more temples?"

"Three, I think . . . Perhaps more next week."

"I want to see the ceremonies completed." Suddenly, he was feeling very mortal—with more than a suspicion that what lay beyond mortality was not what he most fervently desired.

Philby walked slowly toward the loose line of twelve bullyboys, reeking of Chujoan protective scent. They lifted their heads, sniffed the air casually, remained where they were. Surely they could see he was not Chujoan; surely they had minds enough to recognize that scent alone did not guarantee his belonging. But they restrained themselves, and once again added to the mystery of how they functioned in Chujoan society.

He passed between two of them, barely a meter on each side from their claws and fangs barely concealed behind loose lips.

The shamans formed the next loose line. Beyond them lay the edge of the village, and the hut which Kammer had taken, or had been assigned, who could say which. He was on the outskirts, rather than in the center; that might be significant. Perhaps he was not as important to the Chujoans as this peculiar reception ceremony implied; perhaps Chujoan ritual went beyond the simple analogy of enfolding and protection, putting their most valuable icons on the edge of the village rather than in the center.

Perhaps he didn't understand Kammer's meaning at all.

A loose dry breeze blew dust between the shamans' spindly legs. The line parted, as if Philby had ordered the breeze as a signal.

He could feel the casual, unresponsive presence of the bully-boys behind him.

The work he had done in the past week to make this meeting useful—to be able to ask the question he would now ask of Kammer—had taxed his patience to its limit. He had asked five of his ship's biologists, and three of the Japanese doctors and biologists, how much of a risk Kammer might be to crews if they were actually exposed to his physical presence. None had been willing to give a straight answer at first; fear of the wineskin plague had distorted simple rational judgments, leading to hedged bets, hems and haws, a reliance on very fuzzy statistics. Finally Philby had been able to draw a consensus from the scientists and doctors: Kammer was not much of a threat now. If indeed the wineskin plague had begun on Kammer, which was almost universally accepted, then it was likely that they had protected themselves against all possible varieties he might have generated. Unless—and this possibility still haunted Philby, if only for its fearfully nonsensical aspects—unless Kammer or the Chujoans had deliberately created the plague . . .

Kammer could walk among them, if he so chose.

Philby stood outside the mud-brick and reed hut. "Hello," he said. Nothing but silence within. His communications with the Chujoans had led him to believe Kammer was willing to have another meeting—had in fact requested it.

"Hello," he called out again, glancing over his shoulder at the shamans, shivering despite himself. Which was worse—to be ignored as if one didn't exist, or to be recognized by something so intrinsically alien? In some respects, now that he was familiar with the two species, the humanoid Chujoans seemed much more alien than the Boschian Irdizu . . .

"Doing you here?"

Kammer came around the other side of the hut. Philby started, turned slowly, trying to regain dignity, and faced Kammer.

"I've brought a message," Philby said. "From your starship, on its way back to Earth. They intercepted reports that you had been found alive . . ."

Kammer glanced up at the sky speculatively with one pale eye, lips moving. "Must be about two and a half light-years out," he said. "Doing fast by now. Bit-rate way down. Band width doing the very narrow."

"A woman who held you in high regard sends you a message," Philby said. This, he hoped, was the shock that would jolt Kammer back to some human sense of responsibility. "It's rather personal, but its reception by our ship—and the Japanese ship, simultaneously—was hardly private."

"Something to be read, or just spoken?" Kammer asked. Philby interpreted that question as a promising sign. Curiosity, plain English syntax, a tone of some concern. "I know her. I did life with her." He tapped his leathery pate. "In dreams."

"Her name is—"

"Nicole," Kammer said.

Philby said nothing for a time, watching the brown, tortured face reflect some inner realization, some reawakening of old memories.

"What does she say?"

Philby held out a slate. Nicole had convinced the powers that be—apparently her husband, Captain Darryl Washington—that a message of several hundred words was necessary. This had required considerable diversion of resources—turning antennas around, readjustment, expenditure of valuable communications time. Philby had read the message several times. He had no idea what Kammer would make of it. If he had been Kammer—and Kammer still retained any human emotions, a long-shot of supposition—Philby would have been deeply saddened.

Dearest Airy,

I cannot believe what we have heard. That you are alive! By what miracle is not clear to us; we have only been able to receive about three-quarters of the transmissions from Murasaki. We all feel incredibly guilty about leaving you behind. There was no chance of your survival—we knew that, you must believe we knew that! I grieved for you. I punished Darryl for years. This has been cruel to all of us, but especially I think to him. Whom I punish, I feel the most sympathy for . . .

What are you now, after so many years with the Chujoans? Do you still think of us, or have they changed you so much you have forgotten? I cannot tell you all that has happened to us . . . We feel like such cowards, such fools, having left Murasaki just when the rush from Earth was beginning. We should have stayed, but we did not have the heart. What reception we will return home to, I cannot say . . . Perhaps the reception reserved for (L.O.S. 2.4 kb?).

. . .were the better man. I chose you. Know that about me now, Aaron, that in the end, I chose you, my body chose you. Darryl has lived with this, and I think I admire him more now, despite my punishments and inward scorn, for having lived with it.

We have a son, Aaron. You and I. He is your boy. He was born five months ago. I have named him after your father, Kevin. He is healthy and will be a young man when we return to Earth.

He will be told that you are his father. Darryl insists, especially since we've learned you are alive.

That knowledge grinds Darryl down more each night. Who can understand the grief of strong men?

I love you, Aaron.

Nicole

Kammer let the slate drop to the ground, then swayed like an old tree in a slight breeze. "I am not that same person," he said throatily. "He did the dying."

"I think that person is still here," Philby persisted. "You remember Nicole. You remember who you were. And you knew that Carnot would cause great damage. You hit him to stop him."

"I hit him to save him," Kammer said with a sudden heat. "Could not see them do all the dying."

"I don't understand," Philby said, eyes narrowing.

"They gave me this," Kammer said, lifting the stick covered with patchy snug. "Long times past. Years, maybe. I did the bloating too, and the filling with liquids, the twisting of bones. This," he indicated his contorted trunk and limbs, "was not from breaking my back. I did the sickness myself. Body like a skin full of wine. They gave me the stick, and the snug took me over. It found what was making me sick, and it killed them, or tamed them. I got better."

Philby's eyes widened, and for the first time in Kammer's presence, he felt a shiver of awe. What did the Chujoans know—what could they do? He slowly turned to survey the shamans, uncaring and implacable in their loose line between the two humans and the bullyboys.

"Hit him to save him, if he had the brains to know what it was I gave," Kammer said. "I see he did." Kammer's gaze was intense, his eyes seeming darker, more human now. "Perhaps that was when he did the prophet. Bent body, bent mind. Saved from death. Knew, knew."

Softly, shivering slightly, Philby said, "We're going to meet with the God the Physicists, with Carnot. I think it's important that you talk with him."

"Can't go back and do the human thing," Kammer said. "Being this. Knew, knew."

"If you believe his distortions are dangerous—and you must, Aaron, you must!—you cannot refuse us this. Talk with him, tell him what you know. Try to make him stop this insanity. He could destroy all the Genjians have in the way of . . . culture, language, independent thought."

"Never did them," Kammer said.

"Aaron . . ." Philby stepped forward, hands beseeching. He removed his hydrator, to speak directly with Kammer. The cool dry air felt like dust in his throat and he coughed.

Two trolls shoved him roughly away and spilled him on the ground. His mask flew high into the air and came down six or seven meters away. A troll loomed over him, baring its teeth, seeming to grin, examining his form as if it might be a long diversion from the troll's normal mindless boredom.

Kammer stood back, stick lifted as if to defend himself as well against the trolls, and said nothing.

The shamans moved in around Philby. He tried to get up, but the troll casually kicked his arm out from under him and he fell back. He prepared himself to die, but first, he triggered the emergency signal in his belt. That would bring Sheldrake and Thompson; they were armed. If he was dead, they would do nothing but try to retrieve his body; but if he were still alive, they would carve their way through trolls and shamans both to save him.

He considered this for a moment, realized what an ugliness might spread from another such incident—realized that what the Japanese had done, years before, might still linger between Chujoans and humans—and shouted to Kammer, "For God's sake, Aaron, this is awful! Stop them!"

He saw part of Kammer's twisted leg through the parted legs of a troll. The leg moved, then the stick came down with a thud. More snug dropped away from the stick. Fascinated, anesthetized by his terror, Philby watched the fallen patches of growth twist about and crawl along the ground, back to the stick.

"There isn't much I can do," Kammer said. "Lie still."

"Damn it, you're sacred to them! Tell them to stop!"

"I'm hardly sacred," Kammer said. The troll stepped aside and Philby saw Kammer clearly. He was standing away from the trolls, who showed their teeth to him with as much apparent enthusiasm as they did to Philby. "That's what Carnot thought. Doing the Earth and making all like men.

"I'm an experiment, Philby. I thought you were rational and could know that. An experiment, and nothing more."

SCATTERSHOT

In 1979, when James Turner, editor at Arkham House, contemplated buying a collection of my short fiction, he picked out four stories he thought were worthy: "The Wind From a Burning Woman," "Mandala," "The White Horse Child," and "Scattershot."

"Scattershot" was bought originally by Terry Carr for his Universe 8 anthology. Terry was a friendly and charming man, but editorially spare with words; it was enough, in those days, that he bought a story. Terry—and Ben Bova at Analog, and Robert Silverberg—made me feel I was making real progress in those years before any of my novels had sold.

This story features one of my typical strong female characters, and it also shows the influence of James Tiptree, Jr.—an influence I now find slightly peculiar.

Everyone knows now that Tiptree was actually a woman, Alice Sheldon. She wrote fine short storie s and cut quite a swath through the science fiction world in the nineteen seventies. Her biography is fascinating. Suffice it to say that in her stories, she often gave the masculine sex a hard time. She was not an overt lesbian, to my knowledge, but in her journals and spoken diaries, she tells us that the sexual attentions of men made her uncomfortable. She married a much older man, and when he was dying and life to her seemed not worth living, she shot him, and then shot herself. Alice Sheldon was nothing if not pragmatic.

She seemed to enjoy her run at literature a great deal, and the exchanges of letters her stories provoked. She also enjoyed deceiving people, for a time at least, as to her gender.

Many writers, perhaps most, adopt likely quirks to work to the market. In "Scattershot," the quirk I acquired from Tiptree is so small hardly anyone will notice it. But I give the strong male in this story a very hard time, and promote the women characters to almost mythic stature. It seemed right at the time.

Tiptree was wry, witty, and probably deeply misandric. We all miss her, but I no longer want to write like her.

Now, when I write strong women characters, I intend that they be natural and believable, not distorted or mythic. It's tough to beat Alice Sheldon at her own game, and also tough to beat H. Rider Haggard.

Discerning readers might note that this story bears a similarity to "Hardfought." The deep structure is the same, in fact, but the endings are very different.

The teddy bear spoke excellent mandarin. It stood about fifty centimeters tall, a plump fellow with close-set eyes above a nose unusually long for the generally pug breed. It paced around me, muttering to itself.

I rolled over and felt barbs down my back and sides. My arms moved with reluctance. Something about my will to get up and the way my muscles reacted was out-of-kilter; the nerves didn't convey properly. So it was, I thought, with my eyes and the small black-and-white beast they claimed to see: a derangement of phosphene patterns, cross-tied with childhood memories and snatches of linguistics courses ten years past.

It began speaking Russian. I ignored it and focused on other things. The rear wall of my cabin was unrecognizable, covered with geometric patterns that shifted in and out of bas-relief and glowed faintly in the shadow cast by a skewed panel light. My fold-out desk had been torn from its hinges and now lay on the floor, not far from my head. The ceiling was cream-colored. Last

I remembered it had been a pleasant shade of burnt orange. Thus tallied, half my cabin was still with me. The other half had been ferried away in the—

Disruption. I groaned, and the bear stepped back nervously. My body was gradually coordinating. Bits and pieces of disassembled vision integrated and stopped their random flights, and still the creature walked, and still it spoke, though getting deep into German.

It was not a minor vision. It was either real or a full-fledged hallucination.

"What's going on?" I asked.

It bent over me, sighed, and said, "Of all the fated arrangements. A speaking I know not the best of—Anglo." It held out its arms and shivered. "Pardon the distraught. My cords of psyche—nerves?—they have not decided which continuum to obey this moment."

"Same for me," I said cautiously. "Who are you?"

"Psyche, we are all psyche. Take this care and be not content with illusion, this path, this merriment. Excuse. Some writers in English. All I know is from the read."

"Am I still on my ship?"

"So we are all, and *hors de combat.* We limp for the duration."

I was integrated enough to stand, and I towered over the bear, rearranging my tunic. My left breast ached with a bruise. Because we had been riding at one G for five days, I was wearing a bra, and the bruise lay directly under a strap. Such, to quote, was the fated arrangement. As my wits gathered and held converse, I considered what might have happened and felt a touch of the "distraughts" myself. I began to shiver like a recruit in pressure-drop training.

We had survived. That is, at least *I* had survived, out of a crew of forty-three. How many others?

"Do you know . . . have you found out—"

"Worst," the bear said. "Some I do not catch, the deciphering of other things not so hard. Disrupted about seven, eight hours past.

It was a force of many, for I have counted ten separate things not in my recognition." It grinned. "You are ten, and best yet. We are perhaps not so far in world-lines."

We'd been told survival after disruption was possible. Practical statistics indicated one out of a myriad ships, so struck, would remain integral. For a weapon that didn't actually kill in itself, the probability disrupter was very effective.

"Are we intact?" I asked.

"Fated," the Teddy bear said. "I cognize we can even move and seek a base. Depending."

"Depending," I echoed. The creature sounded masculine, despite size and a childlike voice. "Are you a he? Or—"

"He," the bear said quickly.

I touched the bulkhead above the door and ran my finger along a familiar, slightly crooked seam. Had the disruption kept me in my own universe—against incalculable odds—or exchanged me to some other? Was either of us in a universe we could call our own?

"Is it safe to look around?"

The bear hummed. "Cognize—know not. Last I saw, others had not reached a state of organizing."

It was best to start from the beginning. I looked down at the creature and rubbed a bruise on my forehead. "Wh-where are you from?"

"Same as you, possible," he said. "Earth. Was mascot to captain, for cuddle and advice."

That sounded bizarre enough. I walked to the hatchway and peered down the corridor. It was plain and utilitarian, but neither the right color nor configuration. The hatch at the end was round and had a manual sealing system, six black throw-bolts that no human engineer would ever have put on a spaceship. "What's your name?"

"Have no official name. Mascot name known only to captain."

I was scared, so my brusque nature surfaced and I asked him sharply if his captain was in sight, or any other aspect of the world he'd known.

"Cognize not," he answered. "Call me Sonok."

"I'm Geneva," I said. "Francis Geneva."

"We are friends?"

"I don't see why not. I hope we're not the only ones who can be friendly. Is English difficult for you?"

"Mind not. I learn fast. Practice make perfection."

"Because I can speak some Russian, if you want."

"Good as I with Anglo?" Sonok asked. I detected a sense of humor—and self-esteem--in the bear.

"No, probably not. English it is. If you need to know anything, don't be embarrassed to ask."

"Sonok embarrassed by no thing. Was mascot."

The banter was providing a solid framework for my sanity to grab on to. I had an irrational desire to take the bear and hug him, just for want of something warm. His attraction was undeniable—tailored, I guessed, for that very purpose. But tailored from what? The color suggested panda; the shape did not.

"What do you think we should do?" I asked, sitting on my bunk.

"Sonok not known for quick decisions," he said, squatting on the floor in front of me. He was stubby-limbed but far from clumsy.

"Neither am I," I said. "I'm a software expert. I wasn't combat-trained."

"Not know 'software,'" Sonok said.

"Programming. Instructions for machines," I explained.

The bear wrinkled his nose, then got up to peer around the door. He pulled back quickly and scrabbled to the rear of the cabin. "They're here!" he said. "Can shut port?"

"I wouldn't begin to know how—" But then I looked and retreated just as quickly, with a high squeak, to cling to my bunk. A stream of serpents flowed past the hatchway, metallic green and yellow, with spade-shaped heads and dorsal red ovals. The stream passed without even a hint of intent to molest, and Sonok climbed back down the bas-relief pattern.

"What the hell are they doing here?" I asked.

"They are crew member, I think," Sonok said.

"What else is out there?"

The bear straightened. "Have none but to seek," he said solemnly. "Else, we own no right to ask. Not?" The bear walked to the hatch, stepped over the bottom seal, and stood in the corridor. "Come?"

I let go of my bunk, got up, and followed.

A woman is a deep, strange pool to slip into at birth. For the first few months of listening and seeing, her infant mind is a huge dark volume that absorbs all and stores it away. Those months lay down a foundation for role acceptance and rough outlines of attitude, as well as the potential for future achievement—if those watching her are tuned to such sensibilities.

Few are. Most adults, even most parents, just want the girl to fit in and not cause trouble. Listening to adults and observing their actions fills the infant female with hints, preconceptions, borders, and stark warnings: *None of the rest of us can see your imaginary companions, darling . . . . It's something you have to understand.*

And so, from some dim beginning, not *ex nihilo* but out of totality, the girl pares away her infinite self. She whittles at this unwanted piece, that undesired trait. She forgets in time that she was once part of All and trims to a simpler tune, narrowing her music from the endless and symphonic *before.* She forgets those companions who danced on the ceiling above her bed and called to her from the dark. Some of them were friendly; others, even in that dim time, were not pleasant. But they were all *she.*

For the rest of her life, the woman seeks some echo of that preternatural menagerie; in the men she chooses to love, in the tasks she chooses to perform, in the way she tries to be. After thirty years of cutting, she becomes Francis Geneva.

And so begins or concludes other phases of loss. When love dies, another piece is carved away, another universe is sheared off, and the split can never join again. With each winter and spring, spent on or off worlds with or without seasons, the woman's life grows more solid, but smaller.

Now, on this jumbled ship, the parts are coming together again. Old, forgotten companions return from the dark above the child's bed. Beware. They're all the things you lost or let go, and now they walk on their own, out of your control; reborn and indecipherable.

"Are you understanding?" the bear asked.

I shook my head to break my steady, baffled glare at the six-bolted hatch. "Do I understand what?" I asked.

"Of how we are here."

"Disrupted. By Aighors, I assume."

"Yes, for us, too. But how?"

"I don't know," I said.

No one did. We could only observe the results. When the remains of disrupted ships could be found, they always resembled floating garbage heaps—plucked from our universe, rearranged in some cosmic grab bag, and returned. What came back was of the same mass, made of the same basic materials, even—the ultimate perversity!—recombined with a tendency toward order and viability. But in deep space, even ninety-nine percent viability is tantamount to none at all. If the ship's separate elements didn't integrate perfectly—and only one in a hundred thousand instances would—there were no survivors. But oh, how interested we were in the corpses! Most were kept behind a Paper Curtain of secrecy, but word leaked out even so—of ostriches with large heads, blobs covered with blobs of crystalline seawater . . . All snatched out of Terrestrial ships, but from a huge jumble of alternate universes.

And now, my own additions: a living Teddy bear, a herd of parti-colored snakes.

Word also leaked out that of five hundred such incidents, not once had a human body returned intact to our continuum. Terrible odds all around.

Yet here we were.

"Some things still work," Sonok said. "We are heavy the same."

The ship's gravitation was unchanged—I hadn't paid attention to that. "We can still breathe, for that matter," I said. "We're all from one world. There's no reason to think those basics will change."

And that meant there had to be standards for communication, no matter how diverse the forms. Communication was part of my expertise, but thinking about it made me shiver. A ship runs on computers, or their equivalent. How were at least ten different computer systems communicating? Had they integrated with working interfaces? If they hadn't, our time was limited. We would soon be wrapped in darkness and cold and vacuum.

I released the six throw-bolts and slowly opened the hatch.

"Say, Geneva," Sonok mused as we looked into the corridor beyond. "How did snakes get through?"

I shook my head. There were more immediate problems. "I want to find something like a ship's bridge, or at least a computer terminal. Did you see something like those before you found my cabin?"

Sonok nodded. "Other way in corridor. But there were . . . *things* there. Didn't enjoy the looks, so came this way."

"What were they?" I asked.

"One like trash can," he said. "With breasts."

"We'll keep looking this way," I said by way of agreement.

The next bulkhead was a dead end. A few round displays studded the wall, filled like bull's-eyes with concentric circles of varying thickness. A lot of information could be carried in such patterns, given a precise optical scanner to read them—which suggested a machine more than an organism, though not necessarily.

The bear paced back and forth in front of the wall.

I reached out with one hand to touch one of the round displays. Then I got down on my knees to feel the bulkhead, looking for a seam. "Can't see it, but I feel something here—like a ridge in the material."

The bulkhead, displays and all, peeled away like a heart's triplet valve, and a rush of air shoved us into darkness. I instinctively rolled into a fetal curl. The bear bumped against me and grabbed my arm. Some throbbing force flung us this way and that, knocking us against squeaking wet things. I forced my eyes open and unfurled my arms and legs, trying to find a grip. One hand rapped against metal or hard plastic, and the other caught what felt like rope. With some fumbling, I gripped the rope and braced myself against the hard surface. Then I had time to sort out what I was seeing. The chamber seemed to be open to space, but we were breathing, so obviously a transparent membrane was keeping in the atmosphere. I could see the outer surface of the ship, and it appeared a hell of a lot larger than I'd allowed. Clinging to the membrane in a curve, as though queued on the inside of a bubble, were five or six round nebulosities that glowed dull orange like dying suns. I was hanging on to something resembling a ship's mast, a metal pylon that reached from one side of the valve to the center of the bubble. Ropes were rigged from the pylon to stanchions that seemed suspended in midair, though they had to be secured against the membrane. The ropes and pylon supported clusters of head-sized spheres covered with hairlike plastic tubing. They clucked like brood hens as they slid away from us. "*Góspodi!*" Sonok screeched.

The valve that had given us access was still open, pushing its flaps in and out. I kicked away from the pylon. The bear's grip was fierce. The flaps loomed, slapped against us, and closed with a final sucking throb. We were on the other side, lying on the floor. The bulkhead again was impassively blank.

The bear rolled away from my arm and stood up. "Best to try other way!" he suggested. "More easy faced, I think."

I unshipped the six-bolted hatch and we crawled through, then doubled back past my cabin. The corridor, now that I thought of it, was strangely naked. In any similar region on my original ship there would have been pipes, access panels, printed instructions— and at least ten cabin doors.

A few yards beyond my cabin, the corridor curved and the interiors became more diverse. We found several small cubby-holes, all empty.

Sonok walked cautiously ahead. "Here," he said. "Can with breasts was here."

"Gone now," I observed. We stepped through another six-bolt hatch into a chamber with a vague resemblance to a command center. In its larger details, it resembled the bridge of my own ship, and I rejoiced for that small sense of security.

"Can you talk to it?" Sonok asked.

"I can try. But where's a terminal?"

The bear pointed to a curved bench in front of a square, flat surface, devoid of keyboard, speaker, or knobs. Didn't look much like a terminal—though the flat surface resembled a visual dis-play screen—but I wasn't ashamed to try speaking to it. Nor was I abashed when it didn't answer. "No go. Something else."

We looked around the chamber for several minutes but found nothing more promising. "It's *like* a bridge," I said, "but nothing matches specifically. Maybe we're looking for the wrong things."

"Machines run themselves?" Sonok suggested.

I sat on the bench, resting an elbow on the edge of the "screen." Nonhuman technologies frequently use other senses for infor-mation exchange. Where we generally limit machine-human interactions to sight, sound, and sometimes touch, Crocerians use odor, and Aighors control their machines with microwave radiation from their nervous systems. I laid my hand across the screen. It was warm to the touch, but I couldn't detect any varia-tion in the warmth. Infrared is an inefficient carrier of informa-tion for creatures with visual orientation. But snakes use infrared to seek prey—

"Snakes," I said. "The screen is warm. Is this part of the snake ship?"

Sonok shrugged. I looked around the cabin to find other smooth surfaces. They were few. Most were crisscrossed with raised grills. Some were warm to the touch. There were any number of possibilities—but I doubted I would hit on the right one quickly. The best I could hope for was the survival of some other portion of my ship.

"Sonok, is there another way out of this room?"

"Several. One is around gray pillar," he said, pointing. "Another hatch with six dogs."

"What?"

"Six . . ." He made a grabbing motion with one hand. "Like the others."

"Throw-bolts," I said.

"I thought my Anglo was improving," he sulked.

"It is. But it's bound to be different from mine, so we both have to adapt." We opened the hatch and looked into the next chamber. A haze of cloying smoke drifted out and immediately set ventilators to work. The lights flickered feebly, and wrecked equipment gave off acrid smells. The bear held his nose and jumped over the seal for a quick walk through the room.

"Is something dead in here," he said when he returned. "Not like human, but not far. It is shot in head." He nodded for me to go with him, and I reluctantly followed. The body was pinned between two bolted seats. The head was a mess, and there was ample evidence that it used red blood. The body was covered by gray overalls and, though twisted into an awkward position, was obviously more canine than human. The bear was correct in one respect: it was closer to me than whiskered balls or rainbow snakes.

The smoke had almost been cleared when I stepped back from the corpse. "Sonok, any possibility this could be another mascot?"

The bear shook his head and walked off, nose wrinkled. I wondered if I'd insulted him.

"I see nothing like terminal," he said. "Looks like nothing work, anyway. Go on?"

We returned to the previous bridge-like chamber, and Sonok picked out another corridor. By the changing floor curvature, I guessed that all my previous estimates as to ship size were appreciably off. What I'd seen from the bubble had appeared endless, but that might have been optical distortion. There was no way of determining either the shape or size of this collage of vessels.

The corridor dead-ended again, and we didn't press our luck as to what lay beyond the blank bulkhead. As we turned back, I asked, "What were the things you saw? You said there were ten of them, all different."

The bear held up his paws and counted. His fingers were otter-like and supple. "Snakes, number one," he said. "Cans with breasts, two; back wall of your cabin, three; blank bulkhead with circular marks, four; and you, five. Other things not so different, I think now snakes and six-dog hatches go together. Snakes know how to use them. Other things—you and your cabin fixtures, all together. But you add dead thing in overalls, fuzzy balls, and who can say where it ends?"

His Anglo really was improving, and rapidly. "I hope it ends someplace," I said. "I can only face so many variations before I give up. Is there anything left of your ship?"

"Where I was after disruption," the bear said. "On my stomach in bathroom."

Ah, that blessed word! "Where?" I asked. "Is it working?" I'd considered impolitely messing the corridors if there was no alternative.

"Works still, I think. Back through side corridor."

He showed me the way. A lot can be learned from a bathroom: social attitudes, levels of technology, even basic psychology—not to mention anatomy. This one was lovely and utilitarian, with fixtures for males and females of at least three sizes. I made do with the largest. The bear gave me privacy, which wasn't strictly necessary—bathrooms on my ship being coed—but appreciated, none-theless. Exposure to a Teddy bear takes getting used to.

When I was through, I joined Sonok in the hall and realized I'd gotten myself turned around. "Where are we?"

"Is changing," Sonok said. "Where bulkhead was, now hatch. Not sure I see how—is *different* hatch."

And it was, in an alarming way: battle-armored, automatically controlled, and equipped with heavily shielded detection equip-ment. It was ugly and khaki-colored and had no business being inside a ship, unless the occupants greatly distrusted each other.

"I am in anteroom, outside lavatory," Sonok said, "with door closed. I hear loud sound and something like metal cutting, and open door to this."

We stayed away from the new hatch. Vague sounds of machines were still audible, grinding and screaming. Sonok motioned for me to follow. "One more," he said. "Almost forgot." He pointed into a cubbyhole, about a meter deep and two meters square. "Look like fish tank?"

Filling the cubbyhole was a large rectangular tank filled with murky fluid. It reached from my knees to the top of my head.

"Hasn't been cleaned," I said. I touched the glass to feel how warm or cold it was. The tank lighted up, and I jumped back, knocking Sonok over. He rolled into a backward flip and came upright, wheezing.

The light in the tank flickered like a strobe, gradually speeding up until the glow steadied. For a few seconds, it made me dizzy. Then the murk gathered itself together. I bent over cautiously to get a close look. The murk wasn't evenly distributed. It was com-posed of animals like brine shrimp, each no more than a centi-meter long, with two black eyespots at one end, a pinkish "spine," and a feathery fringe rippling between head and tail. They were forming a dense mass at the center of the tank. Ordered dots of luminescence crossed the bottom of the tank, changing colors across a narrow spectrum: red, blue, amber.

"It's doing something," Sonok said. The mass was defining a shape. Shoulders and head appeared, then torso and arms, sculpted in ghost-colored brine shrimp. When the living sculpture was finished, I recognized *myself* from the waist up. I held out my arm, and the mass slowly followed suit. Then I had an inspiration. In my pants pocket I still had a marker for labeling tapas cube blanks. It used soft plastic wrapped in a metal jacket. I took it out and wrote three letters across the transparent front of the tank: WHO. Part of the mass dissolved and re-formed to mimic the letters, the rest filling in behind. WHO they spelled, then added a question mark. Sonok chirped, and I leaned in closer to see better.

"They understand?" he asked. I shook my head. I had no idea what I was playing with.

WHAT ARE YOU? I wrote.

The animals started to break up and return to the general murk. I shook my head in frustration. So near! The closest thing to communication yet.

"Wait," Sonok said. "They group again."

TENZIONA, the shrimp coalesced. DYSFUNCTIO. GUARDATEO AB PEREGRINO PERAMBULA.

"I don't understand. Sounds like Italian—do you know any Italian?"

The bear shook his head.

"'Dysfunctio,'" I read aloud. "That seems plain enough. '*Ab peregrino*'? Something about a hawk?"

"*Peregrine,* it is foreigner," Sonok said.

"Guard against foreigners . . . 'perambula,' as in strolling? Watch for the foreigners who walk? Well, we don't have the grammar, but it seems to tell us something we already know. Christ! I wish I could remember all the languages they filled me with ten years ago."

My marks on the tank darkened and flaked off. The shrimp began to form something different. They grouped into branches and arranged themselves nose-to-tail, upright, to shape a trunk, which then rooted itself to the floor of the tank.

"Tree," Sonok said.

Again they dissolved, then returned quickly to the simulacrum of my body. The clothing seemed different, however—more like a robe. Each shrimp changed its individual color, making the shape startlingly lifelike.

As I watched, the image began to age. The outlines of the face sagged, wrinkles formed in the skin, and the limbs shrank perceptibly.

My arms felt cold, and I crossed them over my breasts; but the corridor was reasonably warm.

Of course, the universe I grew up in isn't really confined in a little girl's mind. But it is one small thread in a vast skein, separated from every other universe by a limitation of constants and qualities, just as death is separated from life by the eternal nonreturn of the dead.

Well, now we know the universes are less inviolable than death, and there are ways of crossing from thread to thread. So these other beings, from similar Earths, are not part of my undifferentiated infancy. That's a weak fantasy for a rather unequipped young woman to indulge in. Still, the symbols of childhood lie all around—nightmares and Teddy bears and dreams held in a tank; dreams of old age and death. And a tree, gray and ghostly, without leaves. That's me. Full of winter, wood cracking into splinters.

How do they know?

A rustling from the corridor ahead. We turned away from the tank and saw the floor covered with rainbow snakes, motionless, all heads aimed at us.

Sonok began to tremble.

"Stop it," I said. "They haven't done anything yet."

"You are bigger," he said. "Not size of dinner."

"They'd have a rough time putting you away, too. Let's just sit this out calmly and see what it's all about." I kept my eyes on the snakes and away from the tank. I didn't want to see the shape age any further. For all the sanity of this place, that image might have kept on going, through death and decay down to bones. Why did it choose me; why not Sonok?

"I cannot wait," Sonok said. "I have not the patience of a snake." He stepped forward. The snakes watched without a sound as the bear slowly approached. "I want to know one solid thing," he called back. "Even if it is whether they eat small furry mascots."

The snakes suddenly bundled backward and started to crawl over each other. Small sucking noises smacked between their bodies. As they crossed, the red ovals met and held firm. They assembled and reared into a single mass, cobralike, but flat as a planarian worm. A fringe of snakes weaved across the belly like a caterpillar's idea of Medusa.

Brave Sonok was undone. He swung around and ran past me. I was too shocked to do anything but face the snakes down, my neck hairs crawling. I wanted to speak but couldn't. Then, behind me, I heard:

"*Sinieux!*"

As I turned, I saw two things, one in the corner of each eye: the snakes fell into a pile, and a man dressed in red and black vanished into a side corridor. The snakes regrouped into a hydra with six tentacles and grasped the hatch's throw-bolts, springing it open and slithering through. The hatch closed, and I was alone.

There was nothing for it but to scream, then cry. I lay back against the wall, getting the fit out of me as loudly and quickly as possible. When I was able to stop, I wiped my eyes with my palms and kept them covered, feeling ashamed. When I looked out again, Sonok stood next to me.

"We have Indian on board," he said. "Big, with black hair in three ribbons"—he motioned from crown to neck between his ears—"and a snappy dresser."

"Where is he?" I asked hoarsely.

"Back in place like bridge. He controls snakes?"

I hesitated, then nodded.

"Go look?"

I got up and followed the bear.

Sitting on a bench pulled from the wall, the man in red and black watched us as we entered the chamber. He was big—at least two meters tall—and hefty, dressed in a black silk shirt with red cuffs. His cape was black with a red eagle embroidered across the shoulders. He certainly looked Indian—ruddy skin, aristocratic nose, full lips held tight as if against pain.

"Quis la?" he queried.

"I don't speak that language," I said. "Do you know English?"

The Indian didn't break his stolid expression. He nodded and turned on the bench to put his hand against a grill. "I was taught in the British school at Nova London," he said, his accent distinctly Oxfordian. "Then I was educated in Indonesia, and so I speak Dutch, High and Middle German, and some Asian tongues, specifically Nippon and Tagalog. But at English I am fluent."

"Thank God," I said. "Do you know this room?"

"Yes," he replied. "I designed it. It's for the Sinieux."

"Do you know what's happened to us?"

"We have fallen into hell," he said. "My Jesuit professors warned me of it."

"Not far wrong," I said. "Do you know why?"

"I do not question my punishments."

"We're not being punished—at least, not by God or devils."

He shrugged. It was a moot point.

"I'm from Earth, too," I said. "From Terre."

"I *know* the words for Earth," the Indian said sharply.

"But I don't think it's the same Earth. What year are you from?" Since he'd mentioned Jesuits, he almost had to use the standard Christian Era dating.

"Year of Our Lord 2345," he said.

Sonok crossed himself elegantly. "For me 2290," he added. The Indian examined the bear dubiously.

I was sixty years after the bear, five after the Indian. The limits of the grab bag were less hazy now. "What country?"

"Alliance of Tribal Columbia," he answered, "District Quebec, East Shore."

"I'm from the Moon," I said. "But my parents were born on Earth, in the United States of America."

The Indian shook his head slowly; he wasn't familiar with it.

"Was there—" But I held back the question. Where to begin? Where did the world-lines part? "I think we'd better learn how well this ship is put together. We'll get into our comparative histories later. Obviously, you have star drive."

The Indian didn't agree or disagree. "My parents knew ancestors from the West Shore, Vancouver," he said. "They were Kwakiutl and Kodikin. The animal, does it have a Russian accent?"

"Some," I said. "Better than it was a few hours ago."

"My people have blood debts against Russians."

"Okay," I said, "but I doubt if you have anything against *this* one, considering the distances involved. We've got to learn if this ship can take us someplace."

"I have asked," he said.

"Where?" Sonok asked. "A terminal?"

"The ship says it is surrounded by foreign parts and can barely understand them. But it can get along."

"You really don't know what happened, do you?"

"I went to look for worlds for my people and took the Sinieux with me. When I reached a certain coordinate in the sky, far along the arrow line established by my extrasolar pierce, this happened." He lifted his hand. "Now there is one creature, a devil, that tried to attack me. It is dead. There are others, huge black men who wear golden armor and carry gold guns like cannon, and they have gone away behind armored hatches. There are walls like rubber that open onto more demons. And now you—and it." He pointed at the bear.

"Not an 'it,'" Sonok said. "I'm an *ours*."

"Small *ours*," the Indian retorted.

Sonok bristled and turned away. "Enough," I said. "You haven't fallen into hell, not literally. We've been hit by something called a disrupter. It snatched us from different universes and reassembled us according to our world-lines, our . . . affinities."

The Indian smiled contemptuously at my obvious ignorance— or madness.

"Listen, do you understand how crazy this is?" I demanded, exasperated. "I've got to get things straight. The beings who did this—in my universe they're called 'Aighors.' Do you know about them?"

He shook his head. "I know of no beings but those of Earth. I went to look for worlds."

"Is your ship a warper ship—does it travel across a geodesic in higher spaces?"

"Yes," he said. "It is not in phase with the crest of the Stellar Sea, but slips between the foamy length, where we must struggle to obey all laws."

That was a fair description of translating from status geometry—our universe—to higher geometries. It was more poetic than scientific, but he was here, so it worked.

"How long have your people been able to travel this way?"

"Ten years. And yours?"

"Three centuries," I said.

He nodded in appreciation. "You know then what you speak."

"I wish I knew it all."

He inclined his head, being gracious for once. "Perhaps there aren't any devils, and we are not in hell. Not this time."

"How do you use your instruments in here?"

"I do not, generally. The Sinieux use them. If you will not be upset, I'll demonstrate."

I glanced at Sonok, who was still sulking. "Are you afraid of the snakes?"

The bear shook his head.

"Bring them in," I said. "And perhaps we should know each other's name?"

"Jean Frobish," the Indian said. And I told him mine.

At his whistled command, the snakes entered and assembled in the middle of the cabin. There were two sets, each made up of about fifty. When meshed, they made two formidable meta-serpents. Frobish instructed them with spoken commands and a language that sounded like birdcalls. Perfect servants, they obeyed faultlessly and without hesitation. They went to the controls at his command and made a few manipulations, then turned to him and delivered, one group at a time, a report in consonantal hisses and claps. The exchange was uncanny and chilling. Jean nodded, and the serpents disassembled.

"Are they specially bred?" I asked.

"Tectonogenetic farming," he said. "They are excellent workers and have no will of their own, since they have no cerebrums. They can remember, and en masse can think, but not for themselves, if you see what I mean." He showed another glimmer of a smile. He was proud of his servants.

"I think I understand. Sonok, were you specially bred?"

"Was mascot," Sonok said. "Can breed for myself, given chance."

The subject was touchy, I could see. I could also see that Frobish and Sonok wouldn't get along without friction. If Sonok had been a big bear—and not a Russian—instead of an ursine dwarf, the Indian might have had more respect for him.

"Jean, can you command the whole ship from here?"

"Those parts that answer."

"Can your computers tell you how much of the ship will respond?"

"What is left of my vessel responds very well. The rest is balky or blank entirely. I was trying to discover the limits when I encountered you."

"You met the people who've been putting in the armored hatches?'

He nodded. "Bigger than Masai," he said.

I now had explanations for some of the things we'd seen and could link them with terrestrial origins. Jean and his Sinieux weren't beyond the stretch of reason, nor was Sonok. The armored hatches weren't quite as mysterious now. But what about the canine? I swallowed. That must have been the demon Frobish killed. And beyond the triplet valves?

"We've got a lot to find out," I said.

"You and the animal, are you together, from the same world?" Frobish asked. I shook my head. "Did you come alone?"

I nodded. "Why?"

"No men, no soldiers?"

I was apprehensive now. "No."

"Good." He stood and approached a blank wall near the gray pillar. "Then we will not have too many to support, unless the ones in golden armor want our food." He put his hand against the wall, and a round opening appeared. In the shadow of the hole, two faces watched with black eyes glittering.

"These are my wives," Frobish said. One was dark-haired and slender, no more than fifteen or sixteen. She stepped out first and looked at me warily. The second, stockier and flatter of face, was brown-haired and about twenty. Frobish pointed to the younger first. "This is Alouette," he said. "And this is Mouse. Wives, acquaint with Francis Geneva." They stood one on each side of Frobish, holding his elbows, and nodded at me in unison.

That made four humans, more if the blacks in golden armor were men. Our collage had hit the jackpot.

"Jean, you say your machines can get along with the rest of the ship. Can they control it? If they can, I think we should try to return to Earth."

"To what?" Sonok asked. "Which Earth waits?"

"What's the bear talking about?" Frobish asked.

I explained the situation as best I could. Frobish was a sophisticated engineer and astrogator, but his experience with other continua—theoretical or actual—was small. He tightened his lips and listened grimly, unwilling to admit his ignorance. I sighed and looked to Alouette and Mouse for support. They were meek, quiet, giving all to the stolid authority of Frobish.

"What woman says is we decide where to go," Sonok said. "Depends, so the die is tossed, on whether we like the Earth we would meet."

"You would like my Earth," Frobish said.

"There's no guarantee it'll be your Earth. You have to take that into account."

"You aren't making sense." Frobish shook his head. "My decision is made, nonetheless. We will try to return."

I shrugged. "Try as best you can." We would face the truth later.

"I'll have the Sinieux watch over the machines after I start instructions," Frobish said. "Then I would like Francis to come with me to look at the animal I killed." I agreed without thinking about his motives. He gave the meta-serpents their orders and pulled down a panel cover to reveal a small board designed for human hands. When he was through programming the computers, he continued his instructions to the Sinieux. His rapport with the animals was perfect—the interaction of an engineer with his tool. There was no thought of discord or second opinions. The snakes, to all intents and purposes, were machines keyed only to his voice. I wondered how far the obedience of his wives extended.

"Mouse will find food for the bear, and Alouette will stand guard with the *fusil. Comprens?*" The woman nodded, and Alouette plucked a rifle from the hideaway. "When we return, we will all eat."

"I will wait to eat with you," Sonok said, standing near me.

Frobish looked the bear over coldly. "We do not eat with tec-toes," he said, haughty as a British officer addressing his servant. "But you will eat the same food we do."

Sonok stretched out his arms and made two shivers of anger. "I have never been treated less than a man," he said. "I will eat with all or not eat." He looked up at me with his small golden eyes and asked in Russian, "Will you go along with him?"

"We don't have much choice," I answered haltingly in kind.

"What do you recommend?"

"Play along for the moment. I understand." I was unable to read his expression behind the black mask and white markings; but if I'd been he, I'd have questioned the understanding. This was no time, however, to instruct the bear in assertion.

Frobish opened the hatch to the wrecked room and let me step in first. He then closed the hatch and sealed it. "I've seen the body," I said. "What do you want to know?"

"I want your advice on this room," he said. I didn't believe that for an instant. I bent to more carefully examine the creature between the chairs.

"What did it do to you?" I asked.

"It came at me. I thought it was a demon. I shot it, and it died."

"What caused the rest of this damage?"

"I fired many rounds," he said. "I was frightened. I'm calm now."

"Thank God," I said. "This—he or she—might have been able to help us."

"Looks like a dog," Frobish said. "Dogs cannot help."

For me, that crossed the line. "Listen," I said tightly, standing back from the body. "I don't think you're in touch with what's going on here. If you don't get in touch soon, you could get us all killed. I'm not about to let myself die because of one man's stupidity."

Frobish's eyes widened. "Women do not address men thus," he said.

"This woman does, friend! I don't know what kind of screwy social order you have in your world, but you had damn well better get used to interacting with different sexes, not to mention different species! If you don't, you're asking to end up like this poor thing. It didn't have a chance to say friend or foe, yea or nay! You shot it out of panic, and we can't have any more of that!" I was trembling.

Frobish smiled over grinding teeth and turned to walk away. He was fighting to control himself. I wondered if my own brains were in the right place. The few aspects of this man that were familiar to me couldn't begin to give complete understanding. I was clearly out of my depth, and kicking out to stay afloat might hasten death, not slow it.

Frobish stood by the hatch, breathing deeply. "What is the dog-creature? What is this room?"

I turned back to the body and pulled it by one leg from between the chairs. "It was probably intelligent," I said. "That's about all I can tell. It doesn't have any personal effects." The gore was getting to me, and I turned away for a moment. I was tired—oh, so tired I could feel the weary rivers dredging through my limbs. My head hurt abominably. "I'm not an engineer," I said. "I can't tell if any of this equipment is useful, or even if it's salvageable. Care to give an opinion?"

Frobish glanced over the room with a slight inclination of one eyebrow. "Nothing of use."

"Are you sure?"

"I am sure." He looked across the room and sniffed the air. "Too much burned and shorted. You know, there is much that is dangerous here."

"Yes," I said, leaning against the back of a seat.

"You will need protection."

"Oh."

"There is no protection like the bonds of family. You are argumentative, but my wives can teach you our ways. With bonds of family, there will be no uncertainty. We will return, and all will be well."

He caught me by surprise, and I wasn't fast on the uptake. "What do you mean, bonds of family?"

"I will take you to wife and protect you as husband."

"I think I can protect myself, thank you."

"It doesn't seem wise to refuse. Left alone, you will probably be killed by such as this." He pointed at the canine.

"We'll have to get along whether we're family or not. That shouldn't be too hard to understand. And I don't have any inclination to sell myself for security."

"I do not pay money for women!" Frobish said. "Again you ridicule me."

He sounded like a disappointed little boy. I wondered what his wives would think, seeing him butt his head against a wall without sense or sensibility.

"We've got to dispose of the body before it decays," I said. "Help me carry it out of here."

"It isn't fit to touch."

My tiredness took over. "You goddamned idiot! Pull your nose down and look at what's going on around you! We're in serious trouble—"

"It isn't the place of a woman to speak thus, I've told you," he said. He approached and raised his hand palm-high to strike. I instinctively raised one arm to deflect his blow, lowered my head, and threw a fist into his abdomen. His slap fell like a kitten's paw and he went over, glancing off my shoulder and twisting my arm into a painful kink. Somehow, he hit his head going down. He was out cold.

I cursed and rubbed the knotted spot, then sat down on the deck to consider what had happened. I'd never had much experience with sexism in human cultures. It was disgusting and hard to accept, but some small voice in the back of my mind told me it was no more blameworthy than any other social altitude. His wives appeared to go along with it. At any rate, the situation was now completely shot to hell. There was little I could do except drag him back to his wives and try to straighten things out when he came to. I took him by both hands and pulled him up to the hatch. I unsealed it, then swung him around to take him by the shoulders.

I retched when one of his shoulders broke the crust on a drying pool of blood and smeared red along the deck.

I miss Jaghit Singh more than I can admit. I think about him and wonder what he'd do in this situation. He is a short, dark man with perfect features and eyes like those in the pictures of Krishna. We formally broke off our relationship three weeks ago, at my behest, for I couldn't see any future in it. He would probably know how to handle Frobish, with a smile and even a spirit of comradeship, but without contradicting his own beliefs. Jaghit had a knack for making a girl's childhood splinters regroup to form the whole log. He could make these beasts and distortions come together again.

Jaghit! Are you anywhere that has seasons? Is it still winter for you? You never did understand the little girl who wanted to play in the snow. Your blood is too hot and regular to stand up to my moments of indecisive coldness, and you could not—would not—force me to change. I was caught between child and my thirty-year-old form, between spring and winter.

Is it spring for you now?

Alouette and Mouse took their husband away from me, spitting with rage. They weren't speaking clearly, but what they shouted in quasi-French made it obvious who they blamed.

I told Sonok what had happened, and he looked very somber indeed. "Maybe he'll shoot us when he wakes up," he suggested. To avoid that circumstance, I appropriated the rifle and took it back to my half-room. There was an intact cabinet, and I still had the key. I didn't lock the rifle in, however; better simply to hide it and have easy access if I needed it.

High time to start being smart and diplomatic, though all I really wanted for the moment was blessed sleep. My shoulder stung like hell, and the muscles still refused to get themselves straight.

When I returned, Sonok walking point a few steps ahead, Frobish was conscious and sitting up in a cot pulled from a panel near the hole. His wives squatted nearby, somber as they ate from metal dishes.

Frobish refused to look me in the eye. Alouette and Mouse weren't in the least reluctant, however, and their gazes threw sparks. They'd be good in a fight, if it ever came to that. I hoped I wasn't their opposite.

"I think it's time we behaved reasonably," I said.

"There is no reason on this ship," Frobish shot back.

"Aye on that," Sonok said, sitting down to a plate left on the floor. He picked at it, then reluctantly ate, his fingers handling the implements with agility.

"If we're at odds, we won't get anything done," I said.

"That is the only thing which stops me from killing you," Frobish said. Mouse bent to whisper in his ear. "My wife reminds me you must have time to see the logic of our ways." Were the women lucid despite their anger, or was he maneuvering on his own? "There is also the possibility that you are a leader. I'm a leader, and at times, it's difficult for me to face another leader. That is why I alone control this ship."

"I'm not a—" I bit my lip. Not too far, too fast. "We've got to work together and forget about being leaders for the moment."

Sonok sighed and put down the plate. "I have no leader," he said. "That part of me did not follow into this scattershot." He leaned on my leg. "Mascots live best when made whole. So I choose Geneva as my other part. I think my English is good enough now for us to understand."

Frobish looked at the bear, expression unreadable. "My stomach hurts," he said after a moment, and turned to me. "You do not hit like a woman. A woman strikes for the soft parts, masculine weaknesses. You go for direct points with knowledge. I cannot accept you as the bear does, but if you will reconsider, we should be able to work together."

"Reconsider the family bond?"

He nodded. To me, he was almost as alien as his snakes. I gave up the fight and decided to play for time.

"I'll have to think about it. My upbringing . . . is hard to overcome," I said.

"We will rest," Frobish said.

"And Sonok will guard," I suggested. The bear straightened perceptibly and went to stand by the hatch. For the moment it looked like a truce had been made, but as cots were pulled out of the walls, I picked up a metal bar and hid it in my trousers.

The Sinieux went to their multilevel cages and lay quiet and still. I slipped into the cot and pulled a thin sheet over myself. Sleep came immediately, and delicious lassitude finally unkinked my arm.

I don't know how long the nap lasted, but it was broken sharply by a screech from Sonok. "They're here! They're here!"

I stumbled out of the cot, tangling one leg in a sheet, and came to a stand only after the Indian family was alert and armed. So much, I thought, for hiding the rifle. "What's here?" I asked, still dopey.

Frobish used his foot to push Sonok away from the hatch and brought the cover around with a quick arm to slam it shut, but not before a black cable was tossed into the room. The hatch jammed on it, and sparks flew. Frobish stood clear and brought his rifle to his shoulder.

Sonok ran to me and clung to my knee. Mouse opened the cages and let the Sinieux flow onto the deck. Frobish retreated from the hatch as it shuddered. The Sinieux advanced. I heard voices from the other side. They sounded human—like children, in fact.

"Wait a minute," I said. Mouse brought her pistol up and aimed it at me. I shut up.

The hatch flung open, and hundreds of fine cables flew into the room, twisting and seeking, wrapping and binding. They plucked Frobish's rifle from his hands and surrounded it like antibodies on a bacterium. Mouse fired her pistol wildly and stumbled, falling into a nest of cables, which jerked and seized. Alouette was almost to the hole, but her ankles were caught and she teetered.

Cables ricocheted from the ceiling and grabbed at the bundles of Sinieux. The snakes fell apart, some clinging to the cables like insects on a frog's tongue. More cables shot out to hold them all, except for a solitary snake that retreated past me. I was bound rigid and tight, with Sonok strapped to my knee.

The barrage stopped, and a small shadowed figure stood in the hatch, carrying a machete. It cleared the entrance of the sticky strands and stepped into the cabin light, looking around cautiously. Then it waved to companions behind, and five more entered. They were identical, each just under half a meter in height—a little shorter than Sonok—and bald and pink as infants. Their features were delicate and fetal, with large gray-green eyes and thin, translucent limbs. Their hands were stubby-fingered and plump as those on a Rubens baby. They walked into the cabin with long strides, self-assured, nimbly avoiding the cables.

Sonok jerked at a sound in the corridor—a hesitant, high-pitched mewing. "With breasts," he mumbled through the cords.

One of the infantoids arranged a ramp over the bottom seal of the hatch. He then stepped aside and clapped to get attention. The others formed a line, pink fannies jutting, and held their hands over their heads as if surrendering. The mewing grew louder. Sonok's trash can with breasts entered the cabin, twisting this way and that like a deranged, obscene toy. It was cylindrical, with sides tapering to a fringed skirt at the base. Three levels of pink and nippled paps ringed it at equal intervals from top to bottom. A low, flat head surmounted the body, tiny black eyes examining the cabin with quick, nervous jerks. It looked like nothing so much as the Diana of Ephesus, Magna Mater to the Romans.

One of the infantoids announced something in a piping voice, and the Diana shivered to acknowledge. With a glance around, the same infantoid nodded, and all six stood up to the breasts to nurse.

Feeding over, they took positions around the cabin and examined us carefully. The leader spoke to each of us in turn, trying several languages. None matched our own. I strained to loosen the cords around my neck and jaw and asked Sonok to speak a few of the languages he knew. He did as well as he could through his bonds. The leader listened to him with interest, then echoed a few words and turned to the other five. One nodded and advanced. He spoke to the bear in what sounded like Greek. Sonok stuttered for a moment, then replied in halting fragments.

They moved to loosen the bear's cords, looking up at me apprehensively. The combination of Sonok and six children still at breast hit me deep, and I had to suppress a hysteric urge to laugh.

"I think he is saying he knows what has happened," Sonok said. "They've been prepared for it; they knew what to expect. I think that's what they say."

The leader touched palms with his Greek-speaking colleague, then spoke to Sonok in the same tongue. He held out his plump hands and motioned for the bear to do likewise. A third stepped over rows of crystallized cable to loosen Sonok's arms.

Sonok reluctantly held up his hands, and the two touched. The infantoid broke into shrill laughter and rolled on the floor. His mood returned to utmost gravity in a blink, and he stood as tall as he could, looking us over with an angry expression.

"We are in command," he said in Russian. Frobish and his wives cried out in French, complaining about their bonds. "They speak different?" the infantoid asked Sonok. The bear nodded. "Then my brothers will learn their tongues. What does the other big one speak?"

"English," Sonok said.

The infantoid sighed. "Such diversities. I will learn from her." My cords were cut, and I held out my palms. The leader's hands were cold and clammy, and his touch made my arm-hairs crawl.

"All right," he said in perfect English. "Let us tell you what's happened, and what we're going to do."

His explanation of the disruption matched mine closely. "The Alternates have done this to us." He pointed to me. "This big one calls them Aighors. We do not dignify them with a name—we're not even sure they are the same. They don't have to be, you know. Whoever has the secret of disruption, in all universes, is our enemy. We are companions now, chosen from a common pool of those who have been disrupted across a century. The choosing has been done so that our natures match closely—we are all from one planet. Do you understand this idea of being companions?"

Sonok and I nodded. The Indians offered no response.

"But we, members of the Nemi, whose mother is Noctilux, we were prepared. We will take control of the aggregate ship and pilot it to a suitable point, from which we can take a perspective and see what universe we're in. Can we expect your cooperation?"

Again the bear and I agreed, and the others were silent.

"Release them all," the infantoid said with a magnanimous sweep of his hands. "Be warned, however—we can bind you in an instant, and we are unlikely to enjoy being attacked again."

The cords went limp and vaporized with some heat and a slight sweet odor. The Diana rolled over the ramp and left the cabin, followed by the leader and another infantoid. The four remaining behind watched us closely, not nervous but intent on our every move. Where the guns had been, pools of slag lay on the floor.

"Looks like we've been overruled," I said to Frobish. He didn't seem to hear me.

In a few hours we were told where we would be allowed to go. The area extended to my cabin and the bathroom, which apparently was the only such facility in our reach. The Nemi didn't seem to need bathrooms, but their recognition of our own requirements was heartening.

Within an hour of the takeover, the infantoids had swarmed over the controls in the chamber. They brought in bits and pieces of salvaged equipment, which they altered and fitted with extraordinary speed and skill. Before our next meal, taken from stores in the hole, they understood and controlled all the machinery in the cabin.

The leader then explained that the aggregate, or "scattershot," as Sonok had called it, was still far from integrated. At least two groups had yet to be brought into the fold. These were the giant blacks in golden armor, and the beings that inhabited the transparent bubble outside the ship. We were warned that leaving the established boundaries would put us in danger.

The sleep period came. The Nemi made certain we were slumbering before they slept, if they slept at all. Sonok lay beside me on the bunk in my room, snucking faint snores and twitching over distant dreams. I stared up into the dark, thinking of the message tank. That was my hidden ace. Did it belong to one of the groups we were familiar with, or was it different, perhaps a party in itself? I wanted to see what it was capable of telling me.

I tried to bury my private thoughts—disturbing, intricate thoughts and sleep, but I couldn't. I was dead weight now, and I'd never liked the idea of being useless. Useless things tend to get thrown out. Since joining the various academies and working my way up the line, I'd always assumed I could play a key role in any system I was tossed into.

But the infantoids, though tolerant and even understanding, were self-contained. As they said, they'd been prepared, and they knew what to do. Uncertainty seemed to cheer them, or at least draw them together. Of course they were never more than a few meters away from a very impressive symbol of security—a walking breast bank.

The Nemi had their Diana, Frobish had his wives, and Sonok had me. I had no one. My mind went out, imagined blackness and fields of stars, and perhaps nowhere the worlds I knew, and quickly snapped back. My head hurt, and my back muscles were starting to cramp. I had no access to hormone stabilizers, so I was starting my period. I rolled over, nudging Sonok into grumbly half-waking, and shut my eyes and mind to everything, trying to find a peaceful glade and perhaps a good memory of Jaghit Singh. But even in sleep all I found was snow and broken gray trees.

The lights came up slowly, and I was awakened by Sonok's movements. I rubbed my eyes and rose from the bunk, standing unsteadily.

In the bathroom, Frobish and his wives were going about their morning ablutions. They looked at me but said nothing. I could feel a tension but tried to ignore it. I was irritable, and if I let any part of my feelings out, they might all pour forth—and then where would I be?

I returned to my cabin with Sonok and didn't see Frobish following until he stepped up to the hatchway and looked inside.

"We will not accept the rule of children," he said evenly. "We'll need your help to overcome them."

"Who will replace them?" I asked.

"I will. They've made adjustments to my machines which I and the Sinieux can handle."

"The Sinieux cages are welded shut," I said.

"Will you join us?"

"What could I do? I'm only a woman."

"I will fight, my wives and you will back me up. I need the rifle you took away."

"I don't have it." But he must have seen my eyes go involuntarily to the locker.

"Will you join us?" he asked.

"I'm not sure it's wise. In fact, I'm sure it isn't. You just aren't equipped to handle this kind of thing. You're too limited."

"I have endured all sorts of indignities from you. You are a sickness of the first degree. Either you will work with us, or I will cure you now." Sonok bristled, and I noticed the bear's teeth were quite sharp.

I stood and faced him. "You're not a man," I said. "You're a little boy. You haven't got hair on your chest or anything between your legs—just a bluff and a brag."

He pushed me back on the cot with one arm and squeezed up against the locker, opening it quickly. Sonok sank his teeth into the man's calf, but before I could get into action the rifle was out and his hand was on the trigger. I fended the barrel away from me and the first shot went into the corridor. It caught a Nemi and removed the top of his head. The blood and sound seemed to drive Frobish into a frenzy. He brought the butt down, trying to hammer Sonok, but the bear leaped aside and the rifle went into the bunk mattress, sending Frobish off balance. I hit his throat with the side of my hand and caved in his windpipe.

Then I took the rifle and watched him choking against the cabin wall. He was unconscious and turning blue before I gritted my teeth and relented. I took him by the neck and found his pipe with my thumbs, then pushed from both sides to flex the blockage outward.

He took a breath and slumped.

I looked at the body in the corridor. "This is it," I said quietly. "We've got to get out of here." I slung the rifle and peered around the hatch seal. The noise hadn't brought anyone yet. I motioned to Sonok, and we ran down the corridor, away from the Indian's control room and the infantoids.

"Geneva," Sonok said as we passed an armored hatch. 'Where do we go?" I heard a whirring sound and looked up. The shielded camera above the hatch moved behind its thick gray glass like an eye. "I don't know," I said.

A seal had been placed over the flexible valve in the corridor that led to the bubble. We turned at that point and went past the nook where the message tank had been. It was gone, leaving a few anonymous fixtures behind.

An armored hatch had been punched into the wall several yards beyond the alcove, and it was unsealed. That was almost too blatant an invitation, but I had few choices. They'd mined the ship like termites.

The hatch led into a straight corridor without gravitation. I took Sonok by the arm and we drifted dreamily down. Pieces of vaguely familiar equipment studded the walls, and I wondered if people from my world were around here. It was an idle speculation. The way I felt now, I doubted I could make friends with anyone. I wasn't the type to establish camaraderie under stress. I was the wintry one.

At the end of the corridor, perhaps a hundred meters down, gravitation slowly returned. The hatch there was armored and open. I brought the rifle up and looked around the seal. No one. We stepped through—and I saw the black in his golden suit, fresh as a ghost. I was surprised; he wasn't. My rifle was up and pointed, but his weapon was down. He smiled faintly.

"We are looking for a woman known as Geneva," he said. "Are you she?"

I nodded. He bowed stiffly, armor crinkling, and motioned for me to follow. The room around the corner was unlighted. A port several meters wide, ribbed with steel beams, opened onto the starry dark. The stars were moving, and I guessed the ship was rolling in space. I saw other forms in the shadows, large and bulky, some human, some not. Their breathing made them sound like predators waiting for prey.

A hand took mine, and a shadow towered over me. "This way."

Sonok clung to my calf, and I carried him with each step I took. He didn't make a sound. As I passed from the viewing room, I saw a blue-and-white curve begin at the top of the port and caught an outline of continent. Asia, perhaps. We were already near Earth. The shapes of the continents could remain the same in countless universes, immobile grounds beneath the thin and pliable paint of living things. What was life like in the distant world-lines where even the shapes of the continents had changed?

The next room was also dark, but a candle flame flickered behind curtains. The shadow that had guided me returned to the viewing room and shut the hatch. I heard the breathing of only one besides myself.

I was shaking. Would they do this to us one at a time? Yes, of course; there was too little food. Too little air. Not enough of anything on this tiny scattershot. Poor Sonok, by his attachment, would go before his proper moment.

The breathing came from a woman, somewhere to my right. I turned to face her general direction. She sighed. She sounded very old, with labored breath and a kind of pant after each intake.

I heard a slight pop of dry lips parting to speak, then the tiny *click* of eyelids blinking. The candle flame wobbled in a current of air. As my eyes adjusted, I could see that the curtains formed a translucent cubicle in the dark.

"Hello," the woman said. I answered weakly. "Is your name Francis Geneva?"

I nodded, then, in case she couldn't see me, said, "I am."

"I am Junipero," she said, aspirating the j as in Spanish. "I was commander of the High-space ship *Callimachus.* Were you a commander on your ship?"

"No," I replied. "I was part of the crew."

"What did you do?"

I told her in a spare sentence or two, pausing to cough. My throat was like parchment.

"Do you mind stepping closer? I can't see you very well."

I walked forward a few steps.

"There is not much from your ship in the way of computers or stored memory," she said. I could barely make out her face as she bent forward, squinting to examine me. "But we have learned to speak your language from those parts that accompanied the

Indian. It is not too different from a language in our past, but none of us spoke it until now. The rest of you did well. A surprising number of you could communicate, which was fortunate. And the little children who suckle—the Nemi—they always know how to get along. We've had several groups of them on our voyages."

"May I ask what you want?"

"You might not understand until I explain. I have been through the *mutata* several hundred times. You call it disruption. But we haven't found our home yet, I and my crew. The crew must keep trying, but I won't last much longer. I'm at least two thousand years old, and I can't search forever."

"Why don't the others look old?"

"My crew? They don't lead. Only the top must crumble away to keep the group flexible. Only those who lead. You'll grow old, too. But not the crew. They'll keep searching."

"What do you mean, me?"

"Do you know what 'Geneva' means, dear sister?"

I shook my head, no.

"It means the same thing as my name, Junipero. It's a tree that gives berries. The one who came before me, her name was Jenevr, and she lived twice as long as I, four thousand years. When she came, the ship was much smaller than it is now."

"And your men—the ones in armor—"

"They are part of my crew. There are women, too."

"They've been doing this for six thousand years?"

"Longer," she said. "It's much easier to be a leader and die, I think. But their wills are strong. Look in the tank, Geneva."

A light came on behind the cubicle, and I saw the message tank. The murky fluid moved with a continuous swirling flow. The old woman stepped from the cubicle and stood beside me in front of the tank. She held out her finger and wrote something on the glass, which I couldn't make out.

The tank's creatures formed two images, one of me and one of her. She was dressed in a simple brown robe, her peppery black hair cropped into short curls. She touched the glass again, and her image changed. The hair lengthened, forming a broad globe around her head. The wrinkles smoothed. The body became slimmer and more muscular, and a smile came to the lips. Then the image was stable.

Except for the hair, it was me.

I took a deep breath. "Every time you've gone through a disruption, has the ship picked up more passengers?"

"Sometimes," she said. "We always lose a few, and every now and then we gain a large number. For the last few centuries our size has been stable, but in time we'll probably start to grow. We aren't anywhere near the total yet. When that comes, we might be twice as big as we are now. Then we'll have had, at one time or another, every scrap of ship, and every person who ever went through a disruption."

"How big is the ship now?"

"Four hundred kilometers across. Built rather like a volvox, if you know what that is."

"How do you keep from going back yourself?"

"We have special equipment to keep us from separating. When we started out, we thought it would shield us from a *mutata*, but it didn't. This is all it can do for us now: it can keep us in one piece each time we jump. But not the entire ship."

I began to understand. The huge bulk of ship I had seen from the window was real. I had never left the grab bag. I was in it now, riding the aggregate, a tiny particle attracted out of solution to the colloidal mass.

Junipero touched the tank, and it returned to its random flow. "It's a constant shuttle run. Each time we return to the Earth to see who, if any, can find their home there. Then we seek out the ones who have the disrupters, and they attack us—send us away again."

"Out there—is that my world?"

The old woman shook her head. "No, but it's home to one group—three of them. The three creatures in the bubble."

I smiled. "I thought there were a lot more than that."

"Only three. You'll learn to see things more accurately as time passes. Maybe you'll be the one to bring us all home."

"What if I find my home first?"

"Then you'll go, and if there's no one to replace you, one of the crew will command until another comes along. But someone always comes along, eventually. I sometimes think we're being played with, never finding our home, but always having a Juniper to command us." She smiled wistfully. "The game isn't all bitterness and bad tosses, though. You'll see more things, and do more, and be more, than any normal woman."

"I've never been normal," I said.

"All the better."

"If I accept."

"You have that choice."

"'Junipero,'" I breathed. "Geneva." Then I laughed. "How do you choose?"

The small child, seeing the destruction of its thousand companions with each morning light and the skepticism of the older ones, becomes frightened and wonders if she will go the same way. Someone will raise the shutters and a sunbeam will impale her and she'll phantomize. Or they'll tell her they don't believe she's real. So she sits in the dark, shaking. The dark becomes fearful. But soon each day becomes a triumph. The ghosts vanish, but she doesn't, so she forgets the shadows and thinks only of the day. Then she grows older, and the companions are left only in whims and background thoughts. Soon she is whittled away to nothing; her husbands are past, her loves are firm and not potential, and her history stretches away behind her like carvings in crystal. She becomes wrinkled, and soon the daylight haunts her again. Not every day will be a triumph. Soon there will be a final beam of light, slowly piercing her jellied eye, and she'll join the phantoms.

But not now. Somewhere, far away, but not here. All around,

the ghosts have been resurrected for her to see and lead. And she'll be resurrected, too, always under the shadow of the tree name.

"I think," I said, "that it will be marvelous."

So it was, thirty centuries ago. Sonok is gone, two hundred years past; some of the others have died, too, or gone to their own Earths. The ship is five hundred kilometers across and growing. You haven't come to replace me yet, but finally, I'm dying, too, and I leave this behind to guide you, along with the instructions handed down by those before me.

Your name might be Jennifer, or Ginepra, or something else, but you will always be me. Be happy for all of us, darling. We will be forever whole.

AFTERWORD

Years later, I would bring back the *Sinieux,* the nested snakes of "Scattershot" in my novel, *Anvil of Stars,* give them a conceptual upgrade, and call them the Brothers.

PETRA

"Petra" is the most extravagant of my theological fantasies, perfect, I think, for an animated feature. Cute gargoyles come to life, as in Disney's Hunchback of Notre Dame. The sex angle is dicey even for the modern Disney, but I'd be willing to compromise a little to see a splendidly animated feature about a world in which, for whatever reason, God's laws no longer apply.

Matt Howarth did a lovely comic adaptation of "Petra" for the program book of the Philadelphia World Science Fiction convention in 2001, where I was Guest of Honor.

This was the first story I sold to Omni under the editorial surveillance of Ellen Datlow. Ben Bova, my worthy editor at Analog, and at this point in charge at Omni, was not enthusiastic, but once again I was about to benefit from an editor moving on . . .

Ben passed the reins of fiction editing to Ellen, and she bought and published "Petra." Ellen seems to like bent theology. So do I.

I strongly suspect that God has a sense of humor and doesn't mind, either.

"'God is dead, God is dead' . . . Perdition! When God dies, you'll know it."

—Confessions of St. Argentine

I'm an ugly son of stone and flesh, there's no denying it. I don't remember my mother. It's possible she abandoned me shortly after my birth. More than likely she is dead. My father—

ugly beaked, half-winged thing, if he resembles his son—I have never seen.

Why should such an unfortunate aspire to be a historian? I think I can trace the moment my choice was made. It's among my earliest memories, and it must have happened about thirty years ago, though I'm sure I lived many years before that—years now lost to me. I was squatting behind thick, dusty curtains in a vestibule, listening to a priest instructing other novitiates, all of pure flesh, about Mortdieu. His words are still vivid.

"As near as I can discover," he said, "Mortdieu occurred about seventy-seven years ago. Learned ones deny that magic was set loose on the world, but few deny that God, as such, had died."

Indeed. That's putting it mildly. All the hinges of our once-great universe fell apart, the axis tilted, cosmic doors swung shut, and the rules of existence lost their foundations.

The priest continued in measured, awed tones to describe that time. "I have heard wise men speak of the slow decline. Where human thought was strong, reality's sudden quaking was reduced to a tremor. Where thought was weak, reality disappeared completely, swallowed by chaos. Every delusion became as real as solid matter." His voice trembled with emotion. "Blinding pain, blood catching fire in our veins, bones snapping and flesh powdering. Steel flowing like liquid. Amber raining from the sky. Crowds gathering in streets that no longer followed any maps, if the maps themselves had not altered. They knew not what to do. Their weak minds could not grab hold . . ."

Most humans, I take it, were entirely too irrational to begin with. Whole nations vanished or were turned into incomprehensible whirlpools of misery and depravity. It is said that certain universities, libraries, and museums survived, but to this day we have little contact with them.

I think often of those poor victims of the early days of Mortdieu. They had known a world of some stability; we have adapted since. They were shocked by cities turning into forests, by their nightmares taking shape before their eyes. Oracular crows perched atop trees that had once been buildings, pigs ran through the streets on their hind legs . . . and so on. (The priest did not encourage contemplation of the oddities. "Excitement," he said, "breeds even more monsters.")

Our Cathedral survived. Rationality in this neighborhood, however, had weakened some centuries before Mortdieu, replaced only by a kind of rote. The Cathedral suffered. Survivors—clergy and staff, worshipers seeking sanctuary—had wretched visions, dreamed wretched dreams. They saw the stone ornaments of the Cathedral come alive.

With someone to see and believe, in a universe lacking any other foundation, my ancestors shook off stone and became flesh. Centuries of stone celibacy weighed upon them. Forty-nine nuns who had sought shelter in the Cathedral were discovered and were not entirely loath, so the coarser versions of the tale go. Mortdieu had had a surprising aphrodisiacal effect on the faithful.

Conjugation happened.

No definite gestation period has been established, for at that time the great stone wheel had not been set twisting back and forth to count the hours. Nor had anyone been given the chair of Kronos to watch over the wheel and provide a baseline for every-day activities.

But flesh did not reject stone, and there came into being the sons and daughters of flesh and stone, including me. Those who had fornicated with the inhuman figures were cast out to raise or reject their monstrous young in the highest hidden recesses. Those who had accepted the embraces of the stone saints and other human figures were less abused but still banished to the upper reaches. A wooden scaffolding was erected, dividing the great nave into two levels. A canvas drop cloth was fastened over the scaffold to prevent offal raining down, and on the second level of the Cathedral the more human offspring of stone and flesh set about creating a new life.

I have long tried to find out how some semblance of order came to the world. Legend has it that it was the archexistentialist Jansard, crucifier of the beloved St. Argentine, who, realizing and repenting his error, discovered that mind and thought could calm the foaming sea of reality.

The priest finished his all-too-sketchy lecture by touching on this point briefly: "With the passing of God's watchful gaze, humanity had to reach out and grab hold the unraveling fabric of the world. Those left alive—those who had the wits to keep their bodies from falling apart—became the only cohesive force in the chaos."

I had picked up enough language to understand what he said; my memory was good—still is—and I was curious enough to want to know more.

Creeping along stone walls behind the curtains, I listened to other priests and nuns intoning scripture to gaggles of flesh children. That was on the ground floor and I was in great danger, people of pure flesh looking on my kind as abominations.

But it was worth it.

I was able to steal a Psalter and learned to read. I stole more books; they defined my world by allowing me to compare it with others. At first I couldn't believe the others had ever existed; only the Cathedral was real. I still have my doubts. I can look out a tiny round window on one side of my room and see the great forest and river that surround the Cathedral, but I can see nothing else. So my experience with other worlds is far from direct.

No matter. I read a great deal but I'm no scholar. What concerns me is recent history—the final focus of that germinal hour listening to the priest. From the metaphysical to the acutely personal.

I am small, barely three English feet in height, but I can run quickly through most of the hidden passageways. This lets me observe without attracting attention.

I may be the only real historian in this whole structure. Others who claim the role disregard what's before their eyes, in search of ultimate truths, or at least Big Pictures.

So if you prefer history where the historian is not involved, look elsewhere. Objective as I try to be, I do have my favorite subjects.

In the time when my history begins, the children of stone and flesh were still searching for the Stone Christ. Those of us born of the union of the stone saints and gargoyles with the bereaved nuns thought our salvation lay in the great stone celibate, who had come to life along with all the other statues.

Of smaller import were the secret assignations between the bishop's daughter and a young man of stone and flesh. Such assignations were forbidden even between those of pure flesh; and as these two lovers were unmarried, their compound sin intrigued me.

Her name was Constantia, and she was fourteen, slender of limb, brown of hair, mature of bosom. Her eyes carried the stupid sort of divine life common in girls that age. His name was Corvus, and he was fifteen. I don't recall his precise features, but he was handsome enough and dexterous: he could climb through the scaffolding almost as quickly as I. I first spied them talking when I made one of my frequent raids on the repository to steal another book. They were in shadow, but my eyes are keen. They spoke softly, hesitantly. My heart ached to see them and to think of their tragedy, for I knew right away that Corvus was not pure flesh and that Constantia was the daughter of the bishop himself. I envisioned the old tyrant meting out the usual punishment to Corvus for such breaches of level and morality—castration. But in their talk was a sweetness that almost masked the closed-in stench of the lower nave.

"Have you ever kissed a man before?"

"Yes."

"Who?"

"My brother." She laughed.

"And?" His voice was sharper; he might kill her brother, he seemed to say.

"A friend named Jules."

"Where is he?"

"Oh, he vanished on a wood-gathering expedition."

"Oh." And Corvus kissed her again.

I'm a historian, not a voyeur, so I discreetly hide the flowering of their passion. If Corvus had had any sense, he would have reveled in his conquest and never returned. But he was snared and continued to see her despite the risk. This was loyalty, love, faithfulness, and it was rare. It fascinated me.

I have just been taking in sun, a nice day, and looking out over the buttresses.

The Cathedral is like a low-bellied lizard, the nave its belly, the buttresses its legs. There are little houses at the base of each buttress, where rainspouters with dragon faces used to lean out over the trees (or city or whatever was down below once). Now people live there. It wasn't always that way—the sun was once forbidden. Corvus and Constantia from childhood were denied its light, and so even in their youthful prime they were pale and dirty with the smoke of candles and tallow lamps. The most sun anyone received in those days was obtained on wood-gathering expeditions.

After spying on one of the clandestine meetings of the young lovers, I mused in a dark corner for an hour, then went to see the copper giant Apostle Thomas. He was the only human form to live so high in the Cathedral. He carried a ruler on which was engraved his real name—he had been modeled after the Cathedral's restorer in times past, the architect Viollet-le-Duc. He knew the Cathedral better than anyone, and I admired him greatly. Most of the monsters left him alone—out of fear, if nothing else. He was huge, black as night, but flaked with pale green, his face creased in eternal thought. He was sitting in his usual wooden compartment near the base of the spire, not twenty feet from where I write now, thinking about times none of the rest of us ever knew: of joy and past love, some say; others say of the burden that rested on him now that the Cathedral was the center of this chaotic world.

It was the giant who selected me from the ugly hordes when he saw me with a Psalter. He encouraged me in my efforts to read. "Your eyes are bright," he told me. "You move as if your brain were quick, and you keep yourself dry and clean. You aren't hollow like the rainspouters—you have substance. For all our sakes, put it to use and learn the ways of the Cathedral."

And so I did.

He looked up as I came in. I sat on a box near his feet and said, "A daughter of flesh is seeing a son of stone and flesh."

He shrugged his massive shoulders. "So it shall be, in time."

"Is it not a sin?"

"It is something so monstrous it is past sin and become necessity," he said. "It will happen more as time passes."

"They're in love, I think, or will be."

He nodded. "I—and One Other—were the only ones to abstain from fornication on the night of Mortdieu," he said. "I am—except for the Other—alone fit to judge."

I waited for him to judge, but he sighed and patted me on the shoulder. "And I never judge, do I, ugly friend?"

"Never," I said.

"So leave me alone to be sad." He winked. "And more power to them."

The bishop of the Cathedral was an old, old man. It was said he hadn't been bishop before the Mortdieu, but a wanderer who came in during the chaos, before the forest had replaced the city. He had set himself up as titular head of this section of God's former domain by saying it had been willed to him.

He was short, stout, with huge hairy arms like the clamps of a vise. He had once killed a spouter with a single squeeze of his fist, and spouters are tough things, since they have no guts like you (I suppose) and I. The hair surrounding his bald pate was white, thick, and unruly, and his eyebrows leaned over his nose with marvelous flexibility. He rutted like a pig, ate hugely, and shat liquidly (I know all). A man for this time, if ever there was one.

It was his decree that all those not pure of flesh be banned and that those not of human form be killed on sight.

When I returned from the giant's chamber, I saw that the lower nave was in an uproar. They had seen someone clambering about in the scaffold, and troops had been sent to shoot him down. Of course it was Corvus. I was a quicker climber than he and knew the beams better, so when he found himself trapped in an apparent cul-de-sac, it was I who gestured from the shadows and pointed to a hole large enough for him to escape through. He took it without a breath of thanks, but etiquette has never been important to me. I entered the stone wall through a nook a spare hand's width across and wormed my way to the bottom to see what else was happening. Excitement was rare.

A rumor was passing that the figure had been seen with a young girl, but the crowds didn't know who the girl was. The men and women who mingled in the smoky light, between the rows of open-roofed hovels, chattered gaily. Castrations and executions were among the few joys for us then; I relished them too, but I had a stake in the potential victims now and I worried.

My worry and my interest got the better of me. I slid through an unrepaired gap and fell to one side of the alley between the outer wall and the hovels. A group of dirty adolescents spotted me. "There he is!" they screeched. "He didn't get away!"

The bishop's masked troops can travel freely on all levels. I was almost cornered by them, and when I tried one escape route, they waited at a crucial spot in the stairs—which I had to cross to complete the next leg—and I was forced back. I prided myself in knowing the Cathedral top to bottom, but as I scrambled madly, I came upon a tunnel I had never noticed before. It led deep into a broad stone foundation wall. I was safe for the moment but afraid that they might find my caches of food and poison my casks of rainwater. Still, there was nothing I could do until they had gone, so I decided to spend the anxious hours exploring the tunnel.

The Cathedral is a constant surprise; I realize now I didn't know half of what it offered. There are always new ways to get from here to there (some, I suspect, created while no one is looking)—and sometimes even new theres to be discovered. While troops snuffled about the hole above, near the stairs—where only a child of two or three could have entered—I followed a flight of crude steps deep into the stone. Water and slime made the passage slippery and difficult. For a moment I was in darkness deeper than any I had experienced before—a gloom more profound than mere lack of light could explain. Then below I saw a faint yellow gleam. More cautious, I slowed and progressed silently. Behind a rusting, scabrous metal gate, I set foot into a lighted room. There was the smell of crumbling stone, a tang of mineral water, slime—and the stench of a dead spouter. The beast lay on the floor of the narrow chamber, several months gone but still fragrant.

I have mentioned that spouters are very hard to kill—and this one had been murdered. Three candles stood freshly placed in nooks around the chamber, flickering in a faint draft from above. Despite my fears, I walked across the stone floor, took a candle, and peered into the next section of tunnel.

It sloped down for several dozen feet, ending at another metal gate. It was here that I detected an odor I had never before encountered—the smell of the purest of stones, as of rare jade or virgin marble. Such a feeling of lightheadedness passed over me that I almost laughed, but I was too cautious for that. I pushed aside the gate and was greeted by a rush of the coldest, sweetest air, like a draft from the tomb of a saint whose body does not corrupt but rather draws corruption away and expels it miraculously into the nether pits. My beak dropped open. The candlelight fell across the darkness onto a figure I at first thought to be an infant. But I quickly disagreed with myself. The figure was several ages at once. As I blinked, it became a man of about thirty, well formed, with a high forehead and elegant hands, pale as ice. His eyes stared at the wall behind me. I bowed down on scaled knee and touched my forehead as best I could to the cold stone, shivering to my vestigial wing-tips. "Forgive me, Joy of Man's Desiring," I said. "Forgive me." I had stumbled upon the hiding place of the Stone Christ.

"You are forgiven," He said wearily. "You had to come sooner or later. Better now than later, when . . ." His voice trailed away and He shook His head. He was very thin, wrapped in a gray robe that still bore the scars of centuries of weathering. "Why did you come?"

"To escape the bishop's troops," I said.

He nodded. "Yes. The bishop. How long have I been here?"

"Since before I was born, Lord. Sixty or seventy years." He was thin, almost ethereal, this figure I had imagined as a husky carpenter. I lowered my voice and beseeched, "What may I do for you, Lord?"

"Go away," He said.

"I could not live with such a secret," I said. "You are salvation. You can overthrow the bishop and bring all the levels together."

"I am not a general or a soldier. Please go away and tell no—"

I felt a breath behind me, then the whisper of a weapon. I leaped aside, and my hackles rose as a stone sword came down and shattered on the floor beside me. The Christ raised His hand. Still in shock, I stared at a beast much like myself. It stared back, face black with rage, stayed by the power of His hand. I should have been more wary—something had to have killed the spouter and kept the candles fresh.

"But, Lord," the beast rumbled, "he will tell all."

"No," the Christ said. "He'll tell nobody." He looked half at me, half through me, and said, "Go, go."

Up the tunnels, into the orange dark of the Cathedral, crying, I crawled and slithered. I could not even go to the giant. I had been silenced as effectively as if my throat had been cut.

The next morning I watched from a shadowy corner of the scaffold as a crowd gathered around a lone man in a dirty sackcloth robe. I had seen him before—his name was Psalo, and he was left alone as an example of the bishop's largess. It was a token gesture; most of the people regarded him as barely half-sane.

Yet this time I listened and, in my confusion, found his words striking responsive chords in me. He was exhorting the bishop and his forces to allow light into the Cathedral again by dropping the canvas tarps that covered the windows. He had talked about this before, and the bishop had responded with his usual statement— that with the light would come more chaos, for the human mind was now a pesthole of delusions. Any stimulus would drive away whatever security the inhabitants of the Cathedral had.

At this time it gave me no pleasure to watch the love of Constantia and Corvus grow. They were becoming more careless. Their talk grew bolder:

"We shall announce a marriage," Corvus said.

"They will never allow it. They'll . . . cut you."

"I'm nimble. They'll never catch me. The church needs leaders, brave revolutionaries. If no one breaks with tradition, everyone will suffer."

"I fear for your life—and mine. My father would push me from the flock like a diseased lamb."

"Your father is no shepherd."

"He is my father," Constantia said, eyes wide, mouth drawn tight.

I sat with beak in paws, eyes half-lidded, able to mimic each statement before it was uttered. Undying love . . . hope for a bleak future . . . shite and onions! I had read it all before, in a cache of romance novels in the trash of a dead nun. As soon as I made the connection and realized the timeless banality, and the futility, of what I was seeing, and when I compared their prattle with the infinite sadness of the Stone Christ, I went from innocent to cynic. The transition dizzied me, leaving little backwaters of noble emotion, but the future seemed clear. Corvus would be caught and executed; if it hadn't been for me, he would already have been gelded, if not killed. Constantia would weep, poison herself; the singers would sing of it (those selfsame warble-throats who cheered the death of her lover); perhaps I would write of it (I was planning this chronicle even then), and afterward, perhaps, I would follow them both, having succumbed to the sin of boredom.

With night, things always become less certain. It is easy to stare at a dark wall and let dreams become manifest. At one time, I've deduced from books, dreams could not take shape beyond sleep or brief fantasy. All too often I've had to fight things generated in my dreams, flowing from the walls, suddenly independent and hungry. People often die in the night, devoured by their own nightmares.

That evening, falling to sleep with visions of the Stone Christ in my head, I dreamed of holy men, angels, and saints. I came awake abruptly, by training, and saw that one had stayed behind. The last of the others flitted outside the round window, whispering and making plans to fly off to heaven. The wraith that had lingered assumed a dark, vague shape in one corner. His breath came new to him, raw and harsh.

"I am Peter," he said, "also called Simon. I am the Rock of the Church, and popes are told that they are heir to my task."

"I'm rock, too," I said. "At least, part of me is."

"So be it, then. You are heir to my task. Go forth and be Pope. Do not revere the Stone Christ, for a Christ is only as good as He does, and if He does nothing, there is no salvation in Him."

The shadow reached out to pat my head. I saw his eyes grow wide as he made out my form. He muttered some formula for banishing devils and oozed out the window to join his fellows.

I imagined that if such a thing were actually brought before the council, it would be decided under the law that the command of a dream saint is not binding. I did not care. The wraith had given me better orders than any I'd had since the giant told me to read and learn.

But to be Pope, one must have a hierarchy of servants to carry out one's plans. The biggest of rocks does not move by itself. So it was that, swollen with power, I decided to appear in the upper nave and announce myself to the people.

It took a great deal of courage to show myself in broad daylight, without my cloak, and to walk across the scaffold's surface, on the second level, through crowds of vendors setting up the market for the day. Some saw me and reacted with typical bigotry. They kicked and cursed at me. My beak was swift and discouraged them.

I clambered to the top of a prominent stall and stood in the murky glow of a small lamp, rising to my full height and clearing my throat, making ready to give my commands. Under a hail of rotten pomegranates and limp vegetables, I told the throng who I was. I boldly told them about my vision. I tried to make myself speak clearly, starting over from the beginning several times, but the deluge of opprobrium was too thick. Jeweled with beads of offal, I jumped down and fled to a tunnel entrance too small for most men. Some boys followed, ready to do me real harm, and one lost his finger while trying to slice me with a fragment of colored glass.

I recognized, almost too late, that the tactic of open revelation was worthless. There are rungs on the high ladder of fear and bigotry, and I was at the very bottom.

My next strategy was to find some way to disrupt the Cathedral from top to bottom. Even bigots, when reduced to a mob, could be swayed by the presence of one obviously ordained and capable. I spent two days skulking through the walls. There had to be a basic flaw in so fragile a structure as the church, and, while I wasn't contemplating total destruction, I wanted something spectacular, something unavoidable.

While I cogitated, hanging from the bottom of the second scaffold, above the community of pure flesh, the bishop's deep gravelly voice roared over the noise of the crowd. I opened my eyes and looked down. The masked troops were holding a bowed figure, and the bishop was intoning over its head, "Know all who hear me now, this young bastard of flesh and stone—"

Corvus, I told myself. Finally caught. I shut one eye, but the other refused to close out the scene.

"—has violated all we hold sacred and shall atone for his crimes on this spot, tomorrow at this time. Kronos! Mark the wheel's progress."

The elected Kronos, a spindly old man with dirty gray hair down to his buttocks, took a piece of charcoal and marked an X on the huge bulkhead chart, behind which the wheel groaned and sighed in its circuit.

The crowd was enthusiastic. I saw Psalo pushing through the people.

"What crime?" he called out. "Name the crime!"

"Violation of the lower level!" the head of the masked troops declared.

"That merits a whipping and an escort upstairs," Psalo said. "I detect a more sinister crime here. What is it?"

The bishop looked Psalo down coldly. "He tried to rape my daughter, Constantia."

Psalo could say nothing to that. The penalty must be castration and death. All the pure humans accepted such laws.

No other recourse.

I mused, watching Corvus being led to the dungeons. The future that I desired at that moment startled me with its clarity. I wanted that part of my heritage that had been denied to me—to be at peace with myself, to be surrounded by those who accepted me, by those no better than I. In time that would happen, as the giant had said. But would I ever see it? What Corvus, in his own lusty way, was trying to do was equalize the levels, to bring stone into flesh until no one could define the divisions.

Well, my plans beyond that point were very hazy. They were less plans than glowing feelings, imaginings of happiness and children playing in the forest and fields beyond the island as the world knit itself under the gaze of God's heir. My children, playing in the forest.

A touch of truth came to me at this moment.

I had wished to be Corvus when he tupped Constantia.

So I had two tasks, then, that could be merged if I was clever. I had to distract the bishop and his troops, and I had to rescue Corvus, fellow revolutionary.

I spent that night in feverish misery in my room. At dawn I went to the giant and asked his advice. He looked me over with his stern, black visage and said, "We waste our time if we try to knock sense into their heads. But we have no better calling than to waste our time, do we?"

"What shall I do?"

"Enlighten them."

I stomped my claw on the floor. "They are bricks! Try enlightening bricks!"

He smiled his sad, narrow smile. "*Enlighten* them," he said.

I left the giant's chamber in a rage. I did not have access to the great wheel's board of time, so I couldn't know exactly when the execution would take place. But I guessed—from memories of a grumbling stomach—that it would be in the early afternoon. I traveled from one end of the nave to the other and, likewise, the transept. I nearly exhausted myself.

Then, traversing an empty aisle, I picked up a piece of colored glass and examined it, puzzled. Many of the boys on all levels carried these shards with them, and the girls used them as jewelry—against the wishes of their elders, who held that bright objects bred more beasts in the mind.

Where did they get them?

In one of the books I had perused years before, I had seen brightly colored pictures of the Cathedral windows.

"*Enlighten* them," the giant had said.

Psalo's request to let light into the Cathedral came to mind.

Along the peak of the nave, in a tunnel running its length, I found the ties that held the pulleys of the canvases over the windows. The best windows, I decided, would be the huge ones of the north and south transepts. I made a diagram in the dust, trying to decide what season it was and from which direction the sunlight would come—pure theory to me, but at this moment I was in a fever of brilliance. All the windows had to be clear. I could not decide which was best.

I was ready by early afternoon, just after sext prayers in the upper nave. I had cut the major ropes and weakened the clamps by prying them from the walls with a pick stolen from the bishop's armory. I walked along a high ledge, took an almost vertical shaft through the wall to the lower floor, and waited.

Constantia watched from a wooden balcony, the bishop's special box for executions. She had a terrified, fascinated look on her face. Corvus was on the dais across the nave, right in the center of the cross of the transept. Torches illumined him and his executioners, three men and an old woman.

I knew the procedure. The old woman would castrate him first, then the men would remove his head. He was dressed in the condemned red robe to hide any blood. Blood excitement among the impressionable was the last thing the bishop wanted. Troops waited around the dais to purify the area with scented water.

I didn't have much time. It would take minutes for the system of ropes and pulleys to clear and the canvases to fall. I went to my station and severed the remaining ties. Then, as the Cathedral filled with a hollow creaking sound, I followed the shaft back to my viewing post.

The executioners honed their blades on stone wheels.

Corvus strained at his ropes, grunting with his fear.

In minutes the canvases were drooping.

Corvus look up, past all fear, eyes glazed.

The bishop sat beside his daughter in the box. With a sudden shout, he pulled her back into the shadows.

In another two minutes the canvases fell onto the upper scaffold with a hideous crash. Their weight was too great for the ends of the structure, and it collapsed, allowing the canvas to cascade to the floor many yards below.

At first the illumination was dim and bluish, filtered perhaps by a passing cloud. Then, from one end of the Cathedral to the other, a burst of light threw my smoky world into clarity. The glory of thousands of pieces of colored glass, hidden for decades and hardly touched by childish vandals, fell upon upper and lower levels at once. A cry from the crowds nearly wrenched me from my post. I slid quickly to the lower level and hid, afraid of what I had done. This was more than simple sunlight. Like the blossoming of two flowers, one brighter than the other, the transept windows astounded all who beheld them.

Eyes accustomed to orangey dark, to smoke and haze and shadow, cannot stare into such glory without drastic effect. I shielded my own face and tried to find a convenient exit.

But the population was increasing. As the light brightened and more faces rose to be locked, like flowers seeking the sun, the splendor unhinged some people. From their minds poured contents too wondrous to be cataloged.

The monsters thus released were not violent, however, and most of the visions were not monstrous. The upper and lower nave shimmered with reflected glories—with dream figures and children clothed in baubles of light. Saints and prodigies dominated. A thousand newly created youngsters squatted on the bright floor and began to tell of marvels, of cities in the East, and times as they had once been. Clowns dressed in fire entertained from the tops of the market stalls. Animals unknown to the Cathedral cavorted between the dwellings, giving friendly advice. Abstract things, glowing balls in nets of gold and ribbons of silk, sang and floated around the upper reaches. The Cathedral became a great vessel filled to overflowing with all the bright dreams hidden inside its citizens.

Slowly, from the lower nave, people of pure flesh climbed to the scaffold and walked the upper nave to see what they couldn't from below. From my hideaway I watched the masked troops of the bishop carrying his litter up narrow stairs. Constantia walked behind, stumbling, her eyes shut in the new brightness.

All the numbly faithful tried to cover their eyes, but none for long succeeded.

I wept. Almost blind with tears, I made my way still higher and looked down on the roiling crowds. I saw Corvus, his hands still wrapped in restraining ropes, being led by the old woman.

Constantia saw him, too, and they regarded each other like strangers, then joined hands as best they could. She borrowed a knife from one of her father's soldiers and cut his ropes away. Around them the brightest dreams of all began to swirl, pure white and blood-red and sea-green, coalescing into visions of all the children they would innocently have.

I gave them a few hours to regain their senses—and to regain my own. Then I stood on the bishop's abandoned podium and shouted over the heads of those on the lowest level.

"The time has come!" I cried. "We must all unite now; we must unite—"

At first they ignored me. I was quite eloquent, but their excitement was still too great. So I waited some more before speaking again, and was shouted down. Bits of fruit and vegetables flew up to again bejewel my rough skin.

"Freak!" they screamed, and drove me away.

I crept along the stone stairs, found the narrow crack, and hid in it, burying my beak in my paws, wondering what had gone wrong. It took a surprisingly long time for me to realize that, in my case, it was less the stigma of stone than the ugliness of my shape that doomed my quest for leadership.

I had, however, paved the way for the Stone Christ. He will surely take His place now, I told myself. So I maneuvered along the crevice until I came to the hidden chamber and the yellow glow. All was quiet within. I met first the monster, who looked me over suspiciously with glazed gray eyes. "You're back," he said. Overcome by his wit, I leered, nodded, and asked that I be presented to the Christ.

"He's sleeping."

"Important tidings," I said.

"What?"

"I bring glad tidings."

"Then let me hear them."

"His ears only."

Out of the gloomy corner came the Christ, looking much older now. "What is it?" He asked.

"I have prepared the way for You," I said. "Simon called Peter told me I was the heir to his legacy, that I should go before You—"

The Stone Christ shook His head. "You believe I am the fount from which all blessings flow?"

I nodded, uncertain.

"What have you done out there?"

"Let in the light," I said.

He shook His head. "You seem a wise enough creature. You know about Mortdieu."

"Yes."

"Then you should know that I barely have enough power to keep myself together, to heal myself, much less to minister to those out there." He gestured beyond the walls. "My own source has gone away," He said mournfully. "I'm operating on reserves, and those none too vast."

"He wants you to go away and stop bothering us," the monster explained.

"They have their light out there," the Christ said. "They'll play with that for a while, get tired of it, go back to what they had before. Is there any place for you in that?"

I thought for a moment, then shook my head. "No place," I said. "I'm too ugly."

"You *are* too ugly, and I am too famous," He said. "I'd have to come from their midst, anonymous, and that is clearly impossible. No, leave them alone for a while. They'll make me over again, perhaps, or better still, forget about me. About us. We don't have any place there."

I was stunned. I sat down hard on the stone floor, and the Christ patted me on my head as He walked by. "Go back to your hiding place; live as well as you can," He said. "Our time is over."

I turned to go. When I reached the crevice, I heard His voice behind, saying, "Do you play bridge? If you do, find another. We need four to a table."

I clambered up the crack, through the walls, and along the arches over the revelry. Not only was I not going to be Pope—after an appointment by Saint Peter himself!—but I couldn't convince someone much more qualified than I to assume the leadership.

It is the sign of the eternal student, I suppose, that when his wits fail him, he returns to the teacher. I returned to the copper giant. He was lost in meditation. About his feet were scattered scraps of paper with detailed drawings of parts of the Cathedral. I waited patiently until he saw me.

He turned, chin in hand, and looked me over. "Why so sad?"

I shook my head. Only he could read my features and recognize my moods.

"Did you take my advice below? I heard a commotion."

"*Mea maxima culpa,*" I said.

"And . . . ?"

I hesitantly made my report, concluding with the refusal of the Stone Christ. The giant listened closely without interrupting. When I was done, he stood, towering over me, and pointed with his ruler through an open portal.

"Do you see that out there?" he asked. The ruler swept over the forests beyond the island, to the far green horizon. I replied that I did and waited for him to continue. He seemed to be lost in thought again.

"Once there was a city where trees now grow," he said. "Artists came by the thousands, and whores, and philosophers, and academics. And when God died, all the academics and whores and artists couldn't hold the fabric of the world together. How do you expect us to succeed now?"

Us? "Expectations should not determine whether one acts or not," I said. "Should they?"

The giant laughed and tapped my head with the ruler. "Maybe we've been given a sign, and we just have to learn how to interpret it correctly."

I leered to show I was puzzled.

"Maybe Mortdieu is really a sign that we have been weaned. We must forage for ourselves, remake the world without help. What do you think of that?"

I was too tired to judge the merits of what he was saying, but I had never known the giant to be wrong before. "Okay. I grant that. So?"

"The Stone Christ tells us His power, his *charge* is running low. The breast of Mary is no longer full, the light of God has been replaced with a different light. If God weans us from the old ways, we can't expect His Son to replace the nipple, can we?"

"No . . ."

He hunkered next to me, his face bright. "I wondered who would really stand forth. It's obvious He won't. So, little one, who's the next choice?"

"Me?" I asked, meekly. The giant looked me over almost pityingly.

"No," he said after a time. "I am the next. We're *weaned!*" He did a little dance, startling my beak up out of my paws. I blinked. He grabbed my vestigial wing-tips and pulled me upright. "Stand straight. Tell me more."

"About what?"

"Tell me all that's going on below, and whatever else you know."

"I'm trying to understand what you're saying," I protested, trembling.

"Dense as stone!" Grinning, he bent over me. Then the grin went away, and he tried to look stern. "It's a grave responsibility. We must remake the world ourselves now. We must coordinate our thoughts, our dreams. Chaos won't do. What an opportunity, to be the architect of an entire universe!" He waved the ruler at the ceiling. "To build the very skies! The last world was a training ground, full of harsh rules and strictures. Now we've been told we're ready to leave that behind and move on to something more mature. Have I taught you any of the rules of architecture? I mean, the aesthetics. The need for harmony, interaction, utility, beauty?"

"Some," I said.

"Good. I don't think shaping the universe anew will require any better rules. No doubt we'll need to experiment, and perhaps one or more of our great spires will topple. But now we work for ourselves, to our own glory, and to the greater glory of the God who made us! No, ugly friend?"

Like many histories, mine must begin with the small, the tightly focused, and expand into the large. But unlike most historians, I don't have the luxury of time. Indeed, my story is far from finished.

Soon our legions—we, the pupils of Viollet-le-Duc—will begin our campaigns. Kidnapped from below, brought up in the heights, taught as I was—most of the children of stone and flesh have been schooled pretty thoroughly.

We'll soon begin returning them, one by one, to the lower levels of the Catherdral, to the forest—to the far horizons.

I teach off and on, write off and on, observe all the time. The next step will be the biggest. I haven't any idea how we're going to do it.

But, as the giant puts it, "Long ago the roof fell in. Now we must push it up again, strengthen it, repair the beams." At this point he smiles to our pupils. "Not just repair them. Not just restore them. *Replace* them! Now *we* are the beams. Flesh and stone have united into a substance so much stronger."

Ah, but then some dolt will raise a hand and inquire, "What if our arms get tired, holding up the sky?"

Our task, I think, will never end.

MANDALA

In the mid-seventies, I was beginning to place stories in a number of fine markets, and had already produced one novel, Hegira, *which was making the rounds of New York publishers. It would be published by Dell in 1979.*

When I sold to Analog *and* Galaxy *and* The Magazine of Fantasy and Science Fiction, *I was very pleased; I had been submitting to these magazines for almost a decade. When I started selling to Terry Carr and Robert Silverberg, I had the feeling I was truly on my way. Hardcover original anthologies were in their prime!*

Due to backlog at Silverberg's New Dimensions, *"Mandala" took several years to get published. I almost immediately added two more stories and sold the book-sized manuscript as* Strength of Stones *to Ace.*

"Mandala" still stands up well on its own. It's a story of not truly belonging to a society one loves, for reasons that nobody will ever quite understand.

The final decade of Earth's twentieth century was cataclysmic. Moslem states fought horrible wars in 1995, 1996, and 1998, devastating much of Africa and the Middle East. In less than five years, the steady growth of Islam during the latter half of the century became a rout of terror and apostasy, one of the worst religious convulsions in human history.

Christian splinter cults around the world engaged in every imaginable form of social disobedience to hasten the long-overdue

Millennium, but there was no Second Coming. Their indiscretions rubbed off on all Christians.

As for the Jews—the world had never needed any reason to hate Jews.

The far-flung children of Abraham had their decade of unbridled fervor, and they paid for it. Marginally united by a world turning to other religions, and against them, Jews, Christians, and Moslems desperately harked back to ages past to find common ground, and ratified the Pact of God in 2020.

Having spoiled their holy lands, there was no place on Earth where they could live together. And so, in the last years of the twenty-first century, they looked outward. The Heaven Migration began in 2113. After decades more persecution and ridicule, the faithful pooled their resources to buy a world of their own. That world was renamed God-Does-Battle, and it was tamed by the wealth of the heirs of Christ, Rome, Abraham and OPEC.

They hired the greatest human architect to build their new cities for them. He tried to mediate between what they demanded, and what would work best for them.

He failed.

The city that had occupied Mesa Canaan now marched across the plain toward Arat. Jeshua watched with binoculars from the cover of the jungle. The city had disassembled just before dawn, walking on elephantine legs, tractor treads, and wheels, with living bulkheads upright, dismantled buttresses given new instructions to crawl instead of support; floors and ceilings, transports and smaller city parts, factories and resource centers, all unrecognizable now, like a slime mold soon to gather itself in its new country.

The city carried its plan deep within the living plasm of its fragmented body. Every piece knew its place, and within that scheme there was no room for Jeshua, or for any man. The living cities had cast them all out a thousand years before.

He lay with his back against a tree, binoculars in one hand and an orange in the other, sucking thoughtfully on a bitter piece of rind. No matter how far back he probed, the first thing he remembered was watching a city break into a tide of parts and migrating. He had been three years old, two by the seasons of God-Does-Battle, sitting on his father's shoulders as they came to the village of Bethel-Japhet to live. Jeshua—ironically named, for he would always be chaste—remembered nothing of importance before coming to Bethel-Japhet. Perhaps it had all been erased by the shock of falling into the campfire a month before reaching the village. His body still carried the marks: a circle of scars on his chest, black with the tiny remnants of cinders.

Jeshua was huge, seven feet tall flat on his feet. His arms were as thick as an ordinary man's legs, and when he inhaled, his chest swelled as big as a barrel. He was a smith in the village, a worker of iron and caster of bronze and silver. But his strong hands had also acquired delicate skills to craft ritual and family jewelry. For his trade he had been given the surname Tubal—Jeshua Tubal Iben Daod, craftsman of all metals.

The city on the plain moved with faultless deliberation. Cities seldom migrated more than a hundred miles at a time or more than once in a hundred years, so the legends went; but they seemed more restless now.

He scratched his back against the trunk, then put his binoculars in a pants pocket. His feet slipped into the sandals he'd dropped on the mossy jungle floor, and he stood, stretching. He sensed someone behind him but did not turn to look, though his neck muscles knotted tight.

"Jeshua." It was the chief of the guard and the council of laws, Sam Daniel the Catholic. His father and Sam Daniel had been friends before his father disappeared. "Time for the Synedrium to convene."

Jeshua tightened the straps on his sandals and followed.

Bethel-Japhet was a village of moderate size, with about two thousand people. Its houses and buildings laced through the jungle until no distinct borders remained. The stone roadway to the Synedrium Hall seemed too short to Jeshua, and the crowd within the hearing chamber was far too large. His betrothed, Kisa, daughter of Jake, was not there, but his challenger, Renold Mosha Iben Yitshok, was.

The representative of the seventy judges, the Septuagint, called the gathering to order and asked that the details of the case be presented.

"Son of David," Renold said, "I have come to contest your betrothal to Kisa, daughter of Jake."

"I hear," Jeshua said, taking his seat in the defendant's docket.

"I have reasons for my challenge. Will you hear them?"

Jeshua didn't answer.

"Pardon my persistence. It is the law. I don't dislike you—I remember our childhood, when we played together—but now we are mature, and the time has come."

"Then speak." Jeshua fingered his thick dark beard. His flushed skin was the color of the fine sandy dirt on the riverbanks of the Hebron. He towered a good foot above Renold, who was slight and graceful.

"Jeshua Tubal Iben Daod, you were born like other men but did not grow as we have. You now look like a man, but the Synedrium has records of your development. You cannot consummate a marriage. You cannot give a child to Kisa. This annuls your childhood betrothal. By law and by my wish I am bound to replace you, to fulfill your obligation to her."

Kisa would never know. No one here would tell her. She would come in time to accept and love Renold, and to think of Jeshua as only another man in the Expolis Ibreem and its twelve villages, a man who stayed alone and unmarried. Her slender warm body with skin smooth as the finest cotton would soon dance beneath the man he saw before him. She would clutch Renold's back and dream of the time when humans would again be welcomed into the cities, when the skies would again be filled with ships and God-Does-Battle would be redeemed—

"I cannot answer, Renold Mosha Iben Yitshok."

"Then you will sign this." Renold held out a piece of paper and advanced.

"There was no need for a public witnessing," Jeshua said. "Why did the Synedrium decide my shame was to be public?" He looked around with tears in his eyes. Never before, even in the greatest physical pain, had he cried; not even, so his father said, when he had fallen into the fire.

He moaned. It was a deep and frightening sound. Renold stepped back and looked up in fear and anguish. "I'm sorry, Jeshua. Please sign. If you love either Kisa or myself, or the expolis, sign."

Jeshua's huge chest forced out a roar. Renold turned and ran. Jeshua slammed his fist onto the railing, struck himself on the forehead, and tore out the seams of his shirt. He had had too much. For nine years he had known of his inability to be a whole man, but he had hoped that would change, that his genitals would develop like some tardy flower just beyond normal season, and they had. But not enough. His testicles were fully developed, enough to give him a hairy body, broad shoulders, flat stomach, narrow hips, and all the desires of any young man—but his penis was the small, pink dangle of a child.

Now he exploded. He ran after Renold, out of the hall, bellowing incoherently and swinging his binoculars at the end of their leather strap. Renold ran into the village square and screeched a warning. Children and fowl scattered. Women grabbed up their skirts and fled for their wood and brick homes.

Jeshua stopped. He flung his binoculars as high as he could above his head. They cleared the top of the tallest tree in the area and fell a hundred feet beyond. Still bellowing, he charged a house and put his hands against the wall. He braced his feet and heaved. He slammed his shoulder against it. It would not move. More furious still, he turned to a trough of fresh water, picked it up, and dumped it over his head. The cold did not slow him. He threw the trough against the wall and splintered it.

"Enough!" cried the chief of the guard. Jeshua stopped and blinked at Sam Daniel the Catholic, then wobbled, weak with exertion. Something in his stomach hurt.

"Enough, Jeshua," Sam Daniel said softly.

"The law is taking my birthright. Is that just?"

"Your right as a citizen, perhaps, but not your birthright. You weren't born here, Jeshua. But it is still no fault of yours. There is no telling why nature makes mistakes."

"No!" He ran around the house and took a side street into the market triangle. The stalls were busy with customers picking them over and carrying away baskets filled with purchases. He leaped into the triangle and began to scatter people and shops every which way.

Sam Daniel and his men followed.

"He's gone berserk!" Renold shouted from the rear. "He tried to kill me!"

"I've always said he was too big to be safe," growled one of the guard. "Now look what he's doing."

"He'll face the council for it," Sam Daniel said.

"Nay, the Septuagint he'll face, as a criminal, if the damage gets any heavier!"

They followed him through the market.

Jeshua stopped near an old gate that led to the village proper. He was gasping painfully, and his face was red as wine. Sweat gnarled his hair. In the thicket of his mind he was searching for a way out, the only way now. His father had told him about it when he was thirteen or fourteen. "The cities were like doctors," his father had said. "They can alter, replace, or repair anything in the human body. That's what we lost when the cities grew disgusted and cast us out."

No city would let any real man or woman enter. But Jeshua was different. Real people could sin. Jeshua could not sin in fact, only in thought. In his confusion the distinction seemed important.

Sam Daniel and his men found him at the outskirts of the jungle, walking away from Bethel-Japhet.

"Stop!" the chief of the guard ordered.

"I'm leaving," Jeshua said without turning.

"You can't go without a ruling!"

"I am."

"We'll hunt you!"

"Then I'll hide, damn you!"

There was only one place to hide on the plain, and that was underground, in the places older than the living cities and known collectively as Sheol. Jeshua ran. He soon outdistanced them all.

Three miles ahead he saw the city that had left Mesa Canaan. The city had paused in its long journey. Its parts had crossed the plain and were gathering in a temporary site this side of Arat, where their highest tips gleamed in the sun, as beautiful as anything ever denied mankind. Rumbling, shivering sections of wall glowed faintly as the sky darkened, and the soft evening air hummed with the internal noises of a city planning to settle soon and resume its solitary life.

With the help of the finest architect humanity had ever produced, Robert Kahn, Jeshua's ancestors had built the cities and made them as comfortable as possible. Huge laboratories had labored for decades to produce the right combination of animal, plant, and machine, and to fit them within the proper designs. It had been a proud day when the first cities were opened. The Christians, Jews, and Moslems of God-Does-Battle could boast of cities more spectacular than any that Kahn had built elsewhere, and the builder's works could be found on a hundred worlds.

The nearest entrances to Sheol opened about two miles away, but Jeshua could not take his eyes off the city. He approached the nearest pieces before night fell and slept in a gully, hidden by a lean-to woven out of reeds. Coming awake to the soft yellow light of dawn, he listened again to the noises, then lifted his head above the gully's muddy rim and studied the city more closely. Some of the parts had formed a defensive ring of rounded, outward-leaning towers, like the petals of a monumental lotus. Inside them rose another ring, slightly taller, and another that was already sprouting a radiance of buttresses. The buttresses supported a platform topped with columns that were segmented and studded like the branches of a diatom. At the city's rising summit, parts of a dome took a shape like the magnified eye of a dragonfly, emanating a corona of diffracted colors. Opal glints of blue and green sparkled along the outer walls.

What if he tried to get inside before the city could find its final site, before it had finished rebuilding? The very thought made Jeshua ache. He stopped several dozen feet from the glassy steps beneath the city's outer petals. Broad, sharp spikes rose from the pavement and smooth garden walls, blocking the steps like thorns. The plants within the garden shrank at his approach. The entire circuit of paving around the city shattered into silicate thorns and bristled. There was no way to enter. Still, he moved closer and faced the tangle of spines, then reached to stroke one. It shuddered at his touch.

"I haven't sinned," he told the city. He knew it was listening. "I've hurt no one, coveted only that which was mine by law." The nested spikes said nothing but grew taller as he watched, until they extended a hundred yards above his head.

Sitting on a hummock of grass outside the perimeter, clasping his stomach to ease the hunger and pressure of his sadness, Jeshua looked up at the city's peak. A thin silvery tower rose from the columns to support a multifaceted sphere. The sunlit side of the sphere formed a crescent of yellow brilliance. The city was refusing him. Nothing had changed. He wasn't special in any way. He had to find another place to hide.

A cold wind rushed through his clothes and made him shiver. He stood and began to walk around the city, picking up speed when the wind carried sounds of people from the expolis, perhaps searching for him.

Jeshua knew from long hikes in his adolescence that a large entrance to the underground passages of Sheol yawned two miles west. By noon he stood in the cavernous opening. Sheol's tunnels had once been service ways for the inorganic cities of twelve centuries before. With the completion of the living cities, all of the old cities had been leveled and their raw material recycled. But the underground causeways would have been almost impossible to destroy, so they had been blocked off and abandoned. Some had filled with groundwater, and some had collapsed. Still others, drawing power from geothermal sources, maintained themselves and acted as if they yet had a purpose. A few had become the homes of disgruntled expolitans, not unlike Jeshua. Others were homes to more dangerous inhabitants.

Some of the living cities, just finished but not completely inspected, had thrown out their human builders during the Exiling, then broken down. Various of their parts—servant vehicles, maintenance robots, transports—had left the shambles and crept into the passages of Sheol, ill and incomplete, to avoid the natural cycle of God-Does-Battle's wilderness and the wrath of the exiles. Most of those parts had died and disintegrated, but a few had found ways to survive, and rumors about them made Jeshua nervous.

He looked around the opening and found a gnarled, sun-blackened vine hard as wood, with a heavy bole. He hefted it, broke off its weak tapering end, and stuck it into his belt where it wouldn't tangle with his legs. Before he scrambled down the debris-covered slope, he looked back. The expolitans from Ibreem were only a few hundred yards behind him. He lurched and ran. Sand, rocks, and bits of dead plants had spilled into the wide tunnel. Water dripped off chipped white ceramic walls, plinking into small ponds. Moss and tiered fungus imparted a shaggy veneer to the walls and supports. The villagers appeared at the lip of the depression and shouted his name. He hid until they stopped shouting, their shadows backing away and fading. Then he resumed his journey.

A few lights still blazed in discrete globes, unlike the diffuse, gentle glow of a wall in a living city. Wiring hissed and crackled around black metal boxes. Tracks began at a buffer and ran off around the distant curve. Black strips, faded and scuffed, marked a walkway. Signs in old English and something akin to the Hebraic hodgepodge spoken in Ibreem warned against deviating from the outlined path. He could read the English more easily than the Hebrew, for Hebraic script had been used. In Ibreem, all writing was in Roman script.

Jeshua stayed within the lines and walked around the curve. A mile into the tunnel, the floor was ankle-deep with muddy water. He had already seen several of God-Does-Battle's native arthropods and contemplated catching one for food, but he had no way to light a fire. He'd left all his matches in Bethel-Japhet, since it was against the law to go into the jungles carrying them unless on an authorized hunt or expedition. He couldn't stand the thought of raw creeper flesh, no matter how hungry he was.

The floor ahead had been lifted by some past seismic event, and then dropped. A lake had formed within the rimmed depression. Ripples shivered with oily slowness from side to side. Jeshua skirted the water, step by step, on broken slabs of concrete. Something long and white waited in the lake's shallows, waving feelers like the soft feathers of a mulcet branch. It had large gray eyes and a blunt rounded head, with a pocketknife assortment of clippers, grabbers, and cutters branching from arms on each side. Water splashed as he stepped on the solid floor of the opposite shore. The undulating feathery nightmare glided swiftly into the depths. Jeshua had never seen anything like it. God-Does-Battle was seldom so bizarre. It had been a straightforward, slightly dry, Earth-like planet, which was why humans had colonized in such large numbers thirteen centuries ago, turning their new home into a grand imitation of the best parts of ten worlds. Some of the terraforming had slipped since then, but rarely so drastically.

Half of the tunnel ahead was blocked by a hulk, thirty feet wide and some fifty long, frozen in rust and decay. A seat bucket rose from a nest of levers and a small arched instrument panel. The hulk, whatever its use, had been man-operated. As a smith and designer of tools, Jeshua saw there were parts on the rail-rider that hadn't come with the original—odds and ends of mobile machinery from one or more of the cities. Part machine, part organism, equipped with treads and grips, they had joined with the tar-baby rail-rider, trying to find a place on the bigger, more powerful machine. They had found only stillness and silence.

In the tunnel beyond, stalactites of concrete and rusted steel bristled from the ceiling. Fragments of pipes and unraveled runs of wire hung from brackets. At one time the entire tunnel must have been filled with them, with room only for rail-riders and maintenance crews walking the same path he was taking. Most of the metal and plastic had long since been stripped by scavengers.

Jeshua walked beneath the jagged end of an air duct and heard a rustling, and then voices, deeper in the tunnel. He cocked his head and listened more closely. Nothing. Then again, too faint to make out. He found a metal can and stood on it, bringing his ear closer.

"Moobed . . ." the duct echoed.

". . . not 'ere dis me was . . ."

"Bloody poppy-breast!"

"Not'ing . . . do . . ." The plastic of the duct was brittle and added a timbre of falling dust to the voices.

Then they stopped. The can crumpled under him and he dropped to the hard floor, yelping like a boy. Unhurt, he rose again on wobbly legs and walked farther into the tunnel. The lighting here was even dimmer. He stepped carefully over the shadow-pocked floor, avoiding bits of tile and concrete, fallen piping, snaking wires, and loose strapping bands. Fewer people had been this way. Vaguely seen things moved off at his approach: insects, creepers wet and dry, rodents, some native, some feral. What looked like an overturned drum became, as he bent closer, a snail wide as two hand spans, coursing on a shiny foot as long as his calf. The white-tipped, cat-slit eyes leaned his way, dark with secret thoughts, and a warm, sickening odor wafted up. Stuck fast to one side was the rotting body of a large beetle.

A hundred yards on, the floor had buckled again. The rutted underground landscape of pools, concrete, and mud smelled foul and felt more foul, squishing between his sandals and feet. He stayed away from the bigger pools, which were surrounded by empty larvae casings and filled with snorkeling insect young.

Already, Jeshua regretted his decision to run away. He wondered how he could return to the village and face his punishment, live within sight of Kisa and Renold—repair the shattered trough and do penance for the stall owners.

Water fell in a cascade ahead. He stopped to listen. The splashing and its echoes drowned out more subtle sounds, but something of a sharp, squabbling nature rose above. Men were arguing—and coming closer. Jeshua moved back from the middle of the tunnel and hid behind a fallen pipe.

A slender young male, dressed in rags, ran and jumped from block to broken block, dancing down the tunnel, arms held out and hands flexing like wing tips. Four other men followed, knife blades gleaming in the dim light. The fleeing boy ran past, saw Jeshua in the shadows, and, startling, stumbled off into black mud.

Jeshua pushed against the pipe and stood to run. A wide piece of concrete tilted under his weight, and through his hand, pressed against the wall, he felt a violent tremor. A massive presence of falling rock and dirt knocked him over and tossed chunks of concrete.

Four shouts were abruptly silenced.

He choked on the dust as he crawled from under the stony

pile. The lights had gone out. Only a putrid, swampy glow remained, coming from a shallow pond. A shadow obscured this blue-green glow, then came closer.

Jeshua stiffened, ready to strike out and roll away.

"Who?" the shadow said. "Go, spek. Shan hurt."

It was the boy. He sounded young, maybe eighteen or nineteen. He was speaking a sort of English, not the tongue Jeshua had learned while visiting Expolis Winston—but he could understand some of it. He thought it might be Chaser English, but there weren't supposed to be chasers in Ibreem.

They must have followed the city.

"I'm running, like you," Jeshua said in Winston dialect.

"Dis me," said the shadow. "Sabed my ass, you did. Quartie ob toms, lie dey t'ought I spek. Who appel?"

"What?"

"Who name? You."

"Jeshua," he said.

Dirt and pebbles scuttled down the mound where the four lay entombed.

"Jeshoo-a," the boy said. "Iberhim."

"Yes, Expolis Ibreem."

"No' far dis em. Stan' an' clean. Takee back."

"I'm not lost. I'm running."

"No' good t'stay. Bugga bites mucky, bugga bites you more dan dey bites dis me."

With his broad hands, Jeshua wiped mud from his pants.

"Slow, you," the boy said. "Brainsick?" The boy advanced. "Dat's it. Slow."

"Just tired," Jeshua said, looking up. "How do we get out of here?"

"Dat, dere an' dere. See?"

"Can't see," Jeshua said. "Not very well."

The boy advanced again and laid a cool, damp hand on his forearm. The hand gripped and tested. "Big, you. Big and slow.

Tight skeez, maybe." Then he backed off. Jeshua's eyes were adjusting and he could see how thin the boy was.

"What's your name?" he asked.

"No' matta. Go 'long wi' dis me now."

The boy led him up the mound of debris and poked around in the pitch black to see if they could pass. "Allry. Dis way." Jeshua pushed through a hole at the top, his back scraping the ceramic roof. The other side of the tunnel was equally dark.

The boy cursed under his breath. "Whole tube down," he said. "Ginger walk, now."

The pools beyond were luminous with the upright glows of insect larvae, some a foot long and solitary; others smaller and gathered in hazes of pale green light. Always there was a soft sucking sound. A thrash of feelers, claws, legs. Jeshua's skin itched at that sound, and he shivered in disgust.

"Sh," the boy warned. "Skyling here, sout' go, tro loud."

Jeshua caught none of this but stepped more lightly. Dirt and tiles fell into the water, and a chitinous chorus complained.

"Got dur here," the boy said, taking Jeshua's hand and putting it against a metal hatch. He had wide gray eyes and a pinched, pale face. "Ope', den go. Compree?"

The hatch slid open with a drawn-out squeal and blinding glare filled the tunnel. Things behind hurried back into the shadows. Jeshua and the boy stepped from the tunnel into a collapsed anteroom open to the last light of day. Vegetation had swarmed into the wet depression, decorating parades of pipe valves and more electrical boxes. As the boy closed the hatch, Jeshua scraped at a metal case with one hand and drew off a layered clump of moss. Four numbers were engraved beneath: "2278."

"Don' finga," the boy warned. A grin spread between narcissus-white cheeks. He was tight-sewn, tense, with wide knees and elbows and little flesh to cover his long limbs. His hair was rusty orange and hung in strips across his forehead and ears. Beneath a ragged vest, his chest bore a tattoo. The boy rubbed his hand across it, seeing Jeshua's interest, and left a smear of mud behind.

"My bran," the boy said. The "brand" was a radiant circle in orange and black, with a central square divided by diagonals. Triangles diminished to points in each division, creating a vibrant skewedness. "Dat put dere long 'go by Mandala."

"What's that?"

"De gees run me, you drop skyling on, woodna dey lissen wen I say, say dis me, dat de polis, a dur go up inna." He laughed. "Dey say, 'Nobod eba go in polis, no mo' eba.'"

"Mandala's a city, a polis?"

"Twenty-nine lees fr' 'ere."

"Lees?"

"Kileemet'. Lee."

"You speak anything else?" Jeshua asked, his face screwed up with the strain of turning instant linguist.

"You, 'Ebra spek, bet. But no good dere. I got better Englise, tone a bit?"

"Hm?"

"I can . . . try . . . this, if it betta." He shook his head. "Blow me ou' to keep up long, do."

"Maybe silence is best," Jeshua said. "Or just nod yes or no if you understand. You've found a way to get into a a polis named Mandala?"

Nod.

"Can you get back there, take me with you?"

Shake, no. Smile.

"Secret?"

"No secret. Dey big machee . . . machine dat tell dis me neba retourn. Put dis on my bod." He touched his chest. "Throw me out."

"How did you find your way in?"

"Dur? Dis big polis, it creep affa exhaus'—sorry, moob afta run outta soil das good to lib on, many lee fro' 'ere, an' squat on top ob place where tube ope' ri' middle ob undaside. I know dat way, so dis me go in, an' out soon afta . . . after. On my—" He slapped his butt. "Coupla bounce, too."

The collapsed ceiling of the anteroom—or skyling, as the boy called it—formed a convenient staircase from the far wall to the surface. They climbed and stood on the edge, where they looked over each other uncertainly. Jeshua was covered with dark green mud. He picked at the caked layers with his fingers, but the mud stuck like glue.

"Maybe, come fine a bit ob wet to slosh."

A branch of the Hebron River showed itself by a clump of green reeds a half mile from the tunnel exit. Jeshua drew its muddy water up in handfuls and poured it over his head. The boy dipped and wallowed and sprayed it from puffed cheeks, then grinned like a terrier at the Ibreemite, mud streaming down his face.

"Comes off slow," Jeshua said, scraping at his skin with clumped silkreeds.

"Why you interest' in place no man come?"

Jeshua shook his head. He finished with his torso and kneeled to let his legs soak. The bottom of the stream was rocky and sandy and cool. He looked up and let his eyes follow the spine of a peak in Arat, outlined in sunset glow. "Where is Mandala?"

"No tell," the boy said. "*My* polis."

"It kicked you out," Jeshua said. "Why not let somebody else try?"

"Somebod alread' tried," the boy informed him with a narrowed glance. "Dat dey tried, and got in, but dey didna t'rough my dur go. Dey—shee—one gol, dat's all—got in widout de troub' we aw ekspek. Mandala didna sto' 'er."

"I'd like to try that."

"Dat gol, she special, she up an' down legen' now. Was a year ago she went and permissed to pass was. You t'ink special you might be?"

"No," Jeshua admitted. "Mesa Canaan's city wouldn't let me in."

"One it wander has, just early days?"

"Hm?"

"Wander, moob. Dis Mase Cain' you mumbur 'bout."

"That's the one."

"So't it don' let dis you in, why Mandala an' differs?"

Jeshua climbed from the river, frowning. "Appel?" he asked.

"Me, m'appel, not true appel or you got like hair by demon grab, m'appel for you is Thinner."

"Thinner, where do you come from?"

"Same as de gol, we follow de polis."

"City chasers?" By Ibreem's estimation, that made Thinner a ruthless savage. "You don't want to go back to Mandala, do you? You're afraid."

"Cumsay, afraid? Like terrafy?"

"Like tremble in your bare feet in the dirtafy."

"No' possible for Thinner. Lead'er like, snake-skin, poke an' I bounce."

"Thinner, you're a faker." Jeshua reached out and lifted him from the water. "Now stop with the nonsense and give me straight English. You speak it—out!"

"No!" the boy protested.

"Then why do you drop all 'thu's' but in your name and change the word order every other sentence? I'm no fool. You're a fake."

"If Thinner lie, feet may curl up an' blow! Born to spek dis odd inflek, an' I spek differs by your ask! Dis me, no fake! Drop!" Thinner kicked Jeshua on the shin but only bent his toe. He squalled, and Jeshua threw him back like a fingerling. Then he turned to pick up his clothes and lumbered up the bank to leave.

"Nobod dey neba treat Thinner dis way!" the boy howled from the river.

"You're lying to me," Jeshua said.

"No! Stop." Thinner stood in the water and held up his dripping hands. "You're right."

"I know I am."

"But not completely. I'm from Winston, and I spoke like a city chaser for a reason. And accurately, mind you."

Jeshua frowned. The boy no longer seemed a boy. "Why try to fool me?" he asked.

"The chasers have been making raids on the farmlands outside of Winston. I'm a freelance tracker. I was keeping tabs on them. A few caught me and I tried to convince them I was part of a clan. I thought you might be one of them, and after speaking to you like that—well, in a tight spot, I keep to my cover."

"No Winstoner has a tattoo like yours."

"That part's true, too. I did find a way into the city, and it *did* mark me and kick me out."

"You still object to taking me there?"

Thinner sighed and crawled out of the stream. "It's not part of my trip. I'm heading back for Winston."

Jeshua watched him cautiously as he dried himself. "You don't think it's odd that you got into a city?"

"No. I tricked it."

"Men smarter than you or I tried for centuries before they gave up. Now you say you've succeeded, and you don't even feel special?"

Thinner put on his ragged clothes. "Why do you want to go?"

"I've got my reasons."

"Are you wanted in Ibreem? A crook? A murderer?"

Jeshua shook his head. "I'm sick," he said. "I was told a city might cure me, if I could find a way in."

"I've met sick pilgrims before," Thinner said. "A few years ago Winston sent a crowd of sick and wounded to a city. Bristled like a fighting cat. No mercy there, you can believe."

"But you have a way, now."

"Okay," Thinner said after an uncomfortable pause. "I'll take you there. It's on the other side of Arat. You've got me a little curious. You look like you should be dumb as a creeper, but you're not—you might even be smart. Besides, you've got that club. Are you desperate enough to kill?"

Jeshua thought about that for a moment, then shook his head. "I doubt it," he said.

"It's almost dark," Thinner said. "Let's camp and start in the morning."

The Mesa Canaan city—the city that had rejected him, now probably to be called the Arat city—had almost finished its reassembly. Its towers rose high above the foothills, glowing warm and sunset-pretty, like a diadem. It seemed to have found a good supply of water in its new valley, perhaps a steady mountain spring. Sensible, Jeshua thought. He made a bed from the reeds and watched Thinner as he laid down his own nest.

Jeshua slept lightly and woke with the dawn. He watched a small insect creep over his chest, inquiring with its finger-long antennae. He gently picked it off, set it on the ground, and cleared his throat.

Thinner jack-in-the-boxed from his nest. "You didn't cut my throat," he said, rubbing his eyes.

"Wouldn't do any good."

"Work like this wears down a man's trust."

Jeshua returned to the river and soaked himself again, letting the chill wallop his face and back in heavy hand-loads. The pressure in his groin was lighter this morning than most, but it still made him grit his teeth. He wanted to roll in the reeds and groan, rut the earth, but it would do him no good. Only the impulse existed.

They agreed on which pass to take through the snow-capped peaks and set out. Jeshua had spent most of his life within sight of the villages of the Expolis Ibreem and became increasingly nervous the farther they hiked. They ascended the steep slope of a wandering ridge, up to the snow line, where Thinner's claim to have tough soles proved true. He walked barefoot over all manner of jagged rocks and broken branches and ice without complaint. At the crest, Jeshua looked back over the plain of reeds and the jungle beyond. With some squinting and hand-shading, he could make out clusters of huts in two villages and the Temple Josiah on Mount Miriam. All else was hidden.

In two days they crossed Arat and a terrain of rolling foothills, which led them to a high, level plateau. As they waded through a thick green field of wild oats, Thinner said, "This used to be called Agripolis. If you dig deep enough, you'll find irrigation systems, fertilizing machines, harvesters, storage bins—the works. It's all useless now. For nine hundred years it wouldn't let any human cross. It finally broke down and those parts that could move, did. Most died."

Jeshua knew a little of the history of the cities around Arat and told Thinner about the complex called Tripolis. Three cities had grouped twenty miles north of the mountains. After the Exiling, one had fragmented and died. Another had successfully left and moved far south. The third had tried to summit the Arat range and failed. The bulk of its wreckage lay in a disorganized, mute clump east of the plateau.

On the far margin of the field, they passed a sad line of bulkheads and buttresses, most hardy of a city's larger members, still supported by desiccated legs or mounted on decayed wheels. Some were a hundred yards long and twenty feet across. Their metal parts had corroded. The organic parts had disappeared, except for an occasional span of silicate wall or internal skeleton of colloid.

"They're not all dead," Thinner said. "I've crossed here before. Some parts can still make the walking difficult."

In the glare of afternoon they hid from an armored, wheeled beast like a great translucent tank. "That's something from deep inside—a mover or loader," Thinner said. Jeshua tried to get closer but Thinner held his arm. "Just let it go. I've learned enough about feral city parts that I'm not going to walk up and poke it."

When the tank thing had passed they moved on, only to encounter creatures less threatening and more shy. The young of Ibreem had been taught enough about cities to identify many of their parts, but Jeshua couldn't name these or guess their functions. They were queer, dreamy creatures: spinning tops, many-legged

"How did you know?" he asked loudly, desperately.

"Now you've got me all confused," the head said. It stopped talking and its eyes closed. Jeshua nudged it with his toe. Nothing. He straightened up and looked for a place to run. The best way would be out. He was a sinner now, a sinner by anger and shame. The city would throw him out violently. Perhaps it would brand him, as Thinner had hinted earlier.

He heard a noise behind him and turned. A small wheeled cart gripped Thinner's head with gentle mandibles and lifted its segmented arms to send the oracle down a chute into its back. It rolled from the mall into a corridor.

Now that he was inside the city, Jeshua wanted more than anything to return to the familiarity of the grasslands and tangible enemies like the city chasers. The sunlight through the entrance arch guided him. He ran for the glassy walkway and found it rising to keep him in. Furious with panic, he raised his club and struck at the spines. They sang with the blows but did not break.

"Please," he begged. "Let me out, let me out!" Jeshua lifted his slumped shoulders and expanded his chest. "I'm afraid!" he shouted at the city. "I'm a sinner! You don't want me, so let me go!"

He squatted on the pavement with club in hand, trembling. The hatred of the cities for man had been deeply impressed upon him. His breathing slowed until he could think again, and the fear subsided. Why had the city let him in, even with Thinner? He stood and slung the club in his belt. There was an answer someplace. He had little to lose—at most, a life he wasn't particularly enjoying.

And in a city there was the possibility of healing arts now lost to the expolitans.

"Okay," he said. "I'm staying. Do anything you want to me. I'm here, and I'm ready for the worst."

He walked across the mall and followed another corridor beyond. Empty rooms with hexagonal doors waited empty and silent on either side. In a broad nave he found a fountain of clear, cool water and drank his fill. Then he spent some time studying the jointing of the lower reaches of arches that supported the vault, running his fingers along the fine grooves. A small anteroom had a soft couch-like protrusion, and he rested there, staring blankly at the ceiling. For a short while he slept. When he awoke, both he and his clothes were clean. As well, a new outfit had been laid out for him—standard Ibreem khaki shirt and short pants with twine belt, more delicately woven than the one he was wearing. His club remained as well. He lifted it. It had been tampered with—and improved. It fitted his grip better now and was weighted to balance well.

A table was set with dishes of fruit and what looked like milk and bread pudding. He had been accommodated in all ways, more than he deserved from any city. This almost gave him the courage to be bold. He took off his ragged clothes and tried on the new set. They fit admirably, and he felt less disreputable. His sandals had been stitched up but not replaced. They were comfortable, as always, but sturdier.

"You've fixed my clothes. How can I fix *myself* here?" he asked the walls. No answer.

Again, he drank from the fountain and moved on to explore further. The ground plan of Mandala's lowest level was relatively simple. It consisted mostly of trade and commerce facilities, with spacious corridors for vehicle traffic, large warehouse areas, and dozens of conference rooms. Computing facilities were also provided. He knew a little about computers—the trade office in Bethel-Japhet still had an ancient pocket model taken from a city during the Exiling. Of course, it didn't work. The access terminals in Mandala were larger and clumsier, but recognizable. He came across a room filled with them. Centuries of neglect had warped them into irregular shapes. He wondered what portions of them, if any, were alive or might still function.

Most of the rooms on the lowest level maintained the sea-floor green motif. The uniformity added to Jeshua's confusion, but after several hours of wandering, he found the clue that provided guidance. Though nothing existed in the way of written directions or graphic signs or maps, by keeping to the left he found he tended to the center; and to the right, the exterior. A Mandalan of ten centuries ago would have known the organization of each floor by education, and perhaps by portable guidebooks or signalers.

Somewhere, he knew, there had to be a central elevator to the upper levels. He followed all left-turning hallways, avoiding obvious dead ends, and soon reached the base of a hollow shaft. The floor of the shaft was tiled with a circular pattern of greens and reds and blues, advancing and flowing beneath his feet like a cryptic chronometer. From the bottom, he craned his neck and looked up through the center of Mandala. High above he saw a bluish circle—the darkling daytime sky, showcasing a single star. Wind whistled down the shaft. No elevator. How would people reach the upper floors?

Maybe the city didn't care any more. It had rebuilt itself so many times its original design might have—

Jeshua heard a faint hum. A speck blocked out part of the skylight and grew as it fell, spiraling like a dropped leaf. It had wings, a wide body for passengers, and an insect head, like the dragonfly buttresses that provided ventilation on Mandala's exterior. Slowing its descent, it lifted its nose and came to a stop in front of him, still several feet above the floor. The transparent wings refracted the floor's changing design. Then he saw that the design was coming to a conclusion, like an assembled puzzle. It formed a mosaic triskelion—a three-winged symbol outlined in red.

The glider waited for him. In its open body there was room for at least five people. He chose the front seat. The glider trembled and moved forward. The insect-head tilted back, cocked sideways, and inspected its ascent. Metallic antennae emerged from the front of the body. A tingling filled the air.

And he began to fly.

The glider slowed at a considerable distance above the floor and came to a smooth stop at a gallery landing. Jeshua felt his heartbeat race as he looked over the black railing, down the thousand feet or so to the bottom of the shaft.

"This way, please."

He turned, expecting to see Thinner again. Instead there waited a device like a walking coat-tree, with a simple vibration speaker mounted on its thin neck, a rod for a body, and three appendages jointed like a mantis's front legs. He followed it.

Transparent pipes overhead pumped bubbling fluids like exposed arteries. He wondered whether dissenting citizens in the past could have severed a city's lifelines by cutting such pipes— or were these mere ornaments, symbolic of deeper activities? The coat-tree clicked along in front of him, then stopped at a closed hexagonal door and tapped its round head on a metal plate. The door opened.

"In here."

Jeshua entered. Arranged in racks and rows in endless aisles throughout the huge room were thousands of constructions like Thinner. Some were incomplete, with their machinery and sealed-off organic connections hanging loose from trunks, handless arms, headless necks. Some had gaping slashes, broken limbs, squashed torsos. The coat-tree hurried off before he could speak, and the door closed behind.

He was beyond anything but the most rudimentary anxiety now. He walked down the central aisle, unable to decide whether this was a workshop or a charnel house. If Thinner was here, it might take hours to find him.

He stared straight ahead and stopped, seeing someone *not* on the racks. At the far end of the room, a figure stood alone, too distant to be made out in detail. Jeshua waited, but the figure did not move. Stalemate.

So he decided to take the first step. The figure darted to one side like a deer. He automatically ran after it, but by the time he'd reached the end of the aisle, it was nowhere to be seen.

"Hide and seek," he murmured. "For God's sake, hide and seek."

He rubbed his groin abstractedly, trying to still the flood of excitement rushing into his stomach and chest. His fantasies multiplied, and he bent over double, grunting. He forced himself to straighten, held out his arms, and concentrated on something distracting.

Then he found a head that looked very much like Thinner's, wired to a board behind the rack. Fluids pulsed up tubes into its neck. The eyes were open but glazed, and the flesh was ghostly. Jeshua reached out to touch it. It was cold, lifeless. He examined other bodies more closely. Most were naked, complete in every detail. He hesitated, then reached down to touch the genitals of a male. The flesh was soft and flaccid. He shuddered. His fingers, as if working on their own, went to the pubic mound of a female figure. He grimaced and straightened, rubbing his hand on his pants with automatic distaste. A tremor jerked up his back.

He was spooked now, having touched the lifeless forms, feeling what seemed dead flesh. What were they doing here? Why was Mandala manufacturing thousands of surrogates? He peered around the racks of bodies, this way and behind, and saw open doors far beyond. Perhaps the girl—it must have been the girl—had gone into one of those.

He walked past the rows. The air smelled like cut grass and broken reed stems, with sap leaking. Now and then it smelled like freshly slaughtered meat, or like oil and metal.

Something made a noise. He stopped. One of the racks. He walked slowly down one aisle, seeing nothing but stillness, hearing only the pumping of fluids in thin pipes and the clicks of small valves. Perhaps the girl was pretending to be a cyborg. He mouthed the word over again. Cyborg. He knew it from his schooling. The cities themselves were cybernetic organisms.

Then he heard rapid footsteps, the staccato slap of bare feet on the floor—someone running away from him. He paced evenly past the rows, looking down each aisle, nothing, nothing, stillness, *there!*

The girl was at the opposite end, laughing at him. An arm waved. Then she vanished.

He decided it was wise not to chase anyone who knew the city better than he did. Best to let her come to him. He left the room through an open door.

A gallery outside adjoined a smaller shaft. This one was red and only fifty or sixty feet in diameter. Rectangular doors opened off the galleries, closed but unlocked. He tested the three doors on his level, opening them one at a time with a push. Each room held much the same thing—a closet filled with dust, rotting and collapsed furniture, emptiness and the smell of old tombs. Dust drifted into his nostrils and he sneezed. Rubbing his nose, he walked slowly back to the gallery and the hexagonal door.

Looking down, he swayed and felt sweat start. The view was dizzying and claustrophobic.

A voice echoed down from above. It was feminine, sweet, and young, singing a song in words he did not completely catch. They resembled Thinner's chaser dialect, but echoes broke the meaning. He leaned out over the railing as far as he dared and looked up. Definitely the girl—five, six, seven levels up. The voice sounded almost childish.

Some of the words reached him clearly with a puff of direct breeze: "Dis em, in solit lib, dis em . . . Clo'ed in clo'es ob dead . . ."

The red shaft vanished to a point without skylight. He shaded his eyes against the city's internal brightness o see more clearly.

The girl backed away from the railing and stopped singing.

He knew he was being teased and that by rights he should be angry. But he wasn't. Instead he felt a loneliness too sharp to sustain. He turned from the shaft and looked back at the door to the room of cyborgs.

Thinner stared back at him, grinning crookedly. "Didn't have chance to welcome," he said in Hebrew. His head was mounted on a metal snake two feet long. His body was a green car with three wheels, a yard long and half a yard wide. The whole arrangement rolled silently on soft tires. "Have any difficulty?"

Jeshua looked him over slowly, then grinned. "It doesn't suit you," he said. "Are you the same Thinner?"

"Doesn't matter, but yes, to make you comfortable."

"If it doesn't matter, then who am I talking to? The city computers?"

"No, no. They can't talk. Too concerned with maintaining. You're talking with what's left of the architect."

Jeshua nodded slowly, though he didn't understand.

"It's a bit complicated," Thinner said. "Go into it with you later. You saw the girl, and she ran away from you."

"I must be pretty frightening. How long has she been here?"

"A year."

"How old is she?"

"Don't know for sure. Have you eaten dinner?"

"No. How did she get in?"

"Not out of innocence, if that's what you're thinking. She was already married before she came here. The chasers encourage marriage early."

"Then I'm not here out of innocence, either."

"No."

"You never saw me naked," Jeshua said. "How did you know what was wrong with me?"

"I'm not limited to human senses, though El knows what I do have are bad enough. Follow me, and I'll find suitable quarters for you."

"I may not want to stay."

"As I understand it, you've come here to be made whole. That can be done, and I can arrange it. But patience is always a virtue."

Jeshua nodded at the familiar homily. "She speaks chaser English. Is that why you were with the chasers, to find a companion for her?"

The Thinner-vehicle turned away from Jeshua. It rolled through the cyborg chamber, and Jeshua followed. "It would be best if someone she was familiar with would come to join her, but none could be persuaded."

"Why did she come?"

Thinner was silent again. They took a spiral moving walkway around the central shaft, going higher. "This is the slow, scenic route," Thinner said, "but you'll have to get used to the city and its scale."

"How long am I going to stay?"

"As long as you want."

They disembarked from the walkway and took one of the access halls to an apartment block on the outer wall of the city. The construction here seemed more recent and the colors more coordinated. The bulkheads and doors were opaque and brightly colored in blue, burnt orange, and purple. The total effect reminded Jeshua of a dreamy sunset. A long balcony in the outer wall gave a spectacular view of Arat and the plains, but Thinner allowed him no time to sightsee. He escorted Jeshua into a large apartment and made him familiar with the layout.

"It's been cleaned up and provided with furniture you should be used to. You can trade it in for somewhere else whenever you want, but you'll have to wait until you've been seen to by the medical units. You've been scheduled for work in this apartment." Thinner showed him a white-tile and stainless-steel kitchen, with food dispensers and basic utensils. "Food can be made or ordered here. There's enough in the cabinets and freezer to customize whatever comes out of the dispensers. Sanitary units are in here and should explain themselves—"

"They talk?"

"No. I mean their use should be self-evident. Very few things talk in the city."

"We were told the cities were commanded by voice."

"Not by most of the citizens. The city itself doesn't talk back.

Only certain units, none like myself—there were no cyborgs when humans lived here. That's a later development. I'll explain in time. I'm sure you're more used to books and scrolls than tapes or trid-vee experiences, so I've left some offprints for you on these shelves. Over here—"

"Seems I'm going to be here for a long time."

"Don't be worried by the accommodations. This may be fancy by your standards, but it certainly isn't by Mandala's. These units were designed for citizens with an ascetic temper. If there's anything you want to know when I'm not here, ask the information desk. It's hooked to the same source I am."

"I've heard of the city libraries. Are you part of them?"

"No. I've told you, I'm part of the architect. Avoid library outlets for the moment. In fact, for the next few days, don't wander too far. Too much too soon, and all that. Ask the desk, and it will give you safe limits. Remember, you're more helpless than a child here. Mandala is not out-and-out dangerous, but it can be disturbing."

"What do I do if the girl visits me?"

"You anticipate that?"

"She was singing to me, I think. But she didn't want to show herself directly. She must be lonely."

"She is." Thinner's voice carried more than a tone of crisp efficiency. "She's been asking a lot of questions about you, and she's been told the truth. But she's lived without company for a long time, so don't expect anything soon."

"I'm confused," Jeshua said.

"In your case, that's a healthy state of mind. Relax for a while; don't let unknowns bother you."

Thinner finished explaining the apartment and left. Jeshua went through the outer door to stand on the terrace beyond the walkway. Light from God-Does-Battle's synchronous artificial moons made the snows of Arat gleam like dull steel in the distance. Jeshua regarded the moons with an understanding he'd never had before.

Humans had brought them from the orbit of another world, to grace God-Does-Battle's nights. The thought was staggering. A thousand years ago, people used to live on the moons. What happened to them when the cities exiled their citizens?

Had the lunar cities done the same thing as the cities of God-Does-Battle?

He went to his knees for a moment, feeling ashamed and primitive, and prayed to El for guidance. He was not convinced his confusion was so healthy.

He ate a meal that came as close as amateur instructions could make it to the simple fare of Bethel-Japhet. He then examined his bed, stripped away the covers—the room was warm enough—and slept.

Once, long ago, if his earliest childhood memories were accurate, he had been taken from Bethel-Japhet to a communion in the hills of Kebal. That had been years before the Synedrium had stiffened the separation laws between Catholic and Habiru rituals. Jeshua's father and most of his acquaintances had been Habiru and spoke Hebrew. But prominent members of the community, such as Sam Daniel, had by long family tradition worshipped Jesus as more than a prophet, according to established creeds grouped under the title of Catholicism. His father had never resented the Catholics for their ideas.

At that communion, not only had Habiru and Catholic worshipped, but also the now-separate Muslims and a few diverse creeds best left forgotten. Those had been difficult times, perhaps as hard as the times just after the Exiling. Jeshua remembered listening to the talk between his father and a group of Catholics—relaxed, informal talk, without the stiffness of ceremony that had grown up since. His father had mentioned that his young son's name was Jeshua, which was a form of Jesus, and the Catholics had clustered around him like fathers all, commenting on his fine form as a six-year-old and his size and evident strength.

"Will you make him a carpenter?" they asked jokingly.

"He will be a cain," his father answered.

They frowned, puzzled.

"A maker of tools."

"It was the making of tools that brought us to the Exiling," Sam Daniel said.

"Aye, and raised us from beasts," his father countered.

Jeshua remembered the talk that followed in some detail. It had stuck with him and determined much of his outlook as an adult, after the death of his father in a mining accident.

"It was the shepherd who raised us above the beasts by making us their masters," another said. "It was the maker of tools and tiller of the soil who murdered the shepherd and was sent to wander in exile."

"To be sure," his father said, eyes gleaming in the firelight. "And later it was the shepherd who stole a birthright from his nomad brother—or have we forgotten Jacob and Esau? The debt, I think, was even."

"There's much that is confusing in the past," Sam Daniel admitted. "And if we use our eyes and see that our exile is made less difficult by the use of tools, we should not condemn our worthy cains. But those who built the cities were also making tools, and the tools turned against us."

"But why?" his father asked. "Because of our degraded state as humans? Remember, it was the Habirus and Catholics—then Jews and Christians—who commissioned Robert Kahn to build the cities for God-Does-Battle and to make them pure abodes for the best of mankind, the final carriers of the flame of Jesus and the Lord. We were self-righteous in those days and wished to leave behind the degraded ways of our neighbors. How was it that the best were cast out?"

"Hubris," chuckled a Catholic. "A shameful thing, anyway. The histories tell us of many shameful things, eh, lad?" He looked at Jeshua. "You remember the stories of the evil that men did."

"Don't bother the child," his father said angrily.

Sam Daniel put his arm around the man's shoulder. "Our debater is at it again. Still have the secret for uniting us all?"

Half-asleep, Jeshua opened his eyes and tried to roll over on the bed. Something stopped him, and he felt a twinge at the nape of his neck. He couldn't see well—his eyes were watering and everything was blurred. His nose tickled and his palate hurt vaguely, as if something were crawling through his nostrils into the back of his throat. He tried to speak but couldn't. Silvery arms wove above him, leaving gray trails of shadow behind, and he thought he saw wires spinning over his chest. He blinked. Liquid drops hung from the wires like dew from a web. From where the drops fell and touched his skin, waves of warmth and numbness radiated.

He heard a whine, like an animal in pain. It came from his own throat. Each time he breathed, the whine escaped. Again the metal things bobbed above him, this time unraveling the wires. He blinked, but it took a long time for his eyelids to open. When the darkness passed, he saw there was a split in the ceiling, from which branches grew down, one coming up under his vision and entering his nose, others holding him gently on the bed, another humming behind his head, making his scalp prickle. He searched for the twinge below his neck. It felt as if a hair was being pulled from his skin or a single tiny ant was pinching him. He was aloof, far above it, not concerned; but his hand still wanted to scratch and a branch prevented it.

His vision cleared for an instant, and he saw green enameled tubes, chromed grips, pale blue ovals being handed back and forth.

"A anna eh uh," he tried to say. "Eh ee uh." His lips wouldn't move. His tongue was playing with something sweet, like hard candy. Years ago he'd gone for a mouth examination—with a clean bill of health—and he'd been given a roll of sugar gum to tongue on the way home.

He sank back into his skull to resume listening to the old talk by the fireside.

"Hubris," chuckled a Catholic.

"Habirus," he said to himself.

"Hubris."

"A shameful thing, anyway—"

"Our debater is at it again. Still have the secret for uniting us all?"

"And raised us from beasts."

Deep, and sleep.

He opened his eyes and felt something in the bed with him. His hand moved to his crotch. It felt as if a portion of the bed had gotten loose and was stuck under his hip, in his shorts. He lifted his hips and pulled down the garment, then lay back, a terrified look coming into his face. Tears streamed from his eyes.

"Thanks to El," he murmured. He tried to back away from the vision, but it went with him, was truly a part of him. He hit the side of his head to see if it was still a time for dreams.

It was real.

He climbed off the bed and stripped away his shirt, then stood naked by the mirror to look at himself. He was afraid to touch it, but of itself it jerked and nearly made him mad with desire. He reached up and hit the ceiling with his fists.

"Great El, magnificent Lord," he breathed. He wanted to rush out the door and stand on the balcony, to show God-Does-Battle he was now fully a man, fully as capable as anyone else to accomplish any task given to him, including—merciful El!—founding and fathering a family.

He couldn't restrain himself. He threw open the door of the apartment and ran naked outside.

"BiGod!"

He stopped, his neck hair prickling, and turned to look.

She stood by the door to the apartment, poised like a jack-lighted deer. She was only fourteen or fifteen, at the oldest, and slender, any curves hidden beneath a sacky cloth of pink and orange. She looked at him as she might have looked at a ravening beast. He must have seemed one. Then she turned and fled.

Devastated in the midst of his triumph, he stood with shoulders drooped, hardly breathing, and blinked at the afterimage of brown hair and naked feet. His erection subsided into a morning urge to urinate. He threw his hands up in the air, returned to the apartment, and went into the bathroom.

After breakfast he squatted uncomfortably on a small stool to face the information desk. The front of the desk was paneled with green slats, which opened as he approached. Sensor cells peered out at him.

"I'd like to know how I can leave," he said.

"Why do you want to leave?" The voice was deeper than Thinner's, but otherwise much the same.

"I've got friends elsewhere, and a past life to return to. There's nothing for me anything here."

"You have all of the past waiting for you, an infinite number of things to learn."

"I just want out."

"I'd allow you to leave anytime."

"How?"

"Well, there could be a problem. Not all of Mandala's systems cooperate with this unit—"

"Which unit?"

"I am the architect. The systems follow schedules set up a thousand years ago. You're welcome to try to leave—I certainly won't do anything to stop you—but it could be difficult."

Jeshua drummed his fingers on the panel. "What do you mean, the architect?"

"The unit constructed to design and coordinate the building of the cities."

"Could you ask Thinner to come here?"

"Thinner unit is being reassembled."

"Is he part of the architect?"

"Yes."

"Where are *you*?"

"If you mean, where is my central position, I have none. I am part of Mandala."

"Does the architect control Mandala?"

"Not all city units respond to the architect. Only a few."

"The cyborgs were built by the architect," Jeshua guessed, and drummed his fingers again, then backed away from the desk. He stood on the terrace, looking across the plains, grinding his teeth. He seemed to always be missing something terribly important.

"Hey!"

He looked up. The girl was on a terrace two levels above him, leaning with her elbows on the rail.

"I'm sorry I scared you," he said.

"Dis me, li'l shock, but all mucky same-same 'ereber dis em go now. Hey, do, I got warns fo' you."

"What? Warnings?"

"Dey got probs here, 'tween Mandala an' dey 'oo built."

"I don't understand."

"No' compree? Lissy dis me, close, like all dis depen' on't: Dis em, was carry by polis 'en dis dey moob, week 'r two ago. Was no' fun. Walk an' be carry, was I. No' fun."

"The city moved? Why?"

"To leeb behine de part dis dey call builder."

"The architect? You mean, Thinner and the information desks?"

"An' too de bods."

Jeshua began to understand. There were at least two forces in Mandala that were at odds with each other—the city and something within the city that called itself the architect. "How can I talk to the city?"

"De polis no' talk."

"Why does the architect want us here?"

"Don' know."

Jeshua messaged his neck to stop a cramp. "Can you come down here and talk?"

"No' now dis you are full a man . . . Too mucky for dis me, too cashin' big."

"I won't hurt you. I've lived with it for all my life—I can live a while longer."

"Oop!" She backed away from the rail.

"Wait!" Jeshua called. He turned and saw Thinner, fully corporeal, standing in the rounded arch to the access hall.

"So she came back, and you've been able to talk to her," Thinner said. "That's progress."

"Yes. Made me curious, too. And the information desk."

"We expected it."

"Then can I get some sound answers?"

"Of course."

"Why was I brought here—to mate with the girl?"

"El! Not at all." Thinner gestured for him to follow. "I'm afraid you're in the middle of a pitched battle. The city rejects all humans. But the architect knows a city needs citizens. Anything else is a farce."

"We were kicked out for our sins," Jeshua said.

"That's embarrassing, not for you so much as for us. The architect designed the city according to the specifications given by humans—but any good designer should know when a program contains an incipient psychosis. I'm afraid it's set this world back quite a few centuries. The architect was made to direct the construction of the cities. Mandala was the first city, and we were installed here to make it easier to supervise construction everywhere. But now we've lost control.

"After a century of building and successful testing, we programmed community control into the city maintenance computers. We tore down the old cities when there were enough of the new to house the people of God-Does-Battle. Problems didn't develop until all the living cities were integrated on a broad plan. They began to compare notes, in a manner of speaking."

"They found humanity wanting."

"Simply put. One of the original directives of the city was that socially destructive people—those who did not live their faith as Jews or Christians—would be either reformed or exiled. The cities were constantly aware of human activity and motivation. After a few decades, they decided everybody was socially destructive in one way or another."

"We are all sinners."

"This way," Thinner directed. They came to a moving walkway around the central shaft and stepped onto it. "The cities weren't capable of realizing human checks and balances. By the time the problem was discovered, it was too late. The cities went on emergency systems and isolated themselves, because each city reported that it was full of deep, dark sinners—antisocials, infidels, heretics. They never coordinated again. It takes people to reinstate the interurban links."

Jeshua looked at Thinner warily, trying to judge the truth of this story. It was hard to accept—a thousand years of self-disgust and misery because of bad design! "Why did the ships leave the sky?"

"This world was under a colony contract and received support only so long as it stayed productive. Production dropped off sharply, so there was no profit, and considerable expense and danger in maintaining contact. There were tens of millions of desperate people wandering all over. Mayhem, violence. After a time, God-Does-Battle was written off as a loss."

"Then we are not sinners, we did not break El's laws?"

"No more than any other living thing."

Jeshua felt a slow hatred grow inside. "There are others who must learn this," he said.

"Sorry," Thinner said. "You're in it for the duration. We'll get off here."

"I will not be a prisoner," Jeshua said.

"It's not a matter of being held prisoner. The city is in for another move. It's been trying to get rid of the architect, but it can't—it never will. It would go against a directive for city cohesion. And so would you if you try to leave now. Whatever is in the city just before a move is cataloged and kept careful track of by watcher units."

"What can any of you do to stop me?" Jeshua asked, his mind made up, as stubborn as if he'd come across a piece of steel difficult to hammer.

He walked away from the shaft exit, wondering what Thinner would try.

The floor rocked back and forth and knocked him on his hands and knees. Streamers of brown and green crawled over a near wall, flexing and curling. The wall came away, shivered as if in agony, then fell on its side. The sections around it did likewise until a modular room had been disassembled. Its contents were neatly packed by scurrying coat-trees, each with a fringe of arms and a heavier frame for loads.

All around the central shaft, walls were being plucked out and rooms dismantled.

Thinner kneeled next to Jeshua and patted him on the shoulder. "Best you come with this unit. I can guarantee safe passage until the city reassembles. Might be months, might be a year."

Jeshua hesitated, then looked up and saw a cantilever arch throwing out green fluid ropes like a spider spinning silk. The ropes caught on opposite bracings and allowed the arch to lower itself. Jeshua stood up on the uncertain flooring and followed Thinner.

"This is only preliminary work," Thinner said as he took him into the cyborg room. "In a few hours the big structural units will start to come down, then the bulkheads, ceiling, and floor pieces, then the rest. By this evening, the whole city will be mobile. The girl will be here in a few minutes—you can travel together if you want. This unit will give you instructions on how to avoid injury during reassembly."

But Jeshua had other plans. He did as Thinner told him, resting on one of the racks like a cyborg, stiffening as the girl came in from another door and positioned herself several aisles down. He was sweating profusely, and the smell of his fear sickened him.

The girl leaned forward and looked at him cautiously. "You know 'at dis you in fo'?" she asked.

He shook his head.

The clamps on the rack closed and held him comfortably but securely. He didn't struggle. Panels beneath the racks retracted, and wheels jutted out. The room was disassembling itself. Shivering with their new energy, the racks elevated and wheeled out their cargo, forming a long train down a hall crowded with scurrying machines. Behind them, the hall came apart and its bulkheads spewed ropes, sprouted grasping limbs and feet, thrust out wheels and treads.

A storm to the south lay a broad gray hat over Arat's snowy peaks. As the day progressed and the city diminished, the front swept near, then over. Low clouds hid the disassembly of the city's upper levels.

All joined into a spectacular dance. With the precision of a bed of flowers closing for the night, the city shrank, drew in, pulled itself down, and packed itself onto wide-treaded beasts with unfathomable jade eyes. The racks were hoisted onto the backs of trailers that resembled low, fat spiders; their many long legs pumped smoothly up and down. A hundred flat-backed spiders carried all the racks, and joined in the long dance with thousands of tractors and cranes.

All the cyborg monsters finally gathered in concentric circles around Mandala, awaiting further instructions. Rain fell on the ranks of machines and half-machines, and the ground became dark with mud and trampled vegetation.

Transparent skins on rigid foam poles elevated over the carriers. Thinner crawled between the racks and approached Jeshua, who by now was stiff and sore.

"We've let the girl loose," Thinner said. "She has no place to go but with us. Will you try to leave?"

Jeshua nodded.

"It'll only mean trouble. But I don't think you'll get hurt." Thinner tapped the rack and the clamps backed away. Night was falling over the storm. Through the trailer skin, Jeshua could see the city's parts and vehicles switch on interior glows. Rain streaks distorted the lights into ragged splashes. He stretched his arms and legs and winced.

A tall tractor surmounted by a blunt-nosed cone rumbled up to the trailer and hooked itself on. The trailer lurched and began to move. The ride on the pumping, man-thick legs was surprisingly smooth.

Mandala marched away through the rain and dark.

By morning, a new site had been chosen.

Jeshua lifted the skin and jumped into the mud. He had slept little during the trek, thinking about what had happened and what he had been told. He was no longer meek and ashamed. The cities were no longer lost paradises. They now had an air of priggishness. They were themselves deeply flawed.

He spat into the mud.

But the city had made him whole again. Who had been more responsible: the architect, the citizens, or Mandala itself? He didn't know and hardly cared. He had been taken care of as any other unit in Mandala would have been, automatically and efficiently. He coveted his new wholeness, but it didn't make him grateful. It should have been his by a birthright of ten centuries. That birthright had been denied by willful blindness among the cities' patrons and designers. He could not accept any of this as perpetual error. His people tended to think in terms of will and responsibility.

The maze of vehicles and city parts fell quiet now, as if resting before the effort of reassembly. The air was misty and gray with a heaviness that further sunk his spirits.

"'Ere dis you go?"

He turned back to the trailer and saw the girl peering from under the skin. "I'm leaving," he said. "I don't belong here. Nobody does."

"Lissy. I tol' de one, T-Thinner to teach dis me . . . teach me how to spek li' dis you. When you come back, I know by den."

"I don't plan on coming back." He looked at her closely. She was wearing the same shift she wore when he first saw her, but a belt had tightened around her waist. He took a deep breath and backed away a step, his sandals sinking in the mud.

"I don' know 'oo you are . . . *who* you are . . . but if Th-Thinner brought you, you must be a good person."

Jeshua widened his eyes. "Why?"

She shrugged. "Dis me just know." She jumped down from the trailer, swinging from a rain-shiny spider leg. Mud splattered up her bare white calves. "If you, dis me, t'ought . . . if I *thought* you were bad, I'd ekspek' you to brute me right now. But you don'. Even though you neba—*never* have a gol before." Her strained speech started to crack and she laughed nervously. "I was tol' abou' you 'en you came. About your prob-lem." She inspected him. "How do you feel?"

"Alive. And I wouldn't be too sure I'm no danger. I've never had to control myself before."

The girl looked him over curiously, coquettishly.

"Mandala, it isn't all bad," she said. "It took care ob you. *Dat's* good, is it no'?"

"When I go home," Jeshua said, drawing a breath, "I'm going to tell my people we should come and destroy the cities."

The girl frowned. "Li' take down?"

"Piece by piece."

"Nobod' can do dat."

"Enough people can."

"No' good in firs' place. No' 'tall."

"It's because of *them* we're like savages now."

The girl shimmied up the spider leg and motioned for him to follow. He lifted himself and stood on the rounded lip of the back, watching her as she walked with arms balancing to the middle of the vehicle.

"Look all dis," she said, and pointed around the ranked legions of Mandala. The mist was starting to burn off. Shafts of sunlight cut through and brightened wide circles of the plain. "De polis, dey are li' not'ing else. Dey are de . . ." She sighed at her lapses. "They are the fines' thing we eba put together. We should try t'save dem."

But Jeshua was resolute. His face burned with anger as he looked out over the disassembly. He jumped from the rim and landed in the pounded mud. "If there's no place for people in them, they're useless. Let the architect try to reclaim. I've got more immediate things to do."

Jeshua stalked off between the vehicles and city parts.

The girl shook her head sadly.

Mandala, broken down, covered at least thirty square miles of the plain.

Jeshua took his bearings from a tall rock pinnacle, chose the shortest distance to the edge, and sighted on a peak in Arat. He walked without trouble for half an hour, and found himself passing through a widely scattered group of city fragments. Grass grew up between flattened trails. With a final sprint, he stood on the edge of all that had once been Mandala. He took a deep breath and looked behind to see if anything was following. He still had his club. He hefted it in one hand and examined it closely, trying to decide what he would do if he were attacked. He then slipped it beneath in his belt. He might need it for the long trip back to the expolis.

Behind him, the far reaches and ranks of transports and parts lurched and swirled like a flowing tide. Mandala was beginning its reconstruction. Best to escape now.

He ran.

The long grass made running difficult, but he persisted until he stepped into a dry creeper burrow and fell. He got up, rubbed his ankle, and continued with a clumsy, springing gait. In an hour he rested beneath the shade of a copse of trees and laughed to himself. Nothing so ridiculous as a whole man fleeing his salvation!

The sun beat down heavily on the plain and the grass shimmered with golden heat. It was no time to travel. Finding a small puddle of rain water in the cup of a rock, he drank from that and then slept.

A shoe gently nudged his ribs.

"Jeshua Tubal Iben Daod," a voice said.

He rolled over and looked into the face of Sam Daniel the Catholic. Two women and another man, as well as three young children, stood behind him, jockeying for position in the coolest shade.

"Have you found peace in the wilderness?" the Catholic asked.

Jeshua sat up and rubbed his eyes. He had nothing to fear. The chief of the guard wasn't acting in his professional capacity—he was traveling, not searching. And besides, Jeshua was returning to the expolis.

"I am calmer, thank you," Jeshua said. "I apologize for my actions."

"It's only been a fortnight," Sam Daniel said. "Has so much changed since?"

"I . . ." Jeshua shook his head. "I don't think you would believe."

'You came from the direction of the traveling city," the Catholic said, sitting on the soft loam. He motioned for the rest of the troop to rest and relax. "Meet anything interesting?"

Jeshua asked, "Why have you come this far?"

"For reasons of health. And to visit the western limb of Expolis Canaan, where my parents live now. My wife has a lung ailment—I think an allergic reaction to the sorghum being planted in the ridge paddies above Bethel-Japhet. We'll keep away until the harvest. Have you stayed in other villages nearby?"

Jeshua shook his head. "Sam Daniel, I have always thought you a man of reason and honor. Will you listen with an open mind to my story?"

The Catholic considered, then nodded.

"I've been inside a city."

Sam Daniel raised his bushy eyebrows. "The one on the plain?"

Jeshua told him most of the story. Then he stood. "I'd like you to follow me. Away from the rest. I have proof."

Sam Daniel followed Jeshua behind the rocks, and Jeshua shyly revealed his proof.

Sam Daniel stared.

"It's real?" he asked.

Jeshua nodded. "I've been restored. I can go back to Bethel-Japhet and become a regular member of the community."

"No one has ever been in a city before. Not for as long as anyone remembers."

"There's at least one other, a girl. She's from the city chasers."

"But the city took itself apart and marched. We had to change our course to go around it or face the hooligans following. How could anyone live in a rebuilding city?"

"There are ways." And he told about the architect and its extensions. "I've had to twist my thoughts to understand what I've experienced, but I've reached a conclusion. We don't belong in the cities, any more than they deserve to have us."

"Our shame lies in them."

"Then they must be destroyed."

Sam Daniel looked at him sharply. "That would be blasphemous. They serve to remind us of our sins."

"We were exiled not for our sins, but for what we are—human beings! Would you kick a dog from your house because it dreams of hunting during Passover—or Lent? Then why should a city kick its citizens out because of their inner thoughts? Or because of a minority's actions? They were built with morals too rigid to be practical. In their self-righteousness, they are worse than the most callous priest or judge. They've caused us needless suffering, and as long as they stand, they remind us of an inferiority and shame that is a lie. We should tear them down to their roots and sow the ground with salt!"

Sam Daniel rubbed his nose thoughtfully. "The cities are perfect and eternal," he said. "If they're self-righteous, they deserve to be. You of all should know that."

"You haven't understood," Jeshua said, pacing. "They are not perfect, not eternal. They were made by men—"

"Papa! Papa!" a child screamed. They ran back to the group. A black, tractor-mounted giant with an angular, birdlike head and five arms sat ticking quietly near the trees. Sam Daniel called his family to the center of the copse and looked at Jeshua with fear and anger.

"Has it come for you?"

Jeshua nodded.

"Then it's all true. Go with it! Leave us be!"

Jeshua stepped forward. He didn't look at the Catholic as he said, "Tell the rest what I've told you. Tell them what I've done, and what I know we must all do."

A boy clung to Sam Daniel's legs and softly moaned.

The giant picked up Jeshua with a clawed arm and set him delicately on its back. It spun around with a spew of dirt and grass, then moved quietly back across the plain to Mandala. When they arrived, the city was almost finished rebuilding. It looked no different from when he'd first seen it, but its colorful, re-emerging order now seemed ugly and pointless. He preferred the human asymmetry of brick homes, wandering fields, stone walls. The city's soft, efficient noises made him queasy. His reaction grew like steam pressure in a boiler, and his muscles felt tense as a snake about to strike.

The giant set him down on the city's lowest level, near the central shaft. Thinner met him there. Jeshua saw the girl on a bridge extending across the circular design.

"If it makes any difference, we had nothing to do with bringing you back," Thinner said.

"If it makes any difference to you, I had nothing to do with returning. Where will you shut me in tonight?"

"Nowhere," Thinner said. "You have the run of the city."

"And the girl?"

"What about her?"

"What does she expect?"

"You don't make sense," Thinner said.

"Does she expect me to stay and make the best of things?"

"Ask her. We don't control her, either."

Jeshua walked past the cyborgs and over the circular design, now disordered again. The girl watched him as he approached. He stopped below the bridge and looked up at her, hands tightly clenched by his waist.

"What do you want from this place?" he asked.

"Freedom," she said. "The choice of what to be, where to live."

"But the city won't let you leave. You have no choice."

"Yes, the city—I can leave whenever I want."

Thinner called from across the mall. "As soon as the city is put together, you can both leave. The inventory is policed only during a move."

Jeshua's shoulders slumped and his bristling stance softened. He had nothing to fight against now, not immediately. Even so, he kept his fists clenched.

"I'm confused," he said.

"Stay for the evening," the girl suggested. "Then will your thoughts come clear."

He followed her to his room near the peak of the city. The room hadn't been changed. Before she left him there, he asked what her name was.

"Anata," she said. "Anata Leucippe."

"Do you get l-lonely in the evenings?" he asked, stumbling over the question like a child in a field of corn stubble.

"Never," she said. She laughed and turned half away from him. "An' now certes am dis em, you no' trustable!"

She left him by the door. "Eat!" she called from the corner of the access hall. "I be back around mid of the evening."

He shut his door, then turned to the kitchen. Being a whole

man did not stop the pain and fear of loneliness. The possibility of quenching was in fact a final turn of the thumbscrew. He paced like a caged bear, thinking furiously but reaching no conclusions.

By midnight he was near an explosion. He waited in the viewing area of the terrace, watching moonlight bathe God-Does-Battle like milk, gripping the railing with a strength that could have crushed wood. He listened to the noise of the city, less soothing than he remembered, neither synchronous nor melodic.

Anata came for him half an hour after she said she would. Jeshua had gone through so many ups and downs of despair and aloofness that he was exhausted. She took his hand and led him to the central shaft. They found hidden curved stairwells and descended four levels to a broad promenade that circled a wide level of the shaft.

"The walkway, it doesn't work yet," she told him. "I'm studying. My tongue, I'm getting your words."

"There's no reason you should speak like me," he said.

"It is difficult. Dis me—I cannot cure a lifetime ob—of talk."

"Your own language is pretty," he said, half-lying.

"I know. Prettier. Alive-o. But—" She shrugged.

Jeshua thought he couldn't be more than five or six years older than she was, by no means an insurmountable distance. He jerked as the city lights dimmed. All around, the walls lost their bright glow and produced in its stead a pale lunar gleam, like the night outside.

"This is what I brough' you here for," she said. "To see."

The ghost-moon luminescence made him shiver. The walls and floor exchanged long, curling threads of light, and from the threads grew spirits, shimmering first like mirages, then settling into translucent steadiness. They came in couples, groups, crowds, and with them were children, animals, birds, and other things he couldn't identify.

They began to move.

They filled the promenade and terraces and walked, talking

in tunnel-end whispers he couldn't quite make out, laughing and looking and being alive—but not in Jeshua's time. They were not solid, not robots or cyborgs. They were spirits from ten centuries past, and he was rapidly losing all decorum watching them come to form around him.

He groaned and tried to escape from the ghosts.

"Sh!" Anata said, taking his arm. "They're just dreams. They don't hurt anybody."

Jeshua clasped his elbows and forced himself to be calm.

"This is what the city desires," Anata said. "'You want to kill it because it keeps out the people, but look—it hurts, too. It *wants*. What's a city without people? Just sick. No' bad. No' evil. Can't kill a sick one, can you?"

Each night, she said, the city reenacted these living memories of the past, no two alike, and each night she came to watch. Jeshua saw the whispering half-life of a billion recorded memories, and his anger slowly, painfully faded. His hands loosened their grip. He could never sustain hatred for long. Now, with understanding still just out of reach, he could only resign himself to a simmer of confusion.

"It'll take me a long, long time to forgive," he said.

"This me, too." She sighed. 'When I was married, I found I could not have children. My husband could not understand. All the other women could have children. So I left in shame and came to the city we had always worshipped. I thought it would be, the city, the only one to cure. But now, I don't know. I do not want another husband. I want to wait for this to *go away*. These dreams, this pain. It is too beautiful to leave while the dreams are still here."

"Go away?"

"The cities, they get old and they wander," she said. "Not all things work good now. Pieces are dying. Soon it will *all* die. Even such as Thinner, *they* die. And no more are being made. The city is too old and too sad to grow new parts.

"So I'll wait until the beauty is gone."

Jeshua looked at her more closely. There was a whitish cast in her left eye. It had not been there a few hours ago.

"It is time for me to sleep," she said softly. "Very late."

She held up her hand, as they had just watched a lady do, a thousand years before. He took her raised hand and led her through the phantoms, up the empty but crowded staircases, then asked her where she lived.

"I don't have just one room," she said. "I sleep in all of them at one time or another. But we can't go back dere." She stopped. "*There*. Can't go back." She looked up at him. "Dis me, canno' spek mucky ob—" She held her hand to her mouth. "I forget. I learned bu' now—I don't know . . ."

He felt a slow horror grind in his stomach.

"Something is wrong," she said. Her voice became deeper, like Thinner's, and she opened her mouth to scream but could not. She tore away from him and backed away. "I'm doing something wrong!"

"Take off your shirt," Jeshua said.

"No." She looked offended.

"It's all a lie, isn't it?" he asked.

"No."

"Then take off your shirt."

She began to remove it. Her hands hesitated.

"Now."

She peeled it over her head and stood naked, with her small breasts outthrust, narrow hips square and bonily dimpled, genitals flossed in feathery brown. A pattern of scars on her chest and breasts formed a circle. Bits of black remained like cinders, like the cinders on his own chest—from a campfire that had never been.

Once, both of them had been marked like Thinner, stamped with the seal of Mandala.

She turned away from him on the staircase, phantoms drifting past and through her. He reached out to stop her but wasn't quick enough. Her foot spasmed under her and she fell, gathering into a twisted ball, down the staircase, up against the railings, to the bottom.

He stood near the top and saw her pale blue fluid and red skin-blood and green tissue leak from a torn leg.

He felt he might go insane.

"Thinner!" he screamed, and turned, calling the name over and over. The lunar glow brightened. The phantoms disappeared. The halls and vaults echoed with his braying cry.

The cyborg appeared at the bottom of the staircase and knelt to examine the girl.

"Both of us," Jeshua said. "Both lies!"

"We don't have the parts to fix her," Thinner said.

"Why did you bring us back? Why not just tell us what we are?"

"Until a few years ago there was still hope," Thinner said. "The city was still trying to correct the programs, still trying to get back its citizens. Sixty years ago it gave the architect more freedom to try to find out what went wrong. We built ourselves—you, her, the others—to go among the humans and see what they were like now, how the cities could accommodate. If we had told you this, would you have believed? As humans, you were so convincing you couldn't even go into other cities, just your own. Then the aging began, and the sickness. The attempt finally died."

Jeshua felt the scars on his chest and shut his eyes, wishing, hoping it was all a nightmare.

"David the smith purged most of the mark from you when you were small and young, that you might pass for human. The city had already put a block on your development, that you might someday be forced to return."

"My father was like me."

"Yes. He carried the scar, too."

Jeshua nodded. "How long do we have?"

"I don't know. The city is running out of memories to repeat. Soon, in less than a century, it will have to give up. It will move like the others one last time, and strand itself someplace where it can die in peace."

Jeshua walked away from Thinner and the girl's body and wandered down an access hall to the terraces on the outer wall. He shaded his eyes against the rising sun and looked toward Arat. There he saw the city that had once occupied Mesa Canaan. It had disassembled and was trying to cross the mountains.

"Kisa," he said.

The wind played with his hair.

ABOUT THE AUTHOR

Greg Bear is the author of over twenty-five books, which have been translated into seventeen languages. He has won science fiction's highest honors and is considered the natural heir to Arthur C. Clarke. The recipient of two Hugo Awards and four Nebula Awards, Bear has been called "the best working writer of hard science fiction" by the *Science Fiction Encyclopedia*. Many of his novels, such as *Darwin's Radio*, are considered to be classics of his generation. Bear is married to Astrid Anderson—who is the daughter of science fiction great Poul Anderson—and they are the parents of two children, Erik and Alexandria. Bear's recent publications include the thriller *Quantico* and its sequel, *Mariposa*; the epic science fiction novel *City at the End of Time*; and the generation starship novel *Hull Zero Three*.

THE COMPLETE SHORT FICTION OF GREG BEAR

FROM OPEN ROAD MEDIA

Available wherever ebooks are sold

OPEN ROAD

INTEGRATED MEDIA

Open Road Integrated Media is a digital publisher and multimedia content company. Open Road creates connections between authors and their audiences by marketing its ebooks through a new proprietary online platform, which uses premium video content and social media.

Videos, Archival Documents, and New Releases

Sign up for the Open Road Media newsletter and get news delivered straight to your inbox.

Sign up now at
www.openroadmedia.com/newsletters